R SRI RAM

Change:
Slow & *Fast*

urate
quratebooks.com

Because everyone has a story to tell

Change: Slow and Fast
R Sri Ram

Published by Qurate Books Pvt. Ltd.

© Qurate Books Pvt. Ltd.

First Published in 2024

ISBN: 978-81-1926-383-7

Printed By Repro India Ltd.

urate
quratebooks.com
Because everyone has a story to tell

Qurate Books Pvt. Ltd.
Goa 403523, India

www.quratebooks.com

Tel: 1800-210-6527, **Email:** info@quratebooks.com

CONTENTS

Swami Swaroopananda is the Global Head of Chinmaya Mission. The mantle of this important responsibility draped his shoulders from 19 January 2017, when Swami Tejomayananda passed on the baton to him. He chairs Central Chinmaya Mission Trust (CCMT), the apex governing body of Chinmaya Mission Centres and Trusts the world over. He is the Chancellor of Chinmaya University (Chinmaya Vishwavidyapeeth) and Chairman of Chinmaya International Residential School in Coimbatore, one of the most well-respected and well-performing residential schools of India.

An able administrator and a dynamic leader, his watchful eye and acumen keeps him abreast with developments of any consequence in the over 300 Centres under his guard. Devotion to his Guru, Swami Chinmayananda, and obeisance to his philosophy, guides his decision making and governance.

FOREWORD

In the landscape of our contemporary world, the subject of change management stands as a prominent and recurrent theme. People constantly change their minds; economic, political and technological realms introduce new variables and, in an instant, we can lose our health, loved ones, and even life itself. Amidst this uncertainty, the question persists: how does one master change?

Ancient Indian wisdom unveils a powerful truth: our world is shaped by the mind. Master it, and you master the world. In this pursuit, nothing surpasses the wisdom of the Bhagavad Gita. It stands as the zenith of self-mastery and leads us to it.

Bhagavan Krishna's counsel emphasises prioritising present actions over fixating on outcomes. Embracing the journey and cultivating positive values like gratitude and acceptance provide stability amidst life's changes. Furthermore, understanding that all we receive contributes to our growth, guided by nature and God, empowers us not only to navigate but to thrive amidst change.

This positivity and freedom from result-driven anxieties sharpens the mind into a potent, focused instrument which can achieve anything. It is pivotal to understand that Lord Krishna did not alter Arjuna's external circumstances; instead, he ignited a profound shift in his mindset and vision.

Moreover, what is highlighted is that our true journey commences when we transcend life's dualities to find enduring inner joy. This realisation liberates us from the sway of change, leading to constant bliss. Guided by the wisdom of this profound scripture we have the potential not only to surpass change but also to achieve the unimaginable, benefitting not only ourselves but the entire world.

On the topic of transformative change, perspectives from various experts converge. It is with genuine delight and respect that I present the work of Dr. R. Sri Ram – a visionary entrepreneur and philanthropist whose four decades of leadership have not only forged sustainable practices but also ignited a beacon of positive change.

Within these pages, we navigate the pivotal moments of 2022, a year characterised by profound change. Dr. R. Sri Ram masterfully presents a finely detailed narrative, inviting reflection on the seismic shifts that unfolded. He argues that understanding these transformative junctures not only piques curiosity but also provides invaluable foresight into the future. This opus transcends mere historical account; it serves as a living testament to the enduring truth: change is the only constant.

I extend my warmest congratulations to Dr. R. Sri Ram on the release of this book, and I have every confidence that "Change – Slow and Fast" will leave an indelible mark on its readers.

Swami Swaroopananda
Global Head, Chinmaya Mission
Chancellor, CVV

Baron Parekh, FBA FAcSS FRSA is a British political theorist, academic, and life peer. He is a Labour Party member of the House of Lords.

He has been a distinguished Professor at the London School of Economics and University of Harvard..

He was Professor of Political Theory at the University of Hull for several years..

He is a fellow of the prestigious British Academy and received the Padma Bushan from the Government of India.

FOREWORD

The year 2022 was one of the most unusual in recent history. It impacted on people all over the world and confirmed once again their unity of interest. They underwent similar suffering and pain, and offered a common response based on feelings of nervousness, vulnerability, incomprehension, and some measure of hope. A mixture of these emotions was played out at both personal and political levels and gave rise to a highly complex attitude to themselves and to the world around them. The author of this book explores this complexity month-by-month with considerable skill and insight and makes a valuable contribution to our understanding. Business and reflective writing do not generally go together. They do so here and therein lies its uniqueness.

Individual chapters provide a narrow and particularist perspective and need to be balanced by a cross-cutting overview. Sri Ram provides it by offering perceptive accounts of global warming, Ukraine, and the life of Queen Elizabeth II. At first sight the last two may seem rather odd, but not in the way in which he discusses and integrates them. Ukraine is not just a war between two countries, but signifies the demise of the old world order and the gestation of a new one. Similarly, the chapter on the Queen is not just about an individual, but about an impressive sovereign who influenced British political life for the longest period in the country's history, and provided a source of unity and stability during years of increasing plurality and social tension.

I am happy to write a foreword for this impressive book. It covers a large part of the world, offers perceptive accounts of a wide range of activities going on in it, and discusses technical issues with great skill. Entries for each month are mutually consistent in their structure and orientation. Major political and economic events are discussed in conjunction with cultural events, and collectively form a general narrative centred on the themes of migration, the European Union and COVID-19. I commend this book to all those interested in making sense of what they have gone through during the past two years, and knowing what kind of a future they might expect.

Bhikhu Parekh
House of Lords
December 2023

This book is dedicated to my three year old grandson Rami who will see immense change in his life time – for the good, I hope.

All proceeds of this book are being donated to The Wings of Hope Children's Charity,

www.thewingsofhope.org

INTRODUCTION

CHAPTER 1

Change has been part of human history from the moment this Universe was created. It has been part of human evolution and is one of the most important features of our lives. We experience change in many ways. The birth of a child brings an immediate change to the parents. The arrival of a newborn baby is overwhelming and joyful to many. However, some events can be devastating when we feel change almost immediately. A sudden accident brings about change instantaneously although the long-lasting effect of that accident and the change it brings is felt over time. Change is therefore both fast and slow. A person winning a substantial amount in a lottery feels the impact of change immediately, but the consequences may be felt over time.

There are also many events in history which at that time seem to profoundly affect us. Yet after just a short period, we slowly tend to forget how we felt and how it affected us directly or indirectly. We are constantly looking forward, but many of the answers to the future can be found in the past. In the next few pages, I will demonstrate how change has occurred at a staggering pace over just a short period of time. Events that took place just a few decades ago have fundamentally changed the world. Yet many of us do not have an appreciation of these events even though we are affected by them profoundly. With the ebb and flow of time, we may have forgotten many recent events that even occurred. I feel an understanding of some of these events and the change that this has brought us will be not only interesting but useful to give us clues to the way ahead.

World War II ended just over eighty years ago with many who witnessed the horrors still alive and many more who were told about it by their parents and grandparents. We felt the war had taught us that Hitler's ethnic cleansing should never happen again. Many institutions were subsequently created to prevent this tragedy from ever occurring. Yet we have seen so many wars in the past century. Ethnic cleansing in the Balkans, religious wars in the Middle East, wars in Africa and now the recent invasion of Russia in Ukraine. The latter is a major theme of this book as the war in Ukraine has changed the World order and geopolitics in many ways we could never have imagined. We have also witnessed dramatic effects of the Gulf wars, the financial shocks of the nineties.

VERY RECENT HISTORY: THE COVID-19 PANDEMIC

Some of us have even forgotten how the Covid 19 pandemic affected our lives. Everyday events like going to the local shops to purchase our daily necessities, travelling to meet loved ones, and going to the local cinema were simply not possible. We were all asked to stay at home - we all spoke of social distancing, wearing face masks, and vaccinations.

The Zoom phenomenon was breathtaking. Suddenly the old, discovered Zoom and began meeting friends and relatives on the internet. We remembered distant friends with whom we began regular conversations. Elderly people suddenly discovered that they do not need to travel to meet loved ones. They began to use all the 'complicated tools' and became savvy internet users. Shopping online, getting your groceries delivered, and even washing every item to prevent any bacteria from entering our protected domain became common occurrences.

A few short years after the pandemic hit, we have somehow forgotten that as recently as 2020 our lives were so different, the speed at which our lives had changed is staggering. Yet just in a few years life has just as fast returned to normal; we no longer need to fill in the dreaded passenger locator forms, and queue up at airports for the staff to scrutinize so many of our documents before being allowed to board a flight. Simple everyday events seemed more complicated in 2020. Although we begrudged these intrusions into our liberties and way of life, we soon accepted them and for months adjusted to remaining at home. Our routines changed to going for walks in our local parks and avoiding even eye contact with anyone. We even began to appreciate the things we never took notice of earlier, like birds singing or admiring nature in its glory. Life took on a different, less rushed, rhythm. Covid-19 and the trauma that it brought were experienced by all. There were no divisions as the rich and poor suffered similarly. Even though at that moment those events seemed difficult, we have tended to gradually forget about these difficulties and those moments we endured forgetting the extent change had occurred and thereafter changed back to what it was before. The pandemic also brought huge changes to the way mankind developed methods to tackle the pandemic. Breathtaking change occurred in the way medical science and the pharmaceutical industry collaborated to bring out a vaccine. Changes in behaviour, changes in the way we worked and met has brought about in many ways permanent changes to our lives. The Covid 19 pandemic therefore deserves a separate chapter to discuss these changes and I have tried to analyse them later in detail.

CHANGES IN HISTORY: THE BRITISH EMPIRE AND SLAVERY

Today many would hardly believe that Britain over a century ago was an undisputed Superpower. As recently as a hundred and fifty years ago Britain controlled 25% of the world. 'The Sun does not set on the British empire' was no exaggeration. From New Zealand, Australia, Hong Kong, Singapore, India, The Middle East, Africa, Europe, and the Americas, Britain had its footprint.

Britain appointed its Governors, Governor Generals who held sway over these colonies and ruled a vast empire with its own system of government decided from Whitehall, London. It was at times a form of benevolent dictatorship and in many domains, the local population was indoctrinated into believing that the British rule was a force for good. Britain imposed its imperial system, making Sterling the predominant currency for trading - the world followed the Greenwich Mean Time (GMT). Precious metals were denominated in Sterling and the British Raj was the mightiest empire ever created in history.

The British Empire was an important event with hundreds of millions affected by it in some way or another. It stretched for over three hundred years and yet it is incredible that this recent part of history is not a compulsory part of the curriculum in schools in Britain. It seems the British are somewhat embarrassed to teach their children this even existed. In contrast, France was the first country to officially recognise slavery as a "crime against humanity" enshrined in a 2001 law that set out to improve the teaching of slavery and the colonial era.

At a debate on whether the British Empire was a force for good, I was astounded to hear that whilst students in the colonies knew more about recent British history students in Britain were taught about The Vikings and other aspects of distant British history which may not be as relevant as the events just a few hundred years ago.

The changes that have occurred in Britain and the colonies is staggering. From being a subject country, many have risen to become global powers. India for instance has overtaken its colonial master and is now the fifth largest economy in the world and fast racing to become the third largest soon. A staggering change in just over 75 years.

I would argue that some part of Britain's role was a force for good. Many countries that were colonies of the British Empire have embraced democracy. India, Australia, Canada, New Zealand, and many countries in Africa now have democratically elected governments. I accept that it has not been a perfect start. There have been many mistakes made and an increasing number of countries have struggled with corruption and a decline in prosperity. However, they have commenced a journey for the better and the example of India, which is now the largest democracy in the world is a shiny one. Change in India has meant that it now leads the world as the fastest large economy on Earth and millions have benefited from its prosperity.

CHANGES IN HISTORY: SPAIN AND PORTUGAL

Let us consider the role that Spain and Portugal played in world history. I believe this is important as both are responsible for massive changes in shaping much of South America, South and Pacific Asia. Neither of them is a member of the G7 group of the richest industrialized countries. Yet a few centuries ago these two European countries were the richest in the world and played a very important role. Spain and Portugal were the first European nations to establish trading empires spanning the world.

CHANGES IN HISTORY: TECHNOLOGY

It seemed only the other day that we carried massive boxes as status symbols – bulky mobile phones existed just a few years ago with trendy 'City types' carrying them to show their status and pecking order. Today you would be ridiculed if you carried these. The iPhone and Samsungs of today pack in hundreds of features that we could have never imagined then.

The mobile phone at that time was a significant invention but all it did was provide audio connection without the need for a landline.

The advent of Vodafone in 1985 as a public company and provider of mobile telephony was historic and changed the way we lived and worked. Who could have predicted the meteoric rise of mobile telephony in our everyday lives, 'Alexa' becoming our friend and butler managing so many gadgets? All this happened because of the cellular technology that Vodafone and other providers offered.

History is a great teacher and many events have repeated itself. There is therefore some merit in understanding and embracing history and the changes that it has brought about. The idea for this book came to me when I realized that we tend to slowly forget important events. I felt there might be a need for a kind of yearly diary laying out the significant events of the year. This would, I hoped, be a useful reference for those of us interested in history. I have been writing this book since the beginning of 2022 and have written chapters based on each month.

The other reason I wrote the book was because I became a grand father for the first time in 2021 when my grand son Rami was born. It was a new experience because of the change he brought to my life. He changed every day, began to talk, crawl and walk. Change was rapidly happening to his life and my family and the more I reflected what these changes meant I began to realise how important it is for us to understand and embrace change. I therefore began to chronicle important events of 2022. Some may criticize me for focusing too little on art, culture and many of the other events that occurred during this year. It is a fair point but I wanted to focus on some areas which make the most impact on society and on ordinary individuals.

Some readers may ask what is the point of this work when there are numerous publications like the Economist that chronicle each month at the end of the year. No doubt these publications are more authoritative and have a large team of researchers. What is the difference? I have delayed publication of this book to include events that occurred in 2023. This provides more evidence that supports my point: events appearing to be comparatively insignificant at that time, and that happen at glacial speed become significant. Small and slowly developing events turn out to become major and catastrophic. I have where possible with evidence elaborated upon such events. There may be some events which have not turned out to be significant and may turn out to be one with the fullness of time. I invite readers to make their own judgments. There are, however, some significant events which deserve special attention. The War in Ukraine, Climate Change, Democracy, the death of HM Queen, Covid 19 Pandemic, and the recent Gaza conflict which have been addressed in separate chapters.

The wise can connect past events and make calculated guesses about the future. Many have made significant breakthroughs in technology, medicine, and the sciences. Elon Musk must have had some defined ideas of how oil prices were shaping Western economies, and our dependency on Russia and the Gulf countries for our energy needs. Historical threats have been made by nations in leveraging their influences. His bet on launching the electric vehicle and investing billions in battery technology seemed quite risky. His timing was perfect with the rise in energy costs, the invasion of Ukraine in February 2022, and the subsequent meteoric rise in oil and energy prices meant that we all rushed into all things electric. His timing was impeccable. Tesla became the most valuable company in the world. 15 years ago, Tesla was not even in the top 20 car manufacturing businesses with Toyota then the largest. In less than 15 years Tesla not only rose to the top but the market capitalization of the company became more than the combined value of the other 9 behind.

Many events initially do not seem to have a pattern but suddenly a pattern seems to emerge with the elapse of time. Geniuses can connect the dots and make predictions making them fabulously successful and wealthy: Bill Gates's vision of putting a computer on every desk; Steve Jobs' idea of designing the humble phone and Elon Musk's bet on battery operated cars, Jeff Bezos and Amazon retailing will go down in history as momentous events. They all pushed the boundaries, learnt from the past, and were able to see connections where others did not. That truly is the mark of a genius – spotting connections and trends where others do not. Tim Berners-Lee, invention of the internet in 1989 has allowed so much knowledge to be accessed easily, well chronicled, and logged for ease of reference. It has changed the way we access knowledge and information.

The Rise of Google and artificial intelligence has made having great knowledge irrelevant. There was a time when we all had to learn and remember so much. Today most information is available at our fingertips on mobile devices. The need to remember has altered, and the key today is to be able to locate information on the net. Tools like Wikipedia, Google, and Chat GPT among others provide free information. So, what would is required to be successful has again changed. Clarity and the ability to find information quickly has become important. Changes in this areas has happened fast and at breathtaking speeds.

Rise of Facebook and other social media platforms: Today most of our lives are affected by social media. A politician who does not have a savvy social media strategy will not succeed. A business without one would find it hard to survive. News travels so fast that managing breaking news has become extremely important both for business and politics. There was a time when the Royal Families were cloaked in mystery, we heard only good things about them. Today the situation has become so very different. We are fed with minute-to-minute happenings inside the staid Palace walls and managing these has become such an important job. Yet these social media platforms did not exist a few years ago. News was available mainly in printed form. We used telegrams to communicate which was slow. The scale of change in the news media is breathtaking. Google, Facebook, Apple, and Microsoft dominate our lives.

CHANGES IN HISTORY: SOCIETY

Oscar Wilde was jailed because he was homosexual. The brilliant Alan Turing, who helped invent the Enigma machine to break the German coded messages during World War Two, had to hide his sexuality and eventually committed suicide. History is riddled with tales of individuals who were simply ostracized due to their sexual orientation. Yet within decades, we are happy to embrace them in our society. We have elected gay politicians to high offices. Many entertainers belong to the LGBT community. This level of change and transformation is staggering.

This century has also seen other huge changes in society. Consider that it was only 59 years ago that the Civil Rights Act of 1964 was passed. This marked a historic milestone in the long struggle to extend civil, political, and legal rights and protection to African Americans, including former slaves and their descendants as well as ending segregation in public and private facilities.

Before 1964 a black person could not travel in the same train compartment as a white person. Interracial marriage was banned. Yet in 2009, less than fifty years, Barrack Obama became the first-ever black President of the USA. The change in attitudes has been transformational. He was awarded the Nobel Peace Prize and broadly admired for his Presidency and won a second term.

The transformation of the US continues with General Charles Brown appointed as the first black Joint Chief of Staff of the US Air Force in 2020 leading over 685,000 men and women. The current Vice President of the United States Kamala Harris is the first Indian American to be elected to the role.

The staggering changes happening could never have been predicted a few years ago. The President of The World Bank, Ajay Banga, and the First Deputy Managing Director of the IMF, Geeta Gopinath are of Indian origin making two of the most powerful financial institutions in the world run by immigrants. Who could have predicted that Rishi Sunak another person of Indian origin would occupy the same chair as the legendary Churchill and Margaret Thatcher?

More recent events have also precipitated social change. Many of us were appalled by the way George Floyd an African American in May 2020 was murdered by the Police in Minnesota, US.

He was simply suspected of handing over a fake $ 20 dollar bill to a local grocery store. Derek Chauvin, one of the four police officers who arrived on the scene, knelt on Floyd's neck for 9 minutes and 29 seconds which caused his death. After his murder, protests against police brutality, especially towards black people, quickly spread across the United States and globally. His dying words, "I can't breathe", became a rallying slogan changing history. In two years, there is a change in people's awareness of the brutality with which Police in the US treat black and racial minorities. It has also precipitated a growing international movement to call out racial discrimination. In what historians describe as an "unprecedented" public reckoning with the British empire, an estimated 39 names – including streets, buildings, and schools – and 30 statues, plaques, and other memorials have been or are undergoing changes or removal since last summer's Black Lives Matter protests in the UK.

Another event which began with the allegations of sexual abuse by Harvey Weinstein has turned out to become a major moment. MeToo is a social movement and awareness campaign against sexual abuse, sexual harassment, and rape culture, in which people publicize their experiences of sexual abuse or sexual harassment. The phrase "Me Too" was initially used in this context on social media in 2006, on Myspace, by sexual assault survivor and activist Tarana Burke. The hashtag #MeToo was used starting in 2017 as a way to draw attention to the magnitude of the problem. The movement began to spread virally as a hashtag on social media. On October 16, 2017, American actress Alyssa Milano posted on Twitter, "If all the women who have been sexually harassed or assaulted wrote 'Me too' as a status, we might give people a sense of the magnitude of the problem,". A number of high-profile posts and responses from American celebrities Gwyneth Paltrow, Ashley Judd, Jennifer Lawrence, and Uma Thurman, among others, soon followed. Widespread media coverage and discussion of sexual harassment, particularly in Hollywood, led to high-profile terminations from positions held, as well as criticism and backlash.

NEGATIVE CHANGES IN HISTORY

Trumpism and the way backward

Yet despite all the spectacular progress that we have made over the past hundred years the advent of Trump has also brought us backward. Take the case of abortion rights. It is an irony that a modern democratic country could so violently pull back. Eminent Justices numbering just 12 can decide the fate of over 150 million women in the USA. To criminalize abortion and take away the fundamental rights of a woman to decide what is right for her and the unborn baby is tragic. Yet Trump and his policies seem to be popular with millions of ordinary Americans.

Rise of Bin Laden, 9/11 and Muslim terrorism on the rise

The tragic terrorist attack on 9/11 recorded 2977 deaths but is dwarfed by around 42,000 deaths in car accidents each year in the US. Yet 9/11 was one of the most profound moments in US history just as Pearl Harbor.

For the first time, the US population understood what terrorism was after experiencing this firsthand. Prior to 2001, the population had read about and listened to various terrorism outrages across the world, the American public did not truly understand what it is to suffer at the hands of a terrorist. Suddenly this incident demanded the Government take urgent and monumental action and the search for Bin Laden, the perpetrator of this ghastly attack, became the Nation's top priority. This single attack changed geopolitics with the US foreign policy's main goal to eliminate fundamental Muslim terrorism. Since 2001, trillions of dollars have been spent in fighting terrorism, changing the landscape of the Middle East.

Geopolitical changes – 2022

The Ukraine war has brought to the forefront a significant shift in geopolitical power.

The dominance of USA and Western alliance in military and economic power is no longer there. Suddenly the war in Ukraine in 2022 became a rallying call to support the US-led alliance. China was very clear they did not want to support this alliance and were on the side of the Russians. Whilst India did not criticize Russia its position was more ambivalent in trying to please both parties without taking sides. India has played its cards well in demanding cheap oil from Russia to fund its economic growth. It has not made enemies but clearly, there is a lot of irritation amongst the Western alliance on this. The cheap Russian oil purchases made by India are funding the war for Russia and that is not tenable in the eyes of many.

The growth of China has been happening for decades. Its export-led manufacturing has managed to capture huge chunks of the Western market for goods. China's economy has skyrocketed. Consider their spectacular growth. In 1985 China had a GDP of just over $ 300 billion. In 2022 its GDP had risen to $ 18,000 billion. During the same period figures for the USA, the dominant power, was just over $ 4,000 billion rising to $ 25,000 billion in 2022. This substantial increase in the amount of money that China has earned has been used to acquire power. They have spent vast amounts on their armies. They have created the Belt and Road initiative to have significant influence in South Asia and Africa.

Launched in 2013 as "one belt, one road", it involves China underwriting billions of dollars of infrastructure investment in countries along the old Silk Road linking it with Europe. The ambition is immense. China is spending roughly $150bn a year in the 68 countries that have signed up to the scheme. Over the years the West did not take this initiative seriously and have been quite sanguine until it was too late.

The project is the clearest expression so far of President Xi Jinping's determination to break with Deng Xiaoping's dictum to "hide our capabilities and bide our time; never try to take the lead". The Belt and Road Forum (with its unfortunate acronym, BARF) is the second set-piece event this year at which Mr Xi will lay out China's claim to global leadership. (The first was a speech against protectionism made at the World Economic Forum in Davos in January). As early as 2014, Wang Yi, the foreign minister, said the initiative was Mr Xi's most important foreign policy. Its ultimate aim is to make Eurasia (dominated by China) an economic and trading area to rival the transatlantic one (dominated by America).

There has also been growth in India. For example, the GDP of India in 1985 was $ 232 billion and the same has shot up to $ 3,700 billion. This is commendable but pales the growth achieved by China. However, India seems to be the flavour of the month as more and more countries prefer dealing with India than China. India has been consolidating its soft power for decades and there is a lot of expectation that the coming decades could finally bring India its long-standing place to become both an economic and political superpower.

UK Politics – The Fall of Boris Johnson and its Impact on Democracy

in June 2023 Boris Johnson, a previous Prime Minister of Britain resigned his seat in Parliament. This was a historic moment not because he was a former Prime Minister of Britain. It was historic because it will impact on how democracies work. The fundamental basis is for our leaders to tell the truth. Democracy expects politicians and leaders to conduct themselves with honesty, accountability, and integrity. We sometimes tolerate politicians lying but the situation takes on a different turn when they lie to Parliament, a body elected by ordinary people to govern – such lies becomes cardinal sins. He was found to have repeatedly and deliberately lied. There is a chapter on this subject.

My monthly diary may seem simply to report events that occurred during that month. Yet when we look back over a period of time, and with the benefit of hindsight, we suddenly realize how profound that footnote in history has become. Wherever there has been significant developments altering the seriousness of that event I have reported it.

Small events, Big Impacts

I have also reported several events in small countries which normally do not merit a great deal of headline news. Yet for people living in Burkina Faso a local terrorist event is catastrophic and shattering. The Western media is dominated by news that is relevant to the West. The resignation of Imran Khan the Prime Minister of Pakistan is another news. However, with the benefit of hindsight, we may see that many such events change world history. The slow build of Al Qaeda some years ago might have been footnotes in the news but seen now after many years we feel how spectacularly these events have changed history and the entire Middle East.

Her Majesty Queen Elizabeth II

Whilst change has been happening at breathtaking speed, one event I have covered is where the staid British Monarchy has provided stability and strength over generations. I have devoted an entire chapter to Her Majesty Queen Elizabeth II. Her death was a very significant event not just for Britain but for the entire world. It has been estimated that her funeral was watched by around four billion people - a testimony to how much her life and death meant to so many far and wide.

The Queen was a remarkable human being having served Britain and the Commonwealth loyally and admirably for over 70 years. She had ascended the throne completely by accident and had to assume the throne suddenly without much training. She, however, managed to invent herself in this important role and became a symbol of continuity and strength. Thousands queued for hours simply to file past her coffin and the messages from the ordinary and the extraordinary were remarkable.

The chapter looks at her young life and how she transformed herself from a happy and carefree woman to taking over such an enormous responsibility when Britain was transforming rapidly from a colonial superpower to its slow but steady demise as one. She, however, remarkably provided Britain with the soft power to remain relevant with her calm and steady Reign stretching over more than seven decades.

The War in Ukraine

I have devoted an entire chapter to the war in Ukraine which commenced by the barbaric assault by Putin in February of 2022 on his brotherly neighbour. The reckless invasion solely to dominate his neighbors with his mighty army was one of the biggest mistakes made in a long time. Putin calculated that his 'special military operation' would last for a couple of weeks and he would have annexed vast parts of Ukraine, entered Kyiv, toppled the Government, and installed his puppet administration. He also calculated that just as his invasion of Crimea in 2014 there would be little or no reaction from the West. He believed this would make him the greatest leader of Russia and his vision of making Russia great again by annexing these territories would be greeted with joy by his subjects. His greatest mistake and gamble has turned out to be a nightmare for him. It has led to huge suffering by millions of Ukrainians displaced from their beautiful homes and made them refugees in foreign lands. It has led to immense suffering by ordinary people across the world by raising energy prices to levels never seen. It has led to suffering by the poor in many parts of the world starved of grains from Ukraine which was the breadbasket of the world. In addition, it has brought untold misery to ordinary Russians who have been forced into this mindless adventure. There are estimates of around 100,000 Russian deaths on the battlefield. The emotional toll for their families helplessly caught up in this war is heart-rending. There are now estimates that due to this high numbers the Russian population already under demographic pressure before the war is expected to decline by 10% resulting in further long-term problems. Putin's madness would result in consequences far and wide and for a very long time.

This invasion has brought untold suffering not only to millions of Ukrainians, but also to millions of ordinary people across the world with the impact of rising energy costs. This invasion has also affected hundreds of millions dependent on food supplies from Ukraine. Further, the war has brought in major changes to modern warfare. It has changed geopolitics in significant ways. The invasion has been headlining news throughout 2022 and therefore merits a detailed analysis in a dedicated chapter – The War in Ukraine.

Global Warming and Climate Change

Our precious planet has evolved over millions of years with mankind existing on it for thousands. Our population has, however, exploded in just over a century causing huge changes to our planet. The UN estimated that the world population reached 1 billion for the first time in 1804. It was another 123 years before it reached 2 billion in 1927. In just a century these numbers have increased to over 8 billion in 2022. This is quite staggering as it took thousands of years for the human population to reach 1 billion. This massive increase in population over a very short time has caused devastating impact on our climate threatening large numbers of species and significantly affecting our planet's temperature and causing global warming.

A starting point some years ago was when global warming and carbon emissions were not even taken seriously other than by scientists. Today due to the significant climate disasters of cyclones, heatwaves, and droughts mainstream politicians and the population have woken up. The COP conferences have further focused the attention of Governments and other organizations who are now considering active measures to address and combat climate change. The situation is dire with predictions of entire countries getting submerged by the rise in sea levels. Countries totally unconnected with emitting carbon are now being penalized. Bangladesh would lose millions of acres as it would get submerged, similarly, several poor countries are now suffering untold hardships. It is a welcome step that the recent COP conference in Egypt has begun to address setting up funds to support these countries. It is an important development not just in 2022 but over several decades. Only now when things are getting worse does there seem to be an urgency and more people and Governments are discussing this important issue. Some are even taking action to tackle it.

This topic, therefore, requires a detailed analysis of how we got to this point and the various actions and remedies that lie ahead. This will be discussed in greater detail in a separate chapter titled Global Warming and Climate Change.

The Palestinian-Israeli conflict in Gazza – October 2023

I was about to submit this book for publication when I had to pause again to include a fast-moving story happening in Gaza in the Middle East. As I have explained, history is littered with incidents which burn slowly for months and years but turn into quick-paced and catastrophic events in a short period of time. The situation in Gaza is an excellent example of this and over the course of this chapter, I will discuss how such events have changed history forever.

Whilst I have talked about change, I end this chapter with a quote from Zhoe Enlai the Chinese Communist statement and Prime Minister of China from 1949 to 1976. He was a remarkable thinker, a Prime Minister, credited for orchestrating China's 'Great leap forward; and known as a great philosopher.

He was asked to comment about the French Revolution which ended in 1799.

His reply – **Too early to commen**t.

Change therefore can be glacial and fast and I invite the readers to the next chapters to decide for themselves.

THE WORLD IN JANUARY 2022

Introduction

The year began with bleak economic forecasts across the globe, as a result of supply chain disruption caused by the ongoing COVID-19 pandemic, causing inflation and oil prices to rise. Russia threatened military action in Ukraine, amassing over one-hundred thousand troops close to Ukraine's borders. Russia denied plans to invade and during bilateral talks demanded NATO halt its eastwards expansion. The West responded by sending weapons and troops to eastern Europe, withdrawing diplomatic staff from Ukraine and threatening sanctions if Russia invaded. Russia also faced trouble on its border, as protests escalated across Kazakhstan over rising fuel prices. In the Middle East, the war between Saudi Arabia and Yemen escalated as the Houthis seized an Emirati ship and carried out a drone attack on the UAE. Turkey continued its regional diplomatic efforts, holding meetings with officials from the UAE to boost its flailing economy. North Korea caused international outrage after conducting three separate missile tests in the month of January, provoking further US sanctions. Afghanistan's economic crisis worsened as the country's banks remain cut off from international financial institutions due to Taliban rule. China stepped up its preparations to host the Winter Olympics, despite controversy over its human rights record. US President Joe Biden marked a year in office, polling low as the US faced a wave of the Omicron COVID-19 variant. West Africa faced its third military coup in eight months as troops ousted the government in Burkina Faso. European countries began lifting all COVID-19 restrictions, despite record cases caused by the spread of the Omicron variant.

This chapter will summarise these important developments across the globe which took place throughout the month of January 2022, providing a factual and concise summary. It will begin with the global economy, before moving to Russia and Central Asia, Europe, the Middle East, Asia and Africa, and finally the COVID-19 pandemic.

In hindsight it is now clear that many of the events that started out as minor one became major global events. For instance the seizing of an Emirati ship and drone attack has escalated over the years since then. The Houthis have become more and more bold and have caused major international challenges. China is being isolated more and more by the West. Its stance on Taiwan, its various human rights abuses and the various stance it has taken in supporting rogue states has further isolated it. The West is clearly very wary about it and has taken measures to curtail its financial power. The rise of Huawei and other Chinese companies will clearly be threatened by its attitude to the West. All this will clearly hurt the Chinese economy already reeling from the effects of the pandemic.

GLOBAL ECONOMY

The **International Monetary Fund** (IMF) has cut forecasts for global economic growth because of disrupted supply chains and the impact of pandemic restrictions. Global growth forecasts for 2022 have been revised down from 5.9 percent in 2021, to 4.4 per cent in 2022 in the face of an anticipated rise in American interest rates and slowing consumer demand in China. Rising energy prices and supply disruptions have resulted in higher and more broad-based inflation than anticipated, notably in the US and in many emerging markets and developing economies.

At the end of January 2022, **oil prices** rose to a seven-year high of $90 a barrel, supported by tight supply and geopolitical tensions in Europe and the Middle East, raising fears of further disruption to supplies. The Organisation of Petroleum Exporting Countries and its allies, known as OPEC+, will meet at the beginning of February 2022 to consider another output increase. The group has struggled to meet its monthly production targets as it restores supply to markets after drastic cuts in 2020.

European **gas prices** jumped after the breakdown of security talks between Russia and the United States raised concerns over supply. Russia stated that talks with the US and NATO had failed to address its security concerns, casting doubt over the prospect of a western diplomatic push to defuse Moscow's threat of military action against Ukraine.

The world's poorest countries face a $10.9bn surge in **debt** repayments this year after many rebuffed an international relief effort and turned to the capital markets to fund their responses to the coronavirus pandemic. A group of 74 low-income nations will have to repay an estimated $35bn to official bilateral and private-sector lenders during 2022, according to the World Bank, up 45 per cent from 2020. One of the most vulnerable countries is Sri Lanka, which is at risk of a possible default this year after the country's sovereign bonds were downgraded. Investors are also concerned about Ghana, El Salvador and Tunisia, among others.

UK **inflation** jumped to 5.4 per cent in December, its highest rate in 30 years, deepening a cost-of-living crisis that is squeezing household incomes and putting more pressure on the Bank of England to raise interest rates. The large annual rise in the consumer price index reflected widespread increases in the cost of most goods and services.

US **stock markets** suffered the worst January since the global financial crisis, as the threat of rising interest rates, slowing corporate earnings growth and geopolitical tensions sent stocks tumbling.

RUSSIA AND CENTRAL ASIA

Russian President Vladimir Putin has threatened possible military action in **Ukraine** after deploying around 127,000 Russian troops close to Ukraine's northern, eastern and southern borders. The forces include between 55 and 60 battalion tactical groups, which are highly mobile and strategically independent assault units. Russia has also begun moving ammunition stockpiles, field hospitals and supporting security services to sites close to the border and is preparing to conduct joint military exercises in Belarus. Russia denies it is preparing an invasion of Ukraine, but Putin has warned he has "all kinds" of options if his demands over Ukraine and NATO's activities in the former Soviet bloc are unmet. Western intelligence suggests Russia is preparing a possible invasion of Ukraine, turning the slow-burning proxy war in Ukraine's eastern Donbas region into a full-blown conflict.

Russian officials held three sets of bilateral talks in mid-January with officials from the **US**, **NATO** and **OSCE** in Geneva and Brussels. Russia demanded pledges from NATO to halt the alliance's eastward expansion, a commitment to never admitting Ukraine and Georgia and limiting troop deployments in former eastern bloc countries. The demands are deemed unacceptable by western capitals. The US and NATO ruled out any concessions over NATO's presence in eastern Europe or Ukraine's potential membership. Dmitry Peskov, spokesperson of Russian president Vladimir Putin, said the talks had been "unsuccessful" despite "positive elements" on issues Moscow did not consider central to its demands. A US official described the talks as "frank and forthright", but said there had been no concessions from either side, and no evidence that Putin was ready to de-escalate the crisis.

The **UK and US** have ordered partial withdrawals from their embassies in **Ukraine**.

Britain ordered a number of its embassy staff and family members to leave Ukraine, stating the security situation in parts of Ukraine was "highly unstable" with clashes between Ukrainian armed forces and Russian-backed armed separatists. The move came after the US ordered family members of its embassy staff to leave Kyiv because of the risk of "significant military action" by Russia. The

US State Department also advised all US citizens in Ukraine to depart immediately. US and European allies are drawing up severe financial, technological and military sanctions ready to be used against Russia for aggression against Ukraine and have sought to expose Russia's plans by releasing selected intelligence. US President Joe Biden announced the US was prepared to send up to 8,500 troops to eastern Europe to deter Russia from invading Ukraine. Other NATO member states have pledged to send equipment and military aid to NATO's eastern member states.

UK Foreign Secretary Liz Truss announced plans to toughen the sanctions regime against **Russian oligarchs** with links to the Kremlin. The new legislation would "significantly strengthen" the UK's ability to deal with Russia's "aggressive action towards Ukraine", Truss said. The move was part of "an unprecedented package of co-ordinated sanctions" that the UK was preparing with its allies. The US followed, drawing up sanctions targeting Vladimir Putin's inner circle and its ties to the west, as Washington broadens the list of financial penalties it and European allies will impose if Russia invades Ukraine.

A state of emergency was declared nationwide in **Kazakhstan** after anger at rising fuel prices escalated into protests in several Kazakh cities, with government buildings set alight and demonstrators overrunning an airport in the former capital Almaty. The protests began peacefully over a dramatic increase in the price of liquid petroleum gas, which many people use to fuel their cars. However, escalated into a wider expression of discontent over corruption and economic inequality in the former Soviet state, marking the biggest uprising in Kazakhstan's post-Soviet history. The government detained almost 8,000 people in response, with 164 people dead, blaming the violence on "terrorists" trained abroad. President Tokayev made an appeal for help to the CSTO, a Russian-led military alliance, consisting of Armenia, Belarus, Kyrgyzstan and Tajikistan, who sent 2,030 troops to Kazakhstan to quell the protests. In an address to parliament after the protests were over, Tokayev vowed to tackle the country's entrenched inequality, blaming his predecessor, Nursultan Nazarbayev, for an economy dominated by a few wealthy oligarchs, while millions of ordinary Kazakhs struggle to make ends meet.

EUROPE

In **Finland**, Prime Minister Sanna Marin used a new year's address to underline that the country reserved the option of seeking NATO membership at any time. Russia's foreign ministry stated that Finland and **Sweden** joining NATO would have "serious military and political consequences that would require and adequate response from the Russian side". Both Finland and neighbouring Sweden are militarily non-aligned but have a growing co-operation with NATO and strong bilateral relationships with members of the alliance such as Norway, the US and UK. Sweden's defence debate has been more subdued than Finland's, largely because the governing centre-left social democrats are against NATO membership. However, Sweden sent hundreds of troops to Gotland, a crucial island in the Baltic Sea, in mid-January amid increased Russian naval activity in the Baltic Sea.

The **Baltic** countries of Estonia, Latvia and Lithuania announced they are sending anti-tank and anti-aircraft missiles to Ukraine as a group of European countries try to help Kyiv defend itself better against potential Russian aggression. The move, which follows a British dispatch this week of anti-tank weapons to Kyiv, highlights a split among European powers about whether to arm Ukraine and risk provoking Moscow.

Dmitry Peskov, spokesperson for Russian president Vladimir Putin, said this week that western arms supplies to Ukraine were "extremely dangerous and do nothing to reduce tensions".

Poland has declared it is willing to take in up to a million refugees from Ukraine if Russia invades. The government in Kyiv has said that between three and five million people could be forced to leave the country, with 1.5 million having already been displaced from their homes by fighting in the east of the country. Ministers in Slovakia and the Czech Republic estimate that tens of thousands of Ukrainian refugees might arrive if Russia attacked. Poland, which shares a 330-mile land border with Ukraine and already has a substantial Ukrainian community, expects to receive considerably more. Poland was reluctant to accept asylum seekers during the 2015 migration crisis and in the stand-off on the Polish-Belarusian border last autumn. In 2020 Poland granted asylum to 2,000 people, compared with 128,590 in Germany and 86,330 in France.

Bosnia faced its most serious political crisis since the civil war ended 25 years ago, triggered by a rise in secessionist talk by the hardline leader of the Bosnian Serb entity Milorad Dodik. Bosnia has been governed by a power-sharing agreement since 1995 between the country's three main ethnic groups: the Bosniaks, the Serbs and the Croats. Dodik has been fomenting nationalist sentiment aimed at securing more rights for the Serb-majority Republika Srpska entity within Bosnia. Nationalist riots broke out as Bosnian Serbs took to the streets to celebrate the Day of Republika Srpska, the January 9th banned holiday marking the creation of a detached Serb parastate in 1992, a precursor to the ethnic cleansing that enveloped the country during the Bosnian War.

British Prime Minister Boris Johnson battled a renewed Conservative threat to his leadership, in the wake of the release of a highly critical report on the party culture at the heart of his government. The report details serious leadership failings in Downing Street, claiming coronavirus restrictions were not followed. Johnson has refused to acknowledge that parties took place and insisted that Covid guidelines were followed.

MIDDLE EAST

Yemen's Houthis have seized an Emirati-flagged ship in the Red Sea, opening up another front with **Saudi Arabia** as the long-running war escalates. The Saudi-led coalition called on the Houthis, who are aligned to Iran, to free the vessel immediately, threatening the "use of force" to secure its release. The incident marks the first Houthi seizure of international shipping since 2019, representing a significant escalation in the Yemeni which Saudi Arabia first intervened in in 2015, leading a coalition of nations, including the United Arab Emirates, seeking to restore the government ousted by the Houthis. The Emiratis withdrew most of their military forces from Yemen in 2019 but in recent weeks a powerful Yemeni faction armed and backed by Abu Dhabi has joined forces battling a Houthi offensive in Marib and Shabwa provinces.

Later in January, the Houthis carried out a drone attack on the **UAE**, causing the explosion of three petroleum tankers near a depot of the national oil company. The tanker explosion killed a Pakistani and two Indian nationals and injured six others. One week after the attack the UAE intercepted three ballistic missiles launched by the Houthis, targeting Abu Dhabi and Dubai. The missile launches coincided with a visit to the UAE by Israeli President Isaac Herzog. Saudi Arabia launched the heaviest air raids for more than two years on the Yemeni capital Sanaa a day later, killing over 70 civilians.

The **United Arab Emirates** will introduce a 9 per cent corporate tax rate, as the Gulf monarchy tries to modernise its economy and adapt to international norms. The new regime, which is set to be introduced from June 2023, would cover all business activities in the UAE except the extraction of natural resources, the finance ministry said in a statement. The UAE confirmed there would be no tax on personal income from employment or real estate and other investments.

Western negotiators have said that talks to rescue the **Iran** nuclear deal are on the point of collapse because Tehran's nuclear programme is advancing faster than diplomatic progress towards an agreement. President Biden said talks were moving forward and it was not time to give up. However, European negotiators have been warning for months that there is little sign of a deal being struck any time soon. Biden promised to re-enter the nuclear agreement, which his predecessor Donald Trump withdrew from in 2018, but asked for extra guarantees from Iran that this would lead to talks on a broader range of security issues, including its wider Middle East policies. A particular sticking point in the latest talks is Iran's insistence that Biden sign a written guarantee that the US will never again pull out of the agreement and reimpose sanctions. Biden says that no US president can bind their successor. The issue is especially important because Trump may stand for the presidency again in 2024. The talks have been further held up by Iranian presidential elections. The victorious candidate, President Raisi, is a hardliner who has expressed scepticism about the deal.

Former **Israeli** Prime Minister Binyamin Netanyahu entered into negotiations with Israel's attorney-general for a plea deal in his corruption trial that could spell the end of his political career. Netanyahu is on trial in three separate graft cases after being indicted in 2019 for fraud, breach of trust and bribery. Netanyahu denies the allegations. Under the deal, Netanyahu would agree to plead guilty to two of the fraud charges, while the third would be dropped along with the bribery charge. He would avoid a prison sentence and instead serve up to six months of community service and pay a substantial fine, and accept a seven-year ban from elected office, effectively ending his political career in disgrace.

Turkish and **Armenian** officials met in Moscow for the first round of talks aimed at normalising relations and reopening the border between the two countries, which has been closed for almost three decades. Both nations hailed the "positive and constructive atmosphere" after the meeting, agreeing to continue negotiations without preconditions, aiming for full normalisation. The normalisation effort is the first since a previous peace effort collapsed in 2009 and is not seeking to address the fraught issue of the Armenian genocide of 1915, which remains a source of deep mistrust between the two nations. The priority is to focus on boosting trade and transport links, and appointing diplomatic representatives. The negotiations come at a time when Turkish President Erdogan, who has suffered growing regional isolation in recent years, is in the midst of a diplomatic push to improve relations with former rivals, including Saudi Arabia, the United Arab Emirates and Egypt.

Turkey and the UAE signed a $5 billion deal to boost Turkey's foreign currency reserves. The nations' two central banks agreed a swap agreement, enhancing bilateral co-operation in financial matters. Officials hope the agreement is a herald of further investment from the Gulf nation. The Crown Prince of Abu Dhabi also committed to invest $10 billion in Turkish local businesses from ADQ, an Abu Dhabi state investment vehicle. Turkey and the UAE spent much of the past decade competing for influence in the region after backing opposing sides in popular uprisings that rocked the Arab world in 2011. But both countries have begun recalibrating their foreign policy over the past year, driven by the election of Joe Biden as US president and the desire to boost their economies.

Turkey, which has a large foreign debt burden, has suffered a renewed dip in its reserves of foreign currency after President Erdogan ordered a series of aggressive interest rate cuts in the final months of 2021 despite soaring inflation. The country's negative real interest rates have put heavy pressure on the Turkish lira, which lost about 45 per cent of its value against the dollar last year.

ASIA

A new report has revealed that **North Korea** has exploited "non-financial" businesses and professions to evade international sanctions. North Korea has proven adept at accessing the global financial system, despite a 15-year US-led international sanctions regime. Sanctions were intensified in 2017 after North Korea tested an intercontinental ballistic missile capable of striking the US mainland. North Korea conducted various missile tests throughout the month of January 2022, launching a "hypersonic gliding warhead" and firing an "advanced" ballistic missile in the same week. Both were short-range missiles, capable of striking South Korea and Japan, but not the mainland US. President Kim Jong-un also ordered a re-examination of the self-imposed moratorium on nuclear and long-range missile testing which Pyongyang announced in 2018, shortly before Kim's first summit meeting with Donald Trump. The move would dramatically increase international tensions and risk a new nuclear crisis in East Asia. The decision comes after three years of diplomatic stalemate in which North Korean demands for an easing of economic sanctions have been ignored by the US. The Biden administration has held out the offer of talks, but rejected North Korean demands for a prior easing of sanctions.

North Korea was announced in January as chair of the UN disarmament conference for four weeks in May and June 2022. The conference is billed as the world's single multilateral forum for disarmament negotiations. The US imposed further sanctions on North Korea in the month of January 2022, targeting six North

Korean nationals, a Russian national and a Russian company for involvement with or provision of support for the regime's weapons programmes. The sanctions drew an angry response from Pyongyang and Beijing, North Korea's closest ally. China's foreign ministry criticised the restrictions as "wilful", arguing that they would "only worsen the confrontational mood".

South Korea's president Moon Jae, whose presidency ends in May, is pressing ahead with his quest to declare an end to the Korean war, despite months of diplomacy that has exposed divisions between Seoul and Washington. Moon told the UN General Assembly in September that a formal declaration to end the war, which was fought from 1950 until the signing of an armistice agreement in 1953, would "mark a pivotal point of departure in creating a new order of reconciliation and co-operation on the Korean peninsula". Yet, the discussions between North Korea, China and the US-led UN have not resulted in the signing of an end-of-war declaration.

Myanmar's deposed leader has been sentenced to four more years in prison, after a secret trial found her guilty of illegal possession of walkie-talkie radios, in the latest step by the country's junta to eliminate her permanently from politics. The charges were among the first to be brought against her after her elected government was ousted in a coup last February. Numerous other criminal prosecutions against her continue. Since her arrest in the early hours of the February 1 coup, she has been charged with a dozen separate crimes, including electoral fraud and breaking the official secrets act. All the claims are dismissed by her lawyers, who say that they are politically motivated and intended by the junta as a means of justifying her illegal detention and removing her from neutralising her status as the country's most popular and adored politician.

Afghanistan's currency, the afghani, has plummeted by a quarter since the Taliban seized power last August, exacerbating an economic crisis that has left millions of people in the import-dependent country facing starvation. In Afghanistan, withdrawing US and allied powers cut off the funding that made up 80 per cent of the government's budget, froze more than $9bn in central bank reserves and enforced sanctions that have paralysed the financial system. Banks have been unable to operate properly and public workers such as doctors and teachers have not been paid. The afghani's weakening has stoked what international aid agencies consider the world's worst humanitarian crisis, pushing prices for essential goods beyond the means of desperate Afghans. More than half the population is facing food insecurity, a disaster exacerbated by the freezing winter. The UN and US last month announced exemptions to allow humanitarian aid into the country. But critics maintain that sanctions are punishing ordinary Afghans rather than the Taliban. The World Bank has come under increasing pressure to release more than $1.2bn in frozen funds to pay teachers and other government workers and prevent the collapse of essential services. Under pressure from countries including the US to avoid transferring cash to the Taliban regime after it took over last August, the World Bank froze money pledged to its Afghanistan Reconstruction Trust Fund, the main conduit for foreign governments and other donors.

In **Pakistan,** the Taliban's victory in neighbouring Afghanistan has unleashed a wave of hardline forces that Imran Khan's government is struggling to control, on and within Pakistan's borders. Apart from the border tensions, these range from surging violence by emboldened domestic extremists to a growing political challenge from Pakistani Islamist parties who identify with the Taliban's views. Pakistan has long been one of the Taliban's most important advocates, from openly supporting its regime before 2001 to allegedly providing a haven to the group during the US war. Prime Minister Imran Khan welcomed the Islamists' military conquest in August and has lobbied for more international assistance for its government. Yet, the Islamist threat is growing at the same time as Khan's government is trying to steer Pakistan through an economic crisis and implement a series of unpopular IMF-mandated austerity measures, all while shoring up his position in preparation for elections next year.

As **China** steps up its preparations for next month's **Winter Olympics,** China's President XI Jinping met the president of the International Olympic Committee in a rare face-to-face encounter with an overseas official, as Beijing maintains strict coronavirus prevention measures ahead of the Games. The build-up to the Olympics has been dominated by China's battle to eliminate coronavirus and stop the spread of the highly infectious Omicron variant. The country last month recorded its highest number of daily cases since early 2020 and imposed a lockdown on about 13m residents in the central city of Xi'an for almost three weeks. The measures were recently relaxed. China's closed-loop system for the Games will limit the movements of participants, and authorities in Beijing have encouraged people in the capital to avoid any contact with vehicles transporting Olympic attendees.

Chinese officials have warned foreign athletes attending the Games against making political statements and have threatened to punish those who speak out. The Games are set to be overshadowed by politics as China is under criticism for its poor human rights record, especially in the far west Muslim region of Xinjiang, and its suppression of civil freedoms in Hong Kong. Under International Olympic Committee (IOC) rules, athletes are "not welcome to make political statements". President Putin of Russia is expected to attend the opening ceremony on February 4 in Beijing. The prime ministers of Mongolia and Pakistan, the president of Argentina and the secretary-general of the United Nations are expected to attend the Games. The US, Britain, Canada and Australia announced a diplomatic boycott over human rights abuses in China.

THE AMERICAS

US President Joe Biden marked one year in office, with polls showing just 40.7 per cent of Americans approve of the job Biden has done in his first 12 months, while 54.1 per cent disapprove. Biden's legislative agenda has also stalled after two Democratic senators joined every Republican in blocking his $1.75tn flagship Build Back Better economic package and landmark legislation to protect voting rights. The US Supreme Court blocked Biden's administration from imposing vaccine mandates on large American companies, in another blow for the president as his government struggles to curb the COVID-19 pandemic.

Venezuela's opposition party won an election for state governor in the state of Barinas, where former President Hugo Chavez was born, dealing a blow to Nicolás Maduro's ruling socialists. The one-off election was brought about by a dispute during regional elections in November, when Maduro's dominant United Socialist Party of Venezuela (PSUV) won 19 out of 23 state governorships nationwide to the opposition's three. The contest in Barinas, the remaining state, was too close to call, although partial results suggested the opposition had won it.

Argentina has secured an outline deal with the IMF to restructure $44.5bn of debt from a record 2018 bailout, removing the threat of an imminent clash with the lender as Buenos Aires tries to bolster its floundering economy. Argentina is facing inflation of more than 50 per cent a year, pressure on its exchange rate, dwindling reserves and billions of dollars of IMF repayments. The lender wanted to draw a line under the failure of its $57bn bailout

AFRICA

Two months after being reinstated as Prime Minister of **Sudan**, Abdalla Hamdok resigned, saying a fresh round of talks was needed with the military about a stalled transition to democracy. The resignation comes after mass street protests against a military coup last October and a deteriorating economy. The military has said it is committed to holding democratic elections in 2023, but progress towards that goal has been slow.

Mali has expelled the French ambassador after a breakdown in relations between the two countries. Thousands of French troops have been stationed in the west African country since 2013 as the former colonial power leads an increasingly overwhelmed regional operation against militants linked to al-Qaeda and Islamic State. A coup in Mali in August 2020 upended President Macron's strategy of gradually handing over responsibility to civilian governments, and relations between the two countries have been fraught since. Relations have sunk to a new low in recent weeks after Mali's transitional government announced plans to delay elections by up to five years and employed the services of Russian mercenaries accused of human rights abuses to fight the insurgents. Macron has announced a gradual downsizing of the French force in Mali from 5,000 to under 3,000, but their complete withdrawal would leave the vast Sahel region open to militants, with no co-ordinated counterinsurgency. Denmark has begun withdrawing special forces troops from Mali, after the west African country's military junta insisted on their departure. The Danish troops only arrived in Mali the week before to join the European counterterror force, but the Malian government said in a statement that "no accord authorises the deployment of Danish special forces".

Neighbouring West African countries have imposed a series of severe sanctions on Mali after its ruling military junta announced a delay in the elections it had pledged to hold in February. The 15-member **Economic Community of West African States** (Ecowas) regional bloc will close its borders to the landlocked country, implement economic sanctions and sever diplomatic ties. The moves come as the international community increases pressure on the junta, which seized power in two coups over the past year. The junta has proposed holding elections in December 2025.

The president of **Burkina Faso** has been overthrown by a group of soldiers in the third military coup in west Africa in eight months. A soldier, surrounded by a dozen armed troops, said on national TV on Monday evening that they had detained President Roch Kaboré, suspended the constitution, dissolved the government and national assembly and closed the country's borders. The announcement came the day after heavy gunfire was reported near the presidential residence and at a number of military barracks in the landlocked country. The soldier said Kaboré was unable to lead in the face of challenges including a jihadist insurgency that has left thousands dead and millions displaced. Al-Qaeda and Isis-linked groups have in just a few years taken over wide swaths of Burkina Faso.

Nigeria has lifted a ban on Twitter after the social media company agreed to open a local office and meet other conditions set out by authorities in Africa's most populous country. The reversal came seven months after Abuja ordered telecoms providers to block Twitter in response to the company removing a post by President Muhammadu Buhari that threatened a violent crackdown on secessionists in the country's south-east. Beyond opening a local office, Twitter agreed to appoint a country head and to pay domestic taxes.

COVID-19 PANDEMIC

The **US** reported record-breaking numbers of COVID-19 infections in the first week of January 2022, driving up hospitalisation rates and causing widespread disruption to flights. The growth in infections comes as Tedros Adhanom Ghebreyesus, director-general at the World Health Organization, said it would be possible to end the pandemic in 2022 if 70 per cent of the global population was vaccinated by the middle of the year.

Humanitarian efforts to assist the South Pacific nation of **Tonga** after a volcanic eruption were hampered nation's determination to keep Covid-19 at bay. The subsea eruption of the Hunga Tonga Hunga Ha'apai volcano, about 65km north of the capital Nuku'alofa, triggered a tsunami that caused substantial damage to the island nation. Tsunami waves also crossed the Pacific Ocean while the eruption, which created an enormous ash cloud, set off a sonic boom that could be heard as far away as Alaska. The government has stressed the need to retain its virtually Covid-free status. Tonga was one of the last countries in the world to record a case of Covid-19 after a traveller from New Zealand tested positive while in quarantine in October, triggering a national lockdown. It remains the only confirmed case in the country. The government has held talks with Australian and New Zealand officials regarding the imposition of strict protocols for humanitarian workers. It is expected to waive the 21-day quarantine period for aid workers.

Austria became the first EU country to make vaccination against COVID-19 compulsory for all adults, after lawmakers voted to approve the measure to curb a surge in infections. The government announced the controversial measure in November 2021, but was forced to make significant concessions in the face of fierce opposition and widespread vaccine scepticism that sparked protests in cities across the country. Under the new law, those who refuse to be vaccinated will face fines of up to €3,600. Those vaccinated would be enrolled in a lottery with the chance of winning up to €500 in vouchers to be spent in Austrian businesses.

The world's top-ranked Serbian tennis player **Novak Djokovic** was deported from Australia after his visa was cancelled by Australia's immigration minister. The deportation order, supported unanimously by a three-judge panel, is the second Djokovic faced in Australia in as many weeks, as he sought to stay in Melbourne to defend his Australian Open title. Djokovic, who has publicly opposed mandatory vaccination against COVID-19 in the past and is not vaccinated, entered the country with a medical exemption. However, he was detained at the airport in Melbourne, as the Australian Border Force argued that the tennis star could not provide sufficient evidence to justify his exemption.

Denmark became the latest European country to lift almost all COVID-19 restrictions, in the latest sign that western European countries are easing or even eradicating strict measures brought in to combat the Omicron coronavirus variant. Denmark follows the UK, Ireland and the Netherlands in easing restrictions as infections remain at record highs across the continent due to the Omicron variant. European countries reacted quickly with varying measures of strictness to the emergence of Omicron in December, but have been relieved in the past few weeks that a much-feared rise in intensive care patients has not materialised.

New Zealand reintroduced tough COVID-19 restrictions as Asia-Pacific countries battle to stop the spread of the Omicron variant. The measures, which include stricter mask wearing and social-distancing rules, follow an outbreak of nine cases among a family that travelled between Auckland and the South Island to attend a wedding. New Zealand has been closed to foreign non-residents since March 2020. The restrictions in New Zealand and other Asia-Pacific countries stand in contrast to Europe. New Zealand was one of the last countries to abandon attempts to eliminate the virus by closing borders and imposing strict lockdowns — leaving China as the only large country still pursuing such a strategy, with its "zero covid" policy.

SOURCES:

https://www.thetimes.co.uk/article/growth-forecasts-hit-by-supply-chain-and-covid-pressures-hgrxxjh3g

https://www.thetimes.co.uk/article/oil-price-hits-seven-year-high-as-tensions-rise-in-europe-and-middle-east-jvpgr59jq

https://www.ft.com/content/6f09cfb7-ea4a-4640-940c-750491703f68

https://www.ft.com/content/4b5f4b54-2f80-4bda-9df7-9e74a3c8a66a

https://www.ft.com/content/9188e191-4c1c-4968-a3af-9a43f086de6b

https://www.ft.com/content/e43e33b5-d4a4-462c-ac3a-5901d3beb278

https://www.ft.com/content/5cf5199c-5538-40b6-a059-d2c795108919

https://www.ft.com/content/28e104d4-bee1-4685-acd1-ff7cd0186ddf

https://www.ft.com/content/3b92e7bf-86fe-47bf-8064-24d8983db02c

https://www.ft.com/content/ccec6995-3029-4f47-a553-328dd7646411

https://www.ft.com/content/8084cae5-1e87-4b0f-8490-c0f10e742b05

https://www.politico.eu/article/secession-threat-bosnia-milorad-dodik-eu-limited-options/

https://www.ft.com/content/3fc94e2e-c954-49b5-bc74-58231f276c7e

https://www.ft.com/content/18cda234-a731-47cd-a664-7ec10ef095df

https://www.ft.com/content/17decdab-653c-4c36-846a-0f0368a7bca5

https://www.ft.com/content/121e42b4-a158-445e-a69f-33d1c7e54d3b

https://www.thetimes.co.uk/article/us-hints-at-gas-deal-as-putin-sends-jets-to-ukraine-border-7fr78q2nm

https://www.thetimes.co.uk/article/protests-in-kazakhstan-five-things-you-need-to-know-869jlkvlk

https://www.thetimes.co.uk/article/kazakhstan-protests-rumblings-in-russias-underbelly-776qfp97k

https://www.thetimes.co.uk/article/kazakhstan-unrest-caused-by-foreign-trained-terrorists-vladimir-putin-claims-0kf97nm9n

https://www.thetimes.co.uk/article/the-times-view-on-the-future-of-kazakhstan-trouble-in-eurasia-x5kg8c5zj

https://www.ft.com/content/c942aad3-e406-4d5d-aa64-cef52da8b70f

https://www.ft.com/content/5a1294b4-b412-473c-a628-0015ee786cf0

https://www.ft.com/content/9dc586f8-5da4-4ff3-b71a-0b88c224a4d3

https://www.ft.com/content/67568ccc-f64a-4b1b-b757-50c212d51837

https://www.ft.com/content/ee9005ee-7269-4081-801a-61011b233e78

https://www.ft.com/content/95c5eea0-53c6-4b07-9720-cbe89f1250e5

https://www.ft.com/content/939ab2fa-4242-4156-b251-84c5e874f311

https://www.thetimes.co.uk/article/saudis-hit-back-at-yemeni-rebels-with-air-raids-on-capital-b727z6982

https://www.ft.com/content/184522cd-b549-41de-946f-1ace28c39213

https://www.ft.com/content/dd6452ea-5316-4b26-af34-d5f7e973cc46

https://www.ft.com/content/493f997e-6e85-4fbd-83b1-f580061a508e

https://www.ft.com/content/7555244a-e78b-4226-98a7-61a5db8319ed

https://www.ft.com/content/f69e837e-a39d-4b6c-add0-f609c8b2f47c

https://www.ft.com/content/789f0799-8583-4cbb-b513-8924561caf74

https://www.ft.com/content/a75a74a9-a017-4c5a-9cc9-fd9c76bac51f

https://www.ft.com/content/4b737e92-1c93-4cfa-b184-6ae19c605fdd

https://www.ft.com/content/5804ff8a-71cf-4ab4-a39d-69ecd56ac8e5

https://www.ft.com/content/e14124f9-1073-4cf4-b9ba-3b819eeb01ac

https://www.ft.com/content/cfe422d1-e9dd-400d-8a97-c36e173e78ec

https://www.thetimes.co.uk/article/iran-nuclear-talks-on-brink-of-collapse-warn-negotiators-zqbqhcdbc

https://www.ft.com/content/8ea4f3ea-cdbf-45ff-b4f1-d77451109453

https://www.ft.com/content/ed5918a8-d699-417b-a0f8-4e947fee3dc7

https://www.ft.com/content/ec08f5d0-bd96-4d19-b0b7-6b9caed2d490

https://www.ft.com/content/65fd1e40-c2cc-4098-81fc-2f3cbe3f66cf

https://www.ft.com/content/02194361-a5b9-4bf0-9147-f36ba7759cf1

https://www.ft.com/content/66b4b395-2b16-4689-bbb1-281dd172ec2a

https://www.ft.com/content/69b8e713-fb8a-4fec-ba86-63c3164df877

https://www.ft.com/content/d4de5b83-c01f-45f3-bc1d-74fe4418dfe4

https://www.ft.com/content/45f7b0a3-d050-4afc-9c12-bdb966d971f6

https://www.ft.com/content/085304e3-474b-4ca7-b48b-4e8a70799e9d

https://www.ft.com/content/1f5dc997-c5ff-456c-b58a-11becaecd892

https://www.ft.com/content/ee37b5b3-81b4-488b-a97b-90c7ed42d4a4

https://www.ft.com/content/4493bcf4-91cf-4550-8c67-16e610208a9c

https://www.thetimes.co.uk/article/north-korea-named-chair-of-un-disarmament-conference-whz6p02js

https://www.thetimes.co.uk/article/kim-defiant-after-latest-round-of-missile-tests-xbfp0kvg9

https://www.thetimes.co.uk/article/north-korea-missile-launch-no-let-up-in-provocation-as-kim-conducts-seventh-test-65phs2rvf

https://www.ft.com/content/dd318eb3-9192-49f9-99c9-b723c2bcb5b8

https://www.thetimes.co.uk/article/north-korea-launches-short-range-ballistic-missile-thx0dls56

https://www.thetimes.co.uk/article/north-korea-carries-out-second-missile-test-in-six-days-tmq3w7kfk

https://www.thetimes.co.uk/article/as-he-turns-38-kim-jong-un-has-the-world-where-he-wants-it-02fvn6lqr

https://www.thetimes.co.uk/article/myanmars-deposed-leader-aung-san-suu-kyi-sentenced-to-four-more-years-in-prison-bmtnxmtn8

https://www.ft.com/content/b1b1711c-33e8-4068-8c83-d45f794f75d4

https://www.ft.com/content/5e2ac2b5-47c5-4f8d-8a57-17bf26d5fc8d

https://www.ft.com/content/d0ff7a30-dbbd-4035-8525-bbd817352775

https://www.ft.com/content/51a61659-8caf-4abc-aca7-4a6808917089

https://www.ft.com/content/9f6fc66d-3efd-4465-84ba-f058b6ea9d43

https://www.ft.com/content/b6d0ea59-8439-4325-a5fe-edce8db9b3dd

https://www.ft.com/content/656c84a1-ca69-4357-a1db-287313989aff

https://www.ft.com/content/84b96b13-18cc-4ad8-9ae9-a86f5d03d81a

https://www.ft.com/content/0b4e2635-8fc3-4015-905f-1160786063f0

https://www.ft.com/content/a12d8bad-523b-48ec-8433-b48d2d4e4b88

https://www.ft.com/content/6c1ac211-df0f-4607-9f1e-c9b15e16d609

https://www.ft.com/content/8963b1ee-9ffb-4f2e-8648-472e641716ba

https://www.ft.com/content/3f692e15-0e78-4fe3-845f-74093fafd904

https://www.ft.com/content/b8555ffb-4a19-415b-8263-bda6c816fa3e

https://www.ft.com/content/42241c55-8437-4a8a-bac7-9ad69b89e832

https://www.ft.com/content/9b2debce-60be-41ab-9427-37d209af1d66

https://www.ft.com/content/c4ce76f9-fe3f-4db6-aefa-1163a11b09a5

https://www.ft.com/content/f31edc79-f7df-48d7-badf-5d074cb19afd

https://www.ft.com/content/70451eee-5163-4348-af1a-82656f7a50fa

https://www.ft.com/content/8f00d054-d66a-409c-9a8e-cd6b0a1012f4

https://www.thetimes.co.uk/article/olympic-games-athletes-making-political-statements-will-be-punished-warns-china-qrt69kwp8

https://www.thetimes.co.uk/article/xi-denies-asking-putin-to-delay-ukraine-invasion-until-after-winter-olympics-rvvrg7rq2

https://www.thetimes.co.uk/article/japan-invests-in-railgun-to-shoot-down-north-korea-missiles-pqm9w59ts

https://www.thetimes.co.uk/article/combat-jet-crash-shakes-taiwans-hopes-of-fighting-off-china-in-the-air-lbl0tv9xx

https://www.thetimes.co.uk/article/narendra-modi-hopes-varanasi-temple-gift-will-make-him-a-shoe-in-at-election-time-7pnfcp6cr

https://www.thetimes.co.uk/article/french-ambassador-expelled-from-mali-sqttdpff5

https://www.ft.com/content/7b7ddd65-d7c4-4d43-a3e3-67df24d22afe

https://www.bbc.com/pidgin/tori-59965740

https://www.ft.com/content/822fb15c-ed74-4cd9-be87-0ef40fe35652

https://www.ft.com/content/fec69667-c9f6-4c14-bc9c-ad2887d0f310

https://www.ft.com/content/81764d61-6a3a-4914-b6d6-69d56d256b2a

https://www.ft.com/content/b654f120-01aa-41b1-92e2-f3017b7845bf

https://www.ft.com/content/f4525017-eb6f-47ee-b05e-d381e1b05407

https://www.ft.com/content/a5efad05-38e0-4043-b39b-2793aaa8e748

https://www.ft.com/content/a8b04d55-e9df-425b-b461-bdccceff9dff

https://www.thetimes.co.uk/article/us-plans-to-cripple-russias-banks-if-it-invades-ukraine-05xldp8c9

https://www.thetimes.co.uk/article/nato-vows-to-send-troops-if-russia-invades-ukraine-7bc92mtq0

https://www.thetimes.co.uk/article/russia-threatens-us-with-a-new-cuban-missile-crisis-unless-nato-stops-eastern-enlargement-fvn8pqckg

https://www.thetimes.co.uk/article/cyberattack-shuts-down-ukraines-government-websites-3brkb02lp

https://www.thetimes.co.uk/article/portugal-investigates-roman-abramovich-citizenship-65bsc2j3c

https://www.thetimes.co.uk/article/kremlin-denies-missiles-are-bound-for-ukraine-83rqbmlj0

https://www.thetimes.co.uk/article/british-anti-tank-weapons-sent-to-defend-ukraine-from-russia-2f5lbzn8v

https://www.thetimes.co.uk/article/britain-fears-tens-of-thousands-dead-if-russia-invades-ukraine-jvzb266pr

https://www.thetimes.co.uk/article/liz-truss-accuses-putin-of-ukraine-puppet-plan-s9xd7dmqc

https://www.thetimes.co.uk/article/kiev-puppet-is-a-part-of-putins-toolkit-in-ukraine-warns-us-b5fnbrssk

https://www.thetimes.co.uk/article/britain-pulls-embassy-staff-out-of-ukraine-over-invasion-fears-9bk3brm5d

https://www.thetimes.co.uk/article/russia-joe-biden-prepares-to-send-8-500-troops-to-eastern-europe-to-prevent-ukraine-invasion-vrdkpj8rk

https://www.thetimes.co.uk/article/ukraine-crisis-hard-to-see-how-putin-can-back-down-says-former-mi6-chief-bd93x2cvn

https://www.thetimes.co.uk/article/ukraine-crisis-britain-readies-troops-and-warns-putin-of-tough-sanctions-klkk2w6sd

https://www.thetimes.co.uk/article/ukraine-crisis-how-russias-military-forged-a-path-to-the-forefront-of-warfare-30lwd52zb

https://www.thetimes.co.uk/article/putin-tells-macron-he-doesnt-want-confrontation-over-ukraine-cd3wb7jnv

https://www.thetimes.co.uk/article/west-is-pushing-us-into-chinas-embrace-says-russian-ambassador-6lqqbcqnn

https://www.thetimes.co.uk/article/liz-truss-plans-tougher-sanctions-on-putins-oligarchs-9cjx9qssh

https://www.thetimes.co.uk/article/poland-ready-for-million-refugees-if-russia-invades-ukraine-dgd36gj2n

https://www.thetimes.co.uk/article/the-west-wants-war-in-ukraine-russia-claims-at-fiery-un-meeting-tcgsxm508

https://www.thetimes.co.uk/article/putin-accuses-us-of-warmongering-as-boris-johnson-visits-ukraine-qv8g9fklw

https://www.ft.com/content/baa50a17-5f6b-47f3-8b79-5667ec6d78ac

https://www.ft.com/content/19cf30eb-9955-4e36-8c21-78f410674846

https://www.ft.com/content/e3e47867-e909-4be8-a2d2-c49b7f9570ff

https://www.ft.com/content/5d6d0b54-bb43-4599-8781-dff316e54497

https://www.ft.com/content/4d128a50-ae12-408e-8cee-c4fd685c50ff

https://www.ft.com/content/c237a37b-eeca-45b1-99b2-746c9d10a059

https://www.ft.com/content/cdd4c096-b534-4b8b-a546-36fac89f66e6

https://www.ft.com/content/7c8c2717-0cd4-4dc4-98d4-2f4be8142804

https://www.ft.com/content/833d3784-57cf-46a4-ade2-8d4ab2a3bae2

https://www.ft.com/content/2d04e7a8-c9f6-475f-8c04-5f2edf0fb5a6

https://www.ft.com/content/426889a6-4fe9-4897-b923-6b3f546c5878

https://www.ft.com/content/4d128a50-ae12-408e-8cee-c4fd685c50ff

https://www.thetimes.co.uk/article/satellite-images-reveal-devastation-of-tonga-volcano-eruption-7mgdcp3dg

https://www.ft.com/content/352efc20-e176-49f8-944d-e7c8f18b98b1

https://www.thetimes.co.uk/article/australian-government-commits-a-1bn-in-scramble-to-save-great-barrier-reef-m7q7319kl

https://www.ft.com/content/c87d1c2d-69b6-4367-b229-38ec0dd159dd

https://www.ft.com/content/5d41778b-1ee5-43a7-a61d-3fa88f4a1e00

https://www.ft.com/content/655d0101-b952-481c-a5bb-503de8ad3fa9

https://www.ft.com/content/80ce45ea-da4f-4655-a934-060c41f82576

https://www.ft.com/content/41830ec7-77a7-4754-bc4b-19f62c11dcc6

https://www.thetimes.co.uk/article/fed-signal-on-higher-rates-soon-triggers-wall-street-sell-off-776s2b363

https://www.thetimes.co.uk/article/us-public-gives-joe-biden-the-thumbs-down-over-covid-g7bx72frd

https://www.thetimes.co.uk/article/capitol-rioters-lament-bad-food-and-cable-tv-in-prison-nc2s67r3r

https://www.thetimes.co.uk/article/joe-biden-fights-republicans-to-end-voter-suppression-krqfrw59l

https://www.thetimes.co.uk/article/joe-biden-wants-to-scrap-filibuster-rule-in-fight-over-anti-voting-laws-m8hzwkjsc

https://www.thetimes.co.uk/article/us-inflation-surges-to-40-year-high-of-7-kxp5qtpjp

https://www.thetimes.co.uk/article/us-supreme-court-blocks-joe-bidens-vaccine-mandates-on-large-businesses-m5tkxnhsm

https://www.thetimes.co.uk/article/republican-national-committee-threatens-to-pull-candidates-from-presidential-debates-2cjbl9wzg

https://www.thetimes.co.uk/article/head-of-far-right-militia-oath-keepers-charged-with-sedition-over-capitol-riots-hhpd79g2r

https://www.thetimes.co.uk/article/donald-trump-still-claims-2020-presidential-election-was-stolen-but-vows-to-fight-in-2024-6dpdt27v7

https://www.thetimes.co.uk/article/texas-synagogue-siege-malik-faisal-akrams-gun-tracked-to-legal-sale-mtq8jgq9q

https://www.thetimes.co.uk/article/joe-biden-admits-defeat-2trn-build-back-better-plan-tjz3g7jwl

https://www.thetimes.co.uk/article/judge-throws-out-gulf-of-mexico-oil-and-gas-sale-over-climate-concerns-c2qrlfn5d

https://www.ft.com/content/4bd223ac-82a4-4ab2-b54a-496213b5cf15

https://www.ft.com/content/9ac4d53c-fafe-4e08-969d-d2ae927bc912

https://www.ft.com/content/16200884-9854-4b98-a48d-0388f53218ac

https://www.ft.com/content/1ac9a0b9-5e93-4d1c-8f9b-d3a16db2467a

https://www.ft.com/content/98b128b5-d722-4425-8391-7f74764d5b68

https://www.ft.com/content/03e918f5-e316-483e-871a-bf47da919340

https://www.ft.com/content/1784bcdc-63ac-4a70-8a9a-f87a0b4c128c

https://www.ft.com/content/7f336082-b9a5-421f-abbb-28add05e585f

https://www.ft.com/content/94360f42-5f19-4491-9c15-d1912886f6ed

https://www.ft.com/content/c9ed3413-1142-44d6-8a23-193ed8fe3d09

https://www.ft.com/content/9d3a39c0-0de2-4e82-ae3e-f0cf8535e9f3

THE WORLD IN FEBRUARY 2022

Introduction

February 2022 was a month which was shaped by the start of Russia's invasion of Ukraine. Putin launched his invasion on 24 February, causing condemnation and retaliatory sanctions from leaders across the world. Russia began its assault on Ukraine by attempting to capture the cities of Kyiv and Kharkiv. Almost half a million Ukrainian s were displaced from their homes in the first few days of the invasion. As a result, global food prices began to soar, as did oil and gas prices, sending markets into chaos. Inflation continued to rise in Europe, as did consumer energy bills. In the lead up to the invasion, foreign leaders, including British foreign secretary Liz Truss and French President Emanual Macron visited Moscow in unsuccessful attempts to stop Putin's war. Elsewhere in the Middle East, the leader of Isis was assassinated by US forces in Syria and Turkey continued its rapprochement with Arab states, with Erdogan visiting the UAE. In China, the Beijing Winter Olympics began against a backdrop of political tension, boycotted by most western leaders over China's abuse of its Uyghur population in Xinjiang. In Africa, France announced its withdrawal from the fight against islamist insurgency

Mali due to disagreements with its military leaders. A coup attempt was thwarted in Guinea-Bissau, following a surge of coups across the region in Mali, Guinea, Chad and most recently in Burkina Faso. In Canada, the "freedom convoy" of protestors continued in Ottawa against covid-19 vaccinations.

WAR IN UKRAINE

At the **UN Security Council**, Russia launched an attack on the US for creating "hysteria" over a potential invasion of Ukraine. This came amid repeated warnings from the US that Vladimir Putin is preparing to attack Ukraine. Russia has made various security demands of the West, including that Nato drop its open-door policy on countries that can join the alliance. US president Joe Biden has rebuffed Russia's requests and has said he is prepared to send troops to Nato members on the eastern flank of the alliance to bolster their defences. Russia has continued to increase the number of troops amassed on the border with Ukraine, despite claims from Russia's president that troops were withdrawing. Russia has concentrated 150,000 troops on its border with Ukraine and in Belarus for military exercises.

In the morning of 24 February **Russian** president Vladimir Putin began a military invasion of **Ukraine**, launching Europe's worst conflict since the second world war. Putin launched a barrage of missile strikes and sent troops and tanks into Ukraine, while warning dire consequences to other countries attempting to get involved. Nato called an emergency meeting of its top decision-making body ahead of an emergency summit of EU leaders to decide further retaliatory measures. Putin denies his intention is to occupy Ukraine, but has said Russia intends to redraw its borders.

The US and western allies announced plans to place **sanctions** on Russia's central bank and remove some of the country's lenders from the Swift global financial messaging system. They vowed to address the issuing "golden passports", which allow wealthy Russians buy citizenship to certain countries and to introduce sanctions on those close to the Russian government.

Russia's Ukraine offensive has exposed deep divisions among world leaders, with some pointedly refraining from condemnation and others maintaining silence. China's decision not to criticise President Putin had been widely expected, but the ambivalence from India, Saudi Arabia, the Gulf states and more than a dozen countries notionally friendlier towards the West is striking. Many have avoided using the term "invasion" or attributing blame to Russia, and still more have declined to say anything at all. Many states in Asia, the Middle East and Africa have either remained silent or issued statements without mentioning Russia. Of the states in southeast Asian, only Singapore expressed support for Ukraine. Kenya and several other African states have vigorously denounced Russia's aggression but the African Union has yet to take a position, and South Africa simply called on "all parties" to negotiate. The Gulf states, which are riding a wave of turbulence the conflict has stirred in the energy markets, have declined to take sides. There have been few endorsements of the invasion, including from Russia's allies. President Lukashenko of Belarus came closest, saying he had made troops available to Moscow. Venezuela pledged "powerful military co-operation" with Russia, and Iran blamed the US and Nato for the war.

Russia's invasion of Ukraine caused **global food prices** to soar, threatening supply chains and pushing up commodities markets that had already hit multiyear highs. Russia and Ukraine combined make up a third of the world's wheat exports. The attack has led to a ban on all commercial vessels in the inland sea of Azov, which connects to the Black Sea, and the closure of Ukrainian ports. Almost 90 per cent of Ukrainian grain exports are transported by sea; the disruption will impact global food supply chains and markets. Wheat and corn prices have risen significantly since the invasion began. Supply chains were already struggling with high demand and rising prices due to poor harvests in countries such as Canada, a key exporter.

Russian's plan for a quick takeover of the Ukrainian cities of **Kyiv** and **Kharkiv** has been met by strong resistance from Ukrainian forces. Ukrainian troops repelled a Russian incursion into the eastern city of Kharkiv as Russia forces continued to slowly encircle the capital Kyiv, where defending troops have retained control despite four days of attacks. The level of resistance from Ukrainian forces, particularly in cities, has come as a surprise to Western officials. The resistance comes as Russian forces have been targeting Ukraine's southern coast, seeking to block Ukraine's access to the Black Sea.

Over half a million Ukrainians have fled the country since Russia began its invasion and more than 100 civilians have been killed. Many more have been internally displaced.

EUROPE

Inflation has reached its highest levels in Europe for the third month in a row. Eurozone countries saw consumer prices increase

by an annual 5.1 percent in January, breaking records. Once again, soaring energy prices played a major role, rising 28.6 percent. Oil prices have spiked as the global economy recovers from the worst of COVID-19 restrictions, while natural gas prices have surged in Europe because of depleted winter reserves, lower supplies from Russia and fears over Russia's offensive in Ukraine. Higher energy bills for consumers have quickly become a political issue in Europe as governments roll out subsidies and tax breaks to soften the blow to household budgets. Higher inflation makes it more expensive for people to buy everything from food to fuel and has been one factor holding back Europe's recovery.

Germany has announced a big shift in defence policy in response to the Russian invasion of Ukraine. Chancellor Olaf Scholz pledged a jump in military spending and a revamp of the armed forces. His government has faced repeated criticism over its reluctance to take a more aggressive position towards Russia. Scholz said recent developments had convinced him that Putin is aiming to build a new Russian empire, and that the defence of peace and democracy in Europe must be strengthened as a result. Scholz pledged to invest €100bn this year in a fund to modernise Germany's military and to boost yearly defence spending above 2 per cent of gross domestic product in the future. As a Nato member, Germany has already pledged to spend 2 per cent of its GDP on defence but, like many of its European allies, it has almost never reached that target. This marks a major turning point for Germany, which under Merkel's 16-year leadership followed a policy of cautious engagement with Russia.

Austria became the first country in the EU to make vaccinations against Covid-19 mandatory for all adults, but questions remain over whether it can sway those sceptical of taking the jab. The upper house of the Austrian parliament, the Bundesrat, formally approved a law that will see those over the age of 18 who decline to take a jab, face penalties of up to 3,600 euros, unless they are pregnant or severely ill. The legislation has been followed with great interest across Europe, where other nations have considered taking a similar step.

President Macron will start his run for a second term as president of **France** and hold a rally to launch a five-week campaign that will cast him as a reliable statesman against a field of mediocre contenders. Aides confirmed that the 44-year-old president will descend from the Elysée Palace into the campaign ring. Macron's long-awaited entry is expected to give new energy to a race that has been under way for months, dominated by three challengers to the right of the centrist president, none of whom has posed a serious threat to his position as favourite.

The Russian foreign minister publicly taunted **UK** foreign secretary Liz Truss as "unprepared", likening their face-to-face meeting on the Ukraine crisis to talking to a deaf person. Truss is the first foreign secretary to visit Moscow in four years, meeting Lavrov to deliver an uncompromising message that Russia should withdraw all its forces from Ukraine's border immediately to prove its professed peaceful intentions. Lavrov questioned the reasons for Truss's visit to Moscow, beyond reiterating Britain's position on sanctions.

British Home Secretary Priti Patel has said President Macron was "absolutely wrong" to blame Britain for the migrant crisis in the Channel. The home secretary rejected Macron's comments blaming Britain's reliance on "illegal" migrant labour for the crisis. Last year brought a record number of arrivals in the UK, more than 28,000, and last month six times as many people came as in the same month last year. Macron wants to establish a legal route for asylum seekers.

MIDDLE EAST & NORTH AFRICA

Iraq has become a major beneficiary of China's Belt and Road Initiative. China is deepening its economic ties across the Middle East through billion-dollar construction and energy contracts. Beijing reached $10.5bn in new construction deals in Iraq last year. Beijing's efforts to foster deeper economic ties with Iraq, Opec's second-largest oil producer, coincides with a growing perception among Arab leaders that the US is disengaging from the Middle East. The US has around 2,500 troops in Iraq in a training and advisory role.

US President Biden announced the leader of **Isis** was killed by an explosion as US special forces launched a night-time raid on his hide-out in north-western Syria. Abu Ibrahim al-Hashimi al-Qurayshi launched explosion as American troops approached his loaction, killing himself and family members. The raid, which lasted about two hours, is one of the biggest US assaults of its type in north-west Syria since special forces conducted an operation in 2019 in which Isis's founder Abu Bakr al-Baghdadi was killed. Qurayshi succeeded Baghdadi as the group's leader.

Official inflation in **Turkey** has reached the highest level since Erdogan came to power two decades ago. This comes as global inflationary pressures combined with the president's unorthodox economic policies have fuelled a surge in prices. The country's consumer price index rose 48.7 per cent in January, up from 36 per cent in December. Erdogan, who was widely credited during his first decade in power with ushering in economic prosperity, has presided over repeated bouts of high inflation in recent years.

Turkey's President Erdogan has signed a deal to strengthen defence co-operation with **Ukraine,** a move which is in defiance to warnings from Moscow. Erdogan signed deals on free trade and defence following talks with President Zelensky in Kyiv. The deals include the joint production in Ukraine of lethal drones, expanding a partnership under which Ukraine has previously bough aerial vehicles from Turkey and deployed them against Russian-backed separatists. During the visit to Kyiv Erdogan reiterated support for the "territorial integrity" of Ukraine and Crimea and offered to act as a mediator between Ukraine and Russia.

Turkish president Erdogan arrived in the **United Arab Emirates** for his first official visit in nine years, building on a rapprochement between the two countries after a decade-long feud in the wake of the Arab uprising. The two countries signed 13 co-operation agreements, one of which was an intention to launch negotiations over a free trade agreement. The UAE has been refocusing on economic development through partnership agreements that aim to boost trade and investment. The visit comes during a shift in foreign policy for Turkey as it tried to ease tensions with its regional neighbours.

The US will restore sanctions waivers related to **Iran's** atomic activity. The move appears to be a goodwill gesture in the lead up to talks aimed at reviving 2015 nuclear accord. The agreement could lead to Russian, Chinese and European companies receiving waivers from the US to engage in civilian nuclear activities. The decision comes as western diplomats warn that time is running out to save the Joint Comprehensive Plan of Action (JCPOA). Former president Donald Trump pulled the US out of the agreement in 2018 and reimposed sanctions on the republic, revoked the waivers in 2020. Analysts in Iran and western capitals see the move on waivers as a confidence building measure by the US, which has been in indirect talks with Iran in Vienna since April to resurrect the agreement.

US President Joe Biden has moved to freeze about $7bn in assets held in the US by the **Afghan** central bank due to the Taliban takeover. The move comes as Biden has vowed to direct $3.5bn to humanitarian aid and preserve the rest for families of victims of the September 11 terror attacks. The move effectively cuts off the Taliban's access to the US financial system and caps months of uncertainty over the Afghan central bank's funds in the US. The Biden administration has faced competing pressures to keep humanitarian assistance flowing to the Afghan people while ensuring that court-ordered pay-outs to families of the victims of the 2001 attacks were honoured.

Libya's parliament appointed a new prime minister in a deal that could produce two rival administrations and deliver a setback to UN plans to unite the North African country. Fathi Bashagha was appointed prime minister by the House of Representatives, which is based in Tobruk in the east, amid frustration stemming from the UN-recognised government in Tripoli failing to hold December elections. Abdul Hamid Dbeibeh, the interim prime minister of the Government of National Unity in Tripoli, rejected Bashagha's appointment and refuses to step down until elections have taken place. This raises the possibility of two rival leaders vying to rule the country. Dbeibeh's government replaced two opposing administrations in the east and west of the country that has been divided since 2014.

The **United Arab Emirates** and **India** signed a free trade deal that will likely double bilateral non-oil trade to $100bn within five years. The comprehensive economic partnership agreement is expected to boost growth, exports and job creation in both nations. The UAE expects the deal to add $9bn to GDP by 2030. It also forecasts an increase of exports to India by 1.5 per cent, or $7.6bn, and imports to the Gulf state rising by $14.3bn, or 3.8 per cent, by the end of the decade. The pact is also expected to deliver a further 14,000 skilled jobs to its workforce over the same timeframe. The deal will enable Indian and Emirati businessmen to apply for government contracts in each country. The deal comes as a success for India, which has been seeking to sign bilateral trade agreements since leaving the pan-Asian RCEP agreement due to concerns over China's membership.

Tunisian police locked the country's Supreme Judicial Council building and blocked staff from entering a day after President Kais Saied dissolved it. The move came after Tunisian judges rejected the President's decision to disband the council that oversees them, raising fears about the independence of the judiciary amid growing concerns over his consolidation of power. Saied announced he was dissolving the Supreme Judicial Council, one of the few remaining state bodies still able to act independently of him. The move capped months of sharp criticism of the country's judiciary, which he accused of corruption and of being infiltrated by his political enemies.

The United Nations Security Council (UNSC) has extended its arms embargo to all Houthi rebels. This comes as the **Yemeni** group faces increased international pressure after a series of recent attacks on Gulf countries. The resolution was proposed by the UAE and extends an embargo to the entire Houthi group. The Emirati mission to the UN welcomed the result of the vote. The move comes days after US President Joe Biden's administration administered new sanctions against a network accused of transferring millions of dollars to the Houthis – and amid a push by the Emirati government for countries to take a tougher stance against the rebels. The Houthis have ramped up their attacks against Saudi Arabia and started directly targeting the UAE in recent weeks.

ASIA

India will increase investment by more than a third in an endeavour to reclaim its place as the world's fastest-growing large economy. The government plans to spend heavily on infrastructure to recover from the covid-19 pandemic. The recent budget unveiled plans for the central bank to launch its own digital currency along with a hefty tax on cryptocurrency profits, indicating that the government was scrapping a mooted proposal to ban the assets. The government expected India's gross domestic product to grow 9.2 per cent in the year ending March and 8 to 8.5 per cent in the 12 months from April, faster than any other large economy. The increased revenue will go towards India's railway network, building highways and rural housing, and to other initiatives such as climate financing.

China joined **Russia** in opposing further expansion of Nato, a significant step up in Beijing's backing for Moscow as the leaders of the two countries agreed to deepen co-operation across a range of security, political and economic areas. With the west opposing Russia's military build-up on the Ukraine border and China's treatment of Uyghurs in Xinjiang, Putin and Xi presented a united front in talks just hours before the opening ceremony of the Beijing

Winter Olympics. Putin hailed China's "unprecedented" co-operation with Russia. The men were pictured side by side. It is the first time that President Xi has met any foreign leader in more than two years. This is Putin's first foreign trip of the year, as the leader did not attend last year's G20 and Cop26 meetings. Putin told Xi that Russia has prepared a new deal to supply China with 10 billion cubic metres of natural gas from its Far East

The Winter Olympics began in **Beijing** against a backdrop of heightened geopolitical tensions. The Games began with a muted opening ceremony that exemplified the closed nature of the games and the country's increasingly complex attempts to defeat coronavirus. The opening ceremony of the games was boycotted by western leaders in protest over China's treatment of its Uighur minority and its clampdown on the democracy movement and free press in Hong Kong.

Myanmar's resistance leaders are pleading with the International Court of Justice in the Hague not to give legitimacy to the country's ruling junta in a case alleging that its soldiers perpetrated genocide against Rohingya Muslims. The ICJ began four days of hearings on the claims of genocide, during the brutal displacement of more than 700,000 Rohingya, who were forced out of Myanmar into Bangladesh in 2017.

But since the hearings began two years ago, the democratically elected government of Aung San Suu Kyi has been overthrown and replaced by a military government. The junta has sent its own legal team to the Hague, despite warning's Myanmar's shadow democratic government to not give them any standing in the case as this would imply a recognition of their legitimacy.

A report by the UN Security Council states that **North Korea** is stealing cryptocurrency to develop its ballistic missile programme and increase capacity to manufacture nuclear warheads. The report follows a series of missile tests by DPRK, including nine tests last month alone. The report cited conclusions by the cybersecurity firm Chainalysis that North Korea stole close to $400 million in at least seven attacks on cryptocurrency platforms last year, although this was less than the estimate of $2 billion from cybertheft in 2019. North Koreas recent missile tests have included medium and short-range ballistic missiles, cruise missiles and hypersonic ballistic missiles whose high speed and manoeuvrability makes it difficult to intercept them with conventional missile defence shields. The country's continued missile testing shows the weakness of US and western policy on the country. The Biden administration has invited the country for talks at any time without preconditions.

The North insists that the US must first "end its hostile policy", code for reducing sanctions, something that it refuses to do.

AFRICA

Security forces in **Guinea-Bissau** thwarted a coup after gunmen attempted to overthrow the west African country's government in an attack that may have been linked to drug trafficking. Heavy gunfire had erupted in the capital Bissau near the government palace, where President Embaló was presiding over a cabinet meeting. This follows a surge in coups across the region, including in Mali, Guinea, Chad and most recently in Burkina Faso. Guinea-Bissau, a former Portuguese colony, is sometimes known as Africa's first narco-state due to the control drug traffickers have exerted over it as a hub for Latin American cocaine moving to Europe.

France and its European and west African allies announced they will shift the focus of their anti-terrorism campaign in the **Sahel** eastward to Niger and south to the Gulf of Guinea after being pushed out of Mali by the country's military rulers. Islamist militants have recently targeted coastal states such as Nigeria and Benin. Nine people were killed in this month in three bomb explosions in northern Benin. France later announced that its forces in Burkina Faso had killed the 40 jihadis responsible.

Mali's military leadership has postponed elections for five years. The move comes during a growing international outcry over the erosion of freedoms under the leadership of the junta, which is supported by Russian mercenaries. The country has been hit by sanctions and relations with its previous military partner France have deteriorated after two successive coups. At the centre of the

Sahel-wide insurgency, which has killed thousands of soldiers and civilians and displaced some two million people, Mali's generals struck a deal with the Wagner Group, a Russian private army linked to the government. Its parliament is dominated by members of the armed forces and has now approved the delay to elections, passing the legislation by 120 votes out of 121. The military's increasing grip on power has unsettled the West and thrown its international counterterrorism effort into doubt after President Macron announced France would withdraw its troops.

A suicide bomber killed 14 people in a restaurant in the **Somali** town of Beledweyne during a round of voting there. The attack was claimed by the Al-Shabaab Islamist militant group, which has been waging an insurgency in the Horn of Africa for years. Security had been tightened in Beledweyne ahead of a first session of voting for parliamentary seats in the constituency, which lies about 340km (210 miles) north of the capital Mogadishu. Al-Shabaab said in a statement that one of its fighters carried out the bombing. Somalia, particularly the capital Mogadishu, has seen a spate of attacks in recent weeks as the country struggles through a long-delayed election process. Witnesses said the huge explosion tore through an open area of the Hassan Dhiif restaurant where people had gathered under trees to eat lunch.

A vessel with a storage capacity of two million barrels of oil exploded off the coast of southern **Nigeria's** Delta state, raising fears of an environmental disaster and concerns about the fate of its crew. The floating production, storage and offloading vessel can process up to 22,000 barrels of oil a day, according to the operator's website.

Thousands of **Eritrean** refugees sheltering at a camp in the Ethiopian Afar region, have fled following an attack on the camp. Unidentified assailants targeted the camp after fighting engulfed the area. The attack is the latest instance of Eritrean nationals living in Ethiopia coming under fire, since conflict erupted and spread from the northern Ethiopian region of Tigray in November 2020. A joint investigation by the UN human rights office and the Ethiopian Human Rights Commission (EHRC) highlighted how Tigrayan and national Ethiopian fighters had put the security and lives of thousands at risk in Shimelba camp, between November 2020 and January 2021.

THE AMERICAS

Argentina secured an outline deal with the IMF to restructure $44.5bn of debt from a record 2018 bailout, removing the threat of an imminent clash with the lender. Argentina faces inflation of more than 50 per cent a year, pressure on its exchange rate and billions of dollars of IMF repayments. The lender wanted to draw a line under the failure of its $57bn bailout, which veered off track after only a year with most of the money already disbursed.

Peru's left-wing president Pedro Castillo announced the third cabinet of his turbulent six months in office, naming a new prime minister and replacing all his top ministers. This comes after a which during which the prime minister, finance minister and interior minister all quit amid allegations that Castillo lacked leadership and had done little to tackle on corruption within his administration. Castillo, a former primary school teacher without experience in public office, will now put his reshuffled cabinet to the opposition-controlled congress for a vote of confidence. Castillo is likely to face further challenges to his rule in the coming months, including possible impeachment. He has already survived a similar attempt.

Two days of heavy rains and the resulting floods have killed at least three people in **Haiti**. Rescuers began evacuating people in high-risk zones, where thousands of homes have been flooded and some 2,500 families have been displaced.

The north of the country has been the hardest hit, with water filling the historic centre of the city of Cap-Haitien, and strong winds downing trees. The rains are the most recent natural disaster to strike the Caribbean nation, where death tolls are often high due to the poor state of housing and lacking infrastructure. The disasters have compounded the dire state of the country's economy, with high rates of crime and insecurity worsened by a political crisis in the wake of the assassination of President Jovenel Moise in July 2021. Authorities said the storm has affected areas that are still trying to recover from a 7.2 magnitude earthquake which hit the country in August, killing more than 2,000 people.

In the **Brazilian** Amazon, deforestation in January of this year was five times as much than in the same month of 2021, the highest

January total since records began in 2015. Environmentalists accuse Brazil's President Bolsonaro of allowing deforestation to accelerate. Trees are felled for their wood and to clear space to plant crops to supply global food companies. During the COP26 summit in Glasgow last year, over 100 governments promised to stop and reverse deforestation by 2030. The latest data calls into question the Brazilian government's commitment to protect the amazon rainforest.

More than 100 people have died in landslides and flash flooding in the **Brazilian** city of Petropolis. The city, which is located in the mountains north of Rio de Janeiro, was hit by torrential rainfall. Houses in hillside neighbourhoods were destroyed and cars swept away as floodwaters raced through the city's streets.

In **Canada,** protesters continue to occupy the centre of the city of Ottawa, stating that they will not leave until all COVID-19 restrictions and mandates, trucking related and beyond, were lifted. The city has been blocked off by protestors who have blockaded the downtown area with trucks and cars. The mayor of has declared a state of emergency and police have described the protests and blockade as a "siege". In January, a relatively unknown group called Canada Unity announced a "freedom convoy" to protest vaccine passports and mandates installed by different levels of government in Canada. This group has unsuccessfully tried to launch such a convoy before, but this time succeeded due to frustration with a new requirement that all truckers crossing the US-Canada border must be vaccinated against Covid-19. Canada's prime minister Trudeau has invoked emergency powers to stop the protests. Trudeau stated he will use powers granted under the Emergencies Act, including the ability to prohibit public assembly and travel.

SOURCES:

https://www.aljazeera.com/news/2022/1/31/un-security-council-set-to-meet-on-ukraine-crisis-liveblog

https://www.aljazeera.com/news/2022/2/24/putin-orders-military-operations-in-eastern-ukraine-as-un-meets

https://www.reuters.com/world/europe/eu-announces-new-russia-sanctions-with-us-others-including-swift-2022-02-26/

https://www.thetimes.co.uk/article/ukraine-invasion-silence-of-world-leaders-shows-moscow-s-long-reach-p379cblbt

https://www.ft.com/content/c0c9fe20-e219-45d4-b029-2cfbaf86a755

https://www.ft.com/content/dd28dd4c-ab02-4f06-a56a-e930d1ce0ffd

https://press.un.org/en/2022/sc14865.doc.htm

https://www.aljazeera.com/economy/2022/2/2/eurozone-inflation-hits-new-record-for-third-month-running

https://www.ft.com/content/ffc46030-51c6-4d87-b81b-457a31fbcdc9

https://www.theguardian.com/world/2022/feb/04/austria-passes-covid-vaccine-mandate-but-question-marks-linger-over-enforcement

https://www.thetimes.co.uk/article/french-election-2022-macron-to-fire-starting-gun-on-campaign-against-mediocre-rivals-hhg0g5zd5

https://www.thetimes.co.uk/article/boris-johnson-and-liz-truss-urge-russia-to-back-down-over-ukraine-d27ns5w8b

https://www.thetimes.co.uk/article/macron-absolutely-wrong-to-blame-britain-for-migrant-crisis-says-patel-0b93wfjb7

https://www.ft.com/content/f2ef2f3f-c663-4ce8-82d8-8c95ba23de97

https://www.ft.com/content/868e266f-5090-40ee-bffe-f1287245c04a

https://www.ft.com/content/8d7e220d-396f-4752-9d69-b3ad30310f01

https://www.ft.com/content/e2b7df41-6dc6-4ed5-88e5-ab0819967138

https://www.ft.com/content/34b89882-8cb4-45aa-b371-4572a313b5ff

https://www.ft.com/content/bfc23f1b-f05b-4dae-91f4-a7d1c87131e5

https://www.ft.com/content/9018de5d-540f-479a-ba43-ab7323a4790c

https://www.ft.com/content/23ba97ab-dd28-46b7-9952-549db90b174d

https://www.ft.com/content/0cc60d7d-8461-4584-b497-508ea3ac8dd0

https://www.bbc.co.uk/news/world-africa-60281864

https://www.bbc.co.uk/news/world-africa-60281864

https://www.aljazeera.com/news/2022/2/28/un-security-council-extends-yemen-arms-embargo-to-all-houthis

https://www.ft.com/content/a0a6cf20-c4c0-43a0-a717-010167dbf1e7

https://www.theguardian.com/world/2022/feb/04/xi-jinping-meets-vladimir-putin-china-russia-tensions-grow-west

https://www.ft.com/content/fe0bf2ee-3245-46c0-805d-a49a5c6d90e4

https://www.thetimes.co.uk/article/hague-court-urged-not-to-recognise-myanmar-junta-in-genocide-case-jfb92815n

https://www.thetimes.co.uk/article/north-korea-stealing-cryptocurrency-to-develop-missile-programme-un-says-sm0rh3pbl

https://www.aljazeera.com/news/2022/2/2/explainer-guinea-bissau-attempted-coup

https://www.ft.com/content/0b3e194f-13e2-49a2-bec0-bcd552dce26b

https://www.thetimes.co.uk/article/mali-junta-delays-elections-by-five-years-jmwn686df

https://www.theguardian.com/world/2022/feb/19/suicide-bombing-kills-in-somali-restaurant

https://www.aljazeera.com/news/2022/2/4/explosion-nigerian-oil-vessel-sparks-fears-major-spill

https://news.un.org/en/story/2022/02/1112232

https://www.ft.com/content/9ac4d53c-fafe-4e08-969d-d2ae927bc912

https://www.aljazeera.com/news/2022/2/1/at-least-three-dead-in-haiti-floods-official

https://www.bbc.co.uk/news/science-environment-60333422#

https://www.geoengineer.org/news/brazil-petrpolis-deadly-landslides-at-least-100-fatalities

https://www.theguardian.com/world/2022/feb/07/ottawa-declares-state-of-emergency-as-canada-trucker-protest-paralyses-city

THE WORLD IN MARCH 2022

Introduction

This was a month that saw the world grappling with the consequences of Russia's invasion of Ukraine. The impacts of this war were far reaching. As Russia continued its military advance into Ukraine, capturing the cities of Kharkiv and Mariupol, Western states were united in their support for Ukraine, sending arms and aid and offering to take in displaced Ukrainian refugees. The United States and European Union announced a range of tough sanctions, aimed at targeting the Russian economy. NATO responded by conducting military exercises in the Arctic.

The world grappled with the shake-up in global energy markets, as EU countries scrambled find alternative energy sources to Russian oil and gas. The rise in energy prices saw inflation and goods prices rise across the globe. Aside from the war in Ukraine, there were political developments elsewhere in the world throughout the month of March, with a change of governments in South Korea and in Chile. In Pakistan, Prime Minister Imran Khan faced a no-confidence vote and Indian Prime Minister Narendra Modi won a series of state-level elections. The economic crisis is Sri Lanka worsened, with protestors storming the presidential palace in response to daily power cuts and shortages. In North Korea, Kim Jong-un tested a powerful new intercontinental ballistic missile. In the Middle East, talks were underway to revive the 2015 Iranian nuclear deal and Israel continued its diplomatic effort to normalise ties with countries in the Middle East. Qatar continued its plans to host the 2022 World Cup, as its Gulf neighbour the United Arab Emirates hosted Syrian leader Bashar Al-Assad for talks. In Europe, British-Iranian dual national Nazanin Nagari-Ratcliffe arrived back in Britain after six years of detention in Iran. In France, President Macron launched his campaign for re-election and Moldova and Georgia officially applied to become EU member states. African nations grappled with a potential food crisis triggered by the war in Ukraine and the officials from the World Health Organisation debated when to officially call an end to the global Covid-19 pandemic.

This chapter will outline these important global events which took place through the month of March 2022, providing a factual and concise summary of key developments. It will begin discussing the war in Ukraine, before moving onto discuss developments in global energy markets. It will then discuss global political developments on a regional basis, beginning with Asia, then the Middle East, Europe, the Americas and Africa. It will summarise developments on climate change and the Covid-19 pandemic before concluding.

THE WAR IN UKRAINE

Russia continued its military advance into **Ukraine**, which began on 24 February 2022 when President Putin announced a "special military operation". Russian forces advanced from Belarus along the banks of the Dnipro River towards the Ukrainian capital Kyiv. This advance was limited by the Ukrainian defence. Russian forces carried out sustained rocket attacks on the city of Kharkiv and heavy shelling on the port city of Mariupol. On 24 March, Russian forces circled and entered central Mariupol, destroying more than

85 percent of the town. Russian forces also captured the city of Kherson, near Odessa, and Russian-backed separatists demolished and captured most of the city of Volnovakha.

By the end of March 2022, over 4.5 million people had been displaced by the war. Many Ukrainians had been internally displaced, with 2.5 million refugees fleeing the country, mostly to neighbouring **Poland**. Britain announced that 200,000 Ukrainians would be eligible to come to the UK, as other European nations announced similar measures to welcome refugees fleeing the war.

On 3 March 2022, a historic vote took place at the **United Nations General Assembly**, demanding that Russia stop its military offensive in Ukraine and immediately withdraw all troops from the country. The vote comes after the assembly held the first emergency session since 1997. In the vote, 141 countries voted to condemn the invasion. Four countries voted against the motion: Russia, Belarus, Eritrea, North Korea and Syria. There were 35 countries which abstained from the vote, including China, India, Pakistan and nearly half of African countries.

The **United States** and its allies responded to the invasion by announcing sanctions on Russia's financial institutions, including disconnecting Russian banks from accessing the SWIFT global financial messaging system. Most notably, Russia's central bank was blocked from using its foreign currency reserves, causing the rouble to decline more than 20 percent against the dollar on 3 March 2022. Globally companies quickly began to withdraw their business from Russia. Most notably, McDonalds announced the closure of its 850 branches across Russia. The first branch opened in Moscow's Red Square in 1990, signifying Russia's opening up to the West after the Cold War.

The **United States** Senate gave final approval for a $13.6bn emergency military and humanitarian aid package for Ukraine and its European allies. The $13.6bn allocates roughly $6.5bn to the Pentagon for military assistance and about $6.7bn for refugees and to provide economic aid to eastern European allies.

The **European Union** announced sanctions on individuals considered close to the Russian government, freezing their assets in EU countries and preventing them from travelling to the bloc. Other countries followed suit in introducing sanctions against government-linked individuals and oligarchs. Roman Abramovich announced the sale of Premier League football club Chelsea, which had been under his ownership for 19 years.

The Foreign Ministers of Russia and Ukraine met for face-to-face talks in **Turkey** on 9 March, in the first high-level contact between the two sides since the Russian invasion began in February. NATO member Turkey is keen to maintain strong relations with both sides despite the conflict. After the talks, Ukraine's Foreign Minister Dmytro Kuleba said he secured no promise from Russian Foreign Minister Sergey Lavrov for a temporary ceasefire to deliver aid to civilians, and the main humanitarian priority of evacuating the hundreds of thousands of people trapped in the besieged port city of Mariupol. Lavrov asserted that Russia wanted to continue negotiations with Ukraine.

The first **Syrian** troops arrived in Russia at the end of March 2022, to join the war against Ukraine. Ukrainian military intelligence estimates that 40,000 Syrians have enlisted to join fight. The pro-regime militia groups have been trained and backed by Russian units since late 2015, when Putin formally intervened in the Syrian war to assist President Assad.

NATO is to conduct its biggest military exercises since the end of the cold war during a period of rising tensions caused by Russia's invasion of Ukraine. Over 30,000 troops will take part from 27 countries which include the USA, UK, Germany and France. The exercise is aimed at helping Norway practise its defence from air, sea, and land. It will take place throughout the Nordic country, and in the Atlantic and North and Norwegian seas. NATO is concerned that Russia may look to destabilise other areas of Europe during its invasion of Ukraine, in an attempt to either distract or divide the alliance, officials have said, and the Arctic, alongside the Baltic states, is seen as a potential target.

GLOBAL MARKETS

Globally, markets suffered severe shocks throughout the month of March as countries grappling with the far-reaching economic consequences of the war and sanctions. Most impacted were **global energy markets**, as Russia is the world's largest exporter of natural gas, second largest exporter of oil and third largest exporter of coal in the world. On 8 March 2022, America announced an embargo on Russian oil, with Britain announcing it would follow suit later this year. This shocked commodities markets, with swings in prices of brent crude and gas. As oil prices rose above $112 a barrel, a number of Western countries urged Opec to increase production. Energy companies, including BP, Shell and ExxonMobil, vowed to stop buying oil from Russia.

EU countries began to seek alternative energy suppliers to Russia and ways to shield consumers from rising prices. Germany signed a long-term agreement with the Gulf state of **Qatar** to supply natural gas. This would significantly reduce Germany's reliance on Russian gas, accounting for over half of its annual supply.

In the **UK**, it was announced that household electricity and gas bills are expected to double for the year 2022-2023. Most UK households will see their annual energy bills go over £3,000 from October 2022 due to a surge in gas and electricity prices. Britain's Chancellor, Rishi Sunak, came under pressure to announce a windfall tax on British energy producers.

The month of March 2022 saw inflation in the **Eurozone** rise to 5.8 percent. Increases in the price of energy were accompanied by higher surges in the cost of services and manufactured goods. Energy prices rose by a record 31.7 per cent, while unprocessed food prices rose 6.1 per cent. Lithuania saw the highest national annual inflation rate at 13.9 per cent, whereas France had the lowest at 4.1 per cent.

ASIA

In **Pakistan**, Imran Khan, the Prime Minister since he took office in 2018, faced a political crisis. Opposition parties prepared a no-confidence vote to remove his Pakistan Tehreek-e Insaf (PTI)-led coalition government. Khan lost his majority in parliament when a key ally quit his coalition government. The opposition requires172 votes in the 342-member National Assembly to defeat Khan. The opposition accuses Khan of corruption and economic mismanagement, amidst high inflation and a weakened currency. No Pakistani prime minister has ever completed a full term in the country's 75-year history, which has been marred by frequent coups by the military. Khan remained defiant in his position and accused the United States of conspiring with the opposition to remove him from his position, allegations the US has denied. Khan claimed Washington wants him deposed as he has been pursuing an independent foreign policy and visited Russia after it launched its invasion of Ukraine.

Khan also faced pressure from Western diplomats to condemn the Russian invasion of Ukraine, after abstaining from the vote in the UN General Assembly. Khan said his country had suffered in the past after supporting NATO and the US-led alliance. Pakistan had faced criticism, resentment and violence domestically, predominantly from conservative Muslims. His words come after a suicide bombing at a Shia mosque in Peshawar, which killed 62 people and in injured over two hundred more.

In **Myanmar**, the deposed elected leader Aun San Suu Kyi plead not guilty to corruption charges accusing her of receiving hundreds of thousands of pounds worth of cash and gold bars from a former political supporter. The charges are part of over a dozen criminal charges brought against Suu Kyi since she was arrested during the military coup which forced her from power in 2021.

In **India**, Narendra Modi came closer to becoming India's longest-serving Prime Minister, after polls suggested his party was heading for a series of victories in state-level elections. As the count came in on 10 March 2022, the BJP held majority vote in the states of Uttar Pradesh, and the smaller states of Goa, Manipur and Uttarakhand. In the medium-sized state of Punjab, voters elected the Aam Aadmi

Party (AAP, with 77 percent of the seats). The voting in Uttar Pradesh is seen by many as a referendum on Modi's popularity. The state has a population of 200 million people and sends 80 MPs to India's 543-seat national parliament.

In **Sri Lanka**, the country's worst economic crisis since its independence in 1948 deepened, with the government announcing 13-hour daily power cuts. Police introduced an overnight curfew after hundreds of protestors attempt to storm President Gotabaya Rajapaksa's private residence amid anger over the worsening economic crisis. Hospitals suspended routine surgeries after running out of medicine supplies. The country had been under severe electricity rationing since the beginning of the month. Foreign currency reserves had fallen by seventy percent in the two years leading to March 2022, leaving Sri Lanka struggling to import essentials, including fuel and food. The country introduced a broad import ban in March 2020 to save foreign currency needed to service its $51bn foreign debt. However, this led to widespread shortages of essential goods and sharp price rises. The government is seeking a bailout from the International Monetary Fund (IMF).

In **South Korea**, voters elected a new President, hardliner Yoon Suk-yeol. Yoon promised to strengthen the country's alliance with the United States and take a sterner position on North Korean aggression, which is likely to add to ongoing tensions around North Korea's test-firing of ballistic missiles. This will bring to an end the engagement policy pursued by Yoon's predecessor, President Moon, who held three meetings with the North Korean leader Kim Jong-un.

North Korea has tested a new intercontinental ballistic missile, marking the first long-range testing in the country since 2017 and drawing international condemnation. Kim Jong-un was reported to have directly guided the test of the Hwasong-17 – a "new type" of intercontinental ballistic missile that is North Korea's biggest to date. He said the country will continue to develop a "nuclear war deterrent" in preparation for a "long-standing confrontation" with the US. The missile flew for 1,090km to a maximum altitude of 6,248.5km to hit a target in the sea. Kim ordered the test due to the "daily-escalating military tension in and around the Korean peninsula". It a significant step in North Korea's development of weapons that might be able to deliver nuclear warheads anywhere in the US.

A passenger plane with 132 people on board has crashed in southern **China**, with no survivors announced so far.. The China Eastern Airlines plane departed from Kunming, on route to Guangzhou. An hour into the journey, the Boeing 737, plummeted more than 20,000 feet in just over a minute. It then regained altitude briefly, before falling rapidly again. The plane crashed near the city of Wuzhou in Teng County, Guangxi province. China's leader, Xi Jinping, called for a prompt investigation into the cause of the crash, the country's first major fatal air disaster since 2010.

MIDDLE EAST

In **Saudi Arabia**, 81 men were executed in one day, the most in a 24-hour period in the history of the kingdom. State media reported that they were convicted of "multiple heinous crimes". The kingdom's human rights record has come under increasing scrutiny in the West since the 2018 killing of Saudi journalist Jamal Khashoggi in the Saudi consulate in Istanbul. It is Saudi Arabia's struct laws on political and religious expression, and its use of the death penalty which are mostly criticised.

Yemen's Houthis rebels have acknowledged a series of attacks on Saudi Arabia after state media in the kingdom reported rocket and drone strikes targeting an Aramco oil depot in Jeddah and other facilities in Riyadh. Saudi Arabia has been leading a coalition of states fighting the Houthis for seven years. The Houthis took control of the Yemeni capital of Sanaa in September 2014. Saudi state media later announced that the coalition fighting in Yemen had begun a military operation, including air attacks on Yemen's Houthi-controlled capital Sanaa, and the Red Sea port city of Hodeidah, to stop attacks on its oil facilities and "protect global energy sources".

On 27 March, **Israel** hosted an unprecedented summit with the leaders of Bahrain, Egypt, Morocco and UAE. In the previous week, Egypt hosted the leaders of Israel and the United Arab Emirates as part of a wider diplomatic effort to normalise ties with Israel and address regional concerns about Iran. Notably absent were representatives from the United States and Saudi Arabia. The Kingdom is yet to normalise ties with Israel.

Erbil, the capital of **Iraq**'s autonomous Kurdish region, was hit by twelve cruise missiles at midnight on 13 March. The Islamic Revolutionary Guard Corps of Iran claimed responsibility, claiming the target was the "strategic centre" of Mossad, Israel's spy agency.

Syrian leader Bashar Al-Assad visited the **United Arab Emirates** in March 2022, his first visit to an Arab country since 2011. The trip coincided with the eleventh anniversary of the Syrian uprising, which began in 2011. Assad met with Sheikh Mohamed bin Rashid al-Maktoum, vice-president and prime minister of the UAE and the ruler of Dubai. The two discussed expanding bilateral relations between their countries. The meeting signals that the Arab world is willing to re-engage with the Syrian President, the latest in a series of diplomatic overtures that point to a shift underway in the Middle East where numerous Arab countries are resuming ties with Assad. The visit drew criticism from Washington.

In Doha, **Qatar**'s capital, the 72nd FIFA Congress took place, the first in-person annual event of football's world governing body since 2019. Qatar is set to host the 2022 football world cup in November. Questions and concerns around Qatar's human rights record dominated the conference. The chief of Qatar's World Cup organising committee, said labour reforms achieved by Qatar have been "historical" and the event would leave "truly transformational social, human, economic and environmental legacies".

In **Iran**, the Iranian Foreign Minister declared that Iran and other world powers were close to reviving the 2015 nuclear deal, which President Donald Trump pullet out of unilaterally in 2018. Negotiations have been ongoing for months in Vienna with Britain, France, China, Germany and Russia to revive the accord, known as the Join Comprehensive Plan of Action (JCPOA), which would limit Iran's nuclear programme in exchange for lifting tough sanctions on Iran's economy. The European Union's coordinator for nuclear talks, Enrique Mora, arrived in Tehran on 26 March. The main remaining issue is the designation of "terror" on the Iranian Islamic Revolutionary Guard Corps by the United States. Mora will travel to Washington to meet American counter-parts after holding talks in Tehran.

In **Turkey**, the annual inflation rate hit a two-year high of 54.4 percent as the government cut interest rates. The Turkish lira has been generally stable since the start of the year, despite losing 44 percent of its value against the dollar in 2021, since the central bank slashed its policy rate under an unconventional policy driven by President Erdogan. Erdogan approach rejects the idea that inflation should be fought by raising primary interest rates, believing this causes prices to rise even higher, contrary to conventional economic thinking. Erdogan insists that lower interest rates will be beneficial for his country's economy, and says patience is needed to see the results of this new and controversial policy.

EUROPE

On 16 March 2022, Nazanin Zaghari-Ratcliffe arrived back in **Britain** after being arrested in **Iran** in 2016 whilst visiting her parents. The dual British-Iranian national spent four years in prison, accused of plotting to overthrow the Iranian regime, a charge she has denied. She returned with Anoosheh Ashoori, fellow dual national arrested in 2017 and accused by the regime of being an Israeli spy. A third prisoner, Morad Tahbaz, a who is a British-American-Iranian national, was released from prison on house arrest to his home in Tehran. The British government negotiated their release, agreeing to settle a historic debt of £394m dating back to 1971, when the Shah of Iran paid for 1,500 British tanks and other equipment, which went undelivered after the Islamic revolution of 1979. The terms of the deal confidential, but the British government says it complies with sanctions and anti-money-laundering rules, and the proceeds can be spent only on humanitarian aid.

In **France**, Emmanuel Macron launched his campaign for re-election, pledging to pursue what he depicted as his successful attempts to reform France since taking office in 2017. Macron also pledged to make France a more "independent nation" by cutting dependence on foreign energy and fossil fuels and double the size of the military reserve. He pledged to raise the retirement age from 62 to 65 and cut taxes to bring unemployment down. Marine Le Pen, his far-right rival in the presidential campaign, vows to curb the cost of living and tackle immigration. Polls predict Macron will beat his rival, but by a smaller margin than in the 2017 election.

Moldova officially applied to become a member of the European Union, a week after the Russian invasion of Ukraine began. Fellow ex-Soviet member state **Georgia** also formally applied for membership of the bloc. Moves by former Soviet countries to build closer relationships with the West have long angered Russia. Moscow is fiercely opposed to the Eastwards expansion of the EU and NATO, which it sees as a direct threat to Russia's security.

THE AMERICAS

In **Canada**, Prime Minister Justin Trudeau looks set to stay in power until 2025 after his Liberal Party signed a coalition agreement with a small left-wing partner. The deal means the New Democratic Party, the fourth largest in parliament, supports the prime minister's centre-left Liberals in confidence votes, including the next four budgets, and on key legislation.

Voters in **Chile** elected the world's youngest president, 36-year-old Gabriel Boric, a former student protest leader. Boric's election brings in Chile's most left-wing government since Salvador Allende, the radical socialist ousted by Augusto Pinochet in a coup in 1973. Chile was rocked by months of unrest in 2019 over inequality, corruption and inadequate social welfare. Many of the protesters' demands echoed those which Boric and his contemporaries had pushed in a student movement which demanded that Chile be rebuilt with the concerns of its people at the core. Boric wants to set up a state development bank and a state-run lithium company. However, his left-wing coalition, even after allying with the centre-left, lacks a majority in Congress, which threatens to hamper his progress.

The **United States** President Joe Biden came under mounting pressure from within his party to end sweeping asylum restrictions put in place in March 2020 to curb the spread of Covid-19. The border policy allows the US to quickly expel asylum seekers and migrant families caught crossing the US-Mexico border. The Biden administration held talks with officials in Costa Rica, Mexico and Colombia in March 2022. Biden called for a new framework on how countries in the Central and South America region can collectively manage migration, aiming to sign a regional declaration on migration and protection in June 2022.

AFRICA

The chief of the **African Development Bank** (AfDB), the continent's largest multilateral lender, announced that the war in Ukraine could trigger a food crisis in Africa. As the war draws into its second month, the prices of natural gas, wheat and fertiliser have risen significantly. Russia and Ukraine combined produce more than a quarter of global wheat exports. Africa is strongly dependent on both countries for grain exports. Wheat imports make up 90 percent of Africa's $4bn trade with Russia and almost half of the continent's $4.5bn trade with Ukraine, according to AfDB. The bank is working on a $1bn emergency food production plan for Africa to avoid food shortages and bring down inflation, to support 20 million farmers access to climate-resilient agricultural technologies to boost food production to feed 200 million Africans.

In Africa, **Burkina Faso** became the latest country to announce a lengthy delay to elections, after Paul-Henri Sandaogo Damiba signed a charter to remain in power for another three years. Damiba came to power in a coup in January 2022. Last month neighbouring Mali confirmed it would not hold elections for up to five years. Burkina Faso has replaced Mali as the epicentre of the jihadist insurgency developing across the Sahel region. President Macron announced in February 2022 that French forces were withdrawing from Mali after the coup and recruitment of Russian mercenaries. The United States has suspended $160 million in aid to Burkina

Faso, whilst the African Union and West Africa's regional bloc, Ecowas, have suspended Burkina Faso's membership.

CLIMATE CHANGE

The **Intergovernmental Panel on Climate Change** (IPCC) published its latest assessment report. The report sets out the current state of knowledge on the known impacts of climate change on humans and ecosystems. It states that at current levels, human action in heating the climate are causing dangerous and widespread disruption, threatening devastation much of the natural world and making many areas uninhabitable. The report says droughts, floods, heatwaves and other extreme weather are accelerating and causing increasing damage. About half the global population, between 3.3 billion and 3.6 billion people, live in areas "highly vulnerable" to climate change. The final section of the report is due to be published in October to set out lessons for governments meeting in Egypt for the UN Cop27 climate summit.

COVID-19 PANDEMIC

Public health experts at the **World Health Organisation** (WHO) have begun discussing how and when to call an end to the global Covid-19 crisis, exploring what would be an important milestone, over two years after the virus first emerged. The discussions are focusing on what conditions would eventually signal that the public health emergency declared in January 2020, is over. Many nations around the world have already taken steps to return to more normal social behaviours, relaxing masking and quarantine guidelines, and opening borders to travel. Yet cases are notably rising in the Asia region, particularly in Hong Kong and China. Researchers have warned that even if Covid-19 cases fall to lower levels, the disease is still likely to cause thousands of deaths annually, and the potential for new, dangerous variants is unpredictable.

China placed 17 million people under lockdown after the worst COVID-19 outbreak in two years. Shenzhen told all residents to stay at home as it struggles to eradicate an Omicron outbreak from the neighbouring city of Hong Kong. A nationwide surge in cases saw local authorities close schools in China's biggest city, Shanghai, and lock down north-eastern cities. Almost 18 provinces are fighting the Omicron and Delta variants. The Chinese state has maintained a strict "zero-COVID" policy, which involves enforcing by swift lockdowns, travel restrictions and mass testing when outbreaks emerge. The latest outbreak, driven by the highly transmissible Omicron variant and a rise in asymptomatic cases, has the efficacy of the "zero-covid" approach.

Hong Kong announced the end of flight bans and plans to reduce quarantine for arrivals, amid mounting frustration China;s strict "zero COVID" policy that has isolated the city from the world. Hong Kong's Chief Executive Carrie Lam announced that authorities will lift flight bans on nine countries including the United Kingdom and the United States and cut hotel quarantine length for incoming travellers with a negative COVID-19 test result.

The Prime Minister of **New Zealand**, Jacinda Arden, announced a major relaxation of the country's strict covid restrictions. From April 2022, vaccine passes for entry to shops and venues will no longer be required and vaccine mandates will be dropped for some public sector workers. New Zealand has reached 95 percent vaccination rate for the eligible population.

CONCLUSION

This chapter has provided a summary of the key global events which shaped the world during the month of March 2022. These events mainly centred on the war in Ukraine and developments which arose as a result of this war, such as shocks in global energy markets and rising inflation across the globe. March was a month which saw the world divided on how to respond to the war, exposing the multipolarity of the current international order.

SOURCES

Al Jazeera

https://www.aljazeera.com/news/2022/3/25/why-is-pakistans-opposition-seeking-pm-imran-khans-removal

https://www.aljazeera.com/news/2022/3/31/tear-gas-as-sri-lanka-protesters-try-to-storm-presidents-house

https://www.aljazeera.com/news/2022/3/3/unga-resolution-against-ukraine-invasion-full-text

https://www.aljazeera.com/sports/2022/3/31/what-happened-at-the-72nd-fifa-congress-in-qatar

https://www.aljazeera.com/sports/2022/3/31/what-happened-at-the-72nd-fifa-congress-in-qatar

https://www.aljazeera.com/news/2022/3/25/saudi-aramco-jeddah-storage-facility-hit-by-attack

https://www.aljazeera.com/news/2022/3/13/china-announces-new-curbs-amid-worst-covid-outbreak-in-two-years

https://www.aljazeera.com/news/2022/3/3/moldova-officially-applies-for-eu-membership

https://www.aljazeera.com/news/2022/3/26/eu-envoy-in-tehran-to-help-finalise-stalled-nuclear-deal-talks

https://www.aljazeera.com/news/2022/3/15/us-seeks-regional-approach-to-migration-and-asylum-seekers

https://www.aljazeera.com/economy/2022/3/11/who-begins-discussing-when-and-how-to-declare-end-of-pandemic

The Economist

https://www.economist.com/briefing/2022/03/05/the-war-in-ukraine-is-going-to-change-geopolitics-profoundly

https://www.economist.com/finance-and-economics/2022/03/12/can-the-world-cope-without-russias-huge-commodity-stash

https://www.economist.com/asia/2022/03/12/narendra-modis-party-triumphs-in-indias-bellwether-state

https://www.economist.com/asia/2022/03/19/sri-lankas-government-is-stoking-inflation-and-indignation

https://www.economist.com/middle-east-and-africa/2022/03/19/with-america-distracted-iran-hits-iraqs-kurds

https://www.economist.com/middle-east-and-africa/2022/03/26/syrias-outcast-dictator-returns-to-the-arab-world

https://www.economist.com/britain/2022/03/17/after-years-in-jail-nazanin-zaghari-ratcliffe-returns-to-britain

https://www.economist.com/europe/2022/03/12/marine-le-pen-hopes-for-another-face-off-against-emmanuel-macron

https://www.economist.com/the-americas/2022/03/19/chiles-new-president-won-from-the-left-can-he-govern-like-that

https://www.economist.com/science-and-technology/the-latest-un-climate-report-is-gloomy-with-some-sunny-patches/21807952

The Financial Times

https://www.ft.com/content/a7263347-f2c2-425b-85d7-0bcbd0091e52

https://www.ft.com/content/1192517b-e405-486f-a743-51b5be356024

https://www.ft.com/content/262801ca-848f-4134-b571-6b73b5338884

https://www.ft.com/content/b7055867-80b2-4187-b4a4-1bf600dcc32b

https://www.ft.com/content/7d62ddb3-73f8-46c4-9cb7-70e43b8f33a2

Foreign Affairs

https://www.foreignaffairs.com/articles/ukraine/2022-03-18/new-economic-containment

The Guardian

https://www.theguardian.com/world/2022/mar/11/gabriel-boric-chile-president-new-era

https://www.theguardian.com/world/2022/mar/18/syrians-join-russian-ranks-in-ukraine-as-putin-calls-in-assads-debt

https://www.theguardian.com/world/2022/mar/24/n-korea-confirms-missile-testing-ahead-of-long-confrontation-with-us

https://www.theguardian.com/world/2022/mar/21/chinese-plane-crashes-guangxi-province-china-eastern-737-wuzhou

https://www.theguardian.com/world/2022/mar/23/a-new-beginning-new-zealand-to-drop-covid-vaccine-passes-and-mandates

The Times

https://www.thetimes.co.uk/article/eu-freezes-assets-of-russian-oligarchs-and-allies-of-putin-h0crbf8ml

https://www.thetimes.co.uk/article/russians-stoic-as-mcdonald-s-shuts-its-doors-hw55x7p8n

https://www.thetimes.co.uk/article/british-visas-for-ukrainian-refugees-doubled-to-200-000-after-outcry-33c5v6xdv

https://www.thetimes.co.uk/article/more-than-2-5-million-people-have-fled-ukraine-since-russian-invasion-ckgh8lc9q

https://www.thetimes.co.uk/article/brent-crude-hits-112-a-barrel-on-supply-fears-as-peace-hopes-fade-crspl0sjs

https://www.thetimes.co.uk/article/aung-san-suu-kyi-denies-absurd-cash-and-gold-bar-corruption-charges-t95tgtmzp

https://www.thetimes.co.uk/article/south-koreans-elect-yoon-suk-yeol-hardliner-who-backs-strikes-on-kim-8kfkpxx7f

https://www.thetimes.co.uk/article/ukraine-invasion-russia-war-latest-lnws2h2rf

https://www.thetimes.co.uk/article/putin-wipes-out-entire-ukrainian-city-of-volnovakha-b28k0lwh7

https://www.thetimes.co.uk/article/burkina-faso-s-dictator-paul-henri-sandaogo-damiba-delays-elections-for-three-years-jf7sd7njk

https://www.thetimes.co.uk/article/imran-khan-lashes-out-over-demands-for-pakistan-to-rebuke-russian-invasion-8b5cmz3tb

https://www.thetimes.co.uk/article/narendra-modi-cements-dominance-over-india-as-bjp-heads-for-victory-in-uttar-pradesh-3jppzv0xw

https://www.thetimes.co.uk/article/saudi-execution-spree-puts-mockers-on-johnsons-oil-plea-2wxh8rdw5

https://www.thetimes.co.uk/article/emmanuel-macron-asks-nation-for-second-term-38tfh6svb

https://www.thetimes.co.uk/article/emmanuel-macron-sets-out-his-vision-for-a-more-independent-france-fdp6phs00

THE WAR
IN UKRAINE

The War in Ukraine is an important event that deserves analysis as it has brought enormous changes.

Change has happened to the landscape of a large country devastated by war. Change has happened to millions of Ukrainians displaced beyond any calculations, having to flee and seek refuge in Poland and other European countries. Change has happened in Russia due to the increasingly dictatorial regime of Putin. A once emerging and prosperous country has become a pariah and sanctions have cost it dearly. Ordinary Russians have suffered too having been asked to go to the front lines only to be killed or wounded in battle.

Change has happened in geopolitics in the world with the Bipolar and Unipolar power structure undergoing significant changes. Change has happened in how wars are conducted with the advent of new technologies such as drone warfare. In the coming pages, I will examine this conflict in detail.

Two brotherly nations are at war with significant consequences. On the one hand, stand the Russians with their nuclear arsenals and huge military assets. On the other hand, we have Ukraine without even a navy to defend itself. It however is a strategic country supplying grains and many important raw materials to the world. A conflict would be devastating to the entire world. It will bring a lot of negative changes to the world. The changes that the world must adopt to food production, energy consumption and the demise of the bipolar world order is significant. The war has opened up various challenges to geopolitics and the old system of the West's dominance of the world order which is being openly challenged across the world.

It is best to deal with this conflict by discussing the following:
1. *Background to the conflict*
2. *NATO expansion, Russian concerns and views*
3. *The war and its trajectory*
4. *Possible end game scenarios*
5. *New geopolitical issues after the war*
6. *The impact of technology on the war and the impact of war on technology*
7. *The impact of the war on international currencies*

Introduction

In late February 2022, Russia launched a full-scale invasion of Ukraine, transforming an eight-year conflict in eastern Ukraine into a war which has displaced millions of Ukrainians and has undermined Europe's security order. Confounding expectations, alongside reinforced military and economic support by Western powers for Ukraine, has forced Russia to reassess its goals in the war. As Russian forces struggle, Moscow has mobilised hundreds of thousands more troops to the frontline, annexed new territories, attacked Ukraine's energy infrastructure and threatened use of the nuclear card. Now months after Russia began its assault on Ukraine, the prospects for peace remain unlikely. Both sides insist peace will come only if the other concedes; Ukraine wants Russia to completely withdraw its forces from the country, including Crimea and regions held in the eastern Donbas, dropping its unilateral claim of annexation. Ukrainian President Zelenskyy signed a decree ruling out any negotiations with President Putin, although he has since stated he is open to negotiations on Ukraine's terms. Russia's position is harder to read; officials say they are willing to negotiate but reject Ukraine's terms without any offer of concessions or proposals. Ukraine has made territorial gains, during a September counteroffensive, and in the south, including the November liberation of Kherson, the regional capital held by Russian troops since early March. However, Kyiv's military capacity is dependent on a steady supply of weapons from the West. Western states have been providing arms and humanitarian support for Ukraine since the war began in February. However, as inflation and interest rates continue to rise across Europe, this support may begin to wane in 2023 and beyond. For now, support for Ukraine remains generally strong, although Kyiv still struggles at times to ensure all forces are adequately equipped. Equally, it is doubtful that Russia can prevail. Moscow reacted to Ukraine's rebound by mobilising some 300,000 men into the army. Comparable numbers have fled the country for fear of being conscripted. Moscow has also begun targeting Ukraine's energy infrastructure with missiles as winter looms. President Putin has appeared to acknowledge Russia was in for a lengthy war. Russia has been issuing consistent reminders to Ukraine and to the West of its nuclear capabilities.

Current predictions for possible outcomes of the conflict suggest that it could drag on for months, if not years, if neither side makes significant territorial gains. Whatever the conflict's outcome, the war has already shaken up the current "rules-based" international order and the global security order. It is clear the unipolar US-dominance which characterised the post-cold war era is over. The world is now moving towards a new global order.

BACKGROUND TO THE CONFLICT

Russia's invasion of Ukraine on 24 February 2022 marked a dramatic escalation of a conflict that had been ongoing for 8 years on eastern Ukraine's border with Russia after Russia's annexation of Ukraine. However, there were various events leading up to 2014 which are essential to contextualising the conflict in Ukraine. To understand the current conflict's background, it is important to address Russia and Ukraine's long shared history.

THE SHARED HISTORY OF UKRAINE AND RUSSIA

The shared history of Ukraine and Russia goes back over a thousand years to a time when Kyiv was the centre of the first Slavic Orthodox state, the Kyivan Rus. It was founded during the ninth century by Viking warrior-traders from Scandinavia (known Varangians or Rus) who mixed with the local east Slavic population.

In the 13th century, most of what is now Ukraine and Belarus, were divided between the Grand Duchy of Lithuania and the Kingdom of Poland, when they invaded from the west in the 16th century. In the 17th century, the war between the Polish-Lithuanian Commonwealth and Imperial Russia divided Ukraine. The west of the Dnieper River came under Polish control and the east under Russian. The west side was later annexed by the Russian Empire in 1793 and a policy of Russification was enforced. As eastern Ukraine came under Russian rule much earlier than Western Ukraine, people in the east tend to have stronger ties to Russia.

The collapse of the Russian Empire in 1917 lead to the creation of the Soviet Ukrainian Republic in 1922, a founding member of the Soviet Union. During WWII, the entire territory of Ukraine was occupied by German troops. Soviet power was restored in 1944, and in 1945 when the United Nations was established, the Ukrainian SSR, along with the USSR, became members of the General Assembly.

The Ukrainian referendum in December 1991 spelled the end of the union; Russia, Ukraine, and Belarus initiated its formal dissolution. In the three decades since the break-up of the Soviet Union, Ukraine has sought to form its own path as a sovereign state, whilst looking to align more with Western institutions, such as the EU and NATO. However, Ukraine has struggled to align internal nationalist divisions within Ukraine with foreign policy. A more nationalist, Ukrainian-speaking population in the West of the country diverges from a mostly Russian speaking population in the East. Uniting the country after 1991 proved to be a difficult task.

The mass protests against the administration of Victor Yanukovych in late 2013 and early 2014 set in motion a succession of profound changes in Ukraine. The pro-Russian administration of Victor Yanukovych was replaced with the pro-Western administration of Petro Poroshenko. The protesters were objecting to the decision by Yanukovych to scrap plans for closer economic ties to the European Union The protests which followed became known as the 'Euromaidan protests', leading to the 'Revolution of Dignity' in 2014 which toppled Yanukovych, who then fled in exile to Russia.

Russia took advantage of the political turmoil in Ukraine in 2014 to take military control over Crimea. Russian authorities calculated that the local Russian majority would support the peninsula's incorporation into Russia, and it formally annexed the peninsula after a disputed local referendum in which Crimeans voted to join the Russian Federation. At the same time, Russia began arming separatists in the Donbas region in southeast Ukraine, another region home to a large number of ethnic Russians and Russian speakers. The Russian annexation of Crimea marked the first time since the Second World War that a European state had annexed the territory of another. More than fourteen thousand people died in the fighting in the Donbas between 2014 and 2021, the deadliest conflict in Europe since the Balkan wars of the 1990s. The conflict marked a clear shift in the politics of global security, marking a shift from the period of unipolar US dominance since the fall of the Soviet Union, to one of multipolar competition between world powers.

NATO EXPANSION

In April of 2016, NATO made public its plan to send four battalions to Eastern Europe, with troops being rotated through Estonia, Latvia, Lithuania, and Poland. This deployment aimed to discourage potential future Russian aggression in other parts of Europe, particularly in the Baltic states. In September 2017, the United States also sent two U.S. Army tank brigades to Poland to reinforce NATO's position in the area. In 2018, the United States introduced fresh sanctions targeting twenty-one individuals and nine companies with connections to the conflict in eastern Ukraine. Additionally, the U.S. Department of State granted approval for the sale of anti-tank weaponry to Ukraine, marking the first time that lethal weapons had been sold since the commencement of the conflict. Later that same year, Ukraine, in collaboration with the United States and seven other NATO nations, participated in extensive air exercises conducted in western Ukraine. These exercises followed Russia's own annual military manoeuvres, which were the most significant since the dissolution of the Soviet Union.

Late in 2021, Western and Ukrainian intelligence agencies released information about a massive build-up of Russian troops on Ukraine's border and the preparation of infrastructure for a possible invasion. Russian authorities maintained that these preparations constituted nothing more than military drills; however, they concurrently delivered an ultimatum to Western nations, requesting written assurances against any additional expansion of NATO to the east. This ultimatum included restrictions on the types of weapons placed in NATO member countries who have joined the alliance since 1997 and a halt to any NATO military cooperation with other post-Soviet states (notably, Ukraine and Georgia). Meanwhile, the Russian media stoked fears about an imminent NATO attack on Russia and a Ukrainian offensive in the Donbas. In January 2022, President Vladimir Putin threatened possible military action in Ukraine after deploying around 127,000 Russian troops close to Ukraine's northern, eastern and southern borders.

NATO EXPANSION: RUSSIA'S PERSPECTIVE

Some Western analysts view Russia's invasion of Ukraine as the culmination of its growing resentment of NATO's post-Cold War expansion into the post-Soviet neighbourhood, Russia's former sphere of influence. Russian leaders are irritated by these changes and repeatedly claim that the United States and NATO have violated pledges they made in the early 1990s not to expand the alliance into the former Soviet bloc. NATO opened its doors to former Warsaw Pact states and ex-Soviet republics in the late 1990s (the Czech Republic, Hungary, and Poland) and early 2000s

(Bulgaria, Estonia, Latvia, Lithuania, Romania, Slovakia, and Slovenia). Russian fears grew in the late 2000s as the alliance stated its intent to admit Georgia and Ukraine at an unspecified point in the future. For Russia, the notion that Ukraine, a pillar of the Soviet Union with strong ties to Russia, would join NATO was a red line that could not be crossed. Russian leaders have viewed NATO's expansion as a humiliating imposition they could not stop.

Russian officials say the US made a pledge not to expand NATO's eastern borders during the rounds of diplomacy that took place after the fall of the Berlin Wall in 1989 and surrounding the reunification of Germany in 1990. US Secretary of State James A. Baker told Soviet leader Mikhail Gorbachev in February 1990 "there would be no extension of NATO's jurisdiction for forces of NATO one inch to the east." Under this promise, Gorbachev agreed to a United Germany's incorporation into NATO. Russian officials affirm this commitment has been repeatedly betrayed since 1990, taking advantage of Russia's tumultuous post-Soviet period and expanding the alliance to Russia's doorstep. Under the agreement brokered by Gorbachev and the West German Chancellor, Helmut Kohl, it was stipulated that forces from other NATO nations were prohibited from being stationed on the territory formerly belonging to the German Democratic Republic (GDR) until after the withdrawal of Soviet forces, and even then, such deployments would be of a temporary nature. Furthermore, there was a clear prohibition on the placement of nuclear weapons.

Western states assert that the diplomacy conducted between the so-called Two Plus Four (East and West Germany plus the United States, France, the Soviet Union, and the United Kingdom) was the future of Germany and the question of whether the soon-to-be unified country would become a NATO member. The discussions focused on various post-unification security options, including the potential for Germany to become part of both NATO and the Warsaw Pact, for Germany to be nonaligned, and even for the Soviet Union to join NATO. The treaty was eventually signed in the summer of 1990 but did not mention NATO's rights and commitments beyond Germany. It did not give any formal guarantees that there would be no further expansion of NATO beyond the territory of a united Germany. There was no expectation in the West that the USSR would collapse a year after the treaty was signed. Its collapse had changed geopolitical reality at a fast pace, exposing a major divergence between the West and Russia on how to manage European security, and on the role of NATO.

From the end of 1993, Russian diplomacy voiced increasing opposition to NATO's further enlargement, but accepted that it could not stop the process, as there was no legal force to the statements by Western leaders. However change was on the cards once Russia became more and more affluent with the rise of energy prices and under the leadership of Putin. The country that Putin was presiding was changing fast and becoming more assertive leading to a more expansionist and aggressive approach. This was therefore the background to the conflict in Ukraine.

COLLAPSE OF THE WARSAW PACT

Another important moment in explaining the current distrust between Russia and NATO were the 1993-94 discussions between the US administration of Bill Clinton and Boris Yeltsin's Russian government. By this period, the Warsaw Pact and Soviet Union had both collapsed. Instead of expanding NATO, Clinton developed a new NATO initiative called the Partnership for Peace, which would be nonexclusive and open to all former Warsaw Pact members and countries outside Europe. It was launched at the NATO summit of January 1994 and more than two dozen countries, including Georgia, Russia, and Ukraine, joined in the following months. However, soon after Clinton began to speak publicly about NATO expansion. NATO's Kosovo campaign in 1999 coincided with a period of extreme weakness in Russia. It represented a crushing defeat for Russian diplomacy, which had persuaded the Yugoslav president, Slobodan Milosevic that Russia could protect Serbia, a supposedly traditional ally, from NATO. The Russian leadership opted to interpret this incident as proof of a resurging Western threat to Russia but took care to differentiate between NATO and the EU. Maintaining amicable ties with the EU held the potential to undermine the transatlantic alliance. Nevertheless, despite the tumultuous events surrounding the 2003 US-led invasion of

Iraq and the increasing challenges in Washington's dealings with Europe, the EU did not warmly embrace Russia.

As NATO expanded in the 2000s, President Putin expressed doubts over whether the alliance would be effective in tackling the security challenges of the day, including international terrorism and the conflict in Afghanistan. New Baltic country members perceived NATO membership as protection from their former Soviet masters. Putin became more outspoken of NATO's expansion into Eastern Europe, calling it a "serious provocation that reduces the level of mutual trust". At the NATO summit in 2008, France and Germany, among others, restrained the US's effort to put Georgia and Ukraine on a path to membership of the Alliance. Despite NATO's ill-advised assurance to both countries in the summit communiqué that they would join NATO, there was in reality no prospect of this ever happening without Moscow's *de facto* consent. In February 2008, Russia stood in opposition to the Western-backed acknowledgment of Kosovo's declaration of independence, denouncing it as a breach of international law that eroded the established framework of international relations. Several months later, marking a shift in Russia's foreign policy direction in 2008, Russian President Dmitriy Medvedev emphasized the Kosovo case and the US-led coalition's invasion of Iraq as two instances where Western nations had undermined international law. In the months that followed, the key issues of contention between Russia and the West included the NATO Bucharest Summit Declaration on Ukraine and Georgia in April 2008 and the US missile defence plans in Europe.

RUSSIA'S SECURITY DEMANDS

In the weeks leading to the 2022 invasion, Russia made several security demands from the United States and NATO, seeking legally binding security guarantees. The draft treaty with the US contained eight articles which have been explained as follows by the Council For Foreign Relations and US television station PBS :

- Article 4 calls for NATO to end its eastward expansion, specifically, deny future membership to ex-Soviet states, such as Ukraine. It would also ban the United States from establishing bases in or cooperating militarily with former Soviet states.

- Article 5 would block both signatories from deploying military assets in areas outside their national borders that "could be perceived by the other party as a threat to its national security." Heavy bombers and "surface warships of any type" shall refrain from being deployed outside the party's national airspace or territorial waters to areas where they could strike the other's territory.

- Article 6 calls for parties to confine their deployments of intermediate- and short-range, ground-launched missiles to their own territories, and only in areas where they could not strike the other's territory.

- Article 7 would block the parties from deploying nuclear weapons outside their respective territories and would require related nuclear weapons infrastructure in third-party countries to be dismantled.

The agreement with NATO contained nine draft articles including:

- Article 4 would effectively divide NATO's Western and Eastern European membership. It would ban NATO countries that were members of the alliance as of 1997 (a grouping that excludes nearly all eastern members) from deploying military assets to "any of the other states of Europe" in excess of what those members had deployed by 1997. Such deployments could only take place "in exceptional cases" and with Russia's consent.

- Article 5 would forbid the parties from stationing intermediate- and short-range, ground-launched missiles in areas that could strike the other parties.

- Article 6 would restrict NATO "from any further enlargement," including admitting Ukraine.

- Article 7 would ban NATO members from conducting any military activity in Ukraine, as well as in other Eastern European states and those in South Caucasus and Central Asia.

Alliance leaders responded that they were open to new diplomacy but unwilling to discuss closing NATO to new members. Western officials feared Russia's demands were deliberately designed to be excessive, intended to be dismissed by Western powers and used as a pretext to launch an invasion of Ukraine. Experts have different stances on why Putin invaded Ukraine, one perspective is that Russia wants to revise the European security architecture to something more favourable to Russian interests. Some experts say Putin's biggest motivating factor was his fear that Ukraine would continue to develop into a modern, Western-style democracy undermining his autocratic regime in Russia. Thus, Putin wants to destabilise Ukraine and to collapse the economy, making neighbours Belarus, Kazakhstan, and even Poland and Hungary doubt whether democracy will be viable in the long-term in their countries too.

1. THE WAR AND ITS TRAJECTORY IN 2022

The war in Ukraine entered its ninth month in December 2022. Since Russia launched its invasion in February 2022, the conflict has been through various phases as Russia's goals and strategy have changed in the face of strong Ukrainian resistance. In its first phase, Russia set out to conquer all of Ukraine and replace its government with a pro-Russian government. In its second phase, Russia refocuses on eastern Ukraine, as Ukraine launches counteroffensives in the north and south, taking back more than 1,000 settlements. In its third phase, Russia re-expands its goals to include Kherson and Zaporizhia. Ukraine uses missiles to devastate Russian ammunition, bases and command posts deep behind the front lines. In its fourth and current phase, the Ukrainian counter-offensive continues in its success and Russia responds by annexing four regions in southern Ukraine and bombarding Ukrainian energy infrastructure with missiles as the winter approaches. An end to the conflict in the near future remains unlikely.

Phase 1

Russia begins its "special military operation", setting out to conquer Ukraine and replace its government. The West responds by imposing wide ranging financial and trade sanctions on Russia.

February 2022: Russian President Vladimir Putin announced his decision to launch a "special military operation" in Ukraine in an early morning speech with land, air and sea invasion. Ukraine's President Volodymyr Zelenskyy gave a brief and defiant national address, declaring martial law and general mobilisation. Zelenskyy refuses a US offer to evacuate, instead requesting ammunition. His now famous words 'I need ammunition not a ride' have become common folklore. Russia's assault on Kyiv, the eastern city of Kharkiv and Chernihiv in the north stalled, as Ukrainian defenders targeted supply vehicles with missiles. The European Union banned selected Russian banks from SWIFT and froze Russian central bank deposits. It also banned Russian aircraft from EU airspace. Oil majors Shell, BP and Norway's sovereign wealth fund pulled out of Russian joint ventures. Ukraine applied to join the EU.

March: A historic vote took place in the first emergency session at the United Nations General Assembly since 1997, demanding that Russia stop its military offensive in Ukraine and immediately withdraw all troops from the country. In the vote, 141 countries voted to condemn the invasion. Four countries voted against the motion: Russia, Belarus, Eritrea, North Korea and Syria. 35 countries abstained from the vote, including China, India, Pakistan and nearly half of African countries. The Foreign Ministers of Russia and Ukraine met for face-to-face talks in Turkey, in the first high-level contact between the two sides since the Russian invasion began in February. Turkey is a NATO member desirous of maintaining good relations with both sides despite the conflict. A 65km Russian military convoy moved towards to the Ukrainian capital, Kyiv, entered the north-western outskirts but faced manpower shortages. Russian forces entered the city of Kherson. Russian forces shelled Europe's biggest nuclear plant in Zaporizhzhia, raising fears of a nuclear disaster. The US Congress approved military and humanitarian aid for Ukraine to the tune of $13.6 bn. A theatre in the southern Ukrainian port city of Mariupol was bombed by Russia resulting in the deaths of 300 civilians taking refuge in it. NATO estimated that Russia lost 7,000-15,000 troops in one month of war and that the number of Russian dead, wounded, captured and missing was 40,000.

Phase 2

Russia turns its attention back to eastern Ukraine, as Ukraine retakes more than 1,000 settlements in the north and south. The US and UK agree to deploy advanced missile systems to Ukraine.

25 March 2022: Russia said it will focus on consolidating its control over the eastern Ukrainian provinces of Luhansk and Donetsk, in an apparent redefinition of its war aims. More than 3.7 million Ukrainians had been made refugees since the start of the war, with 7.1 million internally displaced.

March 29: Russian and Ukrainian negotiators convened in Istanbul, marking their first face-to-face meeting in over three weeks. Ukraine put forward a detailed proposal of neutrality.

April 2022: As Russian troops withdrew from Bucha, a town northwest of Kyiv, dozens of civilian corpses were found on the streets. President Joe Biden of the United States advocated for Vladimir Putin to face a war crimes tribunal due to the alleged Russian involvement in civilian casualties in Bucha. In response, Russia launched cluster munitions at the crowded Kramatorsk railway station, resulting in the tragic death of a minimum of 52 people. Subsequently, the UN General Assembly decided to suspend Russia from its Human Rights Council. Russian forces launched a new, large-scale offensive in east Ukraine to take full control of the Luhansk and Donetsk oblasts. Putin announced triumph in the Mariupol conflict, despite the presence of approximately 2,500 Ukrainian marines who were still entrenched within the Azovstal Steel Plant. Ukrainian forces were shifting towards initiating a counteroffensive in the vicinity of the eastern cities of Kharkiv and Izyum.

May 2022: A Ukrainian counteroffensive north and east of Kharkiv pushed Russian troops 40km back from the city, in the first significant Ukrainian success since winning the battle for Kyiv. Ukrainian forces were transitioning to counteroffensive operations around the eastern cities of Kharkiv and Izyum. The number of Ukrainians made refugees from the conflict reached 6 million. Ukraine's troops advanced to the Russian border 40km north of Kharkiv, and Russian defensive efforts focused on preventing an incursion towards Belgorod in Russia. Ukraine's military declares an end to the Azovstal resistance in the besieged Ukrainian port city of Mariupol, as hundreds of people were evacuated from a steelworks, the last holdout of Ukrainian resistance to Russian forces in the city. The evacuation came after repeated international efforts to broker safe passage for around 1,000 civilians sheltering in underground tunnels in the massive Azovstal Plant.

Ukrainian forces resisted a major Russian assault in the eastern Donbas region and begged the West to supply weapons to help Kyiv turn the tide of the war. Ukraine forces drove Russian troops back from a highway, allowing Kyiv's forces to supply the critical city of Severdonetsk. Russia concentrated its forces on capturing Severdonetsk, the last big city in Luhansk still under Ukrainian control. The city was enduring the most extensive destruction in the war since a Russian siege effectively devastated the southern port city of Mariupol. However, Russia's advance slowed despite what Ukrainian forces described as a tactical retreat under enormous artillery bombardments. The siege of Severdonetsk, marked a strategic shift by Moscow to overwhelm smaller pockets of resistance one at a time after Russia's forces were forced to retreat from central Ukraine and were driven back in the Kharkiv border region north of the Donbas. On the southern front, Ukrainian forces were mounting a counteroffensive aimed at Kherson, compelling Russian forces to retreat eastward of the Inhulets River. Peace negotiations between Russia and Ukraine faltered as Putin intensified his ambition to seize additional territory and incorporate regions his troops have already taken control of in the south-eastern part of the country.

June 2022: NATO Secretary-General Jens Stoltenberg appeared to suggest that Ukraine will have to accept a loss of sovereignty or territory in return for peace, during a press conference in Finland. Ukraine reported the recapture of 1,026 settlements previously under Russian control. In a separate incident, Russian missiles struck a shopping mall in Kremenchuk, located in central Ukraine, resulting in the tragic loss of life, with at least 18 people confirmed dead. Russia defaulted on its sovereign debt for the first time since the

Bolshevik Revolution in 1917, as a 30-day grace period on interest payments expired. NATO Secretary-General Jens Stoltenberg says the alliance is to increase its Readiness Force from 40,000 to 300,000. After being hit by Ukrainian missiles, Russian troops begin to retreat from Snake Island in the Black Sea. One hundred days into the Russian invasion, Ukraine's president Volodymyr Zelenskyy hailed the survival of his country, in the face of an enemy that has devastated the nation, killed thousands of people and impacted food supplies across the world. In a defiant video, Zelenskyy spoke from outside his office in the capital with his top aides at his side. There were now millions of Ukrainian refugees but Ukraine remained in control of Kyiv. The country is braced for a grinding and drawn-out war with its northern neighbour's larger army. Russia had now occupied 20 per cent of Ukrainian territory in the east and south of the country, up from seven per cent previously, and was pressing on with its proclaimed aim of capturing all of the eastern Donbas region.

Phase 3

Russia expands its objectives once again to encompass Kherson and Zaporizhia. In response, Ukraine employs missiles to inflict extensive damage on Russian ammunition depots, military bases, and command centres situated well beyond the front lines.

July 2022: Some 40 countries participated in an International Conference on the Restoration of Ukraine in Lugano, Switzerland, with Ukraine claiming $750bn would be needed. Sergey Lavrov, the Russian Foreign Minister, announced that Russia had broadened its objectives in the conflict, moving beyond its previously stated aim of occupying the two eastern regions of Luhansk and Donetsk. He emphasized the importance of capturing Zaporizhia and Kherson in the southern part of Ukraine. Russia and Ukraine signed a UN-brokered agreement allowing the export of Ukrainian grain through the Black Sea, aimed at averting a global food crisis. Under the deal, Ukraine and Russia have agreed not to attack merchant vessels, civilian vessels or port facilities covered by the agreement. It represented a "de facto ceasefire".

Ukrainian forces damaged the Antonivka vehicle and rail bridges using HIMARS rocket artillery, rendering them unusable for heavy military transport. This helped to cut off forward Russian positions in Kherson.

August 2022: As the Russian-led invasion entered its sixth month, Kyiv's armed forces continued an offensive to retake the Ukrainian city of Kherson. Persistent and enduring resistance by local partisans in Kherson, following Russia's takeover, had compelled Moscow to repeatedly delay its intentions of annexing the region through a referendum. The military aim of the assault is to recapture territory Moscow seized in the early weeks of Russian President Vladimir Putin's invasion. Kherson, a predominantly level region situated at the delta where the Dnipro River meets the Black Sea, holds significant strategic value for Russia as a crucial "land bridge" to Crimea, which Russia annexed from Ukraine in 2014.

Following an agreement reached on July 22 to end a Russian blockade, the first ship laden with Ukrainian grain departed from the port. Ukraine's southern command reported the successful destruction of 24 Russian multiple rocket launchers, a T-62 tank, five armoured vehicles, and an ammunition depot in operations targeting Berislavsky and another location within the Kherson oblast.

Nine Russian warplanes were destroyed on the ground at the airbase of Saky in Crimea, 225km behind the front line, in what appeared to be the first significant Ukrainian attack on a Russian base on the peninsula. Ukraine also destroyed Russian ammunition warehouses in Novooleksiivka in Crimea, 150km south of the front line, and a command post on the southwestern Kherson coast. A series of blasts hit the village of Mayskoye in Crimea when a suspected ammunition storage facility, linked to Russia, ignited, necessitating the evacuation of 3,000 residents. Russia characterized it as "an outcome of sabotage" without specifying responsibility. Meanwhile, Darya Dugina, the daughter of the well-known Russian ultranationalist Alexander Dugin, lost her life in a car bomb explosion near Moscow, in an incident that could potentially have been an assassination attempt targeting her father. Ukraine denied Russia's accusations that it was behind the attack. Ukraine marked its day of independence from Soviet rule and the six-month anniversary of Russia's full-scale invasion. Independence Day events were cancelled as a result of concerns that Russia could escalate attacks to coincide with the celebrations. President Zelenskyy gave a recalcitrant speech, stating Ukraine had been "reborn" when Russia invaded: "We don't care what army you have, we only care about our land. We will fight for it until the end."

The UN Secretary-General, Antonio Guterres, cautioned that any harm to the Zaporizhia nuclear power station would be tantamount to "self-destruction," while Ukraine and Russia pointed fingers at each other for shelling near the facility.

A team from the UN's nuclear watchdog, the International Atomic Energy Agency announced they will head to Ukraine to inspect the Zaporizhzhia nuclear power plant. Europe's largest atomic plant was captured by Russian troops in March but was still operated by Ukrainian staff, and had become a flashpoint in the conflict, with both sides accusing each other of carrying out artillery attacks threatening the stability of its reactors. The IAEA (International Atomic Energy Agency) announced that the mission would investigate the site's damage, assess the operational status of safety and security systems, appraise the well-being of the plant's personnel and perform urgent safeguard activities.

WHAT'S HAPPENED SO FAR IN 2023

There were several significant developments in the first half of 2023. These developments are summarised month-by-month below.

In January 2023, Germany agreed to supply Ukraine with Leopard 2 battle tanks, setting the stage for the United States and other NATO allies to do the same. Russia denounced the move as a "blatant provocation." Ukraine soon began seeking fighter jets, a request rejected by Western leaders. After months of fighting, Ukrainian troops withdrew from the eastern town of Soledar, reversing Russia's military fortunes. Moscow has depicted this battle as crucial for capturing the strategic town of Bakhmut and the coveted Donbas region. Russia and Belarus initiated joint military exercises, fuelling concerns that Moscow might employ its ally to launch a fresh ground offensive in the spring.

In February 2023, the world marked one year since the war began. Zelenskyy marked the anniversary of a year by striking a tone of grim defiance. "We survived the first day of the full-scale war. We didn't know what tomorrow would bring, but we clearly understood that for each tomorrow, you need to fight. And we fought," he said. "[It was] the longest day of our lives. The hardest day of our modern history. We woke up early and haven't fallen asleep since."

In March, intense combat unfolded in Bakhmut, with both sides repeatedly asserting control over the eastern city. Wagner's mercenary force, recently reinforced with new conscripts, experienced heavy casualties in the brutal battle, while Ukrainian forces also suffered significant losses. Ukraine received its first shipment of Western heavy tanks, including British Challengers and German Leopards, providing a valuable boost to the country's armed forces. Polish fighter jets also arrived. Russia announced its intention to relocate tactical nuclear weapons to Belarus, sparking a strong backlash from the EU, which condemned the move as irresponsible and threatened further sanctions. Putin hosted his Chinese counterpart, Xi Jinping, with the two leaders reaffirming their anti-Western alliance.

In April 2023, a significant leak disclosed classified US intelligence concerning the Ukraine war and other matters, revealing Russian internal disagreements regarding Ukrainian casualties, Washington's allegations of UN Secretary-General Antonio Guterres being "excessively accommodating" to Moscow, and the presence of Western special forces operating within Ukraine. The battle for Bakhmut continued unabated, with Yevgeny Prigozhin, the leader of the Russian Wagner mercenary group, asserting that his forces maintain "legal control of the city." He shared a gruesome video of himself beside deceased soldiers and later threatened to withdraw from the critical battle unless the Russian armed forces provided urgently needed ammunition. This situation highlighted his increasing assertiveness and the tensions within Russia's military establishment.

In May 2023, rumours of a potential Ukrainian counteroffensive began to circulate.

EU's High Representative, Josep Borrell, issued a warning that Ukraine could fall within a "matter of days" if Europe does not substantially increase its support. Macron urged NATO to offer concrete security assurances. Tensions between the Russian army and the Wagner military group intensified, with leader Yevgeny Prigozhin accusing the military of abandoning its positions in Bakhmut. The spotlight shifts to South Africa, as the US ambassador to the country accused the South Africans of supplying weapons and ammunition to Russia. Moscow escalated its bombardments on Ukraine, with Kyiv being targeted over 16 times in May.

In June 2023, the Soviet-era Nova Kakhovka dam in Russia-controlled southern Ukraine was destroyed. Zelenskyy attributed this to "Russian terrorists," while Moscow denies any involvement. The incident resulted in the loss of 50 lives, flooded a vast expanse of land—reportedly altering Ukraine's counteroffensive plans—and caused approximately €1.2 billion in damage. Yevgeny Prigozhin and his Wagner mercenaries rebelled against Russia's leadership, leading to a dramatic 36-hour saga during which they captured Russian cities and advanced toward Moscow. The catalyst for this uprising was the Russian Ministry of Defence's attempt to assume control of Wagner, a proposal Prigozhin vehemently rejected. Belarusian President Aleksander Lukashenko brokered an agreement persuading Prigozhin to halt his troops en route to the Russian capital. The arrangement allowed the Wagner leader and his forces to reside in Belarus in exile, shielding him from criminal charges.

In July 2023, the NATO summit convened in Vilnius, Lithuania. Despite heightened expectations from some quarters, the US-led military alliance refrained from providing a precise timetable for Ukraine's membership. Kyiv expressed its disappointment and frustration but secured formal security guarantees and assurances of eventual accession. The controversial decision by the US to send cluster bombs to Kyiv, notorious for causing civilian casualties long after a conflict concludes, triggered a strong reaction from Moscow. Wagner mercenaries commenced training Belarusian troops, raising concerns in neighbouring Poland and Lithuania that Russia's paramilitary forces could employ hybrid tactics against them. US intelligence released a report disclosing that China is likely supplying Russia's war effort in Ukraine with crucial military equipment, such as fighter jet components and jamming devices. Moscow withdraws from the Black Sea grain agreement and initiates bombing Ukraine's export infrastructure, leading to concerns about a looming famine. Ukraine escalated its actions against Moscow by launching drones at the Russian capital, while its troops are engaged in heavy fighting on the ground.

Most significant of these developments are Wagner leader Prigozhin's march on Moscow and Russia's withdrawal from the Black Sea grain initiative. 2023 has seen the most significant threat to Putin's leadership since he came to power over two decades ago. The divisions within the Russian military leadership have been exposed to the world. The collapse of the grain initiative, one of the most significant developments of 2022, shows that diplomacy is failing to resolve the war. Any of the four possible outcomes to the war predicted in the following section remain relevant to the situation to date.

POSSIBLE END GAME SCENARIOS

The outcome of the war Russia's war remains unclear. The Russian military does not appear to be able to wrest control of Kyiv from the Ukrainians or occupy more than a substantial minority of the country. Ukrainian forces have had months of success on the battlefield and could continue to make progress in regaining territory with support from the West. The conflict may also evolve into a protracted struggle, with neither side able to achieve a decisive victory in the foreseeable future. Predicting the outcome of the war is challenging. While the war has been a tragedy for Ukraine and its citizens, it has equally been a catastrophe for Russia, impacting its military, economy, and geopolitical standing. The conflict has significantly weakened Russia's armed forces, marred its global image, disrupted its economic stability, and brought about substantial changes in the geopolitical dynamics Moscow confronts in Europe.

When Putin began his "special military operation" in Ukraine, the assault suggested Russia's objectives were to quickly seize Kyiv presumably deposing the government and occupy as much as the eastern half to two-thirds of the country. The Russian military made advances in southern Ukraine but was unsuccessful in capturing Kyiv. As March came to a close, Russian forces were in a state of withdrawal in the northern regions. Moscow proclaimed its new objective as occupying all of Donbas, consisting of the regions of Luhansk and Donetsk, around a third of which had already been occupied by Russian and Russian proxy forces in 2014. After three months of battle, Russian forces captured most of Luhansk, but they made little progress in Donetsk, and the battlelines appeared to stabilize in August. In September, the Ukrainian army launched two counteroffensives. One in the northeast expelled Russian forces from Kharkiv and pressed assaults into Luhansk. In the south, the second counteroffensive succeeded in November in driving Russian forces out of Kherson city and the neighbouring region, the only area that Russian forces occupied east of the Dnipro River. Despite three months of setbacks, Russia has shown no sign of readiness to negotiate to end the war. The Russians have attempted to mitigate battlefield losses by increasing missile attacks on Ukrainian cities, aimed in particular at their infrastructure.

Whether the Ukrainian military can drive the Russians completely out or at least back to the pre-war lines is unclear. Certain military experts deem this a plausible outcome, one that encompasses the complete liberation of Donbas and Crimea. However, less optimistic predictions are also put forth. According to the U.S. intelligence community, the conflict may persist and transform into a protracted war of attrition. In late November, Ukrainian President Volodymyr Zelensky and his government insisted on conditions that included Russian withdrawal from all Ukrainian territory (including Crimea and all of Donbas), compensation, and punishment for war crimes. However, achieving these demands will prove difficult. Many questions remain.

FOUR POSSIBLE OUTCOMES TO THE WAR

1. **The Russians launch a renewed military offensive to achieve their original military aims.**

In this scenario, Russian forces could launch a new offensive with its 200,000 newly mobilised conscripts. They could attempt to regain the lost parts of Donetsk, move again north-east to Kharkiv and push south towards Odesa, the vital Black Sea port held by Ukraine. This would block all Ukrainian access to the sea and give Russia the foundation for launching further operations in the west of Ukraine. This would mean Russia would achieve its original goal of controlling a swath of land over 200km long from Kharkiv to Odesa, blocking Ukraine off completely from the sea. The Russians could also launch a new assault on Kyiv from Belarus, which remains a staunch ally of Russia. This would also divert Ukrainian forces from their own offensives in the east and south. This is the outcome Putin initially set out to achieve when he launched the invasion in February. Russian troops have since had reverses in the northeast and south of Ukraine, whilst territory they hold in the east and south has taken months to capture and come at a huge cost for Russia. However, Russia does have the capability to launch a new offensive, the likelihood of which is high. It is difficult to predict how successful this offensive will be and what the outcome will be.

2. The Ukrainian counter-offensive continues, pushing the Russians out of Ukrainian territory.

In this scenario, Ukraine would continue its successful offensive in the east and south of the country. With new supplies of arms from the west, Ukrainian troops could recapture the Kherson, Mariupol, Zaporizhia and the besieged city Mariupol, in the south. This would push Russian troops west into Crimea. Ukrainian forces could try and retake the Donbas by launching a double offensive from both the north in Kharkiv and from the South in Mariupol. This would prove arduous as Russian frontline troops in the Donbas hold strong positions and are well-equipped. However, Ukrainian troops could launch continuous long-range strikes, putting pressure on Russian forces and allowing Ukrainian troops to reach the Russian frontier, which would put them within distance to strike Russian bases. This would achieve Ukraine's aim of pushing the Russians back to the pre-2014 boundaries (minus Crimea). This military defeat could cause unrest within the Russian population, potentially leading to Putin being removed in a coup. This could result in a negotiated solution under which Russia removes all troops from Ukraine but is permitted to keep Crimea. Ukraine would renounce its intention to join NATO and the EU, providing a negotiated end to the war. However, the reverse scenario is that the Ukrainian offensive will trigger strong Russian retaliation and the Russian use of nuclear weapons, completely changing the trajectory of the war. In reality, it is unlikely Ukrainian forces will be able to retake all the territory they lost to Russia, despite continued support from the West. The Russians have strong defensive lines along the occupied areas which will be very difficult for Ukrainian forces overcome. There is a fear that the Ukrainian counter-offensive could get over-extended and thus become vulnerable to a counterattack, meaning a complete Ukrainian victory in the short-term is unlikely.

3. The war becomes a ceaseless "frozen conflict", with neither side able to claim victory, dragging on for years.

In this scenario, both sides would hold onto their positions, with the Russians on the east of the Dnieper River and the Ukrainians on the west. Ukrainian forces would fortify their position to prevent further Russian advances, and Russian forces would fortify their position in the east. This situation has existed in the Donbas since 2014; Russian separatists and Ukrainian forces have occupied defensive positions opposite each other along the Line of control. Low level fighting, artillery duels and raids have continued for over eight years, but the line remains largely static. A similar Line of control could come up along the line of the territories that Russia has annexed in eastern Ukraine, which could also become the dividing line between Russia and the rest of Europe. This scenario is currently the most likely, with both sides occupying defensive positions. In this scenario, although Putin won't have achieved his original military goals, the Russian occupation of Donbas and the south will give Russia a degree of military victory. Ukraine will never accept this scenario but won't be able to change it. This would be similar to the Line of control in Kashmir between India and Pakistan which came up in 1948, and eventually became the status quo.

2. World War III: A global war between Russia and NATO.

The war in Ukraine initially began due to Russia's opposition to Ukraine's desire to join NATO, according to Russia. It seems unlikely Ukraine will join the alliance in the near future as this would draw NATO into the conflict under Article 5 of the NATO charter, which states that any attack on any member state is considered as an attack on all. In the meantime, NATO will continue support Ukraine by providing arms and humanitarian aid, without being directly involved in the conflict. However, NATO could be unavoidably drawn into the conflict if Russia uses a chemical, biological or a nuclear weapon, or even conducts a particularly devastating attack on a civilian target. Putin has said he will use a nuclear weapon if NATO enters the war directly, meaning the smallest trigger could majorly escalate the conflict into a global war. This is without a doubt the worst-case scenario involving the use of nuclear weapons by both sides. It seems unlikely NATO will get directly involved in the conflict, but should this happen, it will set the stage for World War III.

CHANGES TO THE GEOPOLITICAL ORDER AS A CONSEQUENCE OF THIS WAR.

Russia's invasion of Ukraine in February 2022 marked a defining moment in changing and reshaping the global geopolitical order at a fast pace. The war in Ukraine is not only a regional war, it represents a rupture in Russia's relationship with the West and a major challenge to the current "rules-based" international order which has existed since the end of World War II. There are many ways this war has affected and will affect the global balance of power.

CHANGES TO ENERGY AND FOOD SECURITY

The war has had a significant impact on global resource markets. Russia and Ukraine are both significant players in global energy, food and fertilizer markets.

Chatham House has collated the following statistics:

Russia is the world's third largest producer and exporter of oil; the second largest producer and the largest exporter of natural gas; and the third largest exporter of coal.

Russia is also the world's largest exporter of wheat and the second largest exporter of sunflower oil.

Ukraine is the largest exporter of sunflower oil, the fourth largest exporter of maize and the fifth largest exporter of wheat.

Russia also dominates global trade in fertilizers: it is the largest exporter of fertilizers overall, the second largest exporter of nitrogenous fertilizers and the third largest exporter of potassic (those containing potassium) fertilizers.

Russia is also an important supplier of metals and minerals, particularly of nickel, palladium, platinum and titanium, as well as aluminium, copper and uranium.

With the conflict in Ukraine unlikely to be resolved in the short term, its impact on global resource markets will continue to strengthen, and with serious 'ripple effects' on economies and societies around the world.

These ripple effects often can very quickly have negative changes in geographies and sectors far removed from the original event. The energy and food security has resulted in various western economies re assessing their energy needs and fast changing the way they are organised to deal with these shocks.

MOVING TOWARDS AN APOLAR WORLD ORDER

Russia's war in Ukraine signals the end of the post-Cold war world order. When the Cold war ended, crisis hit Russia was economically and politically weak. Thus, the world entered a period of unipolarity dominated by the US. In the past decade, the world has changed into a period of multipolarity, characterised by the revival of Russia, the rise of India and China, growing division in the West and the decline of US hegemony. It can be argued that now the world is moving towards a period of apolarity, where no power will be able to dominate any region on its own. The Ukraine war has brought in profound changes to the global geo-politics

RUSSIA WILL MOVE CLOSER TO CHINA

The war in Ukraine will cement Russia's alliance with China, as Russia has been ostracised from the global financial and political system. Russia began its "pivot eastwards" in 2012, realising it was unlikely to be given a say in the European security order and that there were many economic opportunities there. Russia has helped China in the fields of energy, air and sea power, intelligence, and military and foreign affairs, and in return it has received financing and technology. The Economist Intelligence Unit notes that: "for China, an alliance with Russia offers security along its northern border, natural resources and a shared authoritarian approach and attitude to the West".

THE GLOBAL ARMS RACE WILL ACCELERATE

The end of the cold war led to an overall decline in global arms spending, however this has increased again in recent years. China has expanded its nuclear arsenal and Russia, the US, the UK, France and others have modernised theirs. The quantity of nuclear warheads being actively deployed by operational forces is on the rise, marking a reversal of the declining trend that has been observed since 1991. Moreover, the development and deployment of anti-ballistic missile defence systems, anti-satellite weaponry, and hypersonic missiles by major powers are heightening concerns and intensifying the perception of threats among rival nations, thereby fuelling an arms race. The war in Ukraine will lead to more weapons proliferation.

EUROPE MUST DECIDE WHERE IT STANDS IN THE NEW GLOBAL SECURITY ORDER

The war in Ukraine has confirmed for Europe that it must be able to influence what happens on its own continent. The US will remain by far the dominant power in NATO, but the balance is likely to shift in coming years, as European powers, led by France and Germany, become more serious about asserting their interests. Russia's invasion of Ukraine provoked an unprecedented show of unity from the NATO powers, but this unity will begin to wane in time as national and regional interests come to the surface. This has already shown in NATO powers diverging positions on Russian energy exports.

GEOPOLITICAL CHANGES – 2022

The Ukraine war has brought to the forefront a significant shift in geopolitical power.

The dominance of USA and Western alliance in military and economic power is no longer there. The war in Ukraine in 2022 became a rallying call to take sides either support the US-led alliance or The Russians. China was very clear they did not want to support this alliance and were on the side of the Russians. Whilst India did not criticize Russia its position was more ambivalent in trying to please both parties without taking sides. India has played its cards well in demanding cheap oil from Russia to fund its economic growth which has been accelerating in the past decade. India is racing to become the third largest economy in the world from its current position of fifth in 2023.

It has not made enemies but clearly, there is a lot of irritation amongst the Western alliance on this. The cheap Russian oil purchases made by India are funding the war for Russia and that is not tenable in the eyes of many. India has even become a very large supplier of refined products which it is being legally supplying the West. It argues that the crude it buys from Russia has undergone the minimum amount of change and value addition and the final product can no longer be called Russian. It is dichotomy that a large portion of the aviation fuel bought by the West is bought from Indian refineries who in turn had bought the crude at bargain prices from Russia.

The growth of China has been happening for decades. Its export-led manufacturing has managed to capture huge chunks of the Western market for goods. China's economy has skyrocketed. Consider their spectacular growth. In 1985 China had a GDP of just over $ 300 billion. In 2022 its GDP had risen to $ 18,000 billion, an increase of sixty times. During the same period figures for the USA, the dominant power, was just over $ 4,000 billion rising to $ 25,000 billion in 2022 but just six times. In other words, China had grown ten times more in the same period.

Over the years the West did not take China's growth and the threats seriously and have been quite sanguine until it was too late. The US and Western countries were sleep walking whilst China was stealing their thunder right under their eyes. Deng Xiaoping's dictum to "hide our capabilities and bide our time; was so cleverly followed.

There has also been growth in India. For example, the GDP of India in 1985 was $ 232 billion and has shot up to $ 3,700 billion by 2022. This is commendable but pales the growth achieved by China. However, India seems to be the flavour of the month as more and more countries prefer dealing with India than China. India has been consolidating its soft power for decades and there is a lot of expectation that the coming decades could finally bring India its long-standing place to become both an economic and political superpower.

CHANGES TO THE NEW GEOPOLITICAL ORDER

The war in Ukraine has both directly and indirectly caused significant geopolitical changes. Financial Times journalist, Alec Russell has called this the "à la carte world. The position of America as a sole superpower is changing and countries no longer have to enter into specific alliances. Many countries are using this opportunity to play nations off against each other. The Ukrainian war has suddenly brought to the open where countries stand. Would they simply fall behind the US led western alliance or increasingly behind the Russian / Chinese led alliance? Would they align with more than one set of allies?

The role of Turkey is particularly interesting in the context of geopolitical changes resulting from the war. It will sometimes choose to align itself with western nations, but will, at other times take a position perceived to be more sympathetic to Russia. For example, Turkey had long opposed Sweden's admission to NATO until it suddenly reversed its position in the summer of 2023.

 Policy experts from The German Marshall Fund of the United States at Harvard University (GMF) have classified a group of nations as "global swing states", sometimes referred to as "middle powers. "Middle" refers to the physical location of those countries – between the United States of America and China – and they include Saudi Arabia, Turkey, Israel and Germany, as well as Indonesia and India.

Geopolitical changes resulting from the increasingly confrontational relationship between the US and China and the war in Ukraine has allowed these middle nations to redraw partnerships between themselves or with major powers. This often results in increased significance for nations such as Saudi Arabia rather than a completely redrawn geopolitical map of international alliances. An example specific to the war in Ukraine is the position of India. Since Russia's invasion, New Delhi has been making overtures to the West with international diplomacy from Prime Minister Narendra Modi, which it describes as "in its own interests". However, it has also been purchasing oil from Russia. There are even nuanced differences within alliances such as BRICS (Brazil India China and South Africa). China wishes the alliance to be an alternative to the G20 but India is not keen on further integration. The leaderships of the US and India have also become closer diplomatically. As Alec Russell notes: "Such diplomatic dexterity and juggling are on display daily by middle powers around the world. There is now open talk of transformation of the World Bank and IMF. When these institutions were founded in 1944 many of the middle countries did not exist. The global east and south want to renegotiate the world order." The balance of power has been further complicated by the US response to Russia's invasion of Ukraine and the perceived weaponisation of the dollar in sanctions against Russia. Some middle powers are concerned about both China in general and the willingness of the US to use its currency in this way.

THE IMPACT OF THE WAR IN UKRAINE ON MILITARY TECHNOLOGY

The Ukraine war has resulted in changes in the way warfare is conducted with the dramatic increase in the use of drones and other electronic devices.

The Holy Grail for military commanders is to have weapons which are cheap, plentiful and effective. This has eluded military planners for several decades. The GPS-guided artillery shells made by America cost $ 100,000 a unit and although accurate are very expensive.

The War in Ukraine has changed this, as the development of FPV (First-person view) drones has mushroomed around the front line. Ukraine may be massively outnumbered in terms of the traditional stockpiles of artillery, but it has cleverly outgunned the vast Russian army in modern technology. The FPVs, cheaply adapted from consumer electronics and laden with explosives, are very accurate and can wreak havoc on the battlefield. They are controlled by a technician far away from the front line, who can get real-time images of the battlefield enabling the FPV to enter turrets and other enemy positions and strike with precision. Yet these basic drones only cost between $300 - $ 1,000 apiece. In one month alone over 3,000 verified drone strikes were made by the Ukrainian army causing massive damage to the infrastructure of the Russian army. President Zelenskyy has now created the Unmanned Systems Force, which is dedicated to drone warfare and is on track to build between 1 and 2 million drones in 2024. This is possible as most of the components can be bought off-the-shelf and the manufacture can be scaled up significantly. The Ukrainian domestic economy is also being shifted towards increasing the country's drone-making capabilities through public-private partnerships. In the space of a year, Ukraine went from seven drone manufacturers to around eighty.

Drones can offer psychological advantages. Artillery is generally fired in waves. However, a well-protected enemy can hide underground until the bombardment is over and then regroup. But with the use of these drones, one can see where the enemy is when they break cover and hit them. As these drones can hover around without being noticed they become an insidious threat and highly effective as a killing machine.

In one week alone the Ukrainian army destroyed 75 Russian tanks and 101 large guns. Drones however have limitations as the basic drone can be jammed. They also cannot fly in bad weather and only have a short range. They are however effective when used with artillery. The Houthis in Yemen have used these drones to attack merchant shipping in the Red Sea causing havoc to shipping and trade. Iran a large manufacturer of drones has shown how the Houthis can cause significant damage.

To overcome many of the shortcomings of the basic drones both Ukraine and Russia are experimenting with autonomous navigation and target recognition along with artificial intelligence. Even the US Pentagon is embarking on a new generation of low-cost Replicator drones. Research into the production of more sophisticated drones has already begun to avoid jamming with countermeasures installing swapable radio chips making it easy for the controller on the ground to change the radio frequencies. Autonomous object recognition also allows the drone which is cut off by jamming devices to continue its last journey with pre-installed object recognition. The US has developed a drone of this type called Switchblade costing $ 50,000. Apple's former CEO, Eric Shmidt is investing heavily in drone warfare for mass production but also to make them technologically more sophisticated.

WHAT TYPES OF DRONES ARE BEING USED?

At the start of the war, Ukraine deployed large Turkish-made TB2 drones. These were effective in that they could carry several munitions and could penetrate Russian defences for long periods but, over time, Russia was able to adapt and detect these large models. In response, the Ukrainian military moved on to using smaller drones.

These smaller drones have had a significant impact on the war, giving Ukraine the capability to hit more targets as well as increased awareness of the battlefield. These drones are based on technology widely available to civilian populations across the world.

Moscow has deployed homegrown drones, such as the Orion, Eleron-3, Orlan-10, and Lancet, but Western sanctions have inhibited domestic drone production and forced Russia to rely on a supply of Iranian-made FPVs.

Two types of drones are being utilised in this conflict: those with longer endurance times which can be used for reconnaissance and more complex, technically advanced drones which are directed to make high precision strikes in enemy territory. Drones are also being used for humanitarian purposes, including the documentation of war crimes and human rights abuses.

The innovation of drones in the war in Ukraine has illustrated how technology can change the balance of power. While Russia is attempting to build air superiority, including through a partnership with Iran which could result in the production of 6,000 Geran-2 drones by mid-2025, Ukraine will continue to counter that by crowdsourcing inexpensive drones and adapting them in the field. This could certainly tip the balance of power and progress of the war in Ukraine's favour.

Starlink: Impact of Elon Musk's satellites on the war

Starlink is a network of satellites created by SpaceX, owned by US entrepreneur Elon Musk. The first satellites were sent into space in May 2019. So far, it has played a significant role in the war in Ukraine.

SpaceX made Starlink available to Ukraine in the early stages of the war and it is believed that there are around 42,000 Starlink terminals in the country. The network has served a dual purpose. On the battlefield, Ukrainian drones have used it to bomb Russian targets and communicate with each other. It has also been used for civilian communication. President Zelenskyy has used Starlink to keep in touch with his people, and his army and to maintain a presence on the world stage. The satellites have also enabled ordinary Ukrainian citizens to communicate with the outside world. Russia intended to cut off and isolate Ukraine, but Starlink has ensured that this has not happened. Brig. Gen. Steve Butow, director of the space portfolio at the US Pentagon's Defense Innovation Unit noted that "The strategic impact is, it totally destroyed [Vladimir] Putin's information campaign. He never, to this day, has been able to silence Zelenskyy."

Ukraine has acknowledged the importance of the satellite network: Its minister of digital transformation, Mykhailo Fedorov stated in November 2022 that "Starlink technologies have changed this war."

A leaked US intelligence report indicates that Russia has been trying to negate the impact of Starlink, by experimenting with its Tobol electronic warfare systems. These systems were originally put in place to protect Russia's own satellites. It is unclear whether these tests have been successful, but it does show that Moscow is sufficiently concerned about the impact of Starlink on the progress of the war.

CHANGES TO THE IMPACT OF THE WAR IN UKRAINE ON INTERNATIONAL CURRENCIES

The war has brought about changes in several international currencies including the US dollar, Chinese yuan and European Euro.

The USA and the West imposed severe sanctions on Russia in response to the Ukraine invasion. These sanctions included the restriction of Russia from the SWIFT international banking system, making it impossible for Russia to engage in seamless international trade and investment. The United States has also adopted an increasingly confrontational approach to China, and this has brought Russia and China together to counter the dominance of the Dollar. This can be seen in the use of the Yuan. Not only are the Chinese keeping less of their money in dollars and trying to settle as much as possible of their trade in Yuan, but the Chinese currency is also being posited to have a more international role.

At their summit in March 2023, Putin and Xi Jinping talked about promoting the Chinese Yuan and making it the favourite for settlements between Russia and countries in Asia, Africa and Latin America. This would make the second largest economy in the world and the largest energy exporter teaming up to actively dent the US dollar's dominance. Russia has also reduced the percentage of US dollars in its international reserves- from 46% in 2014 to 20% in 2022, increasing the shares of both the yuan and Euro to compensate.

China and Russia are not the only nations attempting to move away from the dollar. The European Union (EU) is also investigating alternative options to the SWIFT banking system, which are not as focused on the US Dollar. India is paying for the majority of its Russian oil in currencies other than the dollar and discussions have been held in Saudi Arabia regarding pricing its oil in yuan. BRICS countries (Brazil India China and South Africa) are looking to implement their own reserve currency. Digital currencies are also gaining popularity and could challenge the dollar as an international currency in time.

Washington Post columnist Fareed Zakaria notes that "The dollar is…suffering from a thousand cuts and right now even with a global political crisis the dollar has weakened which reflects the changes that the Ukraine crisis is bringing to the superpower status that the US dollar enjoyed for decades."

The Ukraine war and resulting Western sanctions on Russia inevitably caused absolute chaos in commodity and currency markets as well as inflation in economies across the world. However, despite the movement away from the US dollars in some regions, the fallout from the war does not appear to have affected that currency's position as the main global reserve currency in at least the near term. This is as a result of its role in international trade invoicing and as the most significant currency in most foreign exchanges.

According to the Financial Times, the biggest threat to the hegemony of the dollar in the longer term may come from countries impacted by the US sanctions avoiding using the dollar in international transactions as a result of the perceived willingness of the US to weaponise the dollar.

Despite the effective continuation as the global reserve currency, this chapter has shown the fallout from the war in Ukraine has had an impact on the US dollar, which could extend further than the money markets. The Open Access Government organisation explains this most succinctly:

"As the dominance of the dollar declines amidst the Russia and Ukraine war, there would be a rebalancing of global economic power, with other currencies like the euro and the Chinese yuan gaining prominence, thus anticipating a more equitable distribution of economic influence and potentially reshaping the geopolitical landscape."

In March 2023, the yuan – also known as the renminbi- became the most widely used currency for China's cross border trade for the first time, replacing the dollar in pole position. Approximately $88 billion of commodities are now being paid for in yuan and Russia's Sovereign Wealth Fund (or war chest) is also using the Chinese currency.

The war in Ukraine has fundamentally changed the economic relationship between Russia and China. Alexander Gabuev, a senior fellow at the Carnegie Endowment for International Peace believes that Putin is now less concerned about Chinese influence over the Russian economy: "Now it's the only rational choice for Russia and for Putin. If depending on renminbi is the lifeline that helps you to be less exposed and less dependent on hostile currencies, then you take this route."

The Euro has also benefitted from Russia's invasion of Ukraine. Foreign demand for the second most important global currency rose significantly in the immediate aftermath of the invasion in February 2022. The requested denominations were predominantly 100-200 Euro bills which are usually used for store of value to be used at a later time. Demand tended to be highest in nations bordering Russia and Ukraine, including Estonia and Finland as well as relatively close neighbours such as Austria and Germany.

CONCLUSION

This chapter has shown the extensive impact of a single event and moment in history – Russia's invasion of Ukraine in February 2022 – on the entire world order as well as technological development.

1   How Moscow has long used the historic Kyivan Rus state to justify expansionism:
     https://theconversation.com/how-moscow-has-long-used-the-historic-kyivan-rus-state-to-justify-
     expansionism-178092

2   Why NATO Has Become a Flash Point With Russia in Ukraine:
     https://www.cfr.org/backgrounder/why-nato-has-become-flash-point-russia-ukraine

     Why NATO and Ukraine are a flash point with Russia 30 years after the end of the
     Cold War:
     https://www.pbs.org/newshour/world/why-nato-and-ukraine-are-a-flash-point-with-russia-30-after-the-end-
     of-the-cold-war

3   Timeline: Six months of Russia's war in Ukraine: https://www.aljazeera.com/
     news/2022/8/24/timeline-six-months-of-russias-war-in-ukraine
     UN resolution against Ukraine invasion: Full text:
     https://www.aljazeera.com/news/2022/3/3/unga-resolution-against-ukraine-invasion-full-text/

     'No progress' as top Russia, Ukraine diplomats talk in Turkey:
     https://www.aljazeera.com/news/2022/3/10/top-russia-ukraine-diplomats-arrive-in-turkey-for-talks/

4   Ukraine says forces holding out against Russian assault on crucial Donbas city:
     https://www.ft.com/content/33c2ebe6-d8a4-478d-9e8e-3d0607e05c31

     Scores of civilians evacuated from Mariupol steelworks in Ukraine:
     https://www.ft.com/content/fa2d1ed8-303e-43b1-a377-737d8f5049db

Volodymir Zelenskyy hails Ukraine's survival after 100 days of war:
https://www.ft.com/content/3ff06ed2-39dc-4a86-80f0-a1d1a91fc742

5   Timeline: Six months of Russia's war in Ukraine:
https://www.aljazeera.com/news/2022/8/24/timeline-six-months-of-russias-war-in-ukraine

6   Anti-mobilisation protests spread in Russia:
https://www.ft.com/content/6b694942-3501-479e-9b6a-0eabd856b45c

Humiliation for Vladimir Putin as Ukrainians liberate key city of Lyman:
https://www.theguardian.com/world/2022/oct/01/humiliation-for-vladimir-putin-as-ukrainians-liberate-key-city-of-lyman

7   Aerial warfare in the Russian invasion of Ukraine:
https://en.wikipedia.org/wiki/Aerial_warfare_in_the_Russian_invasion_of_Ukraine

8   Ukraine war: '2023 will be the year of our victory' says Zelenskyy on first anniversary:
https://www.euronews.com/2023/02/24/ukraine-war-2023-will-be-the-year-of-our-victory-says-zelenskyy-on-first-anniversary

One year into Russian invasion, Ukraine's Zelenskyy vows victory:
https://www.aljazeera.com/news/2023/2/24/one-year-into-invasion-ukraine-mourns-vows-victory

9   The Russia-Ukraine war and its ramifications for Russia:
https://www.brookings.edu/articles/the-russia-ukraine-war-and-its-ramifications-for-russia/

10 The Ukraine war and threats to food and energy security:
https://www.chathamhouse.org/2022/04/ukraine-war-and-threats-food-and-energy-security/

11 The Russia-Ukraine conflict could shake up the global balance of power in 3 big ways, Economist Intelligence Unit says:
https://www.businessinsider.com/russia-ukraine-global-power-balance-shakeup-economist-intelligence-unit-outlook-2022-3

12 The à la carte world: our new geopolitical order
https://www.ft.com/content/7997f72d-f772-4b70-9613-9823f233d18a

13 Alliances in a Shifting Global Order: Rethinking Transatlantic Engagement with Global Swing States
https://www.gmfus.org/news/alliances-shifting-global-order-rethinking-transatlantic-engagement-global-swing-states

14 The à la carte world: our new geopolitical order
https://www.ft.com/content/7997f72d-f772-4b70-9613-9823f233d18a

15 How the Drone War in Ukraine Is Transforming Conflict
https://www.cfr.org/article/how-drone-war-ukraine-transforming-conflict

16 UkraineX:How Elon Musk's space satellites changed the war on the ground
https://www.politico.eu/article/elon-musk-ukraine-starlink/

17 Whatever the fuss over Elon Musk, Starlink is utterly essential in Ukraine
https://www.washingtonpost.com/world/2023/09/08/elon-musk-starlink-ukraine-war/

18 Russia tests secretive weapon to target SpaceX's Starlink in Ukraine
https://www.washingtonpost.com/national-security/2023/04/18/discord-leaks-starlink-ukraine/

19 The dollar is our superpower, and Russia and China are threatening it
https://www.washingtonpost.com/opinions/2023/03/24/us-dollar-strength-russia-china/

20 The US dollar's status is safe for now:
https://www.ft.com/content/87b52eb7-b22f-4382-a882-bf08b37cc31e

21 Is the dominance of the dollar in trouble amid the Russo-Ukraine war?
https://www.openaccessgovernment.org/is-the-dominance-of-the-dollar-in-trouble-amid-the-russo-ukraine-war/160579/

22 Russia Turns to China's Yuan in Effort to Ditch the Dollar
https://www.wsj.com/articles/russia-turns-to-chinas-yuan-in-effort-to-ditch-the-dollar-a8111457

23 The international role of the euro, June 2023
https://www.ecb.europa.eu/pub/ire/html/ecb.ire202306~d334007ede.en.html

SOURCES

https://www.crisisgroup.org/europe-central-asia/eastern-europe/ukraine/b96-answering-four-hard-questions-about-russias-war-ukraine

https://www.cfr.org/backgrounder/why-nato-has-become-flash-point-russia-ukraine

https://www.cfr.org/backgrounder/ukraine-conflict-crossroads-europe-and-russia#chapter-title-0-4

https://www.aljazeera.com/news/2022/8/24/timeline-six-months-of-russias-war-in-ukraine

https://www.nationalgeographic.com/history/article/russia-and-ukraine-the-tangled-history-that-connects-and-divides-them

https://www.historyextra.com/period/general-history/russia-invade-ukraine-history-relationship-crimea-why-conflict-facts/

https://www.cfr.org/global-conflict-tracker/conflict/conflict-ukraine

https://www.brookings.edu/articles/the-russia-ukraine-war-and-its-ramifications-for-russia/

https://www.chathamhouse.org/2021/05/myths-and-misconceptions-debate-russia

https://theconversation.com/how-moscow-has-long-used-the-historic-kyivan-rus-state-to-justify-expansionism-178092

https://www.chathamhouse.org/sites/default/files/2021-07/2021-07-01-ukraine-crony-capitalism-lough.pdf

https://www.chathamhouse.org/2017/10/struggle-ukraine-0/introduction

https://www.graduateinstitute.ch/communications/news/understanding-roots-russia-ukraine-war-and-misuse-history

https://www.economist.com/the-world-ahead/2022/11/14/three-scenarios-for-how-war-in-ukraine-could-play-out

https://pages.eiu.com/rs/753-RIQ-438/images/ten-ways-the-war-in-ukraine.pdf?mkt_tok=NzUzLVJJUS00MzgAAAGI2cPGpmVAbFJWH31zq_fL0wkkjjkqznwH3FucDEETQVXjwHib3tm1TlhqUUM4WDuvQg3RJ7Bg94rXZGF6NuKr8YD0xgRCyC2awNnm75QdnnnRUA

https://www.tehrantimes.com/news/472681/World-moving-towards-apolar-order-professor

https://geographical.co.uk/geopolitics/how-goes-the-war-in-ukraine

https://www.ft.com/content/7997f72d-f772-4b70-9613-9823f233d18a

https://www.euronews.com/2023/01/30/ukraine-war-a-month-by-month-timeline-of-the-conflict-in-2022

https://www.cfr.org/article/how-drone-war-ukraine-transforming-conflict

https://www.politico.eu/article/elon-musk-ukraine-starlink/

https://www.washingtonpost.com/national-security/2023/04/18/discord-leaks-starlink-ukraine/

THE WORLD IN APRIL 2022

Introduction

April 2022 was a month during which the world continued to grapple with Russia's invasion of Ukraine. As Ukrainian forces recaptured the Kyiv region, Russian forces refocused their offensive on the east of Ukraine, particularly the Donbas region, as Ukrainian authorities urged civilians in the region to evacuate. Reports of atrocities committed by Russian soldiers against civilians have sparked global condemnation and further sanctions from the west. In Europe, the three Baltic nations voiced their desire to end dependence on Russian oil and gas, in a move to cut ties from Russia. In Hungary, Victor Orban became the EU's longest-serving leader, winning a fifth term after 12 years in power. In France, Emmanuel Macron defeated far-right rival Marine Le Pen to be re-elected president of France. In the Middle East, warring parties in Yemen announced a truce a year after a Saudi-led military coalition intervened in Yemen to stop the Houthis. Turkish president Erdogan visited Saudi Arabia, signalling the end of the dispute of the killing of Jamal Khashoggi and a broader effort by Erdogan to attract investment into Turkey amidst rising inflation. Israeli forces raided the Al-Aqsa Mosque compound in

East Jerusalem with at least 158 Palestinians injured and hundreds were detained. In Asia, the omicron covid-19 variant continued to spread in Shanghai, with authorities extending the strict lockdown measures across the city. Shehbaz Sharif was elected Pakistan's new prime minister. His return to power shows the influence influence of the nation's two main political dynasties after the dramatic ousting of Imran Khan. The Sri Lankan rupee has plunged to a record low to become the world's worst-performing currency, as the government grapples with looming debt payments, widespread protests and an economic emergency. In the Americas, protests have continued in Peru, with many Peruvians saying they can no longer cope with inflation that is running at 7 per cent, its highest rate in a generation

WAR IN UKRAINE

Ukraine retook the whole of the **Kyiv** region, including several towns near its capital city. Ukraine's armed forces regained control of the entire provincial area from Russian forces. Russia has withdrawn troops from around Kyiv recently after failing push through the Ukrainian defence. Russia is now focusing its offensive on the Donbas region, where it supported a separatist uprising in two breakaway "republics" in 2014, the city of Kharkiv, and other areas in the east of Ukraine.

Ukraine's has those living in the Donbas region and around Kharkiv to evacuate after Russia increased its offensive in eastern Ukraine. Residents of Donetsk and Luhansk provinces have been asked to leave, as well as parts of Kharkiv province. Russia has withdrawn most of its forces from around Kyiv, and has begun sending them to the east of Ukraine. The town of Severdonetsk came under heavy artillery bombardment. As Ukrainian forces braced for a new attack in Donbas, evidence emerged of the killing of civilians in areas around the capital that were previously under Russian control. Images of atrocities in Bucha, a suburb of Kyiv, caused global revulsion this week and have led western capitals to impose more sanctions on Moscow.

Russian missiles were launched, hitting areas near the Ukrainian port city of **Odessa**. Vital infrastructure suffered damage, resulting in fires across multiple locations. Initial reports did not mention any casualties. According to Russia, their missile strikes successfully targeted an oil refinery and three fuel storage facilities, which were allegedly supplying Ukrainian troops near the city of Mykolaiv, where intense battles have taken place. Additionally, disturbing incidents have occurred in Ukraine, with the discovery of mutilated bodies of men, women, and children in the suburb of Bucha, and the unearthing of mass graves in other regions.

The **EU** is planning to implement additional sanctions against Russia in response to emerging reports of atrocities during Russia's military withdrawal from Kyiv. These measures come as a reaction to Russia's actions in Bucha, a city located about 25km north-west of central Kyiv, which was under Russian occupation until recently. The decision for stronger sanctions comes in the wake of strong condemnation from Western nations concerning alleged Russian war crimes against unarmed Ukrainian civilians in the areas surrounding Kyiv, as Russia shifts its focus towards the eastern part of the country.

Several European countries, including Italy, Spain, Sweden, Latvia, and Denmark, have announced the expulsion of numerous Russian diplomats following the allegations of war crimes in Ukraine. Italy expelled 30 Russian diplomats citing "national security reasons," while Spain plans to expel around 25 Russian diplomats and embassy staff due to their perceived threat to the country's interests. Denmark and Sweden will respectively eject 15 and three diplomats for their involvement in "illegal intelligence-gathering operations." The European Union revealed that Belgium is expelling 19 Russian diplomats.

Amidst the ongoing conflict, Russia claims to have "liberated" **Mariupol**, and President Putin has ordered the military to halt an assault on a steel plant, where more than 2,000 Ukrainian fighters were holding out. The Russian forces have instead decided to blockade the industrial plant to prevent any movement. Despite the offer of fair treatment to those who surrender, about 2,000 Ukrainian soldiers continue to resist at the plant. Mariupol's fall to Russia would mark the largest city captured since the invasion began, with an estimated 21,000 lives lost in the intense battle for the strategic port city. Attempts to rescue the roughly 100,000 civilians still trapped there have seen limited success.

In response to the situation, **US President Biden** has requested an additional $33 billion from Congress to support Ukraine, sending a strong signal of the US's determination to end the invasion. The new aid package includes over $20 billion for military assistance, $8.5 billion in direct funding for the Ukrainian government, and $3 billion in humanitarian aid. This comes after a previous package of $13.6 billion in defense and economic aid for Ukraine and its Western allies, which is nearly depleted. Biden also proposed selling assets seized from Russian oligarchs to further increase aid to Ukraine and pledged to assist Bulgaria and Poland in meeting their energy needs after Moscow cut off their gas supply. However, the president requires bipartisan support to pass these additional budget requests. Russia, on the other hand, accuses the US and other countries supporting Ukraine of waging a "proxy war" against it and has warned of potential retaliation.

EUROPE

Lithuania has become the first EU country to completely cut off Russian gas supplies, with the other two Baltic states also temporarily halting the flow in response to Russia's invasion of Ukraine. Lithuania will no longer import Russian gas and will instead rely on liquefied natural gas from its terminal called Independence. Over the past decade, the three Baltic states have been vocal proponents of ending their dependence on Russian oil and gas, even after the invasion of Ukraine. For Lithuania, achieving energy independence marks the final step in severing ties with Moscow. Since re-establishing formal independence in 1990, joining the EU and NATO in 2004, and launching their own LNG terminal in 2014 at the port of Klaipeda, they have been working towards this goal.

The **Organization for Security and Co-operation** in Europe has criticized the electoral advantage given to Viktor Orban after he secured a fourth consecutive term as Hungary's prime minister.

With his Fidesz party winning a decisive majority and securing a fifth overall term, Orban's victory puts him at odds with the EU, which has condemned his erosion of democracy. Preliminary results show Fidesz winning 135 seats, more than a two-thirds majority in parliament. The hard-line nationalist Our Homeland movement was set to enter parliament for the first time with seven seats. Orban, having been in power for 12 years, holds the distinction of being the EU's longest-serving leader, and his leadership has led to the consolidation of control over various aspects of Hungarian life, shaping a self-proclaimed "illiberal democracy" with weakened checks and balances and a business elite closely aligned with the prime minister.

German Chancellor Olaf Scholz faced a setback in the Bundestag as MPs rejected a proposal to make Covid-19 vaccinations compulsory for individuals over the age of 60. The rejection, with 378 MPs voting against the measure while 296 supported it and nine abstained, is a challenge for Scholz's government, despite his endorsement of the bill. Germany's vaccination rate lags behind other major European countries, with only 76% of the population having received two shots and 58.9% having received a booster jab, raising concerns among health experts about the country's readiness for a potential autumn surge in coronavirus infections.

In a letter, the EU Commission warned **Hungary** about rule of law violations that could jeopardize the European budget. The letter marks an escalation in the ongoing dispute between Brussels and Budapest over Hungary's procurement processes and utilization of EU funding. The commission has serious concerns about how EU funds are managed in Hungary, including financial controls, auditing procedures, spending transparency, and measures to prevent fraud and corruption. For over a decade, Hungary has failed to address EU recommendations on spending. As a result of concerns over the rule of law, the EU has withheld approval for Hungary's share of the €800bn NextGenerationEU recovery package for nearly a year. The activation of the conditionality mechanism further exacerbates tensions with Brussels, occurring at a sensitive time due to the conflict in Ukraine.

Emmanuel Macron secured victory over far-right candidate Marine Le Pen and was re-elected as president of **France**. He vowed to address the country's "doubts and divisions" during his second term. Le Pen conceded the election after initial projections showed Macron winning over 58% of the presidential run-off vote. The election saw the highest level of abstention since 1969, with approximately 28% of voters not participating. Macron acknowledged that he would have to govern a nation facing divisions in his second term. His victory came as a relief to France's allies in the EU and NATO amid the ongoing Russian invasion of Ukraine. A win for Le Pen, a Eurosceptic who sought to withdraw France from NATO's military command structure, would have had significant geopolitical consequences similar to Brexit or the election of Donald Trump.

Finland is expected to apply to join NATO within weeks in response to Russia's invasion of Ukraine, despite Moscow's threats of military retaliation if Helsinki pursued membership. The Finnish Prime Minister, Sanna Marin, stated that the country would decide on NATO membership in the spring, as public support for the alliance continues to grow. Finland's relationship with Russia, sharing an 830-mile border, has changed since President Putin's troops invaded Ukraine. Putin had used the prospect of Ukraine joining NATO to justify the invasion, but instead, it has prompted other states, including Finland and Sweden, to consider NATO membership. Russia warned Finland in February to stay out of NATO, threatening "serious military and political consequences."

MIDDLE EAST AND NORTH AFRICA

Yemen's exiled president has transferred control of the country to a new ruling council, marking a significant shift in the Saudi-backed government. President Abd-Rabbu Mansour Hadi has delegated his powers to the presidential council, which includes representatives from various Yemeni factions fighting Iran-backed Houthi rebels. This move appears to sideline the president while Saudi Arabia, leading an Arab coalition in the conflict since 2015, intensifies efforts to find a diplomatic solution to end the seven-year civil war. Riyadh has urged the new council to engage in negotiations with the Houthis, who have been targeting Saudi Arabia with repeated attacks on oil installations, including a recent missile strike on

Jeddah during a Formula One grand prix event. Hadi came to power after protests ousted the country's long-standing dictator, Ali Abdullah Saleh, but his government lost the capital, Sana'a, to the Houthis in 2015, forcing him to spend much of his time in Saudi Arabia.

Warring parties in **Yemen** have accepted a two-month truce, a significant development as it would be the first mutually agreed ceasefire since 2016. The United Nations announced the truce following separate unilateral ceasefires declared by the Houthi rebels and the Saudi-backed government. Escalating missile and drone attacks on Saudi Arabian oil installations and retaliatory airstrikes in Yemen had led to this decision. The war has resulted in the deaths of hundreds of thousands of Yemenis due to disease and malnutrition, and the conflict has reached a stalemate on most fronts.

Turkey is facing economic challenges as its official inflation rate reaches its highest level in 20 years. The Consumer Price Index (CPI) rose by 61% year on year in March, primarily driven by soaring energy and food prices. Food costs increased by 70%, making up a quarter of Turkey's inflation basket, while energy and transport costs rose by almost 103% and 99%, respectively. The rise in commodity prices, influenced by Russia's invasion of Ukraine, has placed additional strain on Turkey's economy, as the country imports most of its oil and natural gas supplies.

A Turkish court has halted the trial of 26 Saudis accused of the murder of journalist Jamal Khashoggi, closing a case that had strained Turkey-Saudi Arabia relations. The trial was transferred to Riyadh with the approval of the Turkish justice ministry, signaling a potential diplomatic reset between the two nations. This decision has drawn criticism from human rights groups. Additionally, Saudi Arabia has begun easing an unofficial embargo on goods from Turkey, further indicating an improvement in bilateral relations. The Turkish arrest warrants for the suspects, who were being tried in absentia, and the Interpol red notices seeking their arrest worldwide were also lifted.

Turkish President Erdogan and Saudi Crown Prince Mohammed bin Salman met during Erdogan's visit to Saudi Arabia, signaling a reconciliation after years of tension caused by the murder of journalist Jamal Khashoggi. While Erdogan never directly accused Prince Mohammed of the murder, he held him responsible for it. The meeting between the two leaders marks a significant shift in their relationship, as both nations aim for a diplomatic reset. Turkey has been making efforts to mend ties with former regional adversaries and attract foreign investment amid economic challenges and upcoming elections.

Lebanon and the IMF have reached a preliminary agreement for a $3 billion loan facility, representing the first step toward easing the country's severe economic and financial crisis that began in 2019. The crisis has resulted in the country's currency losing over 90% of its value, and a significant portion of the population now lives below the poverty line. The bailout is crucial to prevent further economic collapse, but previous talks between the IMF and Lebanese authorities had faced hurdles due to required economic reforms. The Lebanese government has now promised to implement comprehensive reforms, leading to the agreement.

Clashes between **Israeli** security forces and **Palestinians** have erupted at Jerusalem's al-Aqsa mosque compound, a site revered by both Muslims and Jews. These confrontations come amid heightened tensions, the first exchange of fire in Gaza in months, Palestinian attacks in Israeli cities, and an Israeli military operation in the occupied West Bank. Additionally, political uncertainties surrounding the Israeli governing coalition and the confluence of the Muslim Ramadan holiday and the Jewish Passover festival add to the volatile situation. The unrest poses a risk of spreading into Arab Israeli cities, prompting the Israeli police to put reserve forces on alert ahead of planned demonstrations.

ASIA

Shortages of food and medicine have left residents of **Shanghai**, China's largest city, feeling desperate and frustrated as authorities struggle to control a Covid-19 outbreak. Shanghai has adopted Beijing's strict "dynamic zero" Covid strategy and implemented two four-day lockdowns citywide due to the spreading omicron variant. Some Shanghainese have been confined to their homes for more than two weeks, facing restrictions due to positive cases in their buildings, and have relied on government grocery deliveries.

PM Imran Khan has dissolved **Pakistan's** parliament, triggering new elections and plunging the country into a constitutional crisis as he fights to retain power. With his party losing its slim majority in parliament amid discontent over inflation and declining living standards, Khan's opponents rallied support within the National Assembly to remove him through a no-confidence vote. However, the speaker dismissed the motion in absentia, claiming it was unconstitutional. At Khan's request, the president dissolved the National Assembly, and elections are scheduled to be held in 90 days. Elected on a platform of reform and anti-corruption, Khan has struggled to meet expectations, and his ousting represents a victory for Pakistan's prominent political dynasties, the Sharifs and Bhuttos.

Shehbaz Sharif has been elected as **Pakistan's** new prime minister, marking the return to power and influence of the nation's two main political dynasties following Imran Khan's ousting. The supreme court ruled Khan's dissolution of parliament as unconstitutional and ordered the parliament to debate the motion, making Khan the first Pakistan prime minister to be removed by a no-confidence vote. Shehbaz Sharif, the leader of the Pakistan Muslim League-Nawaz party and brother of former prime minister Nawaz Sharif, now assumes office. Pakistan's political landscape is characterized by stark divisions, with Shehbaz Sharif's victory occurring amidst a nearly half-empty chamber after Khan's allies walked out in protest.

Sri Lanka's president, Gotabaya Rajapaksa, has ended emergency rule, which was imposed amidst an economic and political crisis that sparked widespread protests. The decision to revoke the measures came after the country's finance minister resigned within a day of being appointed. Energy blackouts, shortages of essential goods, and soaring prices triggered demonstrations, accusing Rajapaksa's government of economic mismanagement and calling for his resignation. The dissolution of emergency rule signals efforts to contain the crisis, as Sri Lanka faces negotiations with the IMF over its debt pile and dwindling foreign reserves.

New satellite images of a **North Korean** nuclear facility indicate that Pyongyang may be approaching its first nuclear test since 2017, escalating tensions on the Korean peninsula. The images show construction activity, movement of supplies, and personnel activities near a new entrance to the Punggye-ri nuclear test site. North Korea's actions have raised concerns about regional stability and security.

China has maintained a silent stance on allegations of Russian troop atrocities against civilians in Ukraine, balancing its support for Moscow with the global fallout from the invasion. While many countries condemn Russia over documented atrocities in Bucha near Kyiv, the Chinese government has chosen not to address the issue explicitly. China refrains from defining Russia's actions in Ukraine as an invasion and echoes Russia's arguments about security concerns. This position aligns with the "limitless" partnership between China and Russia, grounded in their shared opposition to the US and its global influence.

Hong Kong's Chief Executive, Carrie Lam, has announced that she will not seek a second term, indicating the end of her tumultuous tenure. John Lee, the city's second-highest-ranking official, is likely to enter the race to succeed Lam. Lee, known for his support of Beijing's sweeping national security law imposed on Hong Kong, may potentially succeed her. Hong Kong's chief executives have not served two full five-year terms allowed under the city's Basic Law since the territory's return to Chinese sovereignty in 1997.

Indonesia's blanket ban on palm oil exports has impacted palm oil prices and the Indonesian rupiah, aiming to contain surging food prices due to the war in Ukraine. Indonesia, the world's largest palm oil exporter, joins other countries implementing food export bans amid rising food prices caused by the conflict in Ukraine. Agricultural commodity prices have surged due to disruptions in grain and sunflower oil supplies from Ukraine. As a result, countries relying on international markets for their grains face higher food import costs, while vegetable oil prices have also seen sharp increases, leading to rationing of supplies in some places.

Aung San Suu Kyi, **Myanmar's** former civilian leader, has been sentenced to five years on corruption charges, adding to her existing six-year sentence for various other charges. The deposed leader, who has been in military custody since the coup in February last year, is expected to remain in prison into her mid-eighties, facing a potential total sentence of more than 150 years.

THE AMERICAS

Oklahoma has passed a bill that imposes severe restrictions on abortion, making it nearly illegal in almost all instances. The bill, led by the Republican-led state's House of Representatives, would criminalize performing abortions except in cases of life-threatening medical emergencies. Offenders could face fines of up to $100,000 and up to 10 years of imprisonment. Several US states have recently enacted similar abortion restrictions, as conservative legislatures gain momentum from the anti-abortion movement. Additionally, the conservative-leaning US Supreme Court is considering a case that may overturn the landmark Roe vs. Wade decision, which legalized abortion across the country. Oklahoma's legislature is also considering other bills to tighten access to abortion, including one resembling a Texas statute that enables private citizens to sue those involved in facilitating an abortion.

Costa Ricans elected a former World Bank official, Rodrigo Chaves, as the country's next president after a contentious campaign characterized by low voter turnout. Chaves secured 53% of the vote, defeating former president José María Figueres, who obtained 47%. Chaves, an economist who spent most of his career abroad, positioned himself as a change candidate. He will assume office in May and will need to collaborate with other parties to advance his agenda. Chaves has vowed to renegotiate a $1.8 billion IMF loan obtained last year to support the country's economic recovery from the pandemic and to strengthen trade ties in the Asia-Pacific region and attract more Chinese tourists.

Mexico's president, Andrés Manuel López Obrador, has proposed a sweeping overhaul of the country's election apparatus, raising concerns about potential damage to democracy and granting his party greater control over the electoral system. The proposed constitutional changes seek to dissolve the country's national electoral institute (INE), which oversees elections, replacing it with a directly elected but less well-funded body. The president also aims to reduce public funding to political parties and relax electoral propaganda rules, measures that critics argue may benefit his party, Morena. López Obrador's critics have feared his intentions to prolong his stay in office beyond the one-term, six-year limit or concentrate power, despite his popularity. He has assured that he will step aside in 2024.

Protestors have taken control of **Peru's** Andean city of Cusco to express their anger over the rising cost of living, blocking roads and a railway, which disrupted access to the ruins of Machu Picchu for tourists. The two-day strike in the Cusco region involved thousands of Peruvians protesting the soaring cost of fuel, fertilizers, and food, partly caused by the war in Ukraine. Some protestors used rocks and burning tires to block roads, and the train service between Cusco and Machu Picchu was suspended. The unrest in Cusco follows weeks of protests across the country, indicating growing discontent over inflation, which has reached 7%, the highest rate in a generation. Peruvians are demanding solutions to the economic challenges, and some call for President Pedro Castillo to step down after only nine turbulent months in office.

The Amazon rainforest in **Brazil** experienced the highest deforestation rate ever recorded in the first three months of 2022. A total of 363 square miles of forest were cleared between January and March, marking a 64% increase compared to the same period last year when 221 square miles were cleared. The surge in deforestation has been linked to President Jair Bolsonaro's weakening of environmental protections since taking office in 2019, citing economic development for the Amazon region. A UN climate panel report highlighted the lack of adequate government actions to control greenhouse gas emissions, with deforestation accounting for about 10% of global emissions.

US President Biden's approval rating has dropped to a low of 33% as he grapples with the impact of surging inflation. The poll revealed that approval among key independent voters was only 26%, indicating potential losses for Democrats in the midterm elections. While Biden's approval among Democrats was 76%, it was only 3%

among Republicans, illustrating the deep political polarization that Biden had hoped to address during his presidency. This marks the second time his approval rating has hit this low point in polling by Quinnipiac University, with his disapproval rating slightly higher now at 54% compared to 53% in January. Biden's popularity suffered after the chaotic withdrawal of US troops from Afghanistan last summer.

AFRICA

More than 250 people lost their lives in **South Africa** due to severe flooding, which occurred a day after heavy rains caused roads and houses to be washed away and disrupted shipping from the continent's largest port. The floods struck Kwazulu Natal, South Africa's second-most populous province, making it one of the country's most devastating natural disasters. Durban received over 200 millimeters of rain in a single day, leading to mudslides, sinkholes, and disruptions to Maersk's container operations. Shipping containers floated down submerged motorways, and debris, including a fuel tanker, washed up ashore. Thousands of informal dwellings in townships were destroyed across the province. Scientists and planners have long warned that as one of Africa's most urbanized and unequal countries, South Africa is ill-prepared for the impact of severe storms on the densely populated shack settlements surrounding its major cities.

Outside Russia's embassy in Addis Ababa, volunteers gathered after reports circulated in the **Ethiopian** capital that the embassy was recruiting fighters for the war in Ukraine. This two-day gathering of young men coincided with intelligence reports suggesting that neighboring Eritrea was preparing to send 5,000 conscripts to bolster Russia's ranks. Sergey Lavrov, Russia's foreign minister, visited Eritrea's president shortly before the invasion of Ukraine. Eritrea, known for mandatory and indefinite conscription in its military and civilian workforce, can readily provide numbers and experienced personnel. Eritrea's soldiers have previously fought alongside Ethiopian troops and have been accused of committing atrocities in the 18-month civil war in Ethiopia's northern region of Tigray, where both capitals consider the leadership a common enemy. Eritrea, long isolated as a pariah state by the West, cast one of the five votes against last month's UN resolution condemning Moscow's aggression in Ukraine, alongside Belarus, Syria, North Korea, and Russia itself. Ethiopia's absence from the vote was seen as tacit support for President Putin. The growing influence of Moscow on the continent is reflected in the eight African nations that did not participate in the vote and the 17 abstentions, including South Africa.

SOURCES:

https://www.reuters.com/world/europe/blinken-visits-ukraine-pivotal-moment-kyiv-claims-gains-2022-09-08/

https://www.ft.com/content/0e7c029f-028e-40e3-b4bb-e310a24ada18

https://www.thetimes.co.uk/article/boris-johnson-eager-to-arm-ukraine-for-defence-of-odesa-880x688xk

https://www.ft.com/content/84b82726-d4d0-446c-a409-f61037686315

https://www.thetimes.co.uk/article/russia-threatens-retaliation-after-more-than-140-diplomats-expelled-across-europe-nt8m2wvgm

https://www.thetimes.co.uk/article/russia-uses-bunker-buster-bombs-in-final-assault-on-mariupol-steelworks-3blkbsjn7

https://www.theguardian.com/us-news/2022/apr/28/joe-biden-ukraine-military-aid-us-congress

https://www.theguardian.com/us-news/2022/apr/28/joe-biden-ukraine-military-aid-us-congress

https://www.ft.com/content/efcadd5a-b192-4567-a991-56cd6fd83dae

https://www.theguardian.com/world/2022/apr/03/viktor-orban-expected-to-win-big-majority-in-hungarian-general-election

https://www.ft.com/content/7d0610bf-3cf9-4edd-a392-e9d97dc9fade

https://www.ft.com/content/3377409d-5f54-4d00-bc7c-e4e099bf8f51

 https://www.ft.com/content/3377409d-5f54-4d00-bc7c-e4e099bf8f51

https://www.ft.com/content/0a5a525b-a459-4741-b3d4-ca335cdc2d33

https://www.theguardian.com/world/2022/may/12/finland-apply-join-nato-without-delay-president-pm

https://www.ft.com/content/9c96e5ba-204e-4ff8-b5ef-23dba1611f8c

https://www.aljazeera.com/news/2022/8/2/yemens-warring-sides-agree-to-renew-existing-truce-un

https://www.ft.com/content/19e9541c-e0b6-4a1c-adb3-afc3f8e1a880

https://www.ft.com/content/cddb05e4-e1bb-4bfa-8d75-76f2f1803c32

https://www.ft.com/content/cddb05e4-e1bb-4bfa-8d75-76f2f1803c32

https://www.ft.com/content/96ce82a0-e654-4d57-b10b-5be5ef6beab1

https://www.ft.com/content/4cd0e760-9e28-4b26-bfcc-4abaeeb20949

https://www.ft.com/content/3bd09792-fad7-4f23-a0ff-2b157f111a93

https://www.ft.com/content/3e439a10-860b-4ae6-9070-ad8546da8850

https://www.ft.com/content/8b1707a5-29ff-49b6-85f3-0ce2e86529f9

https://www.ft.com/content/6b90c9ae-1435-4c53-88ce-f2de7e93f1df

https://www.ft.com/content/3a5b7f88-22c6-43f3-85c2-5bb3efd42a06

https://www.ft.com/content/82ef82a3-681d-4ee7-8987-1d851b949590

https://www.ft.com/content/b11fc9ce-569f-4fcc-a26d-e3f0efa34829

https://www.theguardian.com/world/2022/apr/04/hong-kong-leader-carrie-lam-says-she-will-not-seek-second-term

https://www.ft.com/content/38b6df62-e863-4ba1-8274-138ccb2b061b

https://www.thetimes.co.uk/article/aung-san-suu-kyi-sentenced-to-five-years-in-prison-z7hjplck6

https://www.ft.com/content/cee6a170-fa23-47cb-b554-d457d68f225b

https://www.theguardian.com/world/2022/apr/04/costa-rica-presidential-election-rodrigo-chaves

https://news.sky.com/story/peru-protests-leave-thousands-of-tourists-stranded-in-gateway-city-to-machu-picchu-12769717

https://www.thetimes.co.uk/article/joe-biden-approval-rating-hits-new-low-amid-soaring-inflation-9wzzkbsw7

https://www.ft.com/content/b366212d-91e4-48c2-8581-dbee5461da82

https://www.thetimes.co.uk/article/hundreds-of-volunteers-queue-up-in-ethiopia-to-fight-for-russia-w0db6w8cn

THE WORLD
IN MAY 2022

Introduction

This was a month during which the world grappled with the consequences as Russia's invasion of Ukraine extended into its third month. Global energy prices continued increasing as the European Union stepped up its programme of sanctions against Russia. The Russian siege on Ukraine continued, with heavy shelling on the port city of Mariupol and in the Donbas region. Hungary attempted to block to EU's attempt to ban imports of Russian oil, as Russia turned off the gas supply to Poland and Bulgaria. EU countries and the US stepped up their support offers to Ukraine, sending weapons and aid. The Nordic states of Sweden and Finland put aside years of military non-alignment and applied for membership of NATO, despite vocal objections from member-state Turkey. The Omicron COVID-19 variant continued to spread in Asia, as tough restrictions were announced in parts China and throughout North Korea. The Taliban toughened their stance on women's rights in Afghanistan, ordering all women in the country to cover their faces in public. The economic crisis in Sri Lanka worsened as the Prime Minister resigned after weeks of protests and the country defaulted on its foreign debt payments. Iran seized two

Greek oil tankers in the Strait of Hormuz after a Russian-flagged oil tanker was seized the week before for carrying sanctioned Iranian crude. Al Jazeera journalist Shireen Abu Akleh was shot dead in a refugee camp in the occupied West Bank morning during clashes between the Israeli military and Palestinian gunmen. Elections in Lebanon saw Hizbollah and its allies have lost their majority in parliament, meaning a coalition government must be formed. The US Supreme Court is set to overturn the landmark Roe vs Wade ruling that has guaranteed abortion rights across the country for almost five decades.

This piece will summarise these important developments in global current affairs, providing an accurate and concise summary. It will begin discussing developments in the global economy, before moving to the war in Ukraine, Europe, Asia, the Middle East, Africa and the Americas.

GLOBAL ECONOMY

Shell reported its highest ever quarterly profits during the volatility in **global energy markets** which has followed Russia's invasion of Ukraine. Earnings rose to $9.1bn in the first three months of the year, three times the $3.2bn it recorded a year ago. The world's biggest energy companies' earnings have provoked renewed calls from UK politicians for a windfall tax on oil and gas profits. BP reported underlying profits of $6.2bn, its highest since 2008, while Norway's Equinor recorded its highest ever quarterly pre-tax earnings of $18bn.

Saudi Aramco overtakes Apple as the world's most valuable company following high oil prices pushing shares of the world's biggest crude exporter to record levels. The company's market capitalisation is $2.426tn this month, exceeding Apple's. It is the first time that Saudi Aramco has regained the top spot since 2020.

Opec and its allies agreed to a modest crude output increase even as a growing international boycott of Russian oil cast doubt on Russia's ability to continue to meet the cartel's targets. The Opec+ group, which has included Russia since 2016, said it would raise continuing with the plan to gradually replace output cut at the start of the coronavirus pandemic. Brent was trading at more than $113 a barrel, a day after the European Commission proposed a phased-in ban on all imports of Russian crude into EU member states by the end of the year.

WAR IN UKRAINE

The **European Union** is planning further emergency lending to Ukraine. This follows a request by US President Joe Biden to Congress to provide $33bn in military, economic and humanitarian aid for Ukraine. The announcement of the new funds is the latest escalation in tensions between Moscow and the west over Putin's war. The US is taking an increasingly assertive approach to the war. As Russia continues its offensive in eastern Ukraine, the US convened a meeting of over forty countries over increasing weapons aid to Kyiv, and Moscow announced a halt to gas exports Poland and Bulgaria. Russia cut off gas supplies after the two countries refused to comply with a Russian order to settle payments in roubles. Brussels has warned member states that doing so would be in breach of EU sanctions.

More than 100 people have been evacuated from a steelworks in the besieged Ukrainian port city of **Mariupol**, the last holdout of Ukrainian resistance to Russian forces in the city. The evacuation comes after repeated international efforts to negotiate safe passage for civilians sheltering in the Azovstal Plant. Around 1,000 civilians have sought refuge in the steel plant, hiding underground for weeks as Russian strikes and artillery have hit the site. About 100,000 civilians are estimated to be still living in the city.

Ukrainian forces have held off a Russian offensive in the **Donbas** region amidst heavy artillery fire. Ukrainian resistance drove Russian troops back from a highway, allowing Ukrainian forces to supply the city of Sievierodonetsk. Russia is focused on capturing Sievierodonetsk, the last major city in Luhansk still under Ukrainian control. However, its advance has slowed despite what Ukrainian forces described as a tactical retreat under heavy artillery bombardments. Russian forces have surrounded Sievierodonetsk in an attempt to encircle it but have yet to progress further. The siege marks a strategic shift by Russia to overwhelm smaller pockets of resistance. Ukraine believes it can recapture the area once it receives more weapons from the west. Peace talks between the two sides have foundered after Putin hardened his desire to capture more territory and annex areas his forces have already captured in the south-east.

The All England Club, which runs the **Wimbledon** tennis tournament, has banned Russian and Belarussian players from competing in the tournament, citing "unjustified and unprecedented military aggression" in Ukraine. However, the men's and women's tennis tours, both of which have condemned the Russian invasion, warned against "discrimination". The bodies have announced they would strip the upcoming Wimbledon championships of their rankings points.

Russian President Putin has announced double-digit increases to Russia's minimum wage and pensions as rising inflation and sanctions push up the cost of living. Putin admitted Russia faced "difficulties" but denied these were linked to the "special military operation" in Ukraine. Prices of food and other basic items in Russia have risen in the days following Moscow's invasion of Ukraine, when the rouble weakened substantially. Prices have not returned to previous levels. The measures come as the rouble is trading at its highest level since 2018 despite efforts by western countries to put pressure on the Russian economy. Russia's central bank is set to hold an extraordinary meeting at which it is expected to make a further cut in interest rates, which were pushed up to try to protect the economy from sanctions that followed the invasion of Ukraine in February.

European leaders are increasing diplomatic efforts to loosen Russia's hold on Ukraine's grain supplies as the risk of a global food crisis mounts. German chancellor Scholz and French president Macron discussed the situation with Putin in a phone call. Putin told them Russia was willing to find ways to unblock grain exports from Ukraine's Black Sea ports and could increase its own fertiliser and agriculture exports if sanctions are lifted. Ukraine and some of its western allies have accused Russia of blockading the port of

Odesa, holding up the export of large shipments of grain. The risk of a global food crisis has been intensifying since Putin launched his invasion of Ukraine, a major grain producer and exporter.

EUROPE

Germany has requested a phased-in ban on Russian oil imports to the EU, a topic which has divided EU member states. Germany, the EU's biggest economy, was reluctant to target Russian oil at the start of the invasion, but has shifted its position as the war continues. Russian oil accounts for a quarter of the bloc's crude imports. The EU Commission is drawing up its sixth sanctions package against Russia over its war against Ukraine. The measures target Russian oil, Russian and Belarusian banks and more individuals and companies. Gemany favours an oil embargo, whereas some countries, such as Italy, are pushing for other measures such as a price cap or tariff on Russian oil. Poland and the Baltic states are also calling for an outright ban. Hungary and Slovakia's Russian-dependent oil infrastructure and landlocked status mean do not have alternative supply options and would need to overhaul their physical oil-processing network.

Hungary's PM Viktor Orban has warned the EU his government would not sanction Russian oil and gas; 85 per cent of Hungary's gas supply and 65 per cent of its oil is Russian. This is delaying an EU plan to ban imports of Russian oil, which requires unanimity among the EU's 27 member states. The ban would hit crude oil within six months and refined products by the end of the year. But Hungary said it would reject the proposal unless there was an exception for countries which import Russian crude via pipelines. Slovakia and the Czech Republic also have doubts as they rely on the Soviet-era Druzhba pipeline, which transits Ukraine, to import Ural-type crude oil, which their refineries are geared to process.

Hungary's PM, Victor Orban, has a state of emergency. This allows his government rights to rule by decree in response to an "economic crisis" caused the war in Ukraine and Russian sanctions. Orban exercised these emergency powers during the coronavirus pandemic, when critics in Hungary feared a dramatic erosion of democratic rights and civil liberties. However, the government largely conducted business as before, using its comfortable majority in parliament.

Thousands of people attended politically charged May Day marches across **France**, with many protesters angry about re-elected president Emmanuel Macron's plan for a pensions reform. The demonstrations also focused on demands for higher salaries, with the electorate concerned about the cost of living and soaring fuel prices. The protests come a week after Macron defeated far-right leader Marine Le Pen to win a second presidential term. Macron will attempt to win another parliamentary majority in June legislative elections that would enable him to pass reforms.

Migrants continue to arrive in the **UK** by boat after crossing the English Channel, despite the British government's new plan to fly thousands of asylum seekers to Rwanda. More than 6,000 migrants have arrived in the UK on boats mainly organised by criminal gangs so far this year. That compares to more than 28,000 in 2021, and more than 8,000 in 2020. PM Boris Johnson and home secretary Priti Patel recently unveiled the government's plan to send thousands of migrants seeking asylum in Britain to Rwanda. The PM said anyone who had entered Britain through irregular means since January 1 and not sought asylum in a safe third country may be transported Rwanda and assessed there for eventual resettlement. Rwanda initially stands to gain £120mn from the deal with Britain under the country will process and house an unknown number of migrants sent from Britain.

In the **UK**, for the first time in 60 years, the Queen was not able to deliver the annual speech outlining the government's legislative agenda to parliament. Prince Charles read the Queen's Speech instead, in a move that highlighted a gradual transition of duties in the royal family.

Italian Prime Minister Mario Draghi has announced a €14bn economic support package to support vulnerable families, businesses and investment projects cope with risings commodity prices. The government will increase a new windfall tax on energy company profits to fund the measures. The PM said he was determined to help Italian citizens and businesses cope with the disruption caused by Russia's invasion of Ukraine. The measures include a one-off cash payment of €200 for millions of Italians living on low incomes or pensions, energy price subsidies for vulnerable families, tax credits for businesses to cope with higher energy costs, and additional funds for local governments.

Sweden discarded 200 years of military non-alignment and applied to join NATO, alongside its neighbour **Finland**. Russia's invasion of Ukraine has upturned decades of security thinking in the two Nordic countries. Putin has signalled Russia will tolerate Finland and Sweden joining NATO, but warned the Kremlin would respond if the alliance installed military bases or equipment in either country. The Russian president said the proposed NATO enlargement posed "no direct threat for Russia".

ASIA

Beijing announced it is tightening COVID-19 restrictions, closing gyms and cinemas and raising testing requirement during an Omicron outbreak. In Shanghai, tens of millions of people have been restricted to their apartments, signalling **China** remains committed to Xi Jinping's "zero-Covid" policy. However, the head of the World Health Organization has warned that China's zero-Covid strategy is unsustainable; new modelling shows the country risks unleashing a new wave of coronavirus infections and causing 1.6mn deaths if it abandons the policy.

North Korea reports first coronavirus cases since the start of the pandemic and imposes lockdowns of cities. An unspecified number of people in Pyongyang had contracted the Omicron variant of Covid-19. Kim Jong Un ordered all cities to lock down in order to block the transmission of the virus. The borders with China and Russia have been closed since the beginning of the pandemic. Along with Eritrea, North Korea is one of only two countries in the world to have not initiated a Covid-19 vaccination programme, and it has refused offers of vaccines through the World Health Organization's Covax initiative.

Indian PM Modi has been invited as a special guest to the G7 leaders' summit next month, as part of efforts to sway India away from its longstanding alliance with Russia. Germany, which holds the rotating G7 presidency, has also invited the leaders of Indonesia, South Africa and Senegal to the meeting, which will take place in the Bavarian Alps. Germany and India signed a series of bilateral agreements focused on sustainable development that will provide India with €10bn in aid by 2030 to boost the use of clean energy. Germany has been keen to enlist India's support for the tough stance adopted by the US and EU over Russia's invasion of Ukraine. However, Modi has proved reluctant to speak out against Moscow.

In **Afghanistan,** the Taliban have ordered all women to cover their faces in public, the latest in a series of policies targeting women's rights and liberties in the country. The Islamist group's ministry for the propagation of virtue and prevention of vice, a religious police force, announced the restriction, stating that an ideal covering for women was the burka. The garment was previously mandatory under the group's repressive rule in the 1990s. The Taliban also decreed that women should only leave the house when necessary, with the male relatives of rule-breakers liable to face punishment. In March, the Taliban reversed a decision to let teenage girls back to secondary school after having repeatedly claimed they would be allowed back into education.

Sri Lanka's PM has resigned after weeks of protests, leaving the government of his brother, President Gotabaya Rajapaksa, in turmoil during an economic crisis that has taken the country to the brink of default. Mahinda Rajapaksa resigned as clashes escalated after his supporters attacked anti-government demonstrators and the government deployed the military to the streets of Colombo. The president, who imposed a nationwide curfew after declaring a state of emergency last week, asked for his resignation to held stem the protests and pave the way for a cross-party government. Protesters first took to the streets in March, calling for the Rajapaksa family-led government to step down as Sri Lanka entered a crisis, with double-digit inflation and shortages of food, fuel and medicine causing a dramatic decline in living standards. Sri Lanka has suspended international bond payments and began talks with the IMF, World Bank and bilateral creditors including India and

China to restructure debt and take over emergency loans. It owes about $8bn in foreign debt repayments this year.

The **US** and **South Korea** have committed to exploring new steps to reinforce deterrence as North Korea continues to develop nuclear weapons. President Biden is visiting Asia in a bid to reassure allies of the US's commitment to regional security as China pushes for influence. South Korean president Yoon Suk-yeol said during a joint press conference with Biden in Seoul on Saturday that the two leaders had discussed the "timely deployment" of US strategic assets including fighters, bombers and missiles. South Korea is seeking greater reassurance from the US, its closest security ally.

MIDDLE EAST

In **Iran,** President Raisi announced plans to cut back bread subsidies as wheat prices soar globally and Iran tries to steer an economy hit by US sanctions on oil exports. The government will offer citizens coupons to allow them to access bread at subsidised prices, while the rest will be available at market rates. The scheme will later include other goods such as chicken, cheese and vegetable oil. The price of wheat on the global market has jumped since the start of the Russian conflict with Ukraine, adding to the cost of subsidies. Russia and Ukraine account for about 30 per cent of Iran's grain imports. Inflation was already high in the Islamic republic, hitting 39.2 per cent in April.

Iran seizes two Greek oil tankers in one of the world's busiest shipping lanes in retaliation for the capture of a Russian-flagged tanker loaded with Iranian oil last month. Iranian forces boarded the Prudent Warrior, a Greek-owned vessel, in the Strait of Hormuz. The seizure is likely to cause consternation in the oil market and the maritime industry, with oil prices already close to $120 a barrel. Greece is a shipping powerhouse with Greek companies owning almost a quarter of all supertankers. The seizure comes as talks between Tehran and global powers over Iran's nuclear ambitions have stalled in recent months, raising tensions across the Middle East. The Greek foreign ministry described the seizure of the tankers as "acts of piracy". Last month Athens seized the Russian-flagged Pegas oil tanker for carrying sanctioned Iranian crude. In 2019 Iran seized a British-flagged oil tanker shortly after the UK stopped an Iranian vessel in Gibraltar that was carrying crude to Syria. The British-flagged Stena Impero was held in Iran for two months before its release. The Strait of Hormuz, the narrow strategic waterway separating Iran from the Gulf states, is one of the world's most important shipping lanes for crude. Approximately a third of all seaborne oil cargoes pass through each day.

In **Israel,** veteran Al Jazeera journalist Shireen Abu Akleh was shot dead in a refugee camp in the occupied West Bank morning during clashes between the Israeli military and Palestinian gunmen. Al Jazeera hit out at Israel for "deliberately targeting and killing our colleague," and referred to Abu Akleh's death as an "assassination in cold blood". But Israeli military and government officials said it was "likely" Abu Akleh was killed by Palestinian militants who at the time were firing on Israeli forces "wildly and indiscriminately". Abu Akleh was in the Jenin refugee camp in the northern West Bank reporting on an Israeli military raid and the ensuing clashes. She was wearing an armoured flak jacket clearly marked 'Press' when she was shot. The city of Jenin and its adjacent refugee camp have over the past month been the focus of a large Israeli military operation after a spate of Palestinian attacks in Israeli cities that have claimed the lives of 19 people since late March. At least 30 Palestinians have been killed by Israeli forces across the West Bank in the same period.

In **Dubai,** food delivery riders for Talabat have gone on an illegal strike protesting over their low wages as the cost of living sparks widening unrest among the poorest workers in the Gulf state. The unrest comes as fuel prices have soared since the Russian invasion of Ukraine. This has reduced the pay of riders, who purchase their own petrol. With inflation hitting other products such as food, living standards are declining for workers. The Talabat walkout comes after a strike this month in Dubai by employees of rival operator Deliveroo prompted the UK-based firm to drop plans to cut salaries and extend working hours. Strike action and unionised labour are illegal in the UAE. From construction to retail, migrant workers form the backbone of Gulf economies, most of whom travel from south Asia with the aim of remitting funds back to their families.

Sheikh Khalifa bin Zayed al-Nahyan, the **United Arab Emirates'** president and ruler of Dhabi since 2004, has died aged 73. Sheikh Khalifa, who presided over the UAE's rapid economic transformation, had retired from public life after suffering a stroke in 2014. He had handed over decision-making to his half-brother, Sheikh Mohammed bin Zayed al-Nahyan, Abu Dhabi's crown prince. Sheikh Mohammed is poised to become the next president.

Qatar has pledged to invest £10bn in the UK, including in technology, healthcare, infrastructure and clean energy, as the British government entices sovereign wealth fund investment from oil-rich Gulf states. The investment agreement was announced during talks between UK PM Johnson and Sheikh Tamim bin Hamad al-Thani, Qatar's emir. Last year, the UK signed a similar deal with Mubadala, the Abu Dhabi sovereign wealth fund, to invest £10bn. The Gulf states have seen their revenues soar as energy prices have remained high over the past year. Qatar has a long record of investing in the UK and has already invested £5bn in Britain since 2017. It also owns several assets, including Harrods and the Shard skyscraper in London. As the world's top exporter of liquefied natural gas, Qatar's importance to the UK and the rest of Europe has increased in the wake of Russia's invasion of Ukraine. The Gulf state supplies about 40 per cent of the UK's LNG and is in talks to increase its exports to the country.

Turkey's President Erdogan has spoken out against allowing Sweden and Finland to join NATO, putting the two Nordic countries' hopes of joining the western military alliance in jeopardy. Erdogan, whose country has been a Nato member since 1952, said he could not take a "positive view" of the two nations' potential bids for membership. The obstacle was their support for the Kurdistan Workers' party (PKK), which has been embroiled in a decades-long armed insurgency against the Turkish state, he said. The PKK is classified as a terrorist organisation by Ankara, the US and the EU. The Turkish President accused Scandinavian countries of being a "guest house for terrorist organisations", with some countries having Kurdish members of parliament. He also accused the countries of refusing to extradite 30 people accused of terrorism charges in Turkey. Erdogan's position forced NATO to postpone its initial decision to proceed with the two countries' applications. All 30 existing members of NATO have to ratify Finland's and Sweden's applications but that process only starts once the defence alliance issues an accession protocol and formally invites the two countries to join.

In **Lebanon,** Iran-backed group Hizbollah and its allies lost their majority in Lebanon's parliamentary election. Although Hizbollah and its Shia partner Amal retained all of their seats, its main Christian ally and other politicians it relies on to make up its current 71-seat majority lost some of theirs. No one party or bloc has emerged as an outright winner, raising the possibility of further deadlock in the crisis-hit country. These are the first elections since the collapse of the country's economy in 2019 and the 2020 port explosion in Beirut. Lebanon's political parties now need to agree a coalition government, a process that could take several months. The new administration must then negotiate economic reforms needed to unlock billions of dollars in loans and aid to steer Lebanon out of its economic crisis.

AFRICA

In the Horn of **Africa,** an area stretching from northern Kenya to Somalia and of Ethiopia, 20 million people could go hungry this year as delayed rains exacerbate the worst drought in four decades. After three rainy seasons failed and a fourth looks likely to do the same, crops have disappeared and more than a million livestock have died in Ethiopia's south-eastern Somali region alone. One more dry season could turn into the worst drought in a century, just as the region is braced for the devastating fallout of war in Ukraine. The conflict threatens to increase food prices but and push the cost of fertiliser beyond the means of millions of farmers, threatening next year's harvest.

US President Joe Biden has approved the establishment of a small military presence in **Somalia**, reversing the Trump administration's withdrawal of about 750 troops from the country. Biden's decision was made in light of growing concern about the threat posed by al-Shabaab. As well as frequent deadly attacks in Somalia, al-Shabaab has occasionally carried out atrocities in neighbouring countries, such as the 2019 attack on the Dusit complex in Nairobi in which 22 civilians were killed. The group also conducted an attack on a US base in northern Kenya in 2020 in which three American servicemen were killed.

THE AMERICAS

In the **US**, President Joe Biden made a plea for the US to "stand up to the gun lobby" after 19 children and two adults were killed in a shooting at a Texas elementary school. Salvador Ramos, an 18-year-old male resident of the city of Uvalde, had entered Robb Elementary School and opened fire on teachers and students. The shooting in Texas came less than two weeks after a teenager shot and killed ten people at a supermarket in Buffalo, New York. Democrats in Congress have tried to pass stricter measures for years but have encountered steadfast Republican opposition, which has shown no signs of waning even for modest gun control proposals such as more rigorous background checks for the purchase of weapons. Any legislative changes would require clearing a 60-vote threshold in the Senate, meaning at least 10 Republicans would have to be in favour for gun control legislation to advance.

US secretary of state Blinken says Washington will stay focused on China as the most serious threat to the international order despite Russia's invasion of Ukraine. Blinken said China was the only country with the intent and capabilities to reshape the international order and that it was doing so in a way that would undermine global stability. Blinken's comments came as US-China relations are at their worst since the countries normalised diplomatic relations in 1979. In recent months, ties have been strained by Beijing's refusal to condemn Moscow's invasion of Ukraine and by its growing military ties with Russia. This week, Chinese and Russian nuclear-capable bombers flew together over the Sea of Japan as US president Joe Biden was in Tokyo. The speech came on the heels of Biden's first visit to Asia as president, a trip intended to further his strategy of bolstering alliances to counter China. During his visit to Tokyo, Biden said the US would intervene with force to defend Taiwan if it came under attack from China.

Fiji will join the US-led Indo-Pacific Economic Framework just days before China's foreign minister lands in the country. The US welcomed the move by Fiji to become the first Pacific Island nation and 14th member of IPEF, a trade initiative designed to deepen economic ties, which President Joe Biden launched in Japan. The decision provided the US with some relief in its rapidly-escalating battle with Beijing over sway in the Pacific Island nations. The US, Australia, New Zealand and Japan were alarmed when China signed a security pact with Solomon Islands this year. Some security experts believe the deal could pave the way for Beijing to build a naval base that would allow it to project its power further into the Pacific. China is negotiating a security pact with Kiribati, another Pacific island nation 3,000km from Hawaii. Fiji and the other Pacific Nations face dire threats from increasing temperatures and rising sea levels.

A leaked draft ruling indicated the **US** Supreme Court was set to overturn the landmark Roe vs Wade ruling that has guaranteed abortion rights across the country for almost five decades. The nine-member body is not expected to issue its final opinion until June or July. The document, which emerged in a highly unusual leak, triggered immediate outrage among Democratic politicians and groups dedicated to the protection of abortion rights in the US.

The Biden administration will ease restrictions on travel to **Cuba** and lift

Trump-era controls on family remittances amidst an economic crisis on the island and a surge in illegal emigration to the US. The State Department said it would remove the $1,000-per-quarter limit on money sent to family members and will allow non-family remittances to support Cuban entrepreneurs. Scheduled and charter flights will be allowed to locations beyond Havana, the capital. The US will also reinstate the Cuban Family Reunification Parole Program, which has a backlog of more than 20,000 applications, and increase consular services and visa processing. Thousands of people demonstrated on the streets across Cuba in July last year over the faltering economy in the largest such protests seen in decades on the island, leading to many arrests. Trump increased sanctions against Cuba, including the cancellation of permits to send remittances and the punishment of oil tankers bound for the island. In his final days in office he designated Cuba a "state sponsor of terrorism" in part for its support of Nicolas Maduro, the Venezuelan president.

SOURCES:

https://www.ft.com/content/b2713bd1-afa5-4638-ab2d-be0c4e8a7ab7

https://www.ft.com/content/e27fec7b-6afd-4ba4-8e5e-d5d4274f9747

https://www.ft.com/content/64660514-6587-4122-a1ea-464d60a5648f

https://www.theguardian.com/us-news/2022/apr/28/joe-biden-ukraine-military-aid-us-congress

https://www.ft.com/content/fa2d1ed8-303e-43b1-a377-737d8f5049db

https://www.ft.com/content/33c2ebe6-d8a4-478d-9e8e-3d0607e05c31

https://edition.cnn.com/2022/04/20/tennis/kremlin-wimbledon-russian-players-ban-spt-intl/index.html

https://www.ft.com/content/5bad4c29-d4af-4182-a11e-c2ddeaf3b19a

https://www.ft.com/content/5bad4c29-d4af-4182-a11e-c2ddeaf3b19a

https://www.ft.com/content/3e641bb4-176e-40e7-a2ea-6ea92805a6b2

https://www.reuters.com/world/europe/best-we-could-get-eu-bows-hungarian-demands-agree-russian-oil-ban-2022-05-31/

https://www.ft.com/content/c8eedb92-9512-4648-8146-d1450fcbd7e9

https://www.bloomberg.com/news/articles/2022-05-24/hungary-s-orban-declares-state-of-emergency-over-war-economy

https://www.independent.co.uk/independentpremium/world/france-strikes-trains-pensions-macron-b2295827.html

https://www.ft.com/content/55058ac5-1b7c-44d9-8fb0-fab0407a8342

https://www.ft.com/content/32537365-f99a-480d-97b1-313701ada0c0

https://www.ft.com/content/9d077a0a-d3b8-402f-ade4-2ced9afa735b

https://www.ft.com/content/9d077a0a-d3b8-402f-ade4-2ced9afa735b

https://www.pbs.org/newshour/world/sweden-ends-200-years-of-military-neutrality-joins-finland-in-seeking-nato-membership

https://www.aljazeera.com/news/2022/5/12/north-korea-reports-first-covid-outbreak-since-pandemic

https://www.theguardian.com/world/2022/may/07/taliban-order-all-afghan-women-to-wear-burqa

https://www.ft.com/content/f0e78415-66a7-4007-beb3-8dcc347c66b6

https://www.theguardian.com/world/2022/jul/11/sri-lanka-protests-president-gotabaya-rajapaksa-to-quit

https://www.npr.org/2023/04/26/1172116000/u-s-and-south-korea-announce-moves-to-strengthen-alliance

https://www.ft.com/content/15c77929-395a-4f28-a09e-c74c7c46a2ab

https://www.ft.com/content/0bdde91a-21d3-4d97-8879-a79b9bd2b0cf

https://www.aljazeera.com/news/2022/5/11/shireen-abu-akleh-israeli-forces-kill-al-jazeera-journalist

https://www.ft.com/content/17fc356f-4351-4f2d-9001-c9b4c61e4b52

https://news.sky.com/story/uae-president-sheikh-khalifa-bin-zayed-al-nahyan-immortalised-in-name-of-worlds-tallest-building-dies-aged-73-12612387

https://www.ft.com/content/e374a095-d02e-4221-b437-8b8817ad7f89

https://www.aljazeera.com/news/2023/6/14/turkeys-erdogan-defies-pressure-over-swedens-nato-application

https://www.ft.com/content/09d79aad-95fd-4c61-b661-567de126c77c

https://www.ft.com/content/081ac952-48a0-4f67-a597-16b4a98921ba

https://www.aljazeera.com/news/2022/5/16/biden-approves-deployment-of-hundreds-of-us-troops-to-somalia

https://www.ft.com/content/87b64b71-ee56-4eb4-bc0c-b3555e20bcb6

https://www.ft.com/content/976ef1f3-7fef-4738-926f-11f82b1b5422

https://www.theguardian.com/world/2022/jun/24/roe-v-wade-overturned-abortion-summary-supreme-court

https://www.ft.com/content/b9c268f3-3012-4dee-9dbc-13770796565c89

https://www.thetimes.co.uk/article/biden-to-ease-restrictions-on-travel-to-cuba-zbsvssc5q

THE WORLD
IN JUNE 2022

Introduction

June 2022 was a month during which the world continued to grapple with the consequences of Russia's war in Ukraine. As growth slowed worldwide, countries found themselves on the verge of a debt crisis, with interest and inflation rates soaring. Nato stepped up its military response to the invasion, deploying more troops to its Eastern flank and starting the accession process for Finland and Sweden to become member states. In Europe, various leaders found themselves fighting for political survival, with a no-confidence vote in the British Prime Minister Boris Johnson, Bulgarian PM Kirill Petkov and unrest in Estonia. In Asia, the debt crisis in Sri Lanka continued to worsen as the government defaulted on international debts of more than $50bn. In Pakistan faced a balance of payments crisis, requesting support from the IMF and Chinese lenders. North Korea continued to deploy frontline military units close to its border with the South, raising fears of the use of a nuclear weapon. In the Middle East, Turkey's inflation rate continued to rise, as the economic crisis in Lebanon was deemed the worst globally in 150 years by the World Bank. Israel faced political deadlock, as Iran and the EU attempted to revive *the Iranian nuclear deal. There was a flurry of diplomacy in the Gulf, as US President Biden announced a visit to the region and Mohammed Bin Salman held talks with President Erdogan of Turkey. In an historic vote that shook up American society, the US Supreme Court struck down Roe vs Wade, the legal decision which enshrined the constitutional right to an abortion for nearly 50 years in the US. Diplomatic efforts were conducted between Pacific Island Nations and the US were conducted to counteract Chinese military initiatives in the Pacific.*

WAR IN UKRAINE

Ukraine's President, Volodymyr Zelenskyy, celebrated his country's survival after 100 days of enduring a devastating Russian invasion that resulted in thousands of lives lost and posed a threat to global food supplies. In a defiant video, Zelenskyy, flanked by his top aides, spoke from outside his office in the capital, emphasizing the resilience of the Ukrainian people and armed forces. He declared that they have been successfully defending Ukraine for the past 100 days and proclaimed victory.

Recent supplies of advanced weaponry from the US and European countries have bolstered Ukraine's position, allowing Zelenskyy to maintain control of the capital. However, the country remains prepared for a prolonged and arduous war against the larger army of its northern neighbour. Russia's occupation of 20 percent of Ukrainian territory in the east and south, up from seven percent previously, continues as they pursue their goal of capturing the entire eastern Donbas region.

The **World Bank** issued a warning that Russia's war in Ukraine will result in slower-than-expected growth across the developing world in the coming years. This will push millions into extreme poverty and raise the risk of a debt crisis in low and middle-income countries. The pandemic's effects will be exacerbated, leaving 75 million more people in extreme poverty than projected in 2019. The situation is reminiscent of the 1970s, when steep interest rate hikes were used to control inflation, leading to a global recession and debt crises in developing economies. Although the current commodity price shock is less severe, further price increases and ongoing COVID-19 outbreaks could result in steeper interest rate rises and heighten the risk of a broader debt crisis. Central banks worldwide are rapidly raising interest rates in one of the most extensive tightening of monetary policy in decades.

In response to the crisis, Ukraine's central bank has significantly raised its benchmark lending rate from 10 percent to 25 percent. This is the first increase since Russia's full-scale invasion in late February. The move aims to tackle inflation, which soared to 17 percent in May and is on track to exceed last year's average of 10 percent. The increase is intended to safeguard household income and savings in Ukraine's currency, the hryvnia, and prevent the depletion of foreign reserves to protect the exchange rate.

The **G7** leaders have pledged to impose new sanctions on Russia to curtail its ability to import technologies for its arms industry, while also promising to strengthen their security commitments to Ukraine. The group of seven advanced economies intends to expand targeted sanctions, limiting Russia's access to key industrial inputs, services, and technologies. Furthermore, they will impose targeted sanctions on those responsible for war crimes in Ukraine and those exacerbating global food insecurity by stealing and exporting Ukrainian grain. The summit in Germany addresses various crises stemming from Vladimir Putin's invasion of Ukraine, including soaring inflation rates, energy and food supply concerns, and strains on the global economy. Ukrainian President Zelenskyy has cautioned the G7 leaders that Russia intends to solidify its position in Ukraine and launch a renewed offensive during the upcoming winter.

ENERGY

In response to pressure from the US to alleviate a surge in crude oil prices that posed a threat to the global economy, **OPEC** and its allies reached an agreement to accelerate oil production during July and August. Saudi Arabia, under the influence of US pressure, decided to take action to cool down the price rally. The cartel announced a significant increase in output, aiming to produce almost 650,000 more barrels per day in both months, surpassing their initially planned increases of approximately 400,000 b/d. This decision came shortly after the European Union agreed to implement a partial ban on Russian oil imports, heightening concerns about potential energy shortages worldwide as the ongoing invasion of Ukraine by Moscow continues to unsettle markets. Leading OPEC producers, Saudi Arabia and the United Arab Emirates, are expected to be responsible for most of the supply increments, with Riyadh expressing its willingness to increase output to compensate for Russian shortages. These additional supplies signify a departure from the measured supply policy agreed upon during the oil crash triggered by the coronavirus pandemic two years ago, and it follows months of extensive US diplomatic efforts to mend relations with Riyadh.

GLOBAL SECURITY

In response to Russia's invasion of Ukraine, **NATO** is undertaking a sweeping overhaul to bolster its eastern flank and better protect its territories. This historic shift marks a departure from the post-Cold War era when military spending was reduced, and troops were withdrawn from eastern Europe. Now, NATO plans to increase its forces on high alert to 300,000, more than seven times the current number, with a focus on deploying closer to Russia. The alliance aims to shift its strategy from merely deterring invasion to actively defending allied territories. As part of this effort, NATO's pledge to increase the number of troops on high alert across allied countries from 40,000 came concurrently with the G7 leaders' commitment to impose new sanctions in response to the crisis.

Turkey, after six weeks of opposition, has dropped its objections to Finland and Sweden becoming members of NATO. This decision opens the way for the Nordic countries to join the alliance as a response to Russia's invasion of Ukraine. Following hours of trilateral talks brokered by NATO, the three countries, along with Turkey, signed a joint memorandum, overcoming concerns linked to terrorism. The agreement, reached on the eve of NATO's annual summit in Madrid, resolves a dispute that could have overshadowed the event focused on demonstrating unity against Russia, showing support for Ukraine, and introducing the alliance's 10-year "strategic concept," aimed at revamping its approach to defending its eastern European allies.

EUROPE

Scotland's first minister, Nicola Sturgeon, presented plans for an independence referendum on October 19, 2023, as a way to bypass Boris Johnson's refusal to authorize such a vote. Sturgeon stated that her senior legal officer would refer legislation for a "consultative" referendum to the UK Supreme Court to determine if her government had the authority to hold such a vote. If the court ruled against the Scottish government, Sturgeon announced that the UK general election expected in 2024 would essentially become a de facto referendum, with her Scottish National Party focusing solely on the issue of independence.

Following a bruising confidence vote, **UK** PM Boris Johnson managed to survive, but the outcome revealed the extent of division and animosity within his party. Although he secured victory by 211 to 148 in the ballot of Tory MPs, the rebellion left him significantly weakened, with 41 percent of his MPs attempting to oust him. The confidence vote, triggered by the withdrawal of support from over 15 percent of his MPs, resulted in heated criticism and discord among his colleagues.

Croatia's plan to join Europe's single currency received a crucial endorsement as EU officials confirmed that it met the economic criteria for adopting the euro in January 2023. Despite challenges from inflation and public debt caused by the pandemic fallout and Russia's invasion of Ukraine, Croatia's economy remained sufficiently aligned with the rest of the eurozone. EU leaders are expected to approve Croatia's plan to join the euro next year. This achievement represents a significant success for Croatia, which has aimed to adopt the euro since becoming an EU member in 2013.

Bulgaria's government was ousted in a no-confidence vote, plunging the country into renewed political turmoil and delaying the process of EU enlargement to the western Balkans. Prime Minister Kirill Petkov, known for his anti-corruption stance and strong response against Russia's invasion of Ukraine, was toppled in a 123 to 116 vote. The dispute over Bulgaria's veto on the start of EU accession talks with North Macedonia and differences over the budget led to the government's downfall, resulting in the possibility of a fourth election in less than a year.

Tens of thousands of **Georgians** marched in Tbilisi to demonstrate support for their country's EU aspirations and protest against the government. The European Commission's concerns over democratic regression have hindered Georgia's path to EU candidate status. Instead, conditional membership prospects have been proposed, dependent on Georgia's implementation of necessary reforms.

The war in **Ukraine** has forced over half of its Jewish population to flee, according to the chief rabbi of Moscow, Pinchas Goldschmidt. This is the first instance of a senior religious leader from Russia openly criticizing the humanitarian impact of Russia's offensive. The violence has severely affected Jewish life in Ukraine after decades of reconstruction following the Soviet Union's breakup. The majority of Ukraine's Jews, estimated between 40,000 and 400,000 before the war, have sought refuge in other parts of Europe.

Estonia's prime minister, Kaja Kallas, who is renowned for her unwavering support for Ukraine, faces a political battle after dismissing nearly half of her cabinet and accusing her coalition partners of undermining the state's core values. Estonia has been actively supporting Ukraine and has invested significantly in military aid. Kallas' stance on Russia's revanchist ambitions has put her in a precarious position, and her future as prime minister hangs in the balance.

Russia has issued a warning to **Lithuania** regarding the export of EU-sanctioned goods to the exclave of Kaliningrad via rail. Lithuania's restrictions on transit of goods under EU sanctions related to Russia's invasion of Ukraine have triggered tensions. Russia accuses the EU of initiating a blockade of Kaliningrad, and Lithuania's adherence to EU sanctions has become a point of contention between the two countries.

ASIA

As **Sri Lanka's** debt crisis escalates into a humanitarian emergency, the country is seeking food assistance from neighbouring nations. The government has applied for aid from the South Asian Association for Regional Cooperation's food bank, which has historically provided rice and essential staples during food crises. This request underscores Sri Lanka's distressing shift from being an upper-middle-income country, once the most prosperous among its neighbours, to becoming reliant on donations and emergency loans for food, medicine, and fuel. The country defaulted on international debts exceeding $50 billion last month, leading to severe shortages of vital goods as its foreign reserves depleted.

Pakistan's government, led by Prime Minister Shehbaz Sharif, faces protests after increasing fuel prices to secure an IMF loan and avoid a balance of payments crisis. Responding to the IMF's request to remove subsidies, the government raised fuel prices by over a third in two separate moves this month. This measure aims to pave the way for the disbursement of the next $1 billion tranche of a stalled $6 billion IMF loan program. However, this move poses political risks for Sharif's new government, which took power after the ousting of former Prime Minister Imran Khan in a no-confidence vote in April. Amid a painful economic crunch, double-digit inflation, and widespread protests, Pakistan's foreign reserves have fallen below two months' worth of imports, raising concerns of a potential default on foreign debts.

A consortium of Chinese state banks has extended a $2.3 billion loan to **Pakistan** to help the country avoid a foreign payments crisis. The support from China, a close economic and military ally, coincides with Islamabad's announcement of a one-off 10 percent 'super tax' on key industries, aimed at resuming the stalled $6 billion IMF loan package. With this loan, Pakistan's liquid foreign reserves will rise from $8.2 billion to $10.5 billion, which could help stabilize the depreciating rupee. Pakistan began receiving IMF payments in 2019 under a 39-month loan program, but only about half of the agreed $6 billion has been disbursed so far.

The World Health Organization has expressed concern about the deteriorating coronavirus outbreak in **North Korea**, despite the country's claims of control over the situation. The WHO urges North Korean authorities to provide more information about the outbreak to assess potential public health risks for the rest of the world. Medical experts worry about the impact of Covid on North Korea's largely unvaccinated population and its unpreparedness to handle a surge in cases. North Korea is among the two countries that have not initiated a Covid vaccination program.

North Korea's announcement of enhancing frontline military units near the South Korean border has raised concerns about the possible deployment of battlefield nuclear weapons. The decision was made at a three-day meeting of the central military commission, a high-level decision-making body led by Kim Jong-Un. While the announcement did not explicitly mention tactical nuclear weapons, the term "war deterrent" in North Korea's context refers to its nuclear arsenal. The country possesses several nuclear warheads, including hydrogen bombs, and has a missile capacity to reach various parts of the world.

India has seen violent protests from aspiring military recruits in response to the government's plan to replace many permanent positions in the armed forces with four-year contracts. Prime Minister Narendra Modi's "Agnipath" or "Way of Fire" scheme eliminates guaranteed long-term employment and pensions for new military recruits. Thousands of people are outraged by this controversial reform, highlighting India's job crisis, particularly affecting young individuals who view a military career as a pathway to economic security. The protests have led to damage of public property and numerous arrests in various states across the country. Under the new program, recruits aged between 17 and a half and 21 will be hired on four-year contracts, and only a quarter will be retained after this period, while the rest will retire without a pension. The government defends this reform as a way to streamline the armed forces and address the ballooning military pension bill, which consumes over half of the country's defense budget.

MIDDLE EAST & NORTH AFRICA

Turkey's official inflation rate reached a 23-year high last month due to President Recep Tayyip Erdogan's unconventional economic strategy. The consumer price index rose 73.5 percent year on year in May, the highest level since October 1998. Food prices, a growing source of discontent among the public, rose 91.6 percent year on year. Erdogan's opposition to high interest rates led to repeated cuts in borrowing costs, despite rising inflation. He believed this would create a new economic model, leveraging a cheap lira and increased exports to reduce inflation by eliminating the trade deficit.

Lebanese lenders have warned the IMF that a proposed $3 billion rescue plan, which includes seizing their assets from the central bank, is illegal and could severely damage the economy. Lebanon has been devastated by a severe economic crisis, pushing at least 80 percent of its population into poverty. The country's financial collapse is rooted in decades of accrued debt by successive governments. The preliminary agreement for a $3 billion extended fund facility with the IMF includes the appropriation of $60 billion out of $85 billion in banks' foreign currency deposits held at the central bank.

Israel's ruling coalition suffered a setback as it failed to pass a bill on rules governing Jewish settlers in the occupied West Bank. This vote became a critical test of the government's viability, coming two months after the coalition lost its parliamentary majority. The coalition, which includes Jewish nationalists and an Islamist Arab party for the first time, was formed to end Benjamin Netanyahu's decade-long dominance in Israeli politics. Despite trying to avoid contentious issues related to the Israeli-Palestinian conflict, tensions over these matters have caused internal crises within the ruling camp.

Israel is heading for its fifth election in three years after Prime Minister Naftali Bennett and Foreign Minister Yair Lapid declared that they had "exhausted options to stabilize" their coalition government. As part of the coalition agreement, Lapid will become interim prime minister, and elections are likely to be held in October. The eight-party coalition, the most ideologically diverse in Israel's history, has struggled to pass legislation after losing its parliamentary majority and facing defections by MPs.

Iraq's parliament expanded a law criminalizing relations with Israel, making it illegal for citizens to contact Israeli officials on social media, attend gatherings linked to Israel, or visit any Israeli embassy worldwide. This expansion comes eight months after a general election and has generated outrage from Israel and other countries. The law threatens life imprisonment or the death penalty for the worst offenders. The move puts Iraq at odds with neighboring Arab countries that have established diplomatic and economic ties with Israel, highlighting Iran's longstanding influence on Iraqi politics.

Talks to revive the 2015 nuclear accord between **Iran** and leading global powers will resume with initial indirect talks between Tehran and the US. The agreement, known as the Joint Comprehensive Plan of Action (JCPOA), aimed to curb Iran's nuclear activities in exchange for lifting sanctions. However, after the US withdrew in 2018 and imposed stringent sanctions, Iran resumed uranium enrichment, raising concerns about its nuclear activity.

The UN nuclear watchdog's board of governors overwhelmingly passed a resolution criticizing **Iran** for inadequate cooperation regarding its undeclared atomic sites. As diplomatic efforts to save the 2015 accord falter, tensions between Iran and Western powers escalate. Iran recently removed two cameras belonging to the International Atomic Energy Agency from one of its nuclear facilities, seen as a preemptive move ahead of the IAEA's resolution vote. The west accuses Iran of stalling efforts and failing to provide relevant information on traces of atomic material found at some nuclear sites.

Gulf states and other **Islamic countries** have condemned insulting remarks about the Prophet Mohammed made by spokespeople of Indian Prime Minister Narendra Modi's Bharatiya Janata Party (BJP). The comments on television and Twitter have sparked backlash and damaged India's relations with important international partners. The BJP, while denouncing the insults, took action against the spokespersons involved. India has been strengthening trade and partnerships with majority Muslim states in the Gulf, yet critics accuse the government of promoting policies that marginalize India's Muslim minority.

US President Joe Biden will visit **Saudi Arabia** and leaders from nearly a dozen countries on a trip to the Middle East in July. The visit will focus on regional and energy security, expanding Israel's integration in the region, and supporting a two-state solution to the Israeli-Palestinian conflict. Biden will meet with Israeli and Palestinian leaders and explore cooperation with Saudi Arabia to address regional challenges.

The Crown Prince of **Saudi Arabia** was welcomed by **Turkish** President Erdogan in Ankara on his first visit since the murder of journalist Jamal Khashoggi. Erdogan, who previously led international outrage over the killing, demonstrated a U-turn in welcoming the prince with a horse-mounted honor guard. The visit aimed to start a new era of cooperation between the two countries. Prince Mohammed bin Salman's international rehabilitation is evident as he visits various Western allies in the Middle East.

Algeria has severed economic ties with Spain after Spain backed Morocco in a dispute over autonomy for the former Spanish colony of Western Sahara. Algeria's action involves tearing up a "treaty of friendship" signed with Spain in 2002 and rejecting bank transfers from Spain. This escalation of tensions could lead to higher gas prices for Spain, which imports a significant portion of gas from Algeria. The situation has strained relations and involves broader implications for energy supplies in the region.

AFRICA

Two wealthy political veterans, Bola Tinubu and Atiku Abubakar, will vie to become the next president of **Nigeria**. Tinubu, known as the "Godfather of Lagos," emerged as the ruling party's preferred candidate, while Abubakar is representing the main opposition People's Democratic party. Both candidates have reported health issues but declared their fitness to lead the country, which has a population of 210 million and is Africa's most populous and largest oil producer. The election, scheduled for next February, will replace Muhammadu Buhari, the current president and former general, who has been in power since 2015.

THE AMERICAS

In the **US**, the Supreme Court's conservative majority struck down Roe vs. Wade, the landmark legal decision that upheld the constitutional right to abortion for almost 50 years. Justice Samuel Alito authored the decision, upholding a Mississippi state law that bans abortion after 15 weeks and further declaring that the 1973 Roe vs. Wade ruling was incorrect. The ruling has far-reaching implications for American society, politics, and jurisprudence, with anti-abortion advocates celebrating the victory and abortion-rights supporters fearing widespread bans on the procedure in Republican-led states.

The **US and Taiwan** launched the "US-Taiwan Initiative on 21st-century Trade" to deepen economic engagement. This initiative came after the US unveiled the Indo-Pacific Economic Framework, excluding Taiwan due to concerns from some southeast Asian nations about antagonizing China, which claims sovereignty over Taiwan.

US President Biden offered an environmental partnership to **Latin American** leaders to counter Chinese influence in the region. Biden sought to revive a green agenda but faced challenges due to the need to replace Russian oil and gas affected by sanctions. The summit was overshadowed by the exclusion of authoritarian regimes, such as Cuba, Nicaragua, and Venezuela, resulting in some leaders boycotting the gathering.

INDO-PACIFIC

In the Indo-Pacific region, **New Zealand** decided to strengthen military ties with the US to counter China's increasing security threat. The move was seen as remarkable for New Zealand, which historically resisted militarization in the Pacific. Meanwhile, the US, UK, Australia, New Zealand, and Japan launched the "Partners in Blue Pacific" initiative to support Pacific Island nations and enhance their presence in the region amid growing Chinese initiatives.

SOURCES:

https://www.thetimes.co.uk/article/turkey-buries-hatchet-as-erdogan-meets-saudi-prince-mohammed-bin-salman-83lz85c7q

https://www.ft.com/content/3ff06ed2-39dc-4a86-80f0-a1d1a91fc742

https://www.thetimes.co.uk/article/tensions-between-algeria-morocco-and-spain-escalate-over-western-sahara-wpjwfk2bj

https://www.ft.com/content/1cf1cb8a-eb2f-475a-88a0-f49b2e845ffc

https://www.ft.com/content/28650a51-0386-466a-9d7c-bfc9700b9287

https://www.thetimes.co.uk/article/joe-biden-woos-latin-america-away-from-china-6950tlsq9

https://www.ft.com/content/3ff06ed2-39dc-4a86-80f0-a1d1a91fc742

https://www.ft.com/content/6f379a95-21e0-4d25-ba09-c91b1432c584

https://www.ft.com/content/6f379a95-21e0-4d25-ba09-c91b1432c584

https://www.ft.com/content/addbf3ca-9859-47cb-bb8f-56a34aa13930

https://www.ft.com/content/b175b76b-4f3c-4dff-afa8-e61518dbc93f

https://www.ft.com/content/522a1894-155c-4234-860d-b4cf5c965376

https://www.ft.com/content/522a1894-155c-4234-860d-b4cf5c965376

https://www.ft.com/content/bb130bb9-4b75-4626-961a-2c1ed9b0e7f9

https://www.ft.com/content/39caeff3-38cf-44e2-9270-835ab28f13c8

https://www.aljazeera.com/news/2022/6/28/erdogan-to-have-bilateral-talks-with-world-leaders-at-nato-summit

https://www.ft.com/content/26fe73e1-867c-49d6-9a9b-88e10d922386

https://www.ft.com/content/c8fe88a3-df24-4b44-b8bb-64df547f12fb

https://www.politico.eu/article/croatia-join-euro-2023/

https://www.ft.com/content/af56fc79-b477-4541-8543-c994f5e1c41a

https://www.thetimes.co.uk/article/war-has-forced-out-most-of-ukraines-jews-rabbi-claims-72qdxm7sc

https://www.thetimes.co.uk/article/estonian-pm-kaja-kallas-ousts-pro-russia-party-from-coalition-g0bpjp8sp

https://www.ft.com/content/4e211784-83eb-49a2-ba39-8976345a88d5

https://www.ft.com/content/c89a972c-df31-449c-a824-ba3ccd54a4da

https://www.ft.com/content/c89a972c-df31-449c-a824-ba3ccd54a4da

https://www.ft.com/content/4021a65c-99ab-4b53-a357-c0659a8d035c

https://www.ft.com/content/6250c214-cfdc-4b4f-85b3-876666d01ff4

https://www.thetimes.co.uk/article/north-korea-hints-at-deploying-battlefield-nuclear-weapons-tvxc32ffr

https://www.thetimes.co.uk/article/north-korea-hints-at-deploying-battlefield-nuclear-weapons-tvxc32ffr

https://www.ft.com/content/3bfb5571-ca7e-448b-a8fc-82f939d6a4ae

https://www.ft.com/content/3bfb5571-ca7e-448b-a8fc-82f939d6a4ae

https://www.ft.com/content/43899864-9aea-4a4e-bcaa-25c52e5d7db8

https://www.ft.com/content/e44b19fd-ee98-4698-95b5-7b5269899c35

https://www.ft.com/content/a661f59f-4dc0-4d6d-91a3-279d9f1ee0ef

https://www.ft.com/content/18ded427-84ba-461a-b4a5-fa1f81373405

https://www.thetimes.co.uk/article/turkey-buries-hatchet-as-erdogan-meets-saudi-prince-mohammed-bin-salman-83lz85c7q

https://www.ft.com/content/53fd02c5-4392-4347-9c9c-97596dfc8d4d

https://www.business-standard.com/article/economy-policy/india-gcc-group-announce-intention-to-relaunch-fta-negotiations-122112401427_1.html

https://www.ft.com/content/9454a792-db23-4e3e-8cfa-e13553b52468

https://www.ft.com/content/a6de3477-4c70-4aed-a40f-f64238a9b8fa

https://www.ft.com/content/a6de3477-4c70-4aed-a40f-f64238a9b8fa

https://www.ft.com/content/d7849747-8320-442a-8ba1-a7bc053ea7d9

https://www.ft.com/content/77d60298-e393-4e3d-ab7e-3014c2ba87e6

CLIMATE CHANGE AND THE IMPACT OF GLOBAL WARMING

Global warming is a change that is going to be impacted for all of humanity and nature. This is not some wild prediction but an imminent and serious danger. It is therefore an important subject for this book and in the coming pages I will explain some of the facts and why it is important for all of us to understand some of the basics of climate change and how we have got to this place so fast in the past decades.

Although Climate change and the impact of Global warming has been discussed for many years the year 2022 saw many focus on this matter to find lasting solutions. It is a welcome move by the Global community as ignoring climate change could become an existential threat for all of humanity.

The impact of climate change on Earth is arguably the most significant issue of our time. In 2017, the Intergovernmental Panel on Climate Change (IPCC) noted in the context of global warming that "Human emissions and activities have caused around 100% of the warming observed since 1950". [1]

The government of the United States of America has also stated that:

Earth's temperature has risen by 0.14° Fahrenheit (0.08° Celsius) per decade since 1880, but the rate of warming since 1981 is more than twice that: 0.32° F (0.18° C) per decade. [2]

We need to consider the issue and impact of climate change in a number of different ways. In the first instance we need to place the study of climate change and global warming in a historical context. Then consider international cooperation from the perspective of the annual Congress of the Parties (COP) summits. Finally outline environmental innovations which have been designed to combat specific elements of the impact of climate change, often on the most vulnerable regions of our planet.

A BRIEF HISTORY OF CLIMATE CHANGE

Climate change has been a concept for a very long time. In the nineteenth century, some scientific experiments showed that carbon dioxide (CO_2) produced by humans could insulate Earth and lead to an increase in temperature. As early as 1824, French mathematician and physicist, Joseph Fourier, published a paper stating the argument that atmospheric gases create a barrier to trap heat around the earth. Scientific understanding at that point could not explain exactly why this should happen, but thirteen years later, in 1837, Fourier published a further paper that outlined that the

---

1   Why Scientists think 100% of global warming is due to humans
2   Climate Change: Global Temperature

amount of heat trapped in the atmosphere could change over a long period. This, he noted, was a result of both the natural evolution of the earth and the impact of human activity. He predicted:

"The establishment and progress of human society, and the action of natural powers, may, in extensive regions, produce remarkable changes in the state of the surface, the distribution of the waters, and the great movements of the air...Such effects, in the course of some centuries, must produce variations in the mean temperature for such places."

By the 1850s, American scientist and Suffragette, Eunice Newton Foote was conducting experiments on CO_2 in glass cylinders by heating them in the sun. In 1856, she observed that the cylinders containing CO_2 became hotter and retained their heat for longer than those containing other substances. She concluded that this could be replicated on a much larger scale around Earth. "An atmosphere of that gas," Newton Foote believed, "would give to our earth a high temperature." [3]

The reaction to the research of both scientists was greeted with interest and curiosity. However, there was no sense of urgency. In the 1930s, eighty years after Newton Foote's research was published, British engineer Guy Stewart Callendar argued that since the Industrial Revolution, both the United Kingdom and the United States of America had experienced significant increases in temperature. His calculations on warming were based on twice the amount of CO_2 in the atmosphere equalling an increase of around 2 degrees centigrade in the temperature of the planet within the next century. Even though there was now a timescale of sorts attached to global warming and climate change, there was still no sense of urgency from those in power. One hundred years was still perceived to be far enough in the future to warrant real concern. [4]

However, in 1949, the United Nations (UN) began to show awareness of potential climate and environmental issues by holding a Scientific Conference on the conservation and utilization of resources. The increasing awareness and importance of the issue were demonstrated in 1972 at the UN Scientific Conference, also known as the First Earth Summit. The conference adopted a declaration

---

3 How 19th Century Scientists Predicted Global Warming
4   Climate Change History

that "set out principles for the preservation and enhancement of the human environment" and a plan for action with recommendations for environmental action on an international scale. Climate change was also specifically referred to for the first time in an international document: a section on the identification and control of pollutants of broad international significance warned Governments to "be mindful of activities that could lead to climate change and evaluate the likelihood and magnitude of climatic effects."[5]

Seven years later, in 1979, the First World Climate Conference, convened by the World Meteorological Organisation was held in Geneva, Switzerland. At the conclusion of this conference, the agreed Declaration stated:

Having regard to the all-pervading influence of climate on human society and on many fields of human activities and endeavour, the Conference finds that it is now urgently necessary for the nations of the world:
  (a) To take full advantage of man's present knowledge of climate.
  (b) To take steps to improve significantly that knowledge.
  (c) To foresee and prevent potential man-made changes in climate that might be averse to the well-being of humanity.[6]

It was not until the 1980s that climate change, then known as global warming, really entered the consciousness of the public. Environmental organisations such as Friends of the Earth and Greenpeace began to highlight the issue and there were high-profile public campaigns that referred to the hole in the ozone layer and the impact of chlorofluorocarbons (CFCs). Ultimately the use of CFCs was cut in half (1987) and an agreement was put in place to ban them in many countries (1990). It is pertinent to note that during a decade or more large chemicals companies responsible for the production of CFC's with large number of scientists and specialists working for them were in denial. They refused to accept that CFC's were responsible and used their financial might, lobbying resources and public relations companies to avoid taking any responsibility.

This has been the norm in the various debates on climate change where politics, big business and other interest groups have torpedoed good plans proposed by various organisations.

---

5   From Stockholm to Kyoto: A Brief History of Climate Change
6   A History of Climate Activities

It has been argued that, without this ban, the ozone layer would have completely collapsed, and the Earth would be an extra 2.5 degrees hotter than it currently is.[7] 1988 was a particularly significant year in climate change terms. In June, NASA Scientist, James Hansen testified to the United States Congress that "The greenhouse effect has been detected, and it is changing our climate now." [8] Hansen's testimony took place against the backdrop of the hottest summer on record across the world to that point and, in part because of this, the Intergovernmental Panel on Climate Change (IPCC) was formed and met for the first time in November 1988. The United Nations General Assembly also first acknowledged climate change as a "specific and urgent issue".[9]

Conferences and discussions around climate change continued into the 1990s. It began in the first year of the decade, with the second World Climate Conference held in Geneva, Switzerland from 29 October to 7 November 1990. The resulting Declaration committed all parties to:

Urge developed states, which are responsible for 75% of the world emissions of greenhouse gases, to "establish targets and/or feasible national programmes or strategies which will have a significant effect on limiting emissions of greenhouse gases ...";

recognize that the emissions from developing countries must still grow to accommodate their development needs; nevertheless, these states should, with support from the developed nations and international organizations, take action; and call for elaboration of a framework treaty on climate change.[10]

International discussion continued in 1992 when the General Assembly of the United Nations convened the United Nations Conference on Environment and Development, popularly known as the Earth Summit. This established the United Nations Framework Convention on Climate Change (UNFCCC): it aimed to "stabilize

---

7   A 1980s ban on CFCs to heal the ozone layer is also shaving degrees off global warming, study says. The article cites the study The Montreal Protocol protects the terrestrial carbon sink.
The rise of Climate Change Activism?
8   James Hansen's Climate Warning, 30 Years Later
9   From Stockholm to Kyoto: A Brief History of Climate Change
10   The Second World Climate Conference

atmospheric concentrations of "greenhouse gases" at a level that would prevent dangerous anthropogenic interference with the climate system". [11] By the end of the year 158 countries had signed up to the convention and it came into force in 1994; the year before international cooperation started in earnest with the establishment of the annual Conference of the Parties meetings which have been entirely focused on climate change and its impact across the world.

CONFERENCE OF THE PARTIES (COP) 1995 -2022

Conference of the Parties (COP) is an annual gathering of nations to discuss climate change, set targets, and make deals. Individual nations address the conference. This tends to be either a progress report or an appeal by countries most seriously affected by climate change in a given year. The first COP was held in Berlin, Germany in 1995. The venue tends to move for each COP – usually to the country which holds the presidency. If this was not possible, the conference location would default to Bonn, Germany. [12] The three most recent COPs have been held in Glasgow, United Kingdom (COP 26 October – November 2021) and Sharm El-Sheik, Egypt (COP 27 November 2022) and Dubai (COP 28 November 2023)

Over the last 30 years, there have been various significant agreements.

- In Berlin at COP1 in 1995, signatories acknowledged the need to control climate change and to decrease polluting emissions.

- The Kyoto Protocol, which was signed at COP3 in 1997 is one of the most notable achievements of the summits. It committed participating nations to reduce greenhouse gasses in the developed world and established the concept of the carbon market. The carbon market is an attempt to limit greenhouse gas

---

11 From Stockholm to Kyoto: A Brief History of Climate Change
12 Conference of the Parties (COP)

emissions. If a country reaches the pre-determined and agreed limit, then it needs to purchase permits from other signatories.

In 2007, as part of his Reith Lecture series, Jeffrey Sachs, an economist at Columbia University stated, "I believe that by 2010 we will have a post-Kyoto global agreement". [13] Later that year, at COP13 in Bali, a decade after the Kyoto Protocol was signed, it was agreed that the Protocol should be rewritten to include all nations, not only the developed ones. This was followed up in 2011 at COP17 in Durban, where all of the signatories including major polluters and developing nations such as the United States, China, and India, agreed to start decreasing emissions. [14]

This was at least the first step towards the kind of global agreement that Jeffrey Sachs predicted would happen. However, the closest approximation to his prediction would not happen for another eight years, five years longer than he initially expected that it would take.

This significant breakthrough occurred in 2015 at COP21 in Paris. Every nation present unanimously agreed to the following commitments:

substantially reduce global greenhouse gas emissions to limit the global temperature increase in this century to 2 degrees Celsius while pursuing efforts to limit the increase even further to 1.5 degrees;

review countries' commitments every five years;

provide financing to developing countries to mitigate climate change, strengthen resilience and enhance abilities to adapt to climate impacts.

Thus, the Agreement also held participating countries to work towards 'climate neutrality' – removal of Green House Gasses (GHG) and reporting their nationally determined contributions (NDCs) every five years as well as mitigation, or the reduction of carbon emissions. The intention was that each country would aim for increasingly ambitious NDC targets during each five-year cycle. Ultimately, it took almost exactly a year for every country to ratify

13 Jeffrey Sachs: Reith Lectures 2007: Survival in the Anthropocene, Peking University, Beijing, 18th April 2007.
14 Achievements of the Conference of the Parties
   Global carbon markets value surged to record $851 bln last year-Refinitiv

the Paris Agreement. Exactly how to implement the agreement became a focus of subsequent COPs.

In 2016, technical aspects of its implementation dominated the 35 decisions at COP22 in Marrakech, Morocco. [15] COP22 was also notable for the establishment of the Climate Vulnerable Forum by 48 countries from the developing world. In 2022, the membership of the Climate Vulnerable Forum stands at 58: including Kenya, Ghana, Ethiopia, Lebanon, Palestine, Afghanistan, Bangladesh, Costa Rica and Haiti.[16]

One of the most notable achievements of COP23 in Bonn, Germany in 2017 was the establishment of the Powering Past Coal Alliance. This initiative was led by the United Kingdom and Canada and more than 20 countries and states within countries agreed to join. These included Denmark, Finland, Italy and New Zealand plus the US States of Washington and Oregon. The Alliance noted the need to phase out coal by 2030-2050, but members were not committed to doing so by a particular date and the declaration only requires them to restrict financing coal-fired power stations, rather than completely ending it. [17]

COP24 was held in Katowice, Poland in 2018. A large percentage of the discussion again focused on the implementation of the Paris Agreement. The reporting of NDCs was shortened from five years to two. The declaration signed by the parties included the following commitment: to initiate "deliberations on setting a new collective quantified goal a floor of USD 100 billion per year, in the context of meaningful mitigation actions and transparency of implementation and taking into account the needs and priorities of developing countries". [18] This is, of course, a comparatively small step as it is only an agreement to initiate discussions.

The 25th COP meeting in Madrid, Spain in 2019 was largely regarded as a missed opportunity. The main aim of the conference

---

15 The Paris Agreement
    Achievements of the Conference of the Parties
    Key aspects of the Paris Agreement
    Outcomes of COP 22 climate change conference
16 For a full list of countries, see https://thecvf.org/members/
17 COP23: Key outcomes agreed at the UN climate talks in Bonn
18 COP 24 - key outcomes and next steps

was to complete the "Paris rulebook", but the parties failed to reach a consensus on many of the outstanding technical issues.

COP26 AND COP27

The Covid-19 pandemic which raged across the world in 2020, meant that it was not possible to hold a COP that year. So COP26 took place in November and December 2021 in Glasgow, United Kingdom. This congress was perceived to be successful in achieving many of its aims, which were summarised in the Glasgow Pact. These included:

The reaffirmation of the Paris agreement and the acknowledgment that the effects and impact of climate change would be significantly less at 1.5 degrees Celsius than they would be at 2 degrees Celsius.

The urgency of necessary action and the requirement in the present decade for 45% reductions in carbon dioxide emissions in order to reach net zero by 2050. The Glasgow climate pact also requested that participating nations should strengthen their national action plans within the following twelve months rather than the original target of 2025.

The phased reduction of dependence on fossil fuels, especially coal as well as fossil fuel subsidies. This was the first time that action on fossil fuels was specifically addressed, despite the known link between coal, oil, gas, and global warming and climate change.

The pledge for developed countries to contribute $100 Billion dollars for developing countries, which was made at COP24 had not really produced results in the previous two years. The COP26 declaration reaffirmed the pledge with the developed countries setting their own target of 2023 to do this.

The doubling of finance for developing countries to combat the impact of climate change. This would assist with people's lives and livelihoods. Prior to this, the vast majority of the money allocated was used to provide green technology to lessen greenhouse gas emissions.

The ironing out of all the remaining issues from the Paris Agreement: Six years after the Agreement was signed, this finally provided a complete "rule book" for the issue of addressing climate change

The renewed focus and strengthening of the Santiago Network which "connects vulnerable countries with providers of technical assistance, knowledge and resources to address climate risks." A new "Glasgow Dialogue" was established to "discuss arrangements for the funding of activities to avert, minimize and address loss and damage associated with the adverse effects of climate change. "[19]

However, although the results of COP26 and the Glasgow Pact were regarded as highly significant, points of underachievement have also been identified by scientists and other academics. Niklas Hoehne a climate researcher at Wageningen University in the Netherlands, who was present at the conference stated that "COP26 has closed the gap, but it has not solved the problem" and international development students at King's College University of London argued that COP26 failed in a number of ways:

Current commitments put the world on track for 2.4C of warming, a level that would be catastrophic for millions in countries from Bangladesh to the Bahamas. Until industrialised nations commit to action that recognises their overwhelming responsibility for historic emissions, there will be no escaping the impending environmental and ecological crisis.

Even though developed countries finally agreed to meet their commitment to provide $100 billion a year to poorer countries, whether there will not be any strings attached to the money is unanswered. Climate finance cannot be given as loans for it would add more burden in already heavily indebted countries.

India (backed by China) somewhat controversially lobbied for a word change from the 'phasing-out' to the 'phasing-down' of coal due...Many rich industrialised nations have less of a dependency on the ash, and more on oil and gas. Thus, there are still loopholes for countries in the global

---

19 COP26: Together for our planet

north to continue trends of emissions behaviour, while pointing the finger at China and India to reduce theirs.

Food systems, which along with agriculture and the processes that include food processing, transportation, and packaging comprise 25 percent of global emissions. Leaving that issue off the menu for Cop26 will only hinder the battle with curbing the emissions in the long run.

COP26 president, Alok Sharma from the UK Government concluded the congress by summarising the positives and negatives of what it had achieved: *"We are well aware that ambitions have fallen short of the commitments made in Paris… We have kept 1.5 degrees alive. But its pulse is weak, and it will only survive if we keep our promises and translate commitments into rapid action."*[20]

The relative success of COP26 meant that there was a great deal of anticipation surrounding COP27, which took place in November 2022 in Sharm-E-Sheik, Egypt. It attracted a record number of delegates - 45,000- leading some participants to question its purpose. Sunita Narain, director-general of the Centre for Science and Environment, an environmental research organization in New Delhi, believed that the original *raison d'etre*- pushing world leaders towards climate goals and holding them to those goals had been lost. She believed that the COP had been "reduced to a grand spectacle". [21]

COP27 was held in a year of significant climate change events including wildfires across Europe, flooding in Pakistan, prolonged drought in East Africa and record-high temperatures in many parts of the world. The context of the congress was also complicated by the invasion of Ukraine by Russia on 24th February 2022 and the ensuing conflict. Russia is a major gas producer and the curtailing of its exports led to such volatility, shortages, and insecurity in the energy markets, that the International Energy Agency (IEA) referred to it as "the first truly global energy crisis, with impacts that will be felt for years to come".[22] Some of the wealthiest countries in the world reverted to using coal as a substitute for gas until another

---

20 'COP26 hasn't solved the problem': scientists react to UN climate deal
   Reflections on the failures of COP26
21 COP27 climate talks: what succeeded, what failed and what's next
22 6 ways Russia's invasion of Ukraine has reshaped the energy world

source of gas could be located. It was inevitable that the energy crisis would have an impact on COP27 itself.

The goals of the congress were laid out as follows:

Mitigation: All parties, especially those in a position to "lead by example", are urged to take "bold and immediate actions" and to reduce emissions to limit global warming well below 2°C.

Adaptation: Ensure that COP27 makes the "crucially needed progress" towards enhancing climate change resilience and assisting the world's most vulnerable communities.

Finance: Make significant progress on climate finance, including the delivery of the promised $100 billion per year to assist developing countries.

Collaboration: As the UN negotiations are consensus-based, reaching agreement will require "inclusive and active participation from all stakeholders".[23]

The results of the slightly extended summit, were, at best, mixed. The most impactful achievement was the establishment of the "loss and damages fund", including, at least in theory, the funding mechanism for developing countries hardest hit by climate change. A 'transition committee' was also formed to make recommendations at COP28 on "how to operationalize" the new fund. [24] This is a significant achievement because the subject had been discussed at length at previous COPs, but negotiations had been stalled by the United States of America and the European Union, among others "over fears of legal liability for climate damages". [25]

There were also broad agreements on the fundamental priority of "safeguarding food security and ending hunger". This is a subject that had not even been discussed at COP26. However, there is very little in the text of the agreement to indicate how this priority is to receive dedicated funding.

---

23 COP27: Why it matters and 5 key areas for action
24 COP27 Reaches Breakthrough Agreement on New "Loss and Damage" Fund for
    Vulnerable Countries
25 Four Takeaways from the COP27 Climate Conference

COP27 saw a less positive outcome on the issue of fossil fuels, largely prompted by the energy crisis. The final text of the agreement states that the target to keep global warming to 1.5 degrees Celsius above the pre-industrial levels requires "rapid, deep and sustained reductions in greenhouse gas emissions" by 2030. Despite this, the text of the agreement signed at Sharm-El-Sheik does not include any references at all to the phasing out of coal, oil, and gas. However, "new wording was added proposing accelerated development of 'low-emission' energy systems, which many fear will be used to justify further natural-gas development". [26]

In his comments at the closing plenary of COP27, Alok Sharma, who had been the President of COP26 in Glasgow, summed up the failures of the COP27 agreement:

Friends, I said in Glasgow that the pulse of 1.5 degrees was weak.

Unfortunately, it remains on life support.[27]

It is clear then, that the COP summits can be frustrating in both their ambition and their achievements. However, it is equally evident that without the co-operation that COP facilitates, the impact of pollutants and greenhouse gases on the ecosystem of the Earth in the future would be significantly even worse than the most negative current projections indicate.

THE POLITICS OF COP

Many of the commitments which were made, rejected, or made and then not enacted were done so for political or geopolitical reasons.

The role of the United States of America is a good example of this. United States president, Bill Clinton signed the Kyoto Protocol in 1997 but his successor, George W. Bush declared in 1991 that the USA would not be implementing it because he believed it was "fatally flawed in fundamental ways". The pattern of Democrat US

---

26 COP27 climate talks: what succeeded, what failed and what's next
27 COP26 President Alok Sharma's Remarks at the COP27 Closing Plenary

presidents joining and Republican Presidents leaving international climate agreements was repeated with the Paris Agreement. In 2015, Barack Obama signed the United States up, only for Donald Trump to declare that the US would cease to be a signatory upon his election the following year. Trump associated the accord with "onerous restrictions" and that he could not "in good conscience support a deal that punishes the United States." However, like the previous Democratic presidents, Trump's successor, Joe Biden, made climate change a priority. He signed an executive order to re-join the Paris Agreement on his first day in office and this was formally enacted almost exactly a month later on 19th February 2021. [28] Why does it appear that recent Republican presidents are taking the threat of climate change less seriously than their Democrat counterparts? Apart from the Republican ideological stance that places more emphasis on the economy than the environment and the theory that Republicans are in the pay of the fossil fuel industry, one commentator has linked environmental issues to the culture wars. Environmentalism is seen as "woke" and therefore anti-Republican. [29]

The political relationship between China – another major emissions polluter – and climate change and COP is also complicated. Before COP26, it had declared its commitment to carbon neutrality by 2060. However, it is perceived as stalling in the immediate future as a result of uncertain global geopolitics as well as domestic issues including social instability and lack of economic growth. However, without China, it would be impossible for the rest of the world to reach the required 1.5 degrees. [30]

However, during the summit, China and the United States surprised the world by agreeing to work together on climate change issues. This thawing of diplomatic relations was abruptly derailed by the Chinese in August 2022 when the Chinese objected to the visit by US Congress Speaker, Nancy Pelosi to the disputed Island of Taiwan. [31] At COP27, there was renewed hope with "very

---

28 Climate Change History
29 Why Republicans Turned Against the Environment
30 China, climate politics and COP26
31 The US-China climate deal was a rare bright spot in an otherwise thorny relationship. Should it be mended?

constructive" bilateral talks between the United States and China, which were left open to be resumed at a later date. [32]

There are also issues around China and the loss and damage fund. Although China has one of the largest economies in the world, at COP27, it argued that it should be exempted from contributing to the loss and damage fund because it is a developing country. It also pointed out that it had provided help on a completely voluntary basis to countries in Africa and Latin America.[33]

Political issues at COP are not just restricted to geopolitics and individual nations. At COP27 in 2022, there were 636 oil and gas lobbyists in Sharm-El-Sheik which were scattered through the various national delegations. This equated to 100 more lobbyists than at COP26 and that was a larger number of individuals than were represented in the delegations of any individual nation apart from the United Arab Emirates (UAE). This led climate activists to label 'decarbonisation day' at the summit as "a complete oil and gas trade show".[34] International campaigning organisation Global Witness is calling for conflict of interest policies to restrict the number of fossil fuel lobbyists in the room at COP. [35]

It is likely that the high number of fossil fuel delegates, combined with nations who are producers or heavy consumers of fossil fuels, such as Russia and Saudi Arabia precipitated the dropping of the phase out of fossil fuels which had been a commitment made at COP26. One of the architects of the Paris Agreement, Laurence Tubiana, laid the blame for this failure on the host nation, Egypt. He argued that Egypt was trying to protect its regional alliances with major "oil and gas petrostates" and the fossil fuel industries in general. [36]

In common with many other major international events, various groups are generally underrepresented at the COP summits. Before COP 26 in Glasgow, women's activists raised the issue of the lack of female senior leadership: in the UK delegation: for example, at

---

32 COP 27: China and US held 'constructive' climate talks with more to follow, Beijing's envoy says
33 China and US renew commitment to tackling climate crisis but differences remain
34 'Oil and gas trade show' promotes carbon capture at Cop27
35 636 fossil fuel lobbyists granted access to COP27
36 COP27: how the fossil fuel lobby crowded out calls for climate justice

COP25, 10 out of the 12 leaders were men and women took on advisory and organisational roles. By COP26, the following year, the gender balance was not much improved in the UK delegation and the hosting team in Glasgow were all men. [37] Women are not the only under-represented group at the COPs. People from ethnic minorities and those from poorer socio-economic backgrounds are also not present in adequately significant numbers. This is impactful because it is precisely these groups that are most likely to be disproportionately affected by climate change. However, their voices are not being heard as clearly as, say, middle-class European white men. The presence of women is important because, as Friends of the Earth notes "women and children are 14 times more likely than men to suffer direct impacts of natural disasters and climate breakdown yet are regularly shut out of the decision-making that's supposed to change things". This is often because, in many countries, women have fewer political rights than their male peers.

Climate activism in general is also perceived as more difficult for those from ethnic minorities and lower socio-economic groups. This is for a number of reasons including, in the case of ethnic minorities, fear of violence from police if they were to take part in marches and demonstrations. Those of a lower socio-economic status also tend not to have the free time from paid work to take part. They also often don't have the same level of engagement in activities that disrupt the work of others. If these groups are not involved in grassroots environmental activism, then it is highly unlikely that they will progress to a more formal position as a COP delegate or leader. [38]

On occasion, domestic politics can prevent heads of state and ministers from attending COP summits. The most recent example of this comes from the United Kingdom at COP27. At COP26 in Glasgow, the then Prince of Wales gave a speech on behalf of his mother, Queen Elizabeth II. The then-Prince Charles has had a lifelong interest in environmental issues and has helped to raise awareness in the UK. On 8th September 2022, Queen Elizabeth died and her son became King Charles III. Soon after Charles ascended the throne, it was announced that he would not be attending COP27 on the advice of the Government led by the new Prime Minister,

---

37 COP26: Why Are Women Still Missing At The Top Climate Table
38 The lack of diversity at the COP-26 Climate Summit

Liz Truss. It was not constitutionally possible for the King to disregard this advice and the apparent reason for it was that the Government regarded COP as a political event rather than a purely environmental one. Although the UK changed Prime Minister for the second time in 2022 before COP27, and the latest Prime Minister, Rishi Sunak did not appear to have the same objections as his predecessor to King Charles attending COP, it was too late to get the logistics in place for him to do so. Instead, King Charles made a point of holding a reception for environmental figures, activists, and influencers in the UK on the eve of the summit. In the weeks and days preceding COP27 it became increasingly unclear who would actually be the figurehead for the United Kingdom at the summit. As a former chancellor of the exchequer, Sunak focused on the economic situation, announcing that he would not be attending COP27 because he was required to remain in the UK to deal with the cost-of-living crisis. This gave the impression that the United Kingdom placed domestic economic issues above international environmental cooperation. Ultimately, Sunak did attend the summit. His comparatively late decision may have been influenced by former Prime Minister Boris Johnson accepting his invitation to COP27.[39] If so, ironically, the saga ended with a highly political move.

The political saga of the United Kingdom should, of course, be placed in the general context of COP27. Not every world leader was present. Xi Jinping of China and Narendra Modi of India, two of the largest emitters of pollution, did not attend. Vladimir Putin of Russia was also absent as was Anthony Albanese from Australia and Justin Trudeau from Canada. Reasons for non-attendance were not always given. Putin reportedly believed that there were unlikely to be any developments at the summit. If true, it is ironic that Putin's and Russia's actions in invading Ukraine and causing the energy crisis cast such a long shadow over COP27. In spite of Xi Jinping's lack of attendance at COP27, climate negotiation progress was made by the leaders of China and USA at the G20 summit, held, in part, at the same time as COP27. [40]

---

39 Why Rishi Sunak Will Attend COP27 After All—But King Charles Won't
40 Who's attending COP27, and who isn't.
    Some world leaders attend COP27 despite crises, Putin most obvious absentee
    What happened on day nine of COP27? 5 key takeaways from Sharm El Sheikh

It is inevitable that any worldwide Congress of nations will encounter political issues, some of which cannot be resolved. Therefore, the achievements of the summits with global co-operation in spite of individual nations' domestic politics is very positive. The issue of representation at COP and the presence of the fossil fuel lobby are political problems which do need to be addressed but may not have a quick fix.

HOW TO AVOID A CLIMATE CATASTROPHE.

In his book Gates argues that we need to urgently bring down the 51 billion tons of greenhouse gases that the world typically adds to the atmosphere every year.

When the corona virus pandemic struck in 2020 the entire world changed - a substantial number of global activities came to a standstill. This should have considerably reduced the 51 tons of greenhouse gases being emitted in a normal year of activity. Yet this figure just dropped from 51 to about 48 billion tons of carbon emission – a reduction of just 5 percent.

Even when such a profound event strikes bringing the whole world almost to a standstill the reduction of only a five percent reduction in carbon emission is surprising. The emissions did not significantly drop. This demonstrates the need for a rethink as to how we go about reducing emissions.

It is ironic that the world energy industry contributes to about $ 5 trillion a year of revenues. With such a large financial muscle this industry continues to set the agenda on climate change. There was an undeniable link between incomes of countries and energy use with the wealthiest like the US, Qatar using the maximum energy.

What is the solution to address such an existential threat to humanity is something Gates argues passionately.

1. We need to deploy tools that we already have in producing energy from solar, wind and hydro faster and smarter.

2. We need to fund research in rolling out breakthrough technologies to produce essential products like cement, steel etc using less energy and emitting greenhouse gases

Fossil fuels are cheaper than a soft drink. For example, the price of oil at the middle of 2020 was around $ 42 per barrel (a barrel containing 42 gallons) it works out at $ 1 per gallon. If you compare that with the price of 8 litres of soda at $ 6 in a supermarket it works out to $ 2.85 per gallon. This is the dichotomy of the current problem we face. There is therefore an urgency to make alternate energy as cheap or cheaper than fossil fuels. It is critical to produce wind, solar and hydro energy in smarter ways to bring their costs down dramatically.

Almost everywhere people are living longer and healthier. Standards of living are going up and with-it rising demand for energy for cars, roads, building, refrigerators, computer etc. This results in the amount of energy used by each person increasing each year.

Further consider the spectacular growth in population of the world – an increase from 1.6 billion in 1900 to nearly 10 billion by the end of the century. The amount of greenhouse gases being burned is going to be spectacularly more. To see this in context, one needs to appreciate that it took the human population to get to 1.60 billion by 1900 - over thousands of years.

Yet our population has increased from 1.60 billion in 1900 to 8 billion in just 120 years. All this contributes to more energy use and the urgency to produce clean energy is vital. However, with a $ 5 Trillion industry the current fossil fuel industry does not have an incentive to promote rapid change.

We need to accelerate change like what happened in the computer and chip industry. The computer that we have today is a million times more powerful than the one we had in 1970. That kind of change requires investing in R&D and taking various initiatives that the tech industry took decades ago. The question to ask is – do we have the appetite to do this?

The recent war in Ukraine has also started a debate about how we can slightly reduce our energy usage. Currently the world uses

5,000 gigawatts with 20% consumed by the US @ 1,000 gigawatts. There must be many areas this consumption can be reduced. We need to be thinking out of the box with everyone making a genuine effort for the sake of nature. I have heard stories of rich Arabs in the middle east not even shutting their air-conditioners when they go away on holidays. So much of this waste can be eliminated.

What are the current sources of alternate energy.

Fossil fuels produce about 60% of the world's energy with renewables like solar, hydro, wind and nuclear fast becoming more affordable to replace fossil fuels in the years to come.

SOLAR ENERGY

This is free and fantastic but restricted to when the sun shines. Summer months bring in bountiful energy. Costs of solar panels have come down dramatically.

Solar photovoltaics (PV) has seen the sharpest cost decline of any electricity technology over the last decade. A new report by the International Renewable Energy Agency (IRENA) found that between 2010-2019, the cost of solar PV globally dropped by 82%. Across the board the cost of renewables has fallen, with concentrated solar power also seeing a drop of 47%, while onshore wind costs fell 40% and offshore wind 29%.

In 2019 alone, the cost of electricity from solar fell by 13% to just over five pence per kilowatt-hour. This means that by next year globally, there will be up to 1,200GW of existing coal capacity that will cost more to operate than it would to install new solar PV capacity.

This drop now means that costly 500GW coal plants could now be replaced with solar and wind power, and result in an annual saving of £18.6 billion. Additionally, this would reduce global CO_2 emissions by 5% based on figures from 2019. Francesco La Camera, the director-general of IRENA said the new figures show we have reached an important turning point for the energy transition.

The falling cost of solar PV means that while in 2010, it costs £794,990 to obtain 213kW of energy but by 2019 for the same amount you could build a plant producing 1,005kW of energy, according to IRENA. A substantial reduction in costs. This trend is set to continue in 2020, based on auction results and power purchase agreements.

Germany has made impressive efforts through its Energiewende program and set a goal of 60 percent renewables by 2050. The country has spent billions over the past decade expanding its use of renewables, increasing its solar capacity nearly 650 % between 2008 – 2010. It produces so much in the summer that it is unable to use all that it produces and so it transmits its excess to neighbouring Poland and Czech Republic. This brings with it other issues.

WIND ENERGY

There has been significant investment in generating energy from onshore as well as offshore wind.

As per the latest report from the World Economic forum for the first time, wind and solar generated more than 10% of electricity globally in 2021. Fifty countries have now crossed the 10% wind and solar landmark with seven countries joining this elite list in 2021.

Wind power has many advantages. It's constantly renewable, sustainable, and a long-term source of energy provided by nature. The operation of wind turbines does not produce any emissions or require any transportation of fuel. Unlike virtually all other forms of energy production, wind power does not leave any environmental debt for future generations to repay.

Europe and China lead the world in investments in tapping wind energy which is clean and plentiful.

The USA lags significantly although it has plenty of potential for capturing wind energy. It has a huge coastline with most of its major cities by the coast providing an excellent opportunity to tap wind energy. However due to political pressures the wind industry has not taken off like China and Europe

The UK has played a leading role with Ørsted a Danish company investing hugely in one of the largest installed windfarms, Hornsea 2, which is now fully operational. The 1.3GW offshore wind farm comprises 165 wind turbines, located 89km off the Yorkshire Coast, which will help power over 1.4 million UK homes with low-cost, clean and secure renewable energy.

The wind farm is situated alongside its sibling Hornsea 1, which together can power 2.5 million homes and make a significant contribution to the UK Government's ambition of having 50 GW offshore wind in operation by 2030.

The Hornsea zone, an area of the North Sea covering more than 2,000 km2, is also set to include Hornsea 3. The 2.8 GW project is planned to follow Hornsea 2 having been awarded a contract for difference from the UK government earlier this year.

Hornsea 2 has played a key role in the ongoing development of a larger and sustainably competitive UK supply chain to support the next phase of the UK's offshore wind success story. In the past five years alone, Ørsted has placed major contracts with nearly 200 UK suppliers. Ørsted has invested GBP 4.5 billion in the UK supply chain to date and expects to make another GBP 8.6 billion of UK supply chain investments over the next decade.

Ørsted now has 13 operational offshore wind farms in the UK, providing 6.2GW of renewable electricity for the UK – enough to power more than 7 million homes. Hornsea 2 makes a significant contribution to Ørsted's global ambition of installing 30 GW offshore wind by 2030. Ørsted currently has approx. 8.9 GW offshore wind in operation, approx. 2.2 GW under construction, and another approx. 11 GW of awarded capacity under development including Hornsea 3.

Facts about Hornsea 2 Offshore Wind Farm

- 165 wind turbines delivering 1.3 GW of renewable electricity.

- The wind farm spans an area of 462 km2 – equal to more than 64,000 football fields.

- Each wind turbine blade is 81m long and the blade tip reaches more than 200m above sea level

- One revolution of the wind turbine blades can power an average UK home for 24 hours.

- 390km of subsea export cables take the power generated from Hornsea 2 to the shore at Horseshoe Point in Lincolnshire

China is another country making huge inroads in the wind energy industry.

- China is planning the world's largest wind farm, a facility so huge it could power the whole of Norway.

- Chaozhou - a city in China's Guangdong province - has revealed ambitious plans for a 43.3 gigawatt facility in the Taiwan Strait.

- Operating between 75 and 185 kilometres offshore, the 10km long farm will feature thousands of powerful turbines.

- Because of the windy location, these turbines will be able to run between 43 per cent and 49 per cent of the time.

- Work on the project will start before 2025, the province says. Once completed, it will eclipse the world's current largest wind farm. The title is currently held by the Jiuquan Wind Power base in China, a massive site with a 20 gigawatt capacity.

HOW MUCH WIND POWER CAPACITY DOES THE WORLD HAVE?

At the end of 2021, the world's total onshore and offshore **wind power capacity** exceeded 830 GW. China accounts for more than half of this.

In 2021, it installed more offshore wind generation capacity than every other country in the world over the last five years.

China hopes to generate a third of its electricity from **renewables** by 2025. However, it plans to hit net-zero by 2060 - a distant target compared to many other countries.

Sweden is another country making huge investment in wind power.

Markbygden 1101 is one of the largest wind power projects in the world. Located outside Piteå in northern Sweden, the windfarm extends over 450 square kilometres, connected by a 700km road network. Once completed, it will consist of up to 1,101 wind turbines. The project is divided into three main phases, with several sub-projects working simultaneously on assembling the wind turbines. The electricity that the wind turbines produce is fed to nearby 400kV cables and distributed to consumers through Sweden's national grid. Once completed, it will consist of up to 1,101 wind turbines, producing up to 12 TWh per year which is 8% of Sweden's total electricity generation. Markbygden is located on a plateau between two river valleys, allowing for the maximum utilisation of the natural phenomenon of the wind accelerating over hills. This acceleration effect is strongest in winter, which makes northern Sweden an excellent location for onshore wind turbines. The subarctic climate ensures sufficient electricity production during the colder months when electricity consumption peaks. Each kWh produced by wind turbines can replace electricity generated by fossil fuels. Once complete, Markbygden 1101 is expected to generate between 8 and 12 TWh per year. Compared with coal-fired electricity generation, Markbygden 1101 is estimated to reduce carbon dioxide emissions by 8 million tonnes per year.

It is not all doom and gloom and there are many initiatives that many have taken across the world that

ICELAND A COUNTRY WITH HUGE AMBITIONS TO BECOME CARBON NEUTRAL BY 2040

Iceland embraces renewables in a very substantial way which can be the road real ahead for all of us.

In January 2023 my wife and I visited Reykjavik for the first time and were amazed with what we found in this remarkable country. This small island in the Atlantic can be proud of so many unique initiatives that it has taken.

Iceland's unique geology allows it to produce renewable energy relatively cheaply, from a variety of sources. Iceland is located on the Mid-Atlantic Ridge, which makes it one of the most tectonically active places in the world. There are over 200 volcanoes located in Iceland and over 600 hot springs. There are over 20 high-temperature steam fields that are at least 150 °C [300 °F]; many of them reach temperatures of 250 °C. This is what allows Iceland to harness geothermal energy, and these steam fields are used for heating everything from houses to swimming pools. Hydropower is harnessed through glacial rivers and waterfalls, both of which are common in Iceland. Iceland also has an exclusive economic zone measuring some 751,345 km2, which could be used for offshore wind farms.

Iceland is a world leader in renewable energy. 100% of Iceland's electricity grid is produced from renewable resources. In terms of total energy supply, 85% of the total primary energy supply in Iceland is derived from domestically produced renewable energy sources. Geothermal energy provided about 65% of primary energy in 2016, the share of hydropower was 20%, and the share of fossil fuels (mainly oil products for the transport sector) was 15%.

Geothermal power

For centuries, the people of Iceland have used their hot springs for bathing and washing clothes. The first use of geothermal energy for heating did not come until 1907 when a farmer ran a concrete pipe from a hot spring to lead steam into his house. In 1930, the first pipeline was constructed in Reykjavik and was used to heat two schools, 60 homes, and the main hospital. It was a 3 km (1.9 mi) pipeline that ran from one of the hot springs outside the city. In 1943 the first district heating company was started with the use of geothermal power. An 18 km (11 mi) pipeline ran through the city of Reykjavik, and by 1945 it was connected to over 2,850 homes.

Currently geothermal power heats 89% of the houses in Iceland, and over 54% of the primary energy used in Iceland comes from geothermal sources. Geothermal power is used for many things in Iceland. 57.4% of the energy is used for space heat, 25% is used for electricity, and the remaining amount is used in many miscellaneous areas such as swimming pools, fish farms, and greenhouses.

The government of Iceland has played a major role in the advancement of geothermal energy. In the 1940s the State Electricity Authority was started by the government in order to increase the knowledge of geothermal resources and the utilization of geothermal power in Iceland. The agency's name was later changed to the National Energy Authority (Orkustofnun) in 1967. This agency has been very successful and has made it economically viable to use geothermal energy as a source for healing in many different areas throughout the country. Geothermal power has been so successful that the government no longer has to lead the research in this field because it has been taken over by the geothermal industries. The Icelandic government aspires that the nation will be carbon neutral by 2040. The largest obstacles to this are road transport and the fishing industry.

In 2015, the total electricity consumption in Iceland was 18,798 GWh. Renewable energy provided almost 100% of production, with 75% coming from hydropower and 24% from geothermal power.

The main use of geothermal energy is for space heating, with the heat being distributed to buildings through extensive district-heating systems. Nearly all Icelandic homes are heated with renewable energy, with 90% of homes being via geothermal energy. The remaining homes that are not located in areas with geothermal resources are heated by renewable electricity instead.

Iceland is the world's largest green energy producer per capita and largest electricity producer per capita, with approximately 55,000 kWh per person per year. In comparison, the EU average is less than 6,000 kWh. Most of this electricity is used in energy-intensive industrial sectors, such as aluminium production, which developed in Iceland thanks to the low cost of electricity.

Hydropower in Iceland

The first hydropower plant was built in 1904 by a local entrepreneur. It was located in a small town outside of Reykjavik and produced 9 kW of power. The first municipal hydroelectric plant was built in 1921, and it could produce 1 MW of power. This plant single-handedly quadrupled the amount of electricity in the country. The 1950s marked the next evolution in hydroelectric plants. Two plants were built on the Sog River, one in 1953 which produced 31 MW, and the other in 1959 which produced 26.4 MW. These two plants were the first built for industrial purposes and they were co-owned by the Icelandic government. This process continued in 1965 when the national power company, Landsvirkjun, was founded. It was owned by both the Icelandic government and the municipality of Reykjavik. In 1969, they built a 210 MW plant on the Pjorsa River that would supply the southeastern area of Iceland with electricity and run an aluminium smelting plant that could produce 33,000 tons of aluminium a year.

This trend continued and increases in the production of hydroelectric power are directly related to industrial development. In 2005, Landsvirkjun produced 7,143 GWh of electricity total of which 6,676 GWh or 93% was produced via hydroelectric power plants. 5,193 GWh or 72% was used for power-intensive industries like aluminium smelting. In 2009 Iceland built its biggest hydroelectric project to date, the Kárahnjúkar Hydropower Plant, a 690 MW hydroelectric plant to provide energy for another aluminium smelter. This project was opposed strongly by environmentalists.

Iceland is the first country in the world to create an economy generated through industries fuelled by renewable energy, and there is still a large amount of untapped hydroelectric energy in Iceland. In 2002 it was estimated that Iceland only generated 17% of the total harnessable hydroelectric energy in the country. Iceland's government believes another 30 TWh of hydropower could be produced each year, while taking into account the sources that must remain untapped for environmental reasons.

CEMENT, STEEL AND PLASTICS

How does the manufacture of cement, steel and plastics impact global emissions of CO_2

There are three wonder materials that man invented in the recent past which has caused such devastation to global warming.

Steel is manufactured by using iron and carbon. Now carbon is got from coal and iron from the earth's crust. To make steel oxygen is separated from the iron and a tiny bit of carbon is added at very high temperatures. A bit of the carbon grabs onto the oxygen forming carbon dioxide. The trouble is that to make a one ton of steel you produce 1.8 tons of carbon dioxide.

With the world producing 3 billion tons of steel the amount of carbon dioxide emitted is around 5 billion tonnes.

With steel consumption increasing every year due to the demand from a rising population this would inevitably increase each year.

To make cement you need calcium which comes from limestone which contains carbon and oxygen.

When limestone is burned you get calcium but also carbon dioxide. For every ton of cement produced you produce one ton of carbon dioxide

The third wonder product that we all love to use is plastics, but plastics has carbon.

There is one important way that plastics are fundamentally different from cement and steel.

Carbon dioxide is released during the manufacturing process into the atmosphere but when we make plastics half of the carbon stays in the plastic. The problem is plastics take hundreds of years to degrade and stays in the environment. Further plastics that get dumped into landfills and oceans cause huge damage to the marine life and life around us.

We have seen images of turtles eating plastic bags and micro plastics entering into our food chain. Entire species of marine life get affected and some being driven to extinction.

The damage that plastics bring is monumental and that is the reason there have been so many initiatives to ban plastic bags, cups, and other items that we take for granted in our daily life.

NEW MANUFACTURING INITIATIVES
WHICH BRINGS CHANGE AND INNOVATION

Cement

Recently there are many new initiatives being taken. For example, if we can manufacture cement using recycled carbon dioxide captured during the process of making cement and then injecting it back into the cement before it is used at the construction site. Currently this new method is able to reduce carbon emissions by 10% and work is going on to increase this to 33%. Another approach is to make cement out of sea water and the carbon dioxide captured out of power plants which would cut emissions by more than 70%.

Steel – one cool method to steel making is to use clean electricity to replace coal. This is a method called molten oxide electrolysis. Instead of burning iron in a furnace with coke you pass electricity through a cell that contains a mixture of liquid iron oxide and other ingredients. The electricity causes iron oxide to break apart leaving pure iron needed for steel and pure oxygen as a by-product. This ensures that no carbon dioxide is produced.

Cows and Farts

Our population has grown exponentially from 1.60 billion in 1900 to around 8 billion in 2022 in a matter of just 120 years. With the increase in population there has been a steep rise in the demand for meat as the world consumes more. What we have done is to industrial the growth in the population of animals like cows, pigs, sheep to feed human beings.

Unfortunately, this growth in population has caused significant increase in greenhouse emissions as methane produced by the burping and farting of animals causes 28 times more warming per molecule than carbon dioxide over the course of a century. Nitrous oxide another gas emitted causes 265 times more warming.

Each year's emissions of methane and nitrous oxide are the equivalent of more than 7 billion tons of carbon dioxide. Deforestation and other land use adds another 1.6 billion tons of carbon dioxide.

To feed the growing population we have cleverly invented methods to increase food yields significantly. Norman Borlaug was awarded the Nobel prize for the invention of new species of wheat which increased yields significantly by introducing the semi-dwarf wheat. Professor Swaminathan of India introduced the green revolution in India by developing high yielding varieties of rice and crops. These initiatives assist in feeding the huge increases in the population

Environmental Innovation

There are many different individual innovative efforts to mitigate the impact of climate change on the planet. Some of these have been showcased in the Earthshot Prize. This prize is spearheaded by Prince William, the current United Kingdom Prince of Wales and heir to the British throne. It is designed to find and assist innovative solutions to issues around climate change. The winners and runners-up for the awards are good examples of the kind of work that is currently happening and are outlined below.

The aim of the 44.01 project, based in Oman is to remove CO_2 from the atmosphere permanently by converting it into minerals in the form of peridotite rock, which is commonly found in Oman, Europe, Australasia, and America. This mineralisation is a natural process that usually takes a very long time. 44.01's process speeds this process up by pumping carbonated water into the rock. The company aims to mineralise 1000 tonnes per year until 2024 and 1bn tonnes in total by 2040. [41]

Enapter, based in Thailand, has developed green hydrogen technology in the form of AEM Electrolysers which turn renewable electricity into green hydrogen energy that does not produce polluting emissions. The technology has a diverse range of uses within the 50 countries in which the Electrolysers are already sold: including carbon-free ammonia production (United States), aeroplane fuel (United Kingdom), energy storage (Australia), and domestic heating (Netherlands). Enapter is aiming to remove the equivalent of 1.5 tonnes of carbon by 2040 and is hopeful that its Electrolysers will be producing 10% of worldwide hydrogen a decade after that.[42]

The next climate change innovation focuses on the construction industry. This particular industry has had historic issues with the removal of carbon from within its processes. AMPD Energy, based in Hong Kong, has developed an all-electric battery energy storage system called the Enertainer, powered along similar lines to electric vehicles. It is specifically designed to power building sites and equipment such as cranes, hoists, and welders. Each Enertainer

---

41 44.01 Project
42 AEM Electrolyser

reduces CO2 production by 130 tonnes per year as well as removing pollution equivalent to 300 cars. The system has already saved 17000 tonnes of carbon pollution and reduced site running costs by up to 85% as well as noise generation in general. [43]

Concrete is a material that is commonly used in construction and urbanisation across the world. It is so widely used that its production generates 2.8bn tonnes of CO2 emissions every year. This is more in total than every country on the planet except for the United States of America and China. LCM, based in the United Kingdom, has created OSTO a carbon–negative alternative to aggregate, one of the most significant components of concrete. Concrete blocks will be created using OSTO and it is anticipated that it will be used in future house-building projects in the United Kingdom. [44]

Traditional African cookstoves are used by 700 million people across the continent. These cookstoves burn charcoal which causes pollution that contributes to climate change as well as severe respiratory conditions in people. In Kenya, Mukuru Clean Stoves uses cleaner burning fuels for stoves made from a biomass of charcoal but also wood and sugarcane. This reduces pollution compared to an open fire by 90% and 70% compared to a traditional charcoal-burning cookstove. The cost of both the fuel and stove are also significantly less expensive. The company has sold 200,000 cookstoves to date and plans to increase this to one million customers within three years and 10 million in ten years. [45]

Charcoal burning is also common in India. Traditional street ironing services are powered by charcoal-burning apparatus. Aware of the impact of this both on climate change and on human health, Vinisha Umashanka a fourteen-year-old girl, developed a solar-powered street ironing cart. Five hours of solar charge give the iron six hours of energy, so the change from dirty, charcoal-burning, C02-producing energy to clean solar power is certainly justified. The mobility provided by the carts means that street ironers are able to expand the location of their services and the carts are also able to offer built-in phone charging ports as an added form of

---

43 Enertainer
44 OSTO
45 Mukuru Clean Stoves

income. Vinisha intends to develop and expand her innovation across India and into Africa and Asia.[46]

Some climate change innovations are designed to help heal Earth's oceans after decades of overfishing, climate change and pollution. Coral Vita, based in the Bahamas, has devised a method of growing coral on land up to 50 times more quickly than it happens naturally in the sea as part of a reef. The coral is also more resilient to pollution and climate change. Coral Vita is also working on the first-ever coral farm in the Middle East.[47]

The next innovation is also connected to the sea. Notpla, a start-up based in the UK has developed a biodegradable alternative to plastic that is made from seaweed and other plants. Its primary purpose is to reduce plastic waste from food packaging and other sources, and it has the potential to replace 100 million plastic-coated containers across Europe. Notpla has a direct impact on climate change innovation: the seaweed it uses in its farms captures carbon at a faster rate than trees can. [48]

Seaweed and its climate change-fighting properties are a crucial part of another innovation. Seaforester, from Portugal, has pioneered a 'green gravel' which is essentially small pieces of rock covered with seaweed spores and scattered into the oceans and seas. These attach themselves to reefs and the seaweed grows and spreads across the seabed. SeaForester has created mobile seaweed nurseries to be used in coastal areas in countries across the world. [49]

The final ocean-related innovation is designed to prevent plastic and other waste from entering the seas. This is crucial for climate change as decomposing plastic emits greenhouse gases and can affect zooplankton, which helps to break down the carbon in the water. The Great Bubble Barrier, developed in the Netherlands, is a long, perforated tube in a canal, through which air is blown. The resulting 'bubbles' redirect the plastic waste to the surface of the waterway where it is captured by an especially designed collection system. The innovation works well: the bubble barriers have caught 86% of plastic waste in the target areas in the Netherlands. Just

46 Vinisha Umashanka
47 Coral Vita
48 Notpla
49 SeaForester

one of them has stopped 8,000 pieces of plastic waste from entering the sea in a single month. Barriers are soon to be installed in canals and rivers in Germany and Portugal. The aim is to expand the technology to some of the most polluted rivers and seas in the world, especially in Asia. [50]

The provision of electricity is not consistent across the world, and it is not readily available in many of the poorest countries. This affects up to a billion people or one-eighth of the population of Earth. Many of the countries which are suffering from shortages are forced to burn fossil fuels in an attempt to keep up with demand. This inevitably adds to the pollution which exacerbates climate change. Reeddi, a company based in Nigeria, has developed a solar energy capsule that uses a specially optimised lithium battery. The capsules are rented for $0.50 per day from special stations which resemble vending machines in areas that have the greatest need for cheap and clean energy. It currently serves 600 homes, and the number of customers is increasing rapidly.[51]

Energy is at the centre of another innovation. SOLshare is a unique peer to peer energy network based in Bangladesh. Solar panel owners sell excess energy into a microgrid provided by SOLshare for others to buy. This reduces fossil fuel emissions by 30% in those areas as well as generating an income for communities. SOLshare has around 117 grids and has helped 10,000 people in some of the world's most isolated and remote communities.[52]

Climate change will inevitably reduce large parts of Earth to desert conditions. However, a Chinese team hss developed a process called "soilization" which converts dry and barren deserts into green landscapes. Soilization involves applying a paste plus sand to the surface of the earth. This gives it the same scientific properties as soil and plants are able to grow. This is especially useful for crops and farmland. As the crops and plants decay and die off, they help the new soil to become self-sustaining. [53]

---

50 The Great Bubble Barrier
   Would stopping plastic pollution help with climate change? How do we do it?
51 Reeddi Capsules
52 SOLshare
53 Soilization

There are some climate change-combating innovations that use waste and discarded items to create something which is more sustainable. A good example of this is an Indian company called Phool. Flowers from religious festivals in India are already covered with pesticides and then are traditionally thrown into the highly polluted River Ganges after use. This causes the river to become even more polluted. Phool retrieves the waste flowers before they reach and further pollutes the rivers and converts them into Fleather, a sustainable alternative to animal and plastic synthetic leather which is not climate destructive to make. Thirteen thousand tonnes of waste flowers have been collected to date and 90 square feet of Fleather are produced per day. It also employs some of the poorest people in the world as 'flowercyclers' and the company has won contracts with major fashion houses. [54]

The second waste-based climate innovation from India focuses on the agricultural sector. In India, and across much of the developing world, agricultural waste is disposed of by burning it. This causes a large amount of pollution which has an impact on the speed of climate change. Takachar was developed to stop this source of pollution. Instead of burning their waste, farmers attach custom portable machines to their tractors and the technology converts the agricultural waste to products such as bio-products like fuel and fertilizer. These can be sold, thereby also increasing the farmer's income and smoke and pollution emissions are reduced by up to 98%. [55]

Waste-based climate change innovations are also popping up in Africa. Sanergy, based in Kenya, provides dry toilets which do not put extra stress on already overstretched sewerage systems. The company collects the sanitation waste produced by the toilets as well as other organic waste from kitchens and elsewhere. Once at its factory, Sanergy uses black soldier fly larvae to eat and convert the waste into fertilizer and animal feed. It is preventing 50,000 tonnes of waste per year from breaking down and emitting polluting greenhouse gasses into the atmosphere. The aim is to increase the waste conversion to 5 million tonnes by 2027. [56]

---

54 Fleather
55 Takachar
56 Sanergy

Farming and agriculture can both be affected by and contribute to climate change. An innovation from India is the 'greenhouse in a box'. The company, Kheyti, is working to provide an affordable solution for smallholders affected by climate change – especially heatwaves and droughts. The greenhouse in a box is 90% less expensive than a standard greenhouse and it also saves water as the plants require significantly less water – up to 98% less than outdoor plants - and harmful pesticides are not required by crops grown in a greenhouse. This enables farmers to protect their products from climate change and not contribute to it with the use of pesticides. They are also able to double their income. Kheyti is aiming to produce 50,000 'greenhouses in a box' by 2027.[57]

The impact of the release of carbon into the atmosphere is a significant cause of climate change. Lanzatech, a US company, has devised a method that uses bacteria to convert that carbon into useful materials and applications. Their technology is used in production centres such as ethanol plants and steel mills. The resulting consumer products include green fuels, cosmetics, packaging, cleaning products, and textiles. Lanzatech technology has prevented over 190,000 tonnes of CO_2 from being emitted and the company is aiming to have 20 plants in operation by the end of 2024.[58]

The cheapest form of motorised transport in East Africa is the motorcycle taxi, known as the Boda Boda However, these vehicles emit a very large amount of CO_2, a significant contributor to climate change, and are amongst the worst vehicle polluters. Electric vehicles are almost always too expensive for ordinary East Africans to afford. Roam, based in Kenya, is developing affordable and reliable electric vehicles, including buses, which it estimates will save drivers 75% in running costs. To date, it has tested more than 150 prototypes and aims to market its vehicles across Africa. [59]

It is not only companies and organisations that are currently innovating to reduce the impact of climate change. The City of Amsterdam in the Netherlands has committed to establishing a circular economy, in which waste will be cut to zero. Waste can have

---

57 Kheyti
58 Lanzatech
59 Roam

a significant impact on climate change, whether that is through the release of CO_2 and methane through the breaking down of organic waste, the incineration of all types of waste, or the extraction and transportation of plastic waste. By 2030, the city aims to reduce its use of new raw materials by 50% and have a completely circular economy twenty years later. It is planned that waste reduction will occur in the areas of food, products and construction. Several initiatives have already taken place, including, during Covid-19, the city worked with textile companies to reduce the cost of clothing repairs by 80%. This assisted families on tight budgets and reduced clothing waste.[60]

The Italian city of Milan is another urban centre that is working towards eliminating waste: in this instance, specifically food waste. The City of Milan's Food Waste Hubs were established in order to halve food waste by 2030. Food is recovered from supermarkets and canteens across the city and passed to Non-Government Organizations (NGOs) and charities to distribute to those people in most need. Three Waste Food Hubs have been set up and each is responsible for preserving around 130 tonnes of food per year, which is the equivalent of 260,000 meals. This amount of recovered food must certainly have something of an impact on the 30% of the greenhouse gas emissions emitted by the global food industry. [61]

There are other innovations to curb climate change, which are unrelated, as yet, to the Earthshot Prize. Metropolder, based in the United States of America, has created a smart roof. This innovation captures any rain that falls onto it, preventing the flooding associated with climate change events. It then releases that water in times of severe drought. An added benefit is that it can support rooftop gardens, giving city residents the ability to grow food. [62]

Rising water levels and tidal surges are very real threats associated with climate change. Eight hundred million people in 570 cities around the world could be in serious jeopardy if the sea level only rises 0.5 metres in the next 30 years. In Australia, Living Seawalls have been created using a 3D printer. These have a dual function. They are designed to hold back tidal surges, but also their mimicry

---

60 City of Amsterdam Circular Economy
61 City of Milan's Food Waste Hubs
62 Four innovations preparing cities for climate change

of natural habitats provides a home for sealife in the form of creatures and plants. [63]

Trees can remove a significant amount of CO2 from the atmosphere. It is estimated that one single tree is responsible for a 22kg reduction. Growing different species of trees together in a pocket forest can increase that by a further 6%. Using this knowledge, a United States company, SUGi, works around the world to create pocket forests in public parks and other spaces. SUGi uses the Miyawaki method to grow trees and the trees have an 85% chance of flourishing. The project has also developed an app that allows users to "plant, request, gift and track a specific urban forest" from their mobile device. [64]

My own company, Bags of Ethics / Supreme Creations in partnership with the Royal Forestry Society, UK has commenced an initiative called the Green Tree badge (GTB) to encourage primary school children to get involved in nature and trees. The aim is to get at least one million students across the UK to be involved in this project. We are fortunate that the Scouts movement. The Woodland trust. His Majesty's Lord Lieutenants have lent their support on this mammoth target. In my research I learnt that trees are a natural carbon capture and storage machines, absorbing carbon dioxide (CO2) in the atmosphere through photosynthesis then locking it up for centuries. It's why reforestation are touted as key solutions to the climate crisis.

The humble tree is the ultimate carbon sink.

The entire woodland ecosystem plays a huge role in locking up carbon, including the living wood, roots, leaves, deadwood, surrounding soils and its associated vegetation.

Even a young wood with mixed native species can lock up over 400+ tonnes of co2 . add the other benefits of all the species that will live and prosper in these woods is incredible. I cannot tell you how simple it is for each of us to preserve our trees and woods. It is also fun. Can you imagine the joy of seeing your little sapling grow?

---

63 Four innovations preparing cities for climate change
    'Living seawalls' prove eco-engineering's sea legs are strong
64 Four innovations preparing cities for climate change
    SUGi Project Website

Homes in a new social housing estate in Tredegar, Wales, United Kingdom, are being kept warm by a far infrared graphene heating system that looks just like wallpaper. It plugs into a regular socket and includes solar panels and a smart battery, which means it cuts climate change-causing emissions as well as heating bills. It also warms rooms more quickly than traditional heating and is more cost-efficient than a heat pump. This innovation is a significant part of the Welsh Government's strategy to make Wales carbon net zero by 2050. [65]

This diverse range of environmental innovations is in no way a comprehensive survey of all of the work being undertaken in this area. It is both interesting and inspiring that several of the innovations which have been outlined here have been created by ordinary people in the poorest parts of the world most directly impacted by climate change. These innovators are often younger people, thereby also offering a positive message of hope for the future.

REFERENCES

Analysis: Why scientists think 100% of global warming is due to humans – Carbon Brief - *https://www.carbonbrief.org/analysis-why-scientists-think-100-of-global-warming-is-due-to-humans/*

Climate Change: Global Temperature – NOAA Climate.gov - *https://www.climate.gov/news-features/understanding-climate/climate-change-global-temperature*

How 19th Century Scientists Predicted Global Warming – JStor Daily - *https://daily.jstor.org/how-19th-century-scientists-predicted-global-warming/*

Climate Change History – History Channel/History.com - *https://www.history.com/topics/natural-disasters-and-environment/history-of-climate-change*

Back from the brink: how the world rapidly sealed a deal to save the ozone layer – Rapid Transition Alliance - *https://www.rapidtransition.org/stories/back-from-the-brink-how-the-world-rapidly-sealed-a-deal-to-save-the-ozone-layer/*

A 1980s ban on CFCs to heal the ozone layer is also shaving degrees off global warming, study says – CNN - *https://commonslibrary.parliament.uk/the-rise-of-climate-change-activism/*

The Montreal Protocol protects the terrestrial carbon sink. – Nature - *https://www.nature.com/articles/s41586-021-03737-3.epdf*

The rise of climate change activism? – UK Parliament House of Commons Library - *https://commonslibrary.parliament.uk/the-rise-of-climate-change-activism/*

From Stockholm to Kyoto: A Brief History of Climate Change - United Nations (UN Chronicle)- *https://www.un.org/en/chronicle/article/stockholm-kyoto-brief-history-climate-change*

A History of Climate Activities – World Meteorological Organisation - *https://public.wmo.int/en/bulletin/history-climate-activities*

James Hansen's Climate Warning, 30 Years Later – Columbia Climate School - *https://news.climate.columbia.edu/2018/06/26/james-hansens-climate-warning-30-years-later/*

---

65 Wallpaper that heats homes among innovative projects trialled in Wales to tackle climate change and the cost of living crisis

The Second World Climate Conference -UNFCC - *https://unfccc.int/resource/ccsites/senegal/fact/fs221.htm*

Conference of the Parties (COP)-United Nations Climate Change - *https://unfccc.int/process/bodies/supreme-bodies/conference-of-the-parties-cop*

Achievements of the Conference of the Parties – Sustainability For All - *https://www.activesustainability.com/climate-change/achievements-of-the-conference-of-the-parties/?_adin=02021864894*

Jeffrey Sachs: Reith Lectures 2007: Survival in the Anthropocene, Peking University, Beijing, 18th April 2007 - *http://downloads.bbc.co.uk/rmhttp/radio4/transcripts/20070418_reith.pdf*

The Paris Agreement – United Nations - *https://www.un.org/en/climatechange/paris-agreement*

Global carbon markets value surged to record $851 bln last year-Refinitiv – Reuters- *https://www.reuters.com/business/energy/global-carbon-markets-value-surged-record-851-bln-last-year-refinitiv-2022-01-31/*

Key aspects of the Paris Agreement – United Nations Climate Change- *https://unfccc.int/most-requested/key-aspects-of-the-paris-agreement*

Outcomes of COP 22 climate change conference – European Parliament - *https://www.europarl.europa.eu/RegData/etudes/ATAG/2016/593547/EPRS_ATA(2016)593547_EN.pdf*

COP23: Key outcomes agreed at the UN climate talks in Bonn - CarbonBrief - *https://www.carbonbrief.org/cop23-key-outcomes-agreed-un-climate-talks-bonn/*

COP 24 - key outcomes and next steps – Lexology - *https://www.lexology.com/library/detail.aspx?g=e9a3ca16-ab9f-4ddc-ab10-038d487a8b01*

The Gender Action Plan – United Nations Climate Change - *https://unfccc.int/topics/gender/workstreams/the-gender-action-plan*

COP26: Together for our planet – United Nations Climate Action - *https://www.un.org/en/climatechange/cop26*

'COP26 hasn't solved the problem': scientists react to UN climate deal – Nature - *https://www.nature.com/articles/d41586-021-03431-4*

Reflections on the failures of COP26 – King's College London - *https://www.kcl.ac.uk/reflections-on-the-failures-of-cop26*

6 ways Russia's invasion of Ukraine has reshaped the energy world - World Economic Forum - *https://www.weforum.org/agenda/2022/11/russia-ukraine-invasion-global-energy-crisis/*

COP27: Why it matters and 5 key areas for action – World Economic Forum - *https://www.weforum.org/agenda/2022/10/cop27-why-it-matters-and-5-key-areas-for-action/*

COP27 Reaches Breakthrough Agreement on New "Loss and Damage" Fund for Vulnerable Countries – United Nations Climate Change - *https://unfccc.int/news/cop27-reaches-breakthrough-agreement-on-new-loss-and-damage-fund-for-vulnerable-countries*

Four Takeaways from the COP27 Climate Conference – United States Institute of Peace - *https://www.usip.org/publications/2022/11/four-takeaways-cop27-climate-conference*

COP27 climate talks: what succeeded, what failed and what's next - Nature 612, 16-17 (2022) - *https://www.nature.com/articles/d41586-022-03807-0*

COP26 President Alok Sharma's Remarks at the COP27 Closing Plenary – UN Climate Change Conference UK 2021 - *https://ukcop26.org/cop26-president-closing-remarks-at-cop27/*

Paul Krugman: Why Republicans Turned Against the Environment – New York Times - *https://www.nytimes.com/2022/08/15/opinion/republicans-environment-climate.html*

China, climate politics and COP26 – The Lowy Institute - *https://www.lowyinstitute.org/publications/china-climate-politics-cop26*

The US-China climate deal was a rare bright spot in an otherwise thorny relationship. Should it be mended? – CNN - *https://edition.cnn.com/2022/11/10/world/us-china-climate-cooperation-competition-cop27/index.html*

COP 27: China and US held 'constructive' climate talks with more to follow, Beijing's envoy says – South China Morning Post - *https://www.scmp.com/news/china/diplomacy/article/3200305/cop-27-china-and-us-held-constructive-climate-talks-more-follow-beijings-envoy-says*

China and US renew commitment to tackling climate crisis but differences remain – The Guardian - *https://www.theguardian.com/environment/2022/nov/19/china-and-us-renew-commitment-to-tackling-climate-crisis-but-differences-remain*

'Oil and gas trade show' promotes carbon capture at Cop27 – Climate Home News - *https://www.climatechangenews.com/2022/11/13/oil-and-gas-trade-show-promotes-carbon-capture-at-cop27/*

636 fossil fuel lobbyists granted access to COP27 – Global Witness - *https://www.globalwitness.org/en/campaigns/fossil-gas/636-fossil-fuel-lobbyists-granted-access-cop27/*

COP27: how the fossil fuel lobby crowded out calls for climate justice – The Conversation - *https://theconversation.com/cop27-how-the-fossil-fuel-lobby-crowded-out-calls-for-climate-justice-195041*

COP26: Why Are Women Still Missing At The Top Climate Table – Forbes - *https://www.forbes.com/sites/bonniechiu/2021/10/30/cop26-why-are-women-still-missing-at-the-top-climate-table/?sh=699065bb519d*

The lack of diversity at the COP-26 Climate Summit – The Boar - *https://theboar.org/2020/11/diversity-problem-cop-26-climate-summit/*

Why Rishi Sunak Will Attend COP27 After All—But King Charles Won't – Time Magazine - *https://time.com/6227433/rishi-sunak-cop27-king-charles/*

Who's attending COP27, and who isn't – New York Times -*https://www.nytimes.com/2022/11/07/climate/cop27-attendees-egypt.html*

Some world leaders attend COP27 despite crises, Putin most obvious absentee – Egypt Independent - *https://egyptindependent.com/some-world-leaders-attend-cop27-despite-crises-putin-most-obvious-absentee/*

What happened on day nine of COP27? 5 key takeaways from Sharm El Sheikh – Euronews.green - *https://www.euronews.com/green/2022/11/15/what-happened-on-day-9-of-cop27-5-key-takeaways-from-sharm-el-sheikh*

44.01 Project – The Earthshot Prize - *https://earthshotprize.org/winners-finalists/44-01/*

AEM Electrolyser– The Earthshot Prize - *https://earthshotprize.org/winners-finalists/aem-electrolyser/*

Enertainer – The Earthshot Prize - *https://earthshotprize.org/winners-finalists/ampd-enertainer/*

OSTO – The Earthshot Prize - *https://earthshotprize.org/winners-finalists/low-carbon-materials/*

Mukuru Clean Stoves – The Earthshot Prize - *https://earthshotprize.org/winners-finalists/mukuru-clean-stoves/*

Coral Vita – The Earthshot prize - *https://earthshotprize.org/winners-finalists/coral-vita/*

Notpla – The Earthshot Prize - *https://earthshotprize.org/winners-finalists/coral-vita/*

SeaForester – The Earthshot Prize - *https://earthshotprize.org/winners-finalists/seaforester/*

The Great Bubble Barrier – The Earthshot Prize - *https://earthshotprize.org/winners-finalists/the-great-bubble-barrier/*

Would stopping plastic pollution help with climate change? How do we do it? – MIT Climate Portal - *https://climate.mit.edu/ask-mit/would-stopping-plastic-pollution-help-climate-change-how-do-we-do-it*

Reeddi Capsules -The Earthshot Prize - *https://earthshotprize.org/winners-finalists/reeddi-capsules/*

SOLshare – The Earthshot Prize - *https://earthshotprize.org/winners-finalists/solbazaar/*

Soilization – The Earthshot Prize - *https://earthshotprize.org/winners-finalists/desert-agricultural-transformation/*

Fleather – The Earthshot Prize - *https://earthshotprize.org/winners-finalists/fleather/*

Takachar – The Earthshot Prize - *https://earthshotprize.org/winners-finalists/takachar/*

Sanergy - The Earthshot Prize - *https://earthshotprize.org/winners-finalists/sanergy/*

Vinisha Umashanka – The Earthshot Prize - *https://earthshotprize.org/winners-finalists/vinisha-umashankar/*

Kheyti – The Earthshot Prize - *https://earthshotprize.org/winners-finalists/kheyti/*

Lanzatech – The Earthshot Prize - *https://earthshotprize.org/winners-finalists/lanzatech/*

Roam – The Earthshot Prize - *https://earthshotprize.org/winners-finalists/roam/*

City of Amsterdam Circular Economy- The Earthshot Prize- *https://earthshotprize.org/winners-finalists/city-of-amsterdam-circular-economy/*

City of Milan's Food Waste Hubs – The Earthshot Prize- *https://earthshotprize.org/winners-finalists/city-of-milan/*

Four innovations preparing cities for climate change – World Economic Forum - *https://www.weforum.org/agenda/2022/10/innovations-protect-cities-climate-change/*

'Living seawalls' prove eco-engineering's sea legs are strong – World Economic Forum - *https://www.weforum.org/agenda/2022/08/living-seawalls-eco-engineering*

SUGi Project Website - *https://www.sugiproject.com/*

Wallpaper that heats homes among innovative projects trialled in Wales to tackle climate change and the cost of living crisis – Welsh Government - *https://www.gov.wales/wallpaper-heats-homes-among-innovative-projects-trialled-wales-tackle-climate-change-and-cost*

THE WORLD
IN JULY 2022

Introduction

July 2022 was a month during which the world continued to grapple with the effects on Russia's invasion of Ukraine on the global economy and energy markets. Russia cut supplies through its Nord Stream 1 pipeline to Germany, causing gas prices to surge, as Opec struggled to meet the rise in global demand for oil. Meanwhile, Russia and Ukraine struck a deal brokered by Turkey to avert the grain crisis. The war continued to heighten political divisions in Europe, as Hungary requested gas from Russia and Bulgaria expelled Russian diplomats. British PM Boris Johnson resigned after a tumultuous three-year reign. US President Biden visited Israel and Saudi Arabia in an effort to broker ties between the two countries. MBS visited Greece, showing how Western states are deepening their ties with the Gulf monarchy as the oil price crisis continues. Russia stepped up diplomatic efforts in Africa as the food crisis on the continent continues to worsen. Bangladesh approached the IMF for a multi-billion-dollar loan, as the fuel and food crisis continues to effect emerging economies. Pakistan's currency crisis deepened, despite a recent $1.2bn payment from the IMF. Sri Lanka elected a new president after former president

Gotabaya Rajapaksa fled the South Asian Island nation amidst protests over the worsening debt crisis. Former Japanese PM Shinzo Abe died after being shot, causing shock and condemnation globally. North Korea and the United States prepared for their first large-scale joint military exercises in four years.

WAR IN UKRAINE

Russia's foreign minister, Sergei Lavrov, revealed that Moscow's objectives for its invasion of Ukraine have broadened significantly, indicating a desire to annex regions currently under its control. Initially claiming the goal was to "liberate" the eastern Donbas border region during the war's outset in February, Lavrov now admits that Russia's ambitions extend further to include the provinces of Kherson and Zaporizhzhia in southern Ukraine, which are mostly occupied by Russian forces. The Donbas region, on the other hand, is under the control of two Moscow-backed separatist groups in Donetsk and Luhansk. At the war's onset, Russian President Vladimir Putin denied any aspirations to take more of Ukraine, despite a failed assault on Kyiv during the initial weeks of the invasion. However, Lavrov's recent statement suggests a shift in the scope of Russia's military objectives.

Meanwhile, the **International Monetary Fund** (IMF) has downgraded its global growth forecasts and raised projections for inflation, citing overwhelming risks to the economic outlook. The world continues to grapple with the fallout from Russia's invasion of Ukraine, enduring disruptions caused by the ongoing coronavirus pandemic, and facing tightening financial conditions. Central banks are actively trying to contain soaring prices. According to the IMF's revised estimates, global economic growth is expected to slow to 3.2 per cent in 2022, approximately half the pace of last year's expansion. In 2023, further weakening is anticipated, with global growth projected to reach 2.9 per cent. The IMF describes the economic outlook as notably gloomier and characterized by "extraordinary uncertainty," marked by historic inflation peaks and growing challenges to economic growth.

Ukraine's debt restructuring has brought to light the lack of urgency from Kyiv's military supporters in providing the necessary funds to cover a monthly budget shortfall of $5 billion. Despite calls for assistance to fill the gap, allies have largely shown little response, prompting Kyiv to secure preliminary agreements with bondholders and certain western governments. These agreements, if finalized, would postpone debt repayments for two years starting from August 1, freeing up approximately $6 billion. In addition, there has been a 25 per cent devaluation of the hryvnia, which helps alleviate immediate pressure on Ukraine to meet its obligations to foreign creditors. The devaluation was aimed at slowing the rapid depletion of Ukraine's foreign currency reserves caused by citizens who have fled abroad using hryvnia bank cards to withdraw $1.5 billion per month at an artificially cheap rate. However, economists caution that Ukraine still faces significant financial strain, especially with the war necessitating a sharp increase in monthly military spending, rising from $250 million in February to $3.3 billion in May. As a result, the government has already imposed severe spending cuts on essential services to meet its military expenses, and further drastic measures may be required.

In an effort to prevent a **global food crisis**, Kyiv and Moscow have reached an agreement that effectively establishes a ceasefire for cargo ships collecting millions of tonnes of stranded grain from Ukrainian ports. The signing ceremony in Istanbul was praised by UN Secretary-General António Guterres as a "beacon of hope on the Black Sea." The deal aims to stabilize global food prices and bring relief to developing countries on the brink of bankruptcy and vulnerable populations on the verge of famine. Turkey's President Recep Tayyip Erdogan played a central role in negotiating the agreement, and Turkey's military will help monitor Ukrainian ports as part of the deal. While the agreement is seen as a positive step, ongoing fighting in Ukraine and deep mistrust between the two sides may pose significant challenges in upholding the deal. The accord ensures that Ukraine and Russia agree not to attack merchant vessels, civilian vessels, or port facilities covered by the agreement, effectively creating a "de facto ceasefire."

ENERGY

Russia is planning to significantly reduce gas supplies through its largest pipeline to **Germany**, which poses a risk of leaving the continent with insufficient critical supplies as the winter approaches. Gazprom, the state-owned energy group, announced its intention to cut existing flows on the Nord Stream 1 pipeline by half, limiting it to just 20 per cent of its capacity. Last month, the capacity was already reduced to 40 per cent. This move by Russia has been criticized by European politicians who view it as the "weaponization" of gas supplies.

German business confidence has recently hit its lowest level in over two years, indicating that Europe's largest economy is on the verge of a recession. In response to the potential winter electricity crunch caused by Russia's gas supply cuts, Germany is reconsidering its plan to phase out nuclear power by the end of the year. This shift in energy policy would be a significant departure, especially for the Greens, a key component of Chancellor Olaf Scholz's coalition government and historically associated with the country's anti-nuclear movement. Before making a decision on nuclear power, Germany is conducting a stress test to assess the electricity supply's resilience under challenging conditions. The test is expected to highlight potential issues with Bavaria's winter electricity supply, as the state heavily relies on gas and nuclear energy due to a relatively low amount of wind and solar energy despite being a major industrial center.

In response to Russia's actions, **European gas prices** have surged by 30 per cent in just two days. In an effort to mitigate the impact, EU ministers have agreed on a somewhat diluted plan to reduce gas consumption by 15 per cent during the winter. However, certain member states that are less dependent on Russian gas have been granted exemptions. The soaring gas prices underscore the mounting pressure on Europe to seek alternative energy supplies to ensure warmth for homes and maintain industrial operations throughout the upcoming winter.

The **French** government is set to invest €9.7 billion in fully nationalizing EDF, a move aimed at strengthening the nuclear specialist's finances amid an ongoing energy crisis. Currently holding an 84 per cent stake in the company, the government plans to launch a tender offer to acquire the remaining shares and convertible bonds after the summer. The buyout is seen as a means to provide financial support to EDF as it embarks on a significant project to construct six new nuclear reactors in France in the coming years, the largest order in over two decades. Following the announcement of the buyout, trading of EDF shares was temporarily suspended, but they subsequently surged by nearly 15 per cent, reaching a level close to the offer price. Additionally, the government aims to expedite decision-making at EDF, as the company is crucial to France's long-term strategy of reducing carbon emissions, which includes increased investment in nuclear energy.

In the energy sector, **OPEC** (the Organization of the Petroleum Exporting Countries) anticipates global oil demand to rise significantly next year, reaching levels that could strain the cartel's capacity to meet it. The "call on OPEC crude," which refers to the amount of oil the group must produce to satisfy global demand, is projected to reach as high as 32 million barrels per day by the end of the following year. This estimate is close to or even exceeds most assessments of the group's maximum production capacity, raising concerns about a potential global supply deficit in 2023 if oil demand grows as projected by OPEC.

EUROPE

Europe has experienced a chaotic summer travel season with millions of passengers facing flight cancellations and disruptions. The root of the problem lies in chronic staff shortages across various parts of the aviation industry, including airlines, airports, and ground-handling companies responsible for services like check-in and baggage handling. With the lifting of coronavirus travel restrictions, there has been a surge in demand for travel, outpacing the industry's ability to hire new staff. Industrial action, such as the pilot strike at Scandinavian airline SAS leading to bankruptcy, has compounded the issues. Europe has become the epicenter of travel disruptions this summer, with long wait times at airports becoming all too common.

Hungary's foreign minister, Peter Szijjártó, has traveled to Moscow to request additional gas supplies from Russia, a rare visit by a high-level EU official since Russia's invasion of Ukraine. Despite criticism from Western partners, Szijjártó argues that Hungary cannot quickly decouple from Russian energy resources without damaging its economy. Hungary has maintained a neutral stance on the Ukraine conflict, unlike other central European countries supporting Kyiv, and it urges pragmatic relations with Moscow.

Mario Draghi has resigned as **Italy's** prime minister, leading to the dissolution of parliament and triggering snap elections in September. His resignation came after three major parties in parliament boycotted a confidence vote, leaving President Sergio Mattarella with no choice but to dissolve the parliament earlier than scheduled. The move raises concerns about Italy's ability to meet deadlines for accessing EU coronavirus recovery funds, adding to the economic challenges faced by Italy and Europe. The sell-off in Italian debt has intensified following Draghi's resignation, with the yield on the country's 10-year government bond jumping significantly, reflecting the uncertainty ahead.

Lawmakers in **North Macedonia** have approved a proposal aimed at resolving a longstanding dispute with Bulgaria over history and language. This move opens the way for accession talks with the EU and represents a significant step in the EU's expansion in the Western Balkans. As the war in Ukraine has heightened the urgency to complete enlargement and counter increasing Russian influence, the EU has been encouraging the region's countries to set aside historical disputes. North Macedonia's government accepted the French proposals with amendments that ensure Macedonian will be recognized as an official language in the EU and that bilateral issues with Bulgaria will no longer hinder the accession talks. Despite opposition from the walkout by the opposition, the proposal was passed in the country's 120-member parliament with 68 votes. This approval also has implications for Albania's EU membership bid, as progress on North Macedonia's accession plan would unlock Tirana's bid, potentially leading to further expansion in the Western Balkans.

Amid an escalating row over the expulsion of numerous Russian diplomats on espionage concerns, Moscow's ambassador to **Bulgaria** has threatened to sever diplomatic relations by closing its embassy in Sofia. Bulgaria, a member of NATO and the EU, has historically had closer ties with Moscow than other EU allies. However, the country recently announced the expulsion of 70 Russian diplomats, the largest number expelled from any European nation since the invasion of Ukraine. The government's hardline stance on Moscow in response to the Ukraine war has led to the expulsion of about two-thirds of the pre-war Russian diplomatic contingent since February. Russia's ambassador to Bulgaria, Eleonora Mitrofanova, strongly objected to these latest expulsions and called for the Bulgarian government to reverse its decision.

After a tumultuous three-year reign as **Britain's** prime minister, Boris Johnson signaled his departure from the role. He defended his record and blamed Conservative MPs for their decision to force him out of office, describing it as "eccentric." Although he resigned as the Conservative leader, he stated that he would remain as prime minister until his successor is chosen, which is expected to be in September. Potential contenders to succeed Johnson as Tory leader include former chancellor Rishi Sunak, foreign secretary Liz Truss, and defense secretary Ben Wallace. Johnson's term in office was marked by significant events such as Britain's exit from the EU, the Covid-19 pandemic, Russia's invasion of Ukraine, and a cost-of-living crisis. His tenure also included the Conservatives' substantial victory in the 2019 general election, the party's largest in over four decades. However, Johnson faced criticism for his handling of the partygate scandal and his association with former deputy chief whip Chris Pincher, who has since faced disgrace.

MIDDLE EAST & NORTH AFRICA

In a referendum in **Tunisia**, voters have approved a controversial new constitution, despite critics' concerns that the changes undermine the democratic progress initiated after the country's uprising against authoritarian rule in 2011. The new charter grants the populist elected president, Kais Saied, significant powers and was supported by 94.6 per cent of voters, according to the electoral commission. However, the overall voter turnout was low, with less than a third of registered voters casting their ballots, amounting to only 30.5 per cent. Analysts point out that the new constitution weakens checks and balances in the political system, and notably, it states that the president "cannot be questioned" about his actions while performing his duties. The president gains substantial authority over the judiciary and government, including the ability to dissolve parliament and issue laws by decree in its absence. Moreover, the president can extend his term beyond the two terms allowed by the constitution if he perceives the country to be in danger.

Saudi Crown Prince Mohammed bin Salman has engaged in talks with Greek leaders during his first trip to EU states since the murder of journalist Jamal Khashoggi in 2018. This indicates Western leaders' efforts to strengthen ties with the world's leading oil exporter, despite concerns over human rights. During his visit to Athens, Prince Mohammed met with Prime Minister Kyriakos Mitsotakis, and both sides revealed an agreement for a fiber optic and data cable connecting Europe to Asia through Saudi Arabia. Prince Mohammed emphasized the significance of their talks, stating that the visit would bring about significant changes for both countries and the region. Additionally, bilateral agreements on energy, technology, health, and crime-fighting were signed during the visit. The crown prince's trip to Europe underscores the deepening engagement of Western states with him, especially as Russia's invasion of Ukraine has driven oil prices to their highest levels in over a decade.

Saudi Arabia is set to open its airspace to all flights to and from Israel, marking a foreign policy win for US President Joe Biden. Biden, who is hoping to reset US relations with Saudi Arabia during his upcoming trip amid turmoil in the global oil market, praised the Saudi announcement as a "historic decision" and credited his administration for brokering the deal. This move comes after Donald Trump's efforts to broker peace accords between Israel and four Arab countries in the 2020 Abraham Accords, in which Saudi Arabia initially did not participate. However, the kingdom had already allowed some flights to Israel to use its airspace. With this decision, all airlines will have access to Saudi airspace, significantly reducing travel times between Israel and Asia. The announcement followed US-brokered negotiations between Saudi Arabia and

Israel over security arrangements in two Red Sea islands that Egypt had transferred to Saudi Arabia in 2017.

During Biden's first visit to the Middle East as president, he and Israeli Prime Minister Yair Lapid pledged to work together to prevent Iran from obtaining a nuclear weapon. However, they remain divided on how to achieve this goal. The strategic declaration made during the visit commits the US to prevent Iran from acquiring nuclear weapons and collaborate with partners to counter Iran's aggressive and destabilizing activities. While both sides agree on the aim, the method of achieving it remains unclear. Biden advocates for a return to the 2015 deal that addressed Iran's nuclear program and believes diplomacy can be coupled with pressure on Iran to cease using proxy forces in the region.

The US State Department stated that unintentional Israeli gunfire was likely responsible for the death of a prominent **Palestinian**-American journalist, Shireen Abu Akleh, who was killed while covering an Israeli military raid in the occupied West Bank. Both Palestinian officials and Al Jazeera, for whom she worked, blamed Israeli soldiers for her death. However, Israeli officials rejected the notion of intentional targeting and suggested she may have been hit by either Palestinian or Israeli fire during the shootout. The US Security Coordinator, after reviewing Israeli and Palestinian investigations into the shooting, concluded that gunfire from Israeli Defense Forces (IDF) positions was likely responsible for her death.

Amid rising concerns, **Turkish** inflation has reached nearly 80 per cent, raising warnings that the country may be caught in a spiral of escalating prices and wages. Consumer prices rose 78.6 per cent year on year in June, with President Recep Tayyip Erdogan's unconventional monetary policy and the disruption caused by the war in Ukraine on food and energy imports taking a heavy toll. This marks the largest annual increase since 1998, though slightly below analysts' consensus forecast of 80 per cent. Erdogan, who opposes the widely accepted view that raising interest rates curbs inflation, has ordered the central bank to maintain its benchmark borrowing rate far below the level of inflation. Consequently, the Turkish lira has lost 48 per cent of its value against the dollar in the past 12 months, leading to soaring prices in a country heavily reliant on imports, particularly energy. The situation has been further exacerbated by a surge in energy and commodity prices following Russian President Vladimir Putin's invasion of Ukraine.

AFRICA

Zambia's official creditors, led by China, have agreed to grant debt relief to the country, paving the way for an IMF bailout and setting an example of how Beijing can collaborate with other lenders to address the risk of widespread defaults across emerging markets. A committee of creditors co-chaired by China and France stated their commitment to negotiate restructuring terms with Zambia under a G20 framework for coordinating debt relief. This development was welcomed by the IMF's managing director, Kristalina Georgieva, as it will unlock a $1.3 billion IMF loan to support Zambia's financial recovery. However, Zambia still needs to negotiate the exact terms of the relief and reach a similar agreement with private creditors.

Russian Foreign Minister Sergei Lavrov recently visited Egypt, the Republic of Congo, Uganda, and Ethiopia during a time when African countries are grappling with soaring food and fertilizer prices. Despite attempts by the West to isolate Moscow due to the conflict, Lavrov's warm reception in Africa showcased the Kremlin's considerable influence on the continent. This influence was evident when 17 African countries abstained from a UN General Assembly vote to condemn the invasion of Ukraine, with eight others absent and only one voting against. In recent years, Moscow has established a thriving arms and security business in various countries and deployed mercenaries to regions like the Sahel, as well as mining groups to nations such as Sudan and the Central African Republic.

In response to the worst-ever rolling blackouts in Africa's most industrialized economy, the **South African** government has collaborated with the private sector in an emergency plan. They have removed controls on companies generating their own power outside the monopolistic Eskom to address the crisis. President Cyril Ramaphosa emphasized the need for a wave of new private generation to rescue the country's grid from recent intense power cuts that have severely impacted the economy and citizens' lives.

Frequent breakdowns and illegal strikes at Eskom's aging coal stations have caused prolonged power outages, adding pressure on the ruling African National Congress. South Africa also plans to double its procurement of renewable energy this year to over 5,000 megawatts and incentivize those with rooftop solar panels to sell power to Eskom in an effort to alleviate the problem of load-shedding.

ASIA

China has escalated its campaign of threats and military maneuvers in an attempt to dissuade Nancy Pelosi from visiting Taiwan. This potential visit would mark the first time a US House of Representatives Speaker has visited the island in 25 years. Beijing has publicly warned of "forceful countermeasures" and has increased naval and air force activities in the region. Chinese officials have even suggested the possibility of a military response. The situation has raised concerns among analysts, who believe that Beijing and Washington may be heading into a new crisis over Taiwan. The long-standing conflict over Taiwan has been frozen since China's Nationalist government fled to the island in 1949, and now the US is closely assessing whether the friction could lead to a dangerous escalation and potential war with Beijing.

North Korean leader Kim Jong Un has accused the US and South Korea of bringing the Korean peninsula to the "brink of war" as they prepare for their first large-scale joint military exercises in four years. In a speech marking the anniversary of the end of the Korean War in 1953, Kim threatened to use nuclear weapons to "wipe out" South Korean forces in the event of a confrontation. North Korean state media reported that their armed forces are fully prepared to respond to any crisis, and their nuclear war deterrent is ready to mobilize its absolute power according to its mission. The joint military exercises between the US and South Korea, set to take place next month, will include aircraft carrier strike drills and amphibious landing training. These exercises come after previous years of scaled-down and computer-simulated training following a summit between Kim and then-US President Donald Trump.

Japan has raised concerns over increased military cooperation between Russia and China in a defense white paper. The paper warned that an isolated Moscow could draw closer to Beijing in the aftermath of the conflict in Ukraine. The Japanese defense ministry is seeking additional funding to address the threats posed by China, Russia, and North Korea. The white paper highlighted the importance of monitoring the activities of Russian armed forces and expressed alarm over joint nuclear bomber exercises conducted by China and Russia over the Sea of Japan since 2019. In May, Japan was particularly concerned when strategic bombers from both countries carried out an exercise during a Quad summit attended by US President Joe Biden in Tokyo. The white paper release coincides with the government's preparation for a review of the country's national security strategy.

Bangladesh has approached the IMF for a multibillion-dollar loan, becoming the latest South Asian country seeking international financial assistance due to rising global food and fuel prices straining emerging economies. The IMF confirmed that negotiations for a program, under the "Resilience and Sustainability" facility to help countries adapt to climate change, are underway. While local media in Bangladesh reported the government's request as $4.5 billion, the IMF did not comment on the package size, stating that it will be part of the program design discussions. Nearby countries like Sri Lanka and Pakistan have also sought assistance due to inflation, dwindling foreign reserves, and political upheaval.

Pakistan's currency faced its worst week in over two decades, with the Pakistani rupee declining by 7.6% to the dollar, raising concerns that the country might follow Sri Lanka into defaulting on foreign repayments. The recent $1.2 billion loan disbursement from the IMF may not be sufficient to avert a balance of payments crisis, leading to worries among investors about the country's economic stability. Pakistan's bonds have been among the worst performers in emerging markets this year.

In **Pakistan**, Imran Khan's party won 15 out of 20 seats in Punjab's by-elections, indicating a significant victory that puts him on track to force early parliamentary polls just months after being ousted from office. Khan's Pakistan Tehreek-i-Insaf party garnered support from voters who expressed frustration over soaring living costs.

The result is significant since Punjab is considered the political stronghold of the Sharif family, former Prime Minister Nawaz Sharif, and his brother Shehbaz Sharif. Khan's victory occurred shortly after he lost a vote of no confidence, which he alleged was a foreign-orchestrated coup.

India elected Droupadi Murmu, a tribal woman, as its president, making her the first from a historically marginalized population to hold the position. As a member of the Santhal tribe, Murmu's election marks an important milestone for indigenous groups that have faced discrimination in India. India's presidency holds some vital powers, including the right to appoint the prime minister in case of a hung parliament.

Japan's Bharatiya Janata Party (BJP) regained control of Maharashtra, the country's richest state, by forming a partnership with rebel lawmakers who brought down the state government. Maharashtra is a crucial political prize for the BJP as it consolidates power ahead of the 2024 general election. After weeks of political drama, the BJP agreed to form a new administration with nearly 40 breakaway legislators from the regional Hindu nationalist Shiv Sena party, with whom they are now joint partners in the government.

Sri Lankan parliamentarians elected Ranil Wickremesinghe as the country's president, risking further protests that could complicate urgent bailout talks with the IMF. Wickremesinghe won with 134 votes in the 225-seat parliament. Sri Lanka has been facing demonstrations due to soaring prices and fuel shortages, which led to the ouster of former president Gotabaya Rajapaksa. The country has substantial overseas debt, with the largest share owed to private bondholders, multilateral lenders, and other countries.

The killing of former **Japanese** prime minister Shinzo Abe sparked global condemnation. Abe, who was Japan's longest-serving prime minister, was shot and killed in Nara. World leaders, including US President Joe Biden and Secretary of State Antony Blinken, expressed shock and sadness at his assassination. Abe was known for his role in forming the "Quad" group, a partnership aimed at countering China's assertiveness in the region, consisting of Australia, India, Japan, and the US.

THE AMERICAS

In **Brazil**, prominent executives, public figures, and artists have launched a campaign in support of democracy amid increasing attacks by far-right President Jair Bolsonaro on the country's electronic voting system ahead of the October elections. The campaign represents the first unified response from Brazilian civil society to Bolsonaro's divisive rhetoric, including his claims of potential election fraud with the electronic ballots that contributed to his election in 2018. Critics accuse Bolsonaro of attempting to pave the way for contesting the election results. Opinion polls show Bolsonaro trailing his main rival, former left-wing leader Luiz Inácio Lula da Silva, by 10 to 15 percentage points, although the gap is expected to narrow in the coming months.

El Salvador has announced plans to repurchase $1.6 billion of its sovereign bonds to alleviate concerns of default in the country. This move comes after El Salvador adopted bitcoin as legal tender last year. President Nayib Bukele tweeted about sending two bills to the national assembly to secure funds for a transparent and voluntary purchase offer to bondholders. The buyback will be executed at market prices and is expected to begin in approximately six weeks. The government will finance the repurchase using special drawing rights from the IMF and a $200 million loan from the Central American Bank for Economic Integration.

SOURCES:

https://www.ft.com/content/84c4beae-fbd6-4d1e-aeb5-5d147b9621a4

https://www.ft.com/content/67ce86b5-163d-4204-a973-ab1528af473c

https://www.ft.com/content/126de7b0-cf7a-4703-9429-6c63cb162b02

https://www.ft.com/content/b193dc11-5069-41f5-ba86-2a83ea78f911

https://www.ft.com/content/cc422ece-92b3-41fa-a05c-900270bfe824

https://www.ft.com/content/cc422ece-92b3-41fa-a05c-900270bfe824

https://www.theguardian.com/business/2022/jul/19/france-to-pay-nearly-10bn-to-fully-nationalise-edf

https://www.ft.com/content/f29ef92d-7a3b-4599-bdb4-a3c35ebe2696

https://www.euronews.com/travel/2023/02/24/travel-chaos-will-flight-delays-and-cancellations-return-this-summer

https://www.ft.com/content/bc68bae2-dbac-4e0c-a424-531258c094e6

https://www.telegraph.co.uk/world-news/2022/07/26/saudi-crown-prince-visits-europe-first-time-since-jamal-khashoggis/

https://www.ft.com/content/f38b44d5-d18e-4fe5-b521-10cdf36a3653

https://www.scmp.com/news/china/diplomacy/article/3225251/zambia-has-struck-debt-deal-china-and-other-major-creditors-how-will-it-work

https://www.ft.com/content/20f4ee66-8a1a-406a-85ff-9d755fdc9c9b

https://www.state.gov/on-the-killing-of-shireen-abu-akleh/

https://www.ft.com/content/44ca7e19-b34e-46d6-9d5a-28bc03bad8ad

https://www.ft.com/content/1c3ec6d1-4391-41e7-b37f-f191c8d8e683

https://www.ft.com/content/31f9fbd5-996a-4c24-8c5d-3fcf824c0d93

https://www.ft.com/content/4061b75f-66c0-4a51-9a26-c9fd539c6624

https://www.ft.com/content/b34ccc3d-4f2d-4cff-9762-a651ea001022

https://www.ft.com/content/c37d9dd8-ca47-4d20-b83e-83daa6786b4d

https://www.aljazeera.com/news/2022/8/11/brazilians-protest-for-democracy-as-bolsonaro-threatens-election

https://www.theguardian.com/world/2022/jul/08/shinzo-abe-japans-former-prime-minister-dies-after-being-shot

https://www.ft.com/content/23d39cec-188e-4ec1-ae01-dd599a77b835

THE WORLD IN AUGUST 2022

August 2022 was a month during which the world continued to grapple with the consequences of Russia's war in Ukraine. Ukrainian armed forces prepared to retake the Russian-occupied city of Kherson, as the US pledged an addition $1bn of military aid to Ukraine. A team from the IAEA headed to Ukraine to inspect the Zaporizhzhia nuclear power plant amidst fears of an accident at the Russian-occupied site. EU nations pledged to cut gas usage by 15 percent due to fear of Russia cutting off supplies over the winter. Finland and Sweden's application for Nato membership came closer to ratification. In Asia, the economic crisis continued in Sri Lanka, as flooding devastated Pakistan, killing over 1000 people. Chinese Premier XI Jinping looked set to be voted in for a third term, as the Chinese government strongly opposed a visit to Taiwan by US House speaker Nancy Pelosi. Iran and the US continued efforts to revive the 2015 nuclear deal. Political unrest in Iraq resulted in the deaths of over 30 people in Baghdad. The UAE and Iran restored diplomatic ties, as did Turkey and Israel. In the US, the House of Representatives has approved Biden's $700bn climate, health and tax bill, a monumental legislative win for the US president ahead of this year's primaries. In Africa, Kenya held a presidential election. Fighting erupted in northern Ethiopia, ending a months-long ceasefire.

RUSSIA AND UKRAINE

As the Russian-led invasion reached its sixth month in **Ukraine**, Kyiv's armed forces continued their offensive to reclaim the city of Kherson. Persistent partisan resistance in Kherson has forced Moscow to repeatedly postpone plans to annex the region through a referendum. The military objective of the assault is to recapture territory seized by Moscow during the initial weeks of Vladimir Putin's invasion, with troops sweeping in from the Crimean Peninsula to the south. Kherson, situated on the delta where the Dnipro River flows into the Black Sea, holds strategic importance for Russia as a "land bridge" to Crimea, annexed from Ukraine in 2014.

A team from the International Atomic Energy Agency (IAEA), the UN's nuclear watchdog, will head to Ukraine to inspect the **Zaporizhzhia nuclear power plant**. The plant has been a key battleground in the conflict, facing repeated attacks and raising concerns about potential catastrophic accidents. Captured by Russian troops in March, the plant is still operated by Ukrainian staff. The IAEA mission aims to assess damage, evaluate safety and security systems, examine the conditions of the plant's staff, and carry out urgent safeguard activities.

To bolster Ukraine's defense efforts, the **US** will send $1 billion in additional military aid, representing the largest equipment drawdown since the war's inception. The package includes ammunition for high mobility artillery rocket systems (Himars), tens of thousands of rounds of artillery and mortar ammunition, anti-armour systems, and armoured medical treatment vehicles. Under President Joe Biden's administration, the US has now provided approximately $9.8 billion in security aid to Ukraine. As Kyiv prepares for a fresh southern offensive to retake Kherson and challenge Russia's control of the Dnipro River, both sides continue to engage in a war of attrition, characterized by bloody artillery duels in the south and the far eastern Donbas region.

The **Russian FSB** security service has accused Ukraine of being responsible for a car bombing that killed the daughter of a prominent supporter of President Vladimir Putin. A Ukrainian woman, Natalya Vovk, was accused of planting the car bomb before fleeing to Estonia. The attack has led to calls for reprisals against Ukraine from Alexander Dugin, a far-right ideologue, and other prominent nationalists. However, Ukraine denies any involvement in the incident.

Mikhail Gorbachev, the last leader of the Soviet Union, passed away at the age of 91 after a "serious and long-term illness" at Moscow's central clinical hospital. His burial took place at Novodevichy cemetery in Moscow alongside his late wife Raisa. Gorbachev's death received a mixed global reaction, with international praise for his role in ending Soviet authoritarianism and facilitating peaceful reunification in Europe. However, he was reviled in his homeland for presiding over the bloc's acrimonious collapse in 1991. Current Russian President Vladimir Putin issued a brief statement expressing "deepest condolences," but did not mention Gorbachev's historical role. Reaction in Russian state media was relatively muted compared to responses from Western leaders.

During a review conference at the UN headquarters in August 2022, Russia blocked the adoption of a joint declaration on the **Nuclear Non-Proliferation Treaty** (NPT). The draft text expressed "grave concern" over military activities around Ukrainian power plants, including Zaporizhzhia, and Ukraine's loss of control over such sites, posing safety risks. The conference also discussed other contentious issues such as Iran's nuclear program and North Korean nuclear tests, but no agreement on substantive matters was reached, mirroring the 2015 review conference.

EUROPE

European energy ministers have reached a unanimous EU-wide plan to reduce gas consumption in the event of a complete shut-off of Russian supplies. The deal commits the 27 EU nations to cut 45bn cubic meters of gas use between August 1, 2022, and March 31, 2023, equal to a 15% decrease from the bloc's average consumption over the previous five years. Hungary, the only dissenting vote, requested more gas deliveries from Russia. However, European Commission officials warned that opt-outs negotiated in the final compromise, accounting for national energy mixes, could risk falling short of the 15% target. Island states like Malta, Cyprus, and Ireland, with no direct connection to the European grid, and countries connected to Russia's electricity systems, will benefit from full exemptions from the target.

The EU has brokered an agreement between **Serbia** and **Kosovo** to ease travel restrictions between the two nations, reducing tensions in the western Balkans. This marks limited symbolic progress in the decades-long dispute over Kosovo's statehood and the coexistence of ethnic Albanians and Serbs, which led to sporadic violent protests along the border. Kosovo, formerly a Yugoslav province, declared independence in 2008, with over 100 nations recognizing it, but Serbia and several EU countries, including Spain, Greece, and Romania, have refused to accept it.

Finland will host talks involving Sweden and Turkey, marking the first three-way meeting on the Nordic countries' Nato membership bids. Sweden has experienced a shift in tone, deporting individuals wanted by Turkey and facing demands for extradition in exchange for support. Finland and Sweden have sought quick accession processes in Nato due to Russia's invasion of Ukraine, but Turkey has threatened to withhold approval unless extradition demands are met.

The US Senate has ratified **Finland** and **Sweden's** accession to Nato, a significant step bringing the Nordic countries into the military alliance amid the ongoing conflict between Russia and Ukraine. All 30 Nato members must approve a country's inclusion, and this vote, receiving bipartisan support, is a crucial milestone for Finland and Sweden, formerly neutral powers who adapted their stance in response to Russian aggression.

The prime ministers of **Estonia** and **Finland** have called on the EU to stop issuing tourist visas to Russians as a new sanctions measure following Russia's invasion of Ukraine. Both countries share borders with western Russia and have observed an increase in Russian tourists entering through other EU countries and using their airports to travel further in the bloc via the Schengen free travel area. The matter will be formally discussed at the next EU summit, with some member states considering restrictions on Russian travelers while keeping borders open within Schengen.

A Home Office study reveals a collapse in EU citizens migrating to the **UK** for work since Britain's departure from the bloc, while the number of non-EU citizens gaining work visas has surged. In the year to June 2022, a record 1.1 million visas were granted, with 331,233 for work-related purposes, up 72% since 2019. India, Nigeria, and the Philippines accounted for the highest number of skilled migrants, and only 12% of skilled migrants arriving on new "worker" visas came from the European Economic Area and Switzerland. Before Brexit, EU nationals did not require work visas, with 71% of people migrating for work in 2015 coming from the bloc.

ASIA

Sri Lankan President Ranil Wickremesinghe has unveiled a budget aimed at securing an IMF support deal and guiding the bankrupt country out of a severe economic crisis. The budget includes tax hikes and bolstering social safety schemes. Wickremesinghe, who assumed office last month after his predecessor Gotabaya Rajapaksa fled amidst significant anti-government protests, presented his first budget outlining plans to increase value-added tax from 12% to 15%, enhance central bank independence, and reallocate government funds towards relief programs to address the country's debt and inflation. Sri Lanka defaulted in May 2022, becoming the first Asia-Pacific nation to do so in over two decades due to depleted foreign reserves unable to cover overseas debt totalling over $50 billion. The president seeks a multibillion-dollar IMF bailout to facilitate debt restructuring and foster a gradual recovery. Negotiations with the IMF team in Colombo are underway, and Wickremesinghe hopes for a preliminary agreement next month.

In **Pakistan**, more than 1,000 people have lost their lives, and over a million homes have suffered damage due to the worst flooding in a decade. Torrential rains and floods have wreaked havoc in three provinces—Sindh, Balochistan, and Khyber Pakhtunkhwa—out of the four provinces in the country. Sindh experienced nearly eight times the average rainfall for August, leading to the destruction of rice and cotton crops. The impact has affected more than 30 million people, approximately 15% of the population, forcing thousands to abandon their homes. South Asia has witnessed extreme weather events, including heatwaves followed by heavy rains that claimed thousands of lives in India, Bangladesh, and Afghanistan. The floods have exacerbated Pakistan's financial woes. In response to the disaster, the IMF approved a $1.1 billion bailout package, reviving a stalled assistance program. However, the introduction of austerity measures by Prime Minister Shehbaz Sharif's government, which includes a significant increase in domestic fuel prices, has sparked political tensions and proved unpopular among the 220 million population. The country is grappling with soaring inflation, with sensitive food and fuel prices rising 45% compared to the previous year.

Political tensions rise in **Pakistan** as terrorism charges are filed against former Prime Minister Imran Khan for comments made in a speech. Khan's loyalists vow to resist efforts to arrest him, and his lawyers plan to challenge the charges. The police accuse Khan of terrorizing officials, while the country's information minister accuses him of inciting violence and rebellion. The media regulator bans broadcasting Khan's speeches, and Khan claims his talks are blocked on YouTube. Khan was removed from office in April through a no-confidence vote, leading to a new coalition government led by Prime Minister Shehbaz Sharif's Pakistan Muslim League (N).

North Korea has declared a "victory" over Covid-19, three months after the regime acknowledged the virus outbreak in the country. North Korean leader Kim Jong Un referred to the official death toll of 74 people as a "miracle" and thanked health officials for following the regime's orders and validating its policies. Meanwhile, Covid-19 cases are increasing in China, which remains committed to its "zero-Covid" strategy.

In **Afghanistan**, the US carried out a drone strike that killed al-Qaeda leader Ayman al-Zawahiri, marking the first known counter-terrorism operation in the country since it fell to the Taliban last year. Zawahiri, who took over al-Qaeda after Osama bin Laden's death in 2011, was targeted in Kabul after intelligence revealed the location of his family's safe house. Zawahiri, a former leader of the Egyptian Islamic Jihad before its merger with al-Qaeda, was believed to be responsible for various terrorist attacks, including the USS Cole attack in Yemen and the September 11, 2001 attacks in the US.

Thailand's Prime Minister Prayuth Chan-ocha has been suspended from office as the country's highest court investigates whether he exceeded his eight-year term limit. In a surprising ruling, the constitutional court voted five to four to suspend the former general until a final decision is made, with Prayuth having 15 days to present his case for remaining in office. During the suspension, Prawit Wongsuwan, a close political ally of Prayuth, will serve as acting prime minister.

In **China**, the Communist Party is preparing for its most significant gathering of the decade in mid-October. The event will secure President Xi Jinping's leadership positions, potentially granting him an unprecedented third term in power. Xi, who has been in charge of China since 2012, is regarded as the nation's most influential leader since Mao Zedong. The 20th congress of the party will reappoint Xi as its leader and head of the Central Military Commission. His claim to unchallenged authority is further likely to be strengthened by his reappointment as state president at the annual session of China's parliament early next year.

China has imposed unspecified sanctions on Nancy Pelosi and her family following her visit to Taiwan, despite the US not officially recognizing Taiwan as an independent state. Pelosi's arrival in Taipei, the highest-ranking US official's visit in 25 years, sparked tensions between China and the US. China considers Taiwan its territory and opposes its independent engagements with foreign governments. The sanctions on Pelosi are largely symbolic in nature.

THE MIDDLE EAST

The US has warned that there are still "gaps" between the US and **Iran** regarding a draft agreement to salvage the 2015 nuclear accord. Although efforts to revive the deal have shown progress with EU-mediated indirect talks in Vienna this month, a "final draft" of the agreement was discussed, and the crisis was initially triggered by Trump's withdrawal from the deal in 2018 and subsequent sanctions on Iran. Biden's administration pledged to rejoin the deal and lift certain sanctions if Iran, which is enriching uranium close to weapons-grade levels, complies with the accord. However, despite 16 months of negotiations, both sides have yet to reach an agreement on crucial issues.

In Baghdad, **Iraq**, at least 30 people were killed during clashes between followers of a prominent Shia cleric and militia groups tied to his rivals, resulting in chaos in the capital. The unrest followed Moqtada al-Sadr's declaration of his withdrawal from politics, prompting his loyalists to take to the streets and breach the heavily fortified green zone, where government buildings, foreign embassies, and the parliament are located. Iraq has been facing a severe crisis since 2003, with Sadr's followers blockading parliament for over four weeks due to the government's prolonged deadlock. Despite winning the largest share of seats in the October 2021 elections, Sadr was unable to form a majority government as he refused to cooperate with his fellow Shia rivals, leading to increased discord between Shia groups that have ruled Iraq since 2003.

After a six-year hiatus, the **United Arab Emirates** (UAE) will restore full diplomatic relations with Iran, marking a significant rapprochement. The UAE has engaged in tentative diplomacy for three years, seeking to ease tensions following the US's withdrawal from the nuclear deal with Iran in 2018. The UAE, a crucial US ally, aimed to improve relations with Iran after incidents of commercial shipping attacks near its waters near the strategic Strait of Hormuz, and also attributed drone and missile attacks on Saudi Arabia's oil infrastructure in 2019 to Iran and its proxies. Both the UAE and Saudi Arabia have accused Iran of being a destabilizing force in the region, leading to their involvement in opposing sides of conflicts, particularly in Yemen. Recently, fellow Gulf state Kuwait reinstated its ambassador in Tehran, and Saudi Arabia has also engaged in talks with Iran in attempts to improve relations with the Islamic republic.

Turkey and **Israel** are set to restore diplomatic ties after a four-year hiatus, aiming to strengthen relations with neighboring countries in the volatile region. Tensions between the two nations have persisted for over a decade, largely due to President Erdogan's criticism of Israel's treatment of Palestinians. In 2018, both countries expelled each other's ambassadors following protests in Gaza, further straining relations. However, Erdogan has been working to mend ties across the Middle East, reconciling with Arab states and western allies, which has helped alleviate some of Turkey's economic challenges. Talks to restore ties with Israel began earlier this year when President Isaac Herzog visited Turkey, and the restoration of diplomatic relations is seen as a positive step towards stability in the region.

Israel and **Palestinian** Islamic Jihad have reached a ceasefire agreement, bringing hope for an end to the recent escalation in hostilities between Israel and Gaza militants. The ceasefire, brokered by Egypt, came after three days of intense fighting during which both sides exchanged fire. Though the conflict resulted in the deaths of 44 Palestinians, including children and women, no Israeli casualties were reported. Israel stated its intention to respond strongly if the ceasefire is violated, while Islamic Jihad also reserved the right to retaliate to any Israeli aggression. The recent clashes have been less severe than last year's 11-day war between Israel and Hamas, as Hamas, which governs Gaza, refrained from getting involved in the current conflict.

The deepening ties between **Turkish** President Erdogan and Russian President Putin have raised concerns among Western states, who fear that Turkey's cooperation with Russia could lead to punitive measures against the NATO member if it aids Russia in bypassing sanctions. Following a meeting in Sochi, Erdogan and Putin pledged to enhance cooperation on trade and energy, with Turkey agreeing to pay for Russian gas in roubles. They also discussed expanding banking ties and settlements in roubles and lira. Furthermore, there were discussions about Russia's Mir payment card system, which allows Russian tourists in Turkey to pay with cards when Visa and Mastercard operations in Russia are suspended. These developments have sparked worries among Western officials about potential efforts to circumvent sanctions.

During a literary event in the US, **author Salman Rushdie** was stabbed on stage, sustaining a wound to the neck. He was promptly airlifted to the hospital by helicopter. The incident has links to Rushdie's controversial book, "The Satanic Verses," published in 1988, which depicted the Islamic Prophet Mohammed in a way that sparked immense controversy. As a result, the book was banned in Iran, and Ayatollah Ruhollah Khomeini issued a fatwa in 1989, calling for Rushdie's death.

In **Saudi Arabia**, a women's rights activist named Nourah bint Saeed al-Qahtani has been given the harshest sentence ever by the country, resulting in 45 years of imprisonment. Her conviction in the Specialised Criminal Court was based on charges related to her activities on social media, including "tearing the social fabric" and "violating public order." The specifics of the accusations are not widely known, but this comes shortly after another activist, Salma al-Shehab, received a 34-year prison sentence, believed to be the kingdom's severest such penalty.

Saudi Aramco, the Saudi Arabian oil company, has broken its previous quarterly profit record, benefiting from surging energy prices driven by Russia's invasion of Ukraine. In the second quarter, net income soared to $48.4 billion, marking a 90 percent year-on-year increase, and the company's highest earnings since its listing in 2019. Despite increased demand and limited spare capacity, Saudi Aramco kept its dividend steady for the third quarter. It aims to expand oil and gas production, with a target of reaching 12.3 million barrels per day by 2025. Western nations have urged Saudi Arabia, the de facto leader of OPEC, to increase production, but the kingdom will do so only if demand rises.

A tragic incident in Cairo, **Egypt**, saw 41 people losing their lives in a fire at a Coptic Orthodox church. Human rights advocates and public figures are calling on the Egyptian government to reform laws that are perceived as discriminatory and restrict the building of churches in the country, which may have contributed to the fire. In 2016, a new law was introduced to govern church construction, shifting decision-making to local governors. However, the law imposes stringent requirements for churches to qualify for permits and lacks an appeals process in cases of permit rejections.

THE AMERICAS

The $700bn climate, health, and tax bill, which has been championed by **US** President Joe Biden and congressional Democrats, has been approved by the House of Representatives, marking a significant legislative victory for the president and his party. Following its final passage in the US Senate, the lower chamber of Congress voted on the legislation. White House officials are celebrating the bill's passage through Congress as a major achievement for Biden, demonstrating his determination to push forward with an ambitious economic agenda despite challenges during the negotiations. They also expressed optimism that this victory could improve the president's low approval ratings leading up to the November midterm elections. Named the Inflation Reduction Act, the $700bn legislation includes substantial funding for clean energy incentives, allows the government to negotiate drug prices for seniors, and introduces tax measures such as a 15 per cent minimum tax rate and a 1 per cent excise tax on corporations. It also allocates additional funding to the Internal Revenue Service to bolster tax enforcement on the wealthy, a move that has drawn criticism from Republicans.

In **Colombia**, Gustavo Petro, a former urban guerrilla who faced imprisonment for his political beliefs in the 1980s, has been sworn in as the country's president, leading what is likely to be the most left-wing government in Colombia's history. The inauguration ceremony was filled with symbolism as Petro, 62, took the presidential oath in Bogotá's Plaza de Bolívar, an iconic location outside Congress and opposite the Palace of Justice. Petro's history is connected to a violent incident that occurred in 1985 when the urban guerrilla group he belonged to stormed the palace, resulting in approximately 100 deaths during the army's attempt to retake it. In his speech, Petro reiterated promises from his election campaign, emphasizing the need for a comprehensive overhaul to transform Colombia into a place of potential and life after decades of bloody conflict. Adding to the historical moment, Francia Márquez, Petro's running mate, was also sworn in as Colombia's first black vice-president. Born in poverty in the violence-ridden southwest region of the country, she is an environmental activist and a recipient of the prestigious Goldman Prize in 2018. The ceremony stood out from tradition as butterfly motifs in Colombia's national colors of yellow, blue, and red were projected on screens flanking the stage, and thousands of people were allowed into the square, breaking with previous government handover practices.

AFRICA

In **Kenya**, Deputy President William Ruto has been declared the winner of the presidential election, but the outcome is contested by his main rival's supporters and some election commissioners. Ruto secured 50.5 per cent of the vote, while former Prime Minister and veteran opposition leader Raila Odinga, who was endorsed by outgoing President Uhuru Kenyatta, received 48.8 per cent. The election, which was fiercely contested, is considered a significant event for Kenya's stability and is among the most important on the African continent this year.

Northern **Ethiopia** has seen a resurgence of fighting, ending a months-long ceasefire and shattering hopes for peace in a conflict that has already resulted in thousands of casualties and displaced millions of people. The escalation complicates plans for peace talks between Prime Minister Abiy Ahmed's government and the Tigray People's Liberation Front (TPLF), the party that controlled Tigray and ruled Ethiopia for three decades. Both sides deny initiating the hostilities, each blaming the other. The conflict, which began in November 2020, has tarnished the international support for Nobel Peace Prize laureate Abiy, who dispatched troops to crush the TPLF after they allegedly attacked a garrison in Tigray's capital, Mekelle. The civil war has also led to a loss of billions in donor support and duty-free access to the US for Ethiopia, one of the major economies in East Africa.

In Mogadishu, the capital of **Somalia**, nearly two dozen people were killed during a 30-hour assault by Islamist militants al-Shabaab on a hotel frequently visited by local politicians. The attackers used bombs and gunfire in the first major attack by the group this year. Somali forces eventually entered the hotel, rescuing 106 people. Al-Shabaab, a long-standing terror group aiming to overthrow the government, claimed responsibility for the attack. This incident marks the first significant offensive by al-Shabaab since former leader Hassan Sheikh Mohamud returned to the presidency in early June.

The **Democratic Republic of Congo** has criticized Rwanda after a report submitted to the UN Security Council presented "solid evidence" that Kigali's armed forces are supporting rebels in the mineral-rich country. The M23 group, predominantly composed of Congolese Tutsis, resurfaced late last year, initiating an offensive in eastern Congo, leading to deaths and mass displacements. Around 170,000 people have been displaced by the violence since November. The situation has incited local anger, resulting in deadly protests against UN peacekeepers operating in eastern Congo. Rwanda has consistently denied supporting the M23, instead accusing Kinshasa of backing the FDLR, a group with Hutus accused of the 1994 genocide against Tutsis in Rwanda. The M23 claims to protect Tutsis from militant Hutu groups like the FDLR. In the 1990s, Rwanda and Uganda invaded Congo, leading to devastating wars and producing various active militias, contributing to the ongoing conflict that has intensified in recent months.

SOURCES:

https://www.ft.com/content/0b13ad42-ec41-449a-aa90-3e1a46700639
https://www.ft.com/content/94a711ff-d4db-41b6-abd4-066c2c7cfe09
https://www.ft.com/content/da098a8d-8115-4cbd-924c-01184b32b990
https://www.ft.com/content/23690584-97de-4453-a0cb-1dbb7e34c3ae
https://www.theguardian.com/world/2022/aug/30/mikhail-gorbachev-dies-soviet-leader-92
https://www.aljazeera.com/news/2022/8/27/russia-blocks-final-draft-of-nuclear-disarmament-treaty-at-un
https://www.aljazeera.com/news/2022/8/27/russia-blocks-final-draft-of-nuclear-disarmament-treaty-at-un/
https://www.ft.com/content/8abdc56d-9b8e-417d-8e49-82684f9f8357
https://www.ft.com/content/60f877b4-fed9-49d7-bfb8-087e380601cb
https://www.ft.com/content/957b7696-9079-452a-809f-9c6fecc351dd

https://www.ft.com/content/a0b788d8-7dd6-4a61-a624-772e0516a41c

https://www.euronews.com/2022/08/09/finland-and-estonia-call-for-eu-ban-on-tourist-visas-for-russians

https://www.ft.com/content/4d5c3294-19cf-4bab-854b-7070f7612fb1

https://www.thetimes.co.uk/article/court-suspends-thai-pm-in-row-over-how-long-he-can-hold-office-rgkt0djv6

https://www.ft.com/content/9f62035b-65a9-48bb-b9b9-ab69cfe627e9

https://www.ft.com/content/9f62035b-65a9-48bb-b9b9-ab69cfe627e9

https://www.aljazeera.com/news/2022/8/5/china-sanctions-us-house-speaker-nancy-pelosi

https://www.ft.com/content/fd6c8a9f-ccce-4dae-8e04-5503decc31bc

https://www.ft.com/content/49dc0b76-b6f6-43b3-aa70-c4e7f39d6bcb

https://www.ft.com/content/236a5b61-1b61-403c-aa96-b439632f9dc8

https://www.ft.com/content/c4c8f9ce-fd5e-453d-b8d9-3db0c31d7189

https://www.eurasiantimes.com/3-key-reasons-why-turkey-is-keen-to-reset-its-ties-with-india/

https://www.ft.com/content/c4c8f9ce-fd5e-453d-b8d9-3db0c31d7189

https://www.ft.com/content/44aab156-b012-490b-92bd-0eb7f6ebdaf8

https://www.ft.com/content/00badf9e-f0d9-417f-9aec-9ac1c2207835

https://www.ft.com/content/604de885-8cb8-40d3-afca-16b71f741c31

https://www.thetimes.co.uk/article/nourah-bint-saeed-al-qahtani-saudi-feminist-jailed-for-45-years-over-social-media-posts-zg8dndhv9

https://www.aljazeera.com/news/2022/8/20/egypts-copts-want-changes-to-law-after-deadly-church-fire/

https://www.ft.com/content/3c6a0c9a-0e4c-4494-88f8-d4c44cd04aa8

https://www.ft.com/content/2045ffc9-fbbf-4c80-876e-d4dcd8c23baa

https://www.ft.com/content/b0f4bae7-962e-42ea-891d-e34d176690ef

https://www.ft.com/content/b0c6d5f7-b3f3-43ec-bcd0-a10d2780a26f

https://www.theguardian.com/world/2022/aug/15/william-ruto-declared-winner-of-kenya-presidential-election-amid-dispute

THE WORLD IN SEPTEMBER 2022

Introduction

September 2022 was a month during which the world continued to grapple with the far-reaching consequences of Russia's war in Ukraine. Debt-ridden countries, such as Zambia and Sri Lanka, sought help from the IMF to tackle their economic crises. Russia announced plans to annex four Ukrainian regions after Russian-led sham referendums took place. Putin announced plans to mobilise 300,000 Russian men, sparking protests across Russia. Europe continued to grapple with energy-supply problems, as Russia cut off gas supplies from the Nord Stream 1 pipeline to Germany. Britain's longest reigning monarch, Her Majesty, Queen Elizabeth II passed away aged 96. Her son, Charles III, succeeded her as King. Liz Truss was sworn in as the new British prime minister. The IMF stepped in to criticise the Truss's plan to implement £45bn of debt-funded tax cuts. Georgia Meloni became Italy's first female prime minister, leader of the most right-wing government since WWII. The death of the 22-year-old Mahsa Amini in police custody sparked protests across Iran and the world about the country's strict female dress code. Saudi Crown Prince MBS was appointed prime minister of the Kingdom by his father, King Salman. Fighting broke out over conflict between Armenia and Azerbaijan in Nagorno-Karabakh. The Shanghai Cooperation Organisation met in Uzbekistan, with Putin, Xi Jinping and Modi in attendance. The army seized power in Burkina Faso in the second military coup of the year.

GLOBAL ECONOMY

The **IMF** has reached a record high in its lending to economically troubled countries, acting as the lender of last resort amid multiple crises that have led at least five nations into default, with more likely to follow suit. The pandemic, Russia's actions in Ukraine, and a significant surge in global interest rates have prompted numerous countries to seek IMF assistance. Experts predict that further substantial interest rate increases by major central banks in the market will raise borrowing costs worldwide, posing a risk of triggering a severe recession. Currently, the IMF's total commitments, including loans agreed upon but not yet dispersed, have surpassed $268 billion. A recent report highlights that 55 of the world's poorest countries are facing a daunting challenge of repaying debts amounting to $436 billion between 2022 and 2028, with approximately $61 billion due this year and in 2023, followed by nearly $70 billion in 2024. Countries like Zambia and Sri Lanka, which defaulted during the pandemic along with Lebanon, Russia, and Suriname, are currently in negotiations with the IMF for bailouts as part of their debt restructuring efforts. Additionally, Ghana, Egypt, and Tunisia are in early discussions for seeking similar financial support. Notably, the IMF approved a $1.1 billion bailout for Pakistan at the end of August, while Argentina is set to receive $3.9 billion as part of its $41 billion program. The mounting financial challenges and debt restructuring efforts underscore the severity of the global economic situation, with the IMF playing a crucial role in providing crucial financial lifelines to countries grappling with various crises.

RUSSIA AND UKRAINE

Vladimir **Putin** has announced his plans to annex four regions in South-eastern Ukraine, despite Russia not having full control over these areas. This significant escalation of the conflict with Kyiv involves signing "treaties" with Russia-appointed occupation officials and delivering a "substantial speech" at the ceremony in the Kremlin. Russia's forces orchestrated highly stage-managed votes in parts of Ukraine's Donetsk, Luhansk, Kherson, and Zaporizhzhia regions under their control, claiming that locals overwhelmingly voted to join Russia with margins of up to 99 per cent. However, Ukraine and its western allies have dismissed these "sham referendums," which, in some cases, involved armed "brigades" taking ballot boxes to people's homes. President Volodymyr Zelenskyy of Ukraine has vowed a "tough" military response to Russia's annexation attempts and called on Russians, especially ethnic minorities in the Caucasus region and Siberia, who were protesting against forced mobilization, to resist Putin's actions.

Protests against Vladimir Putin's decision to mobilize the armed forces' reserves have spread across Russia, marking a significant display of public discontent since the invasion of Ukraine in February. In Dagestan, an impoverished, mostly Muslim region in the North Caucasus, locals blocked highways and clashed with police while chanting "No to war!" The unrest reflects widespread anger at Putin's call-up of hundreds of thousands of men into the Russian army, the country's first military mobilization since World War II. Arson attacks targeted army recruitment offices in 16 Russian regions in the days following the announcement, and over 2,240 people have been arrested for protesting against the mobilization decree. There have been reports of thousands of Russians attempting to flee the country amid unconfirmed rumors of potential border closures for draft-eligible men.

Both **Kazakhstan** and **Georgia** have declared their willingness to welcome Russians fleeing conscription, with queues of mainly young men gathering at their borders seeking refuge. Kazakhstan's President Tokayev emphasized the humanitarian aspect of keeping the country's doors open to Russian refugees, signaling disapproval of Moscow's invasion of Ukraine and its conscription laws. Kazakhstan has also stated its non-recognition of any possible annexation of occupied regions in Ukraine and has dispelled rumors about extraditing individuals to Russia if they receive call-up notices or are accused of evading conscription.

Vladimir Putin has expressed criticism towards a grain deal signed with **Ukraine**, which allowed agricultural products to be released from the country, easing a global food crisis. Despite his government's military assault on Ukraine, Putin blamed the terms of the deal brokered in July for the global grain shortages, especially impacting poorer nations, rather than acknowledging Russia's war against Ukraine, a significant grain exporter. He argued that the grain shipments from Ukraine's Black Sea ports, made possible by the deal, were not going to poorer countries but to Europe. However, all Black Sea grain shipments are documented by the UN, which mediated the deal, and its records show that over 2 million metric tons of grain have been transported from Ukrainian ports on 87 voyages since the deal's inception.

Russia's gas supplies to Europe through the **Nord Stream 1** pipeline will not fully resume until the "collective west" lifts sanctions imposed on Moscow due to its invasion of Ukraine. Russia attributed the lack of gas deliveries through the critical pipeline, which transports gas from St Petersburg to Germany via the Baltic Sea, to sanctions imposed by the EU, UK, and Canada. Although Russia continues to claim technical issues as the cause of gas supply cuts, this recent statement is a clear demand from the Kremlin, indicating that they want the EU to remove sanctions before resuming full gas deliveries. European leaders have dismissed Russia's claims of technical faults and accused Moscow of using energy exports as a weapon in response to western sanctions. Gazprom, Russia's state-run gas monopoly, stated that gas supplies through Nord Stream 1 were halted due to technical faults related to repairing German-made turbines in Canada. This announcement followed the G7 nations' efforts to introduce a price cap on Russian oil exports.

EUROPE

Her Majesty, **Queen Elizabeth II**, Britain's longest-reigning monarch, passed away aged 96, shocking Britain and the world. She served as monarch for over seventy years, celebrating her platinum jubilee earlier this year. She had represented continuity and stability for Britain from the post-war era into the 21st century, acting as a unifying figure at times of crisis. Her son, Prince Charles, succeeded her on the throne as King Charles III. More than a million people travelled to London for her state funeral, which drew in audiences of some four billion people globally. World leaders gathered in London for the funeral at Westminster Abbey, which was hailed as the biggest diplomatic event of the century and concluded the ten-day national mourning period.

Liz Truss emerged victorious in the race to become the **UK's** next prime minister after a hard-fought battle. Her priority is to finalize a two-year energy relief package costing up to £100bn for households and businesses. Truss secured her position by winning 81,326 votes from Conservative party members, defeating her rival Rishi Sunak's 60,399 votes in the seven-week contest to succeed Boris Johnson. After meeting the Queen at Balmoral, Truss returned to London to announce her cabinet and address the economic crisis. She is the 56th prime minister and the fourth Tory leader in just over six years. Additionally, she is the third female premier in Britain's history, following Margaret Thatcher and Theresa May. Truss aims to cap energy prices with a costly market intervention to prevent hardships for households and businesses as average household bills are set to rise from almost £2,000 to over £3,500 in October.

Amid market chaos in the **UK**, the Bank of England disclosed plans to purchase government bonds to safeguard the economy from Chancellor Kwasi Kwarteng's policies. These policies, which include borrowing and tax cuts, have led to fluctuations in sterling and increased costs for the government and mortgage holders. The IMF criticized the UK's £45bn debt-funded tax cut plan, urging the government to "re-evaluate" it, warning that the "untargeted" package could exacerbate soaring inflation, resulting in higher borrowing costs and slower growth.

Germany and the United Arab Emirates reached an agreement for the UAE to supply liquefied natural gas to Germany as part of Chancellor Olaf Scholz's regional tour to secure alternatives to Russian energy. The Abu Dhabi National Oil Company will supply German utility RWE with 137,000 cubic meters of LNG, marking the first delivery to the under-construction import terminal on the north-west coast at Brunsbüttel. With Russia's invasion of Ukraine, Germany has been actively seeking energy imports from non-Russian sources. The oil-rich UAE, despite being a relatively modest gas exporter, aims to double its LNG production to 12 million tonnes per year by 2026.

Italy held its first autumn election in over a century, with far-right parties leading the race to form the next government. One of the new government's initial tasks will be to negotiate a price cap on Russian-imported gas with other EU countries. However, voter turnout is expected to be lower than 65%, reflecting disenchantment with the three coalition governments formed since the last election, each led by someone without prior political experience.

Giorgia Meloni made history as **Italy's** first female prime minister, leading the country's most right-wing government since World War II after a successful general election. Preliminary results show the Brothers of Italy party leading with 26%, followed by Meloni's allies Matteo Salvini's League at 9%, and Silvio Berlusconi's Forza Italia at 8%. The coalition's combined share of over 40% is expected to secure majorities in both houses of parliament, thanks to electoral law favoring party alliances. Meloni has distanced her party from its fascist roots, focusing on migration issues and defending the Christian, heterosexual family.

The EU proposed withholding €7.5bn in funding from **Hungary** due to rule of law violations involving corruption in awarding public contracts. The European Commission's recommendation seeks to suspend approximately one-third of Hungary's cohesion funding, which supports less economically developed parts of the EU. Hungary is set to receive €22bn in cohesion funds until 2027. The country is also seeking additional grants and loans under the EU's Covid-19 recovery fund, which could also be impacted if rule of law issues are not addressed. Brussels aims to address budgetary risks arising from a lack of transparency in awarding contracts, shortcomings in tackling corruption, and weaknesses in prosecuting misuse of European funds in Hungary.

France is expected to expedite the repatriation of ISIS brides after the European Court of Human Rights condemned the country for not bringing back two mothers from Syria. This ruling could serve as a precedent for families of other detained women to challenge France and other European states that refuse their repatriation. Although the court cannot compel France to bring the women back, it ordered President Macron's government to reconsider their return refusal. The court stated that there is "no general right to repatriation," but the women should have had the opportunity to contest the decision before an independent body, which French courts had denied, claiming no jurisdiction over Syria.

MIDDLE EAST & CENTRAL ASIA

Mahsa Amini, a 22-year-old **Iranian** woman from the Kurdish town of Saqqez, tragically died after her arrest by the morality police for not fully complying with Islamic dress regulations while visiting Tehran with her brother. Although she was wearing a headscarf and long coat, she was still arrested outside a metro station. The police claimed that she had a "heart attack" and was immediately taken to a nearby hospital, but images of her in a coma circulated on social media, sparking public outrage at the authorities' intensified crackdown on young women. The morality police, responsible for promoting virtue, displayed CCTV footage of Amini in a room receiving lessons on morality, where she collapsed after discussing her coat with a female officer. Pro-reform women see the hijab as oppressive, leading to nationwide protests and calls from all political spectrums to end the policing of women's clothing.

Saudi Crown Prince Mohammed bin Salman has replaced King Salman as prime minister through a royal decree, further consolidating the son's role as the kingdom's de facto ruler. King Salman, 86, remains the head of state, but the decree elevates the ambitious crown prince, who has overseen economic reforms, to become head of government. Prince Mohammed's promotion has been a subject of speculation, and while it solidifies his position, Saudi domestic and foreign policies are not expected to drastically change. Additionally, Prince Mohammed's brother, Prince Khalid, was promoted to defense minister, while another brother, Abdulaziz bin Salman, remains the energy minister.

Lebanon is set to re-peg its currency for the first time in 25 years, substantially reducing its value against the dollar in an effort to meet the IMF's demand to align the peg closer to the black-market rate and restore confidence in the financial system. The Lebanese pound has been pegged to the US dollar at L£1,507 since 1997, but the new rate of L£15,000 to the dollar will be implemented on November 1, 2022. This move is contingent on the adoption of a financial recovery plan, which aims to address the more than $70bn financial sector crisis caused by the government's debt default. The currency has drastically depreciated by over 95% since the country's financial crisis began in 2019.

In the face of escalating armed robberies by desperate depositors seeking access to their savings, **Lebanon's** banks will remain closed "indefinitely." Amid the deepening financial crisis and widespread poverty, the banking sector has frozen deposits and limited withdrawals for more than two years. This has sparked anger and discontent among the Lebanese population, who blame the financial sector and the central bank for the crisis.

Israel's military has acknowledged a "high possibility" that one of its soldiers unintentionally killed the veteran Palestinian-American journalist Shireen Abu Akleh. Abu Akleh, a well-known Al Jazeera correspondent across the Middle East, tragically lost her life while covering an Israeli military raid in Jenin, occupied West Bank, in May this year. Her death sparked global outrage and brought attention to Israeli operations in the region. While Palestinian officials blamed Israeli soldiers for her killing, Al Jazeera accused Israel of deliberately targeting her. A senior Israel Defense Forces (IDF) official stated that Abu Akleh might have been mistakenly shot by an IDF soldier, who did not recognize her as a journalist during an exchange of fire with militants. The distressing scenes at her funeral, where Israeli riot police allegedly mistreated mourners, further intensified international criticism, prompting examinations and media reconstructions of the incident.

In what would mark the most significant political change in **Kazakhstan** since gaining independence from the Soviet Union, the president has called for snap elections this year and proposed limiting the president's tenure to a single seven-year term. This decision follows violent anti-government protests earlier this year, the deadliest in the nation's history. The next presidential election, previously scheduled for 2024, could see the president's term change pending approval from the country's parliament. Additionally, the president announced bringing forward parliamentary elections from 2025 to the next year, enabling the public to give the government a mandate for reforms in response to the January protests. Nursultan Nazarbayev appointed Tokayev as acting president after stepping down from his 29-year rule in March 2019. Tokayev later won a five-year presidential term in an election. However, discontent, fueled by the influence of the Nazarbayev family and political/business elites, led to massive January protests, resulting in over 200 deaths and prompting the government to seek Russian assistance in quelling the violence.

Following a night of renewed violence on their border, **Armenia** has accused **Azerbaijan's** military of advancing into its territory, with numerous casualties reported. The worst fighting between the two countries in two years involved artillery, mortar, and drone strikes on civilian and military targets in Armenia, according to Yerevan's defense ministry. While Azerbaijan confirmed the clashes, they claimed it was in response to provocations. Armenia's prime minister, Nikol Pashinyan, reported at least 49 troop casualties and informed the country's parliament that fighting was still ongoing after Azerbaijan attacked Armenia's positions overnight. Both sides blamed each other for the escalation, adding to longstanding hostility, including previous wars in the 1990s and 2020, over the disputed Nagorno-Karabakh region.

ASIA

During a meeting between **Indian** Prime Minister Narendra Modi and Russian President Vladimir Putin in Uzbekistan, Modi emphasized that the current time is "not an era of war." For the first time, Putin publicly acknowledged India's concerns about the conflict, similar to his response to Chinese President Xi Jinping. These exchanges at the Shanghai Cooperation Organisation gathering in Samarkand mark Russia's most public recognition of China and India's unease regarding the implications of the Ukraine invasion. While both Xi and Modi have tried to remain neutral on the Ukraine issue, their strong ties with Russia are crucial to Putin's efforts to demonstrate Moscow's significance on the global stage. Putin's newfound deference to Modi and Xi's concerns highlights Russia's increasing reliance on their willingness to purchase its exports, especially after western nations imposed sanctions due to the invasion. The conflict in Ukraine has caused disruptions in food and raw energy supplies to India and led to the evacuation of many Indian medical students from Ukraine. India has generally refrained from extensive public commentary on the war.

In an effort likely to escalate the country's deepening communal tensions, **Indian** Prime Minister Narendra Modi has banned the Popular Front of India (PFI), a leading Muslim group, and its affiliates for five years. The ban follows the arrest of over 200 of its members and searches of top leaders' premises. The Indian Ministry of Home Affairs accused the PFI of involvement in "serious offences, including terrorism and its financing." Additionally, eight other groups working on behalf of the Muslim minority population, which constitutes around 200 million of India's nearly 1.4 billion people, were also banned. Islam is the second-largest religion in predominantly Hindu India. Established in 2006 as a counterweight to Hindu nationalist groups, the PFI is mostly active in southern India but has a wide network across several states, including in the northern regions and the capital, New Delhi.

The **Philippines** and the US are intensifying military cooperation, with plans to double the number of troops participating in joint exercises next year, amid Manila's considerations regarding its role in a potential conflict with China over Taiwan. For their primary annual bilateral military exercise, Balikatan, the US and the Philippines will deploy 16,000 forces next year. The increased cooperation follows China's growing military activity around Taiwan, which has raised concerns among senior Filipino officials. As a result, they are backing a revitalization of the country's alliance with the US, which weakened when former President Rodrigo Duterte attempted to pivot towards China in 2016.

Sri Lanka has initiated debt negotiations with its bilateral and private creditors with the aim of making substantial progress in the talks to unlock a $2.9bn IMF loan by the year's end. In May, Sri Lanka became the first nation in the Asia-Pacific region to default in over two decades. President Ranil Wickremesinghe's government needs to make headway in debt relief talks with various creditors, including private bondholders and countries like China, Japan, and India. To finalize the bailout, the IMF requires Sri Lanka to demonstrate financing assurances from bilateral creditors and engage in "good faith" discussions with private creditors. The country's foreign debts amount to around $50bn, with the largest portion owed to private bondholders at almost $20bn. Additionally, Sri Lanka owes more than $7bn to China and smaller sums to Japan and India.

Hong Kong is set to end its stringent hotel quarantine requirement for incoming travelers, a policy that adversely affected the city's status as a financial hub, battered its economy, and prompted an exodus of residents. The requirement, which mandated visitors and residents to quarantine in hotels for up to three weeks, had been in place for two and a half years, effectively isolating the city from the rest of the world and mainland China. The city's Chief Executive, John Lee, announced that incoming travelers would now undergo testing and monitoring for three days after arrival. Hong Kong had been following a version of Beijing's strict zero-Covid-19 policy, though it avoided the severe lockdowns seen in Chinese megacities. However, after experiencing a devastating wave of the Omicron variant and a change in leadership, authorities have gradually eased restrictions.

North Korean leader Kim Jong Un has legally established his country's status as a nuclear power and permitted the use of pre-emptive strikes. This move comes as the regime seeks to capitalize on escalating tensions between the US and Russia and China in order to shift its policy. Kim pledged to never engage in talks to relinquish his nuclear weapons after the law was passed by the Supreme People's Assembly. Despite comprehensive UN sanctions imposed in response to a nuclear test and intercontinental ballistic missile launch in 2017, North Korea's illicit ballistic missile program has continued to grow in size and sophistication. These sanctions were agreed upon by all five permanent members of the UN Security Council, including the US, Russia, and China. However, in the aftermath of Russia's invasion of Ukraine, Pyongyang and Moscow have grown closer, and Russia has turned to North Korea for the purchase of rockets and artillery shells due to western sanctions impacting Moscow's weapon supply. Additionally, North Korea, alongside Russia, was one of four countries to oppose a UN general assembly resolution condemning the invasion of Ukraine this year.

The US plans to sell $1.1bn in weapons to **Taiwan**, including 60 Harpoon anti-ship missiles, as part of its efforts to strengthen the country's defenses amid escalating military pressure from China. The Biden administration has notified Congress about the proposed sale, which includes 100 Sidewinder air-to-air missiles and support for a surveillance radar program. This notification marks the first American arms package following China's increased military pressure on Taiwan, which occurred after US House Speaker Nancy Pelosi's visit to the island last month. In response to Pelosi's visit, China fired missiles over Taiwan into waters east of the island, including some that landed in Japan's exclusive economic zone. Following the exercise of unprecedented scale during Pelosi's visit, China has maintained higher levels of military activity around Taiwan compared to before her trip.

THE AMERICAS

Chile's left-wing president, Gabriel Boric, held discussions with political leaders and members of congress to find a way to salvage plans for a new constitution after voters overwhelmingly rejected a proposal that investors feared would impact the country's pro-market economic model. In the mandatory plebiscite, nearly 62 percent of Chileans spurned the new charter, with an unexpectedly high turnout of almost 86 percent. This referendum result represents a setback for former student protest leader Boric, who had strongly advocated for the now-rejected rewrite. Boric's left-wing coalition had relied on the new constitution to introduce progressive reforms in areas such as tax, pensions, and social welfare. Despite recognizing the result, the president pledged to make renewed efforts to rewrite the constitution, stating that the vote provided a clear mandate to do so.

A man was arrested after he aimed a gun at the vice-president of **Argentina**, Cristina Fernández de Kirchner, in what appeared to be an assassination attempt outside her home in Buenos Aires. The incident, broadcast live on television, occurred as Kirchner was walking through a crowd of supporters. The trigger was pulled, but no shot was fired. Kirchner, a left-wing politician and former president of Argentina, is currently facing a corruption trial related to allegations of misusing state funds during her time in office. The case has attracted both supporters and critics, leading to large crowds gathering outside her home. Kirchner denies the charges.

Hurricane Ian, one of the most powerful storms to hit the US mainland, struck south-west **Florida** with high winds, rain, and storm surges as it weakened and moved inland. The storm left more than 2 million homes and businesses without power as it made landfall, bringing "catastrophic" 150mph (240km/h) winds and a deadly storm surge of up to 18 feet. Residential areas in Fort Myers Beach and other coastal cities were heavily affected, with buildings damaged and extensive tree and power line damage. The utility company Florida Power and Light warned residents in Ian's path to prepare for days without power.

Cubans have approved a comprehensive "family law" code that would grant same-sex couples the right to marry and adopt, while also redefining rights for children and grandparents. The measure, which contains over 400 articles, was approved with 66.9% of the vote, though there was unusually strong opposition on the Communist party-governed island, particularly from the growing evangelical movement. Despite an extensive government campaign in favor of the measure, including informative meetings and media coverage, many Cubans voiced their resistance. Cuban elections, where only the Communist party is allowed to participate, typically produce victory margins exceeding 90%. The new code includes provisions for surrogate pregnancies, enhanced rights for grandparents regarding grandchildren, protection for elderly individuals, and measures against gender violence.

AFRICA

Members of **Burkina Faso's** army have taken control of state television, announcing the ousting of military leader Paul-Henri Damiba, the dissolution of the government, and the suspension of the constitution and transitional charter. Captain Ibrahim Traore stated that a group of officers removed Damiba due to his failure to address the worsening Islamist insurgency. He also declared indefinite closure of borders and suspension of all political and civil society activities. This is the second takeover in eight months for the West African state. Damiba had come to power in a coup in January that deposed democratically elected president Roch Marc Kaboré. Despite promises to enhance security, violence has persisted, and discontent with his leadership has grown. Recently, Damiba addressed the UN general assembly in New York, defending his January coup as a matter of national survival, even if it was seen as "reprehensible" by the international community.

Egypt, the host of the upcoming UN climate summit (COP27) in Sharm-El-Sheikh in November, has called on countries to put aside tensions over the Ukraine war and focus on the climate crisis. The summit aims to hold companies accountable for the promises made during the COP26 summit in Glasgow the previous year. However, expectations for the meeting have been dampened due to the discord caused by Russia's invasion of Ukraine, resulting in economic and political damage worldwide. Additionally, a diplomatic freeze between the US and China, the top two greenhouse gas emitters, over Taiwan, has cast a shadow over the talks.

The International Monetary Fund has approved a $1.3 billion loan to **Zambia** as the country strives to rebuild its crisis-hit economy after defaulting on its foreign debts in 2020. Zambia's economic woes, attributed to years of mismanagement and corruption, were exacerbated by the Covid-19 pandemic, leading to unsustainable debt levels. The bailout follows extensive negotiations between Lusaka and its major creditors, including France, the UK, and China, with western private lenders accounting for nearly half of the country's debt payments. President Hakainde Hichilema, in office for a year, has been at the forefront of the negotiations, leading to a reduction in inflation and some recovery of the country's currency value.

SOURCES:

https://www.ft.com/content/eddedee3-669d-42cc-9597-33609a8bff99

https://www.ft.com/content/eddedee3-669d-42cc-9597-33609a8bff99

https://www.ft.com/content/2a2243cb-d386-4e34-9c34-3ddbbd84acc9

https://www.aljazeera.com/news/2022/9/28/russia-set-to-annex-ukraine-regions-after-sham-vote

https://www.aljazeera.com/news/2022/9/21/russian-group-calls-for-protests-against-putins-war-mobilisation

https://www.ft.com/content/00ee8cef-446b-4042-9278-a7603965a698

https://www.ft.com/content/2624cc0f-57b9-4142-8bc1-4141833a73dd

https://www.bbc.co.uk/news/uk-61585886

https://www.theguardian.com/politics/2022/sep/05/liz-truss-wins-tory-leadership-race-to-become-britains-next-pm

https://www.ft.com/content/0065dfcc-4519-41b6-9883-92e7ff13777d

https://www.thetimes.co.uk/article/giorgia-meloni-set-to-become-italys-first-female-prime-minister-as-voters-lurch-right-vpp2nhwcp

https://www.ft.com/content/b510fcd7-396d-4909-a91f-2221f9c55a0b

https://www.thetimes.co.uk/article/france-loses-isis-brides-case-at-european-court-of-human-rights-sjqtzxjpl

https://www.theguardian.com/global-development/2022/sep/16/iranian-woman-dies-after-being-beaten-by-morality-police-over-hijab-law

https://www.ft.com/content/26fc5c57-dc8f-4af5-b465-f14ae46ea65b

https://www.ft.com/content/75d21ae6-f508-4af3-91a9-c6a783b83c02

https://www.aljazeera.com/news/2022/9/28/india-bans-muslim-group-pfi-for-alleged-terror-links

https://www.ft.com/content/f8bb5f5d-c0a3-43d1-a31b-ba9c13a54ef7

https://www.ft.com/content/d0ac0361-c101-4605-ba22-ee20f9f92233

https://www.thetimes.co.uk/article/dozens-dead-in-worst-fighting-between-armenia-and-azerbaijan-for-two-years-bsjlb3nsz

https://www.ft.com/content/f76daf68-64f4-462e-990a-1c66bec85882

https://www.ft.com/content/a1fdea5c-a4da-4734-8fd3-ea3cd14c7187

https://www.ft.com/content/b7c9f822-e873-4647-b5cc-5d44786a7002

https://www.thetimes.co.uk/article/argentinas-vice-president-narrowly-escapes-assassination-clx0xkgpp

https://www.aljazeera.com/economy/2022/9/23/hong-kong-to-scrap-controversial-quarantine-policy

https://www.ft.com/content/23784a2e-7ed7-4f37-8921-eb5112683c33

https://www.ft.com/content/025349c0-2c1b-441a-b945-607094dec56d

https://www.theguardian.com/global-development/2022/sep/02/crisis-hit-zambia-secures-13bn-imf-loan-to-rebuild-stricken-economy

https://www.ft.com/content/9c295755-eadf-48a9-9818-6afa1bcbe498

https://www.ft.com/content/7875e3c6-abd6-4839-ac11-5428fdb3aae9

https://www.theguardian.com/us-news/2022/sep/28/hurricane-ian-millions-florida-path-deadly-cyclone

https://www.theguardian.com/world/2022/sep/26/cubans-vote-in-favour-of-family-law-reform-that-will-allow-same-sex-marriage#%3A~%3Atext%3DCubans%20have%20approved%20a%20sweeping%2Cthe%20Communist%20party%2Dgoverned%20island

https://www.theguardian.com/world/2022/sep/30/burkina-fasos-military-leader-ousted-in-second-coup-this-year

https://www.theguardian.com/environment/2022/sep/28/cop27-egypt-hosts-urge-leaders-set-aside-tensions-ukraine-climate

THE LIFE AND REIGN OF HER MAJESTY, QUEEN ELIZABETH II

I have included a full chapter about Her Majesty The Queen for two reasons. The first is as this book addresses the concept of change it is remarkable how change has been both slow and fast in her life. She is the embodiment of very little change and has ruled Britain maintaining the staid traditions of this old Monarchy.

She however has also presided over a period of substantial changes in the world. Britain has changed so much from being a White Colonial Superpower to a multicultural nation. Britain has even embraced a Prime Minister of Indian origin when only a few decades ago this country was a subject colony of the British Empire.

She has in many ways been the true embodiment of change both glacial and fast. An analysis of her life and reign is fascinating in how she managed to balance both so skilfully and for so long. Despite all the controversies in her families lives and the changes to Britain's Global power she remained much loved not just in Britian but throughout the whole world. She was above controversies and hugely admired as was evident in her funeral where millions showed their genuine affection for her.

She ruled for longer than any other Monarch in British history, becoming a much loved and respected figure across the globe. For over 70 years, Her Majesty was a dedicated Head of the Commonwealth, linking more than two billion people worldwide. She felt a very strong personal connection to the organisation, forming close relationships with many Commonwealth leaders and visiting all but two Commonwealth countries during her reign. She was the most widely travelled monarch in the world, visiting over 110 countries during her lifetime.

Queen Elizabeth II acceded to the throne on 7th February 1952 at the young age of only 25. Although the call to the throne was unexpected after the sudden death of her father George VI, she had been preparing for the role since her father came to the throne. George VI had become King unexpectedly, after the abdication of his brother, Edward VIII in 1936. From that moment, the Queen had known she would be monarch one day. She felt a very strong sense of duty towards the role, feeling it was bestowed upon her by God. Her strong Christian faith is something that remained with her throughout her reign, as she acknowledged the importance of her role as Supreme Governor of the Church of England. The Queen reigned over a period of great change and development for both Britain and the world.

The great challenge of change she faced during her long reign as monarch was that the continuities and certainties of monarchy that were taken for granted at the time of her accession, were tested in a fast-changing world during her reign, far beyond the walls of Buckingham Palace. The monarchy faced much instability during her reign, from political crises in the UK and abroad, to personal crises within her own family, most notably the death of Diana Princess of Wales in 1997. However, despite these changes, the

Queen remained a continuous figure of stability in the UK, an eternal presence in the lives of her subjects. The monarchy prevailed through many challenges during her reign, learning to adapt to the rapidly changing times. There was a real effort to bring the monarchy up to date in time for the millennium; a century which saw the Queen celebrate her Golden and Platinum Jubilees, in 2002 and 2022 respectively. Although the new century also brought various challenges to the monarchy, the Queen remained a devoted monarch to Great Britain and the Commonwealth until her death on 8 September 2022.

THE DEATH OF THE KING

Early in 1952, The Queen and her husband embarked on an extensive foreign tour. It was in East Africa, in Kenya, that they received the shattering news from home on 6th February 1952. Princess Elizabeth's father, King George VI, had passed away unexpectedly in his sleep. Just one week before, the King had waved off the princess at the airport in London as she embarked on a tour intended to take her across the world. In the summer of 1951, the health of King George VI entered into a serious decline, and Princess Elizabeth represented him at the Trooping the Colour and on various other state occasions. Upon receiving news of his death, Elizabeth, now queen, flew at once back to England to meet her ministers. The first three months of her reign, the period of full mourning for her father, were passed in comparative seclusion. But in the summer, after she had moved from Clarence House to Buckingham Palace, she undertook the routine duties of the sovereign and carried out her first state opening of Parliament on November 4, 1952. The transition and change was both ordered and orderly. The Queen viewed the mantle of sovereign as a continuation of her role as princess; she felt she was born along a river of history which flowed along an unchanging course. This was partly illusory as the monarchy operated in an ever-changing public sphere that would challenge it. Her father had been a different kind of king from his father, and his grandfather. Nonetheless, the idea of tradition being sustained was fundamental to her. The monarchy that Queen Elizabeth inherited in 1952 was still very much a Victorian organisation, in a very different world to that which the monarchy inhabits now. The monarchy preferred very little change and had continued this tradition for generations. The Queen's coronation was held at Westminster Abbey on June 2, 1953. It was the first state occasion to be televised lived. This had never happened before and this change marked a seismic shift in opening up the mystique of Royalty. There were 20 million viewers, most of whom didn't have their own television set, making it more of a communal event, as across the country there were street parties. The coronation also coincided with the first successful ascent of mount Everest, which was by a New Zealander; the atmosphere of public celebration thus embraced the wider Commonwealth. Although the celebration was rooted in the past, a radically different era had dawned. The most striking feature of the reign of Elizabeth II was the speed and pace of social change, which the monarchy had to adapt to.

THE MODERN MONARCH

By the mid-1960s, the family of the Queen and the Duke of Edinburgh had taken shape in the public mind. This was a solid marriage and the births of their children, Charles, Anne, Andrew and Edward solidified the Victorian image of a dedicated family. The national anthem was still played in cinemas at the end of the evening, but beyond the palace walls social change had speeded up. Popular taste was on the move and the 60s sounded utterly different; the Beatles and the Rolling Stones personified transformation, the theme of the decade and the monarchy needed to keep up as best it could. The reign of Queen Elizabeth II was a period of remarkable cultural development and change. At various points throughout her monarchy, Britain was at the forefront of the arts, in music, painting, literature and theatre. The age of television came at the moment of her coronation. A new epoch arrived with her coronation, the Elizabethan era, bringing excitement about a new era of change with it. The televised coronation was a real major cultural event for people, with many people buying televisions specifically for the event. Within months, television had become the new medium for the Queen and she embraced this change. The royal message became a televised event following the success of the coronation.

The era of mass media had arrived. The Queen, as an early adopter of television was quick to reflect this cultural shift in her delivery, praising invention and innovation. Society over her era changed its attitude, becoming far less differential. One way of broadening the appeal of the arts was through royal patronage. The Queen fulfilled the role of figurehead for scores of cultural organisations, many reflected their regal endorsement in their titles, such as the Royal College of Music and Royal College of Arts.

The cultural landscape was vastly changing in Britain; the Beatles revolutionised not just pop music, but the whole of British culture. Suddenly, the focus was on the 'British invasion', as it was known in America. There was a revolution taking place in music, fashion, art and various other industries. The 1960s marked a significant shift in British culture, from the late 1950s to late 1960s there was a phenomenal change in the position of the visual arts in the culture with the arrival of young artists like David Hockney. The Queen herself was arguably not particularly interested in the arts, but she did help to create a climate in which new values were tolerated, when she could have encouraged a much more conservative attitude. If the Queen wasn't personally part of the sweeping social changes of the 1960s, her image was certainly used as the image of Britain both at home and abroad; she had become a cultural icon. She is arguably the most portrayed individual in history, it is difficult to portray the significance of that. She was the first monarch in the era of mass media. There are popular images, press images, paparazzi images of her, combined with fine art. The Andy Warhol portrait showed he was interested in her as an icon of celebrity, stripping all depth away from the Queen's image, making her image and endlessly reproducible commodity. There were two or three official portraits of the Queen painted every year, most of them highly respectful. For her golden jubilee in 2002, the official portrait was commissioned from the Commonwealth Secretariat, from the late Nigerian artist Chinwe Chukwuogo-Roy. Portraiture since the Queen's accession has been one of the real binding factors in the Commonwealth; every Commonwealth embassy will display a portrait of the Queen. She is not wearing the formal robes in the portrait, instead wearing normal clothes, portraying a more modern monarch. The Queen was devoted to the Commonwealth and strove to promote it as a cultural entity in the broadest sense, initiating an interest in the different cultures, traditions and ways of life in the family of nations. The novelist Ben Okri described the Commonwealth of nations as "liberating because it brought many cultures together, but you could not really honestly get away from the fact of the colonial presence. But so many novels mention her, directly or indirectly, her presence, her visit. She is a steady character that runs like a melody in the background of many Commonwealth novels… She was very interested in Commonwealth writers and she herself initiated many celebrations of Commonwealth writers. She had a beneficial and stimulating role on Commonwealth literature of the twentieth and twenty-first century".

Part of the reason the Queen's image is so embedded in our culture is the fact that in Britain, and in many Commonwealth countries, is that we carry an image of her around with us on coins and banknotes and on stamps. But images of the Queen were not limited to the pictorial. The 1980s television show 'Spitting Image' had a puppet of her. And in comedy shows she is often impersonated by a look-a-like. The persona of her majesty was also portrayed in drama on many occasions, by Helen Mirren for example in the 2006 drama 'The Queen' and the 2013 play 'The Audience' written by Peter Morgan, who later wrote the television series 'The Crown'. The Queen reigned over a vastly changing cultural landscape. She had an extraordinary pervasive presence through her reign, which was benign and tremendously stabilising, providing a stabilising presence to the conscience of her people. During her reign, the arts became a majority interest, rather than a minority interest.

During this period of vast cultural change, pressure was growing for changes in the ways the Queen and Royal family came across to the public. The Queen's duty of service to the nation and Commonwealth mattered profoundly to her, but how that duty was carried out now mattered just as much. The historian John Grigg, the son of a formed colonial governor of Kenya, published an appeal to the monarchy to modernise itself, causing a big stir. He deprecated the Queen's public manner, saying she sounded like a "priggish school girl", her speaking style he said was "pain in the neck". Predictably, he was denounced for his trouble, but as a member of the House of Lords as Lord Altringham, his criticism stung. The aftermath of the Suez crisis of the 1950s, events which made plain that Britain's continued pretensions to be a great power were exposed to almost a sham, became associated with the remarks of John Grigg.

The royal family's break from the past, when it came, was popular outside of the palace gates. To some courtiers, it was painful and would always be a source of regret. When the television film 'Royal Family' was shown in 1969, people had seen nothing like it before; they were permitted a glimpse of the life of the royal family. Scenes were filmed showing preparations for state ceremonies, to the Queen sitting on a tartan rug having a picnic with Princess Anne grilling the sausages. For the court, showing a few family conversations on television was a near revolution, although it was thought to have been encouraged by the Duke of Edinburgh who had sympathy with the view that the palace windows had to be opened to let in a little fresh air. The consort's public reputation for impatience wasn't an invention, and for a monarch who grew with Edwardian and Victorian memories fresh in her family, the sheer weight of history tended to smother innovation. The Queen's biographer Sarah Harris describes a Queen whose instincts were almost bound to make her suspicious of change. "She was always a conservative person whose instinct was always for privacy. Many of those around the royal family knew that the old ways were changing and there was little point in pretending they weren't sooner or later, the light had to shine. Thus, the monarchy went into the risky business of agreeing to make the film. Risky, because it was later claimed the monarchy had been weakened, the useful mystique around it had but punctured. But at the time the opposite seemed true; this was royalty apparently in tune with the age, becoming slightly less stuffy". The institution was still the family, 'the firm' George VI had called it. But how strong would it be in the face of further challenges? This The Queen understood that she had to change.

THE MARRIAGES OF THE QUEEN'S CHILDREN

In highly successful and happy union, the Queen herself was married to Prince Phillip for over seventy years, but for her children the story was very different, with very public and sometimes bitter separations. Twenty-five years after she married Prince Phillip, the Queen used her silver wedding celebration in 1972 to extol the virtues that she considered the essence of the modern royal family, presenting the monarchy and family as one. Royal weddings were public celebrations; Princess Anne and Mark Phillips in 1973, Prince Andrew and Sarah Ferguson in 1986, and above all the Prince of Wales and Lady Diana Spencer in 1981. Prince Edward married Sophie Reece-Jones in 1999. Their marriage was the only which survived the times. In the unravelling of the others, the royal family found itself under the merciless gaze of a press that was no longer willing to draw a discrete veil over personal problems in this most public of families. The Queen was surprised to discover that many of her subjects, not to mention a popular press, developed an insatiable appetite for stories about the marital problems of her family. Buckingham Palace couldn't smother the fascination because the royal family had been presented previously as something almost magical. When Prince Charles, heir to the throne, led Lady Diana Spencer down the aisle of St Paul's Cathedral in the summer of 1981, the ceremony was remarkable. The couple basked in popularity and the curiosity of the world. Princess Diana established herself as a new type of princess, glamourous, warm, emotionally expressive and hugely popular. The births of Princes William and Harry, and the way in which Diana was perceived to be bringing them up as less remote from everyday life, won her a great deal of praise. There were many images of Diana working for charitable causes, from the notable cause of men with aids, to the international campaign against landmines. Diana had brought huge changes to the Royal household reflecting society. But Diana's life was also troubled, much of it ruthlessly documented in the press. The pain she suffered from eating disorders, her estrangement from the royal family and distance that opened up with her husband won her a great deal of sympathy, but criticism too. As the marriage crumbled, it was almost as if the monarchy itself was crumbling too. The Prime Minister John Major announced the separation in the House of Commons in December 1992. Prince Charles himself confessed to infidelity and Diana did the same during an infamous panorama interview with Martin Bashir on BBC1 in 1995. This interview which was subsequently discovered to have been obtained by deception. As scandalous tales circulated, remarkably, the Queen herself felt compelled to write to her eldest son and daughter-in-law urging them to divorce. The Supreme Governor of the Church of England, to the dismay of traditionalists, now had to formally accept a new morality. The divorce finally came in 1996. The Queen reluctantly had to change and this could never have been anticipated just a few years before. She was forced to change and went with the flow.

1992: A TURBULENT YEAR FOR THE ROYAL FAMILY

The collapsing first marriage of the Prince of Wales wasn't an isolated event in 1992. As well as the tribulations of Charles and Diana, the Princess Royal divorced Captain Mark Phillips, and the Queen's second son, Andrew Duke of York, separated from his wife Sarah Ferguson. To have maintained that all of this had nothing to do with the monarch herself would not only have stretched credulity, but it would also have run counter to the palace's own strategy developed over the previous three decades. To have three divorces in one family certainly undermined the Queen's confidence in the royal family as the template for modern marriage, because they had set up the royal family as the institution of the monarchy, not the Queen. This was very much the Queen's doing and was evolved over the 1950s and 1960s as a way in which the concept of royalty would maintain its public appeal and become the symbol of ordinary British people living the moral life. When that began to crack in the 1980s, it was bound to be catastrophic for the royal family and the Queen personally. It was a big shock for the Queen as her own family life had been uncomplicated and happy, she was therefore taken by surprise by the marital problems of her children. The year 1992 culminated in a devastating fire at Windsor Castle, where the Queen spent most of her time. After the fire, in the midst of a huge public row about the cost of restoration and who would meet it, the Queen agreed that she would in the future pay taxes. It had been the worst year of her reign. After 1992, there was a real attempt to look at the way the institution of monarchy worked, and there were changes. It was a time when Buckingham Palace was open to the public and there was a financial settlement. The personal trauma of those years did eat away at the old belief in monarchy. When the Queen reached her 70th birthday in 1996, her son and heir was in the midst of negotiating his divorce, and the public mood was often hostile. For the first time in her reign, two serious newspapers, the Independent and the Guardian argued against the continuation of the monarchy. Yet, the Republican case had never become a mainstream political view. Twenty years earlier, critics of the Queen and the monarchy itself had often been anarchists and punk rockers. Different voices were now starting to be heard, although it seemed clear that the great majority of the public preferred the status quo. However, the age of awe and deference was long gone. The Queen's response was what it had always been; measured. She never sought to present her reign as innovative or adventurous; it was conducted carefully and steadily. She brought about change at times at glacial pace but had the perfect touch with society and the changes they would accept.

THE QUEEN AND HER FAITH

Two central themes of Queen Elizabeth's life and her reign came together at her coronation: her personal faith, and her understanding of her public role, not just as monarch, but as religious leader. Her faith was the foundation, as she described it herself, the "bedrock" of all that she did. She felt she had been chosen by God in her role as Queen. The churches' teachings were a critical factor during turning points in her life, sometimes in unexpected ways. She only became Queen because of the church teaching on divorce. Her uncle was forced to abdicate the throne because he wanted to marry a divorced American socialite, Wallace Simpson. The Church of England since the reformation has had a very hard line on divorce, despite the many marriages of Henry VIII, who founded the Church of England. His marriages were annulled, which meant they never happened in the eyes of the church. After that, the Church of England took a harder line on divorce than virtually any other church in the world. When Edward VIII accepted that he couldn't be Supreme Governor of the Church of England, at the same time as flouting church teachings on divorce, many people felt he failed in his duty. By the time the Queen's father became king, the young Princess Elizabeth was already well-schooled on religious teachings. Another religious influence on the Queen's life was from her husband, Prince Phillip. Phillip was more exploratory about his faith, with an element of agnosticism, but he was undoubtedly a spiritual man who believed in a God. The couple loved talking about spiritual matters together. The Queen felt she had been chosen by God in her role as monarch, and that remained in the Queen's mind throughout her reign, that she had been placed to do a particular job as Supreme Governor of the Church of England also. For example, in the year of her coronation, the Queen's younger sister Princess Margaret became engaged to the recently divorced Peter Townsend, an RAF officer and fighter pilot who was serving in the royal household. Because the princess was in the line of succession to the throne, she needed the Queen's permission to marry, and when the relationship became public, it caused a constitutional crisis for the Queen. The church, the cabinet and even many members of the Commonwealth came out against the marriage. The Queen was placed in a very difficult position; she did not say Princess Margaret could not marry, but instead advised the couple to wait. Ultimately, the strain proved too much for the couple; two and a half years after becoming engaged, the relationship ended. The Queen did have a crisis of conscience, torn between giving her sister what she wanted and her faith, following the church's teachings closely and not wanting to stray from these teachings. Her role as Supreme Governor of the Church of England put her at the pinnacle of the complex and ancient institutional structures which link the Church of England with the nation's life and politics. It meant she was a very visible presence during big church occasions.

Her private faith took place away from the church and large state occasions, whether she was at Balmoral or Sandringham she unfailingly attended a Sunday service, wanting to be treated as an ordinary parishioner. Church life in rural parishes may not have changed greatly during the Queen's long reign, but the religious landscape around them went through a revolution. The United Kingdom is much more secular than it was when she was crowned, and other faiths such as Hinduism, Sikhism, Buddhism, Islam and Judaism play a much more prominent role than they once did. The Church of England changed too; the most radical step it took during her reign was the decision to ordain women, first in 1992 as priests and later as bishops, with the Queen taking a clear interest in this decision. The Queen came to terms with the changing world, living in the present, open to the future. Three of the Queen's four children divorced in 1992; her country had come a long way since divorced forced her uncle from the throne, and so had she, becoming more relaxed. For example, in her attitude towards Camila, accepting Camila as her husband's consort and played an active role later in her life in endorsing Camila, endorsing a divorced woman as sovereign. The Queen's faith was never shaken but came out in a real way through the death of her mother, the Queen mother. The Queen spoke more freely about her personal faith in public during the later years of her life, particularly in her Christmas messages, describing it as the "bedrock of her life". This was interesting, as the society around her did not speak of faith very easily. She said the teachings of Christ "have served as my inner light"; her faith was the foundation of all that she did.

THE DEATH OF DIANA, PRINCESS OF WALES

One of the darkest moments of the Queen's reign came in August 1997, when very early one Sunday morning she was awakened at Balmoral to be told that Diana Princess of Wales had been involved in a car crash in Paris and was dead. Diana was 36 years old when she died. Her death caused an unprecedented outpouring of public grief in the United Kingdom and worldwide, and her funeral was watched by an estimated 2.5 billion people. Her death had an astonishing impact on the monarchy. The fevered public mood led directly to a root and branch reassessment of the monarchy and the way it presented itself to the public. The Princess of Wales's death happened completely out of the blue and was a shock which really affected the Queen. The public reaction was extraordinarily difficult to understand from Balmoral, where the Queen and other members of the royal family were. It was a moment where the institution and the Queen herself was in the frame, that had not been the case before. It was a very significant moment in her reign; it was first and foremost a tragedy for her eldest son and his children, as well as for Diana's family. But it was also the occasion for a public outpouring, which combined an astonishing display of affection for the princess with a blast of criticism for the family from which she was thought by many to have been cruelly excluded. Flowers were strewn in front of the royal palaces and books of condolences were opened around the world. In London, admirers of all ages queued for hours to lead tributes and pay their respects to a woman with whom they apparently felt a real connection. Television and radio schedules were abandoned, newspapers and magazines published thick commemorative editions. The atmosphere was fraught. The Princess' tragic death, epitomised in Elton John's tribute at her funeral, transfixed the country. Diana's death brought further changes to the Monarchy and the Queen had to quickly step in line with these changes if she had to maintain the public's admiration.

ENTERING THE NEW MILLENNIUM

After 1997, the time was ripe to make real changes in the palace. Over the five-year period after the death of Diana, there was a calculated change programme within the palace according to Lord Janvrin, the Queen's private secretary at the time. The palace wanted the change to be imperceptible, not to have a huge modernisation campaign, but instead to look at the way the engagements were done, and to bring a greater sense of informality and more proactive engagement with the media, and to bring more professional people into the palace. There was a real attempt to bring the institution up to date. The idea that things had to move on was something the Queen supported and embraced. After the princess' funeral, the Queen after the celebration of her fiftieth wedding anniversary showed a willingness to talk more personally than she would have been willing to do only a few years before. The greatest ability within the royal family in the years after Diana's death, together with the carefully managed response to a more outwardly expressive and emotional public, helped to counteract some of the excessive remoteness of the monarchy. Whereas the 1990s had proved testing and led to a souring of the public mood, with all the family's domestic problems, the decision to pay taxes, the destructive fire at Windsor, attitudes had sweetened noticeably by the time of the Queen's Golden Jubilee in 2002. This was confirmed first of all in the public reaction to the death of her sister, Princess Margaret, and then only six weeks later, the death of the Queen Mother, aged 101. The Queen herself recognised the mood in a special televised message of thanks on the eve of her mother's funeral. She said: "The extent of the tributes huge numbers of you have paid my mother the past few days has been overwhelming. I have drawn great comfort from so many individual acts of kindness and respect. At the ceremony tomorrow, I hope that sadness will blend with a wider sense of thanksgiving. Not just for her life, but for the times in which she lived, a century for this country and the Commonwealth, not without its trials and sorrows, also one of extraordinary progress, full of courage and examples of service, as well as fun and laughter. This is what my mother would have understood, because it was the warmth and affection of people everywhere which inspired her resolve, dedication and enthusiasm for life".

The Queen's public stoicism and dignity were hallmarks of the funeral service itself, and it was in part that consistently impressive ability to point the way to overcoming national grief and setbacks, that helps to explain her success as a monarch. The Queen's reign, partly because it was so long, but also because of the quite formidable characteristics of her personality, will be seen as one of the great reigns of the last 200 years, despite the context of a declining role for the monarchy and a declining role for Britain. It is interesting to compare her reign with that of the other two great monarchs of Great Britain, namely Elizabeth I and Queen Victoria. They are both seen as having been great monarchs, a great deal due to the fact they happened to be on the throne when Britain was expanding commercially, artistically and in terms of empire. Whereas, Elizabeth II presided over a period during which the realms over which she reigned had been shrinking, along with the importance of the role. Ben Pimlott, a historian of post-WWII Britain believes she will be remembered as a woman of great strength and great ability to carry on regardless, through some very difficult times. That great strength, the resilience, was indeed embedded in her character. Only three weeks after her mother's funeral, the Queen addressed both house of parliament in Westminster Hall at the start of a tour of the country to mark her Golden Jubilee. "I would like to thank people everywhere for the loyalty, support and inspiration you have given me over these fifty unforgettable years. I would like to express my pride in our past and my confidence in our future. I would like above all to declare my resolve to continue with the support of my family, to serve the people of this great nation of ours to the best of my ability through the changing times ahead". As usual it was assured and dignified, words of resonance in that jubilee year, turning a major page for the monarchy.

In the Queen's last years as head of state, far from slowing down, she remained astonishingly active, at the heart of national life, from sporting celebration, to public health emergency. There was personal heartbreak too. But first, in the spring of 2005, good news involving her eldest son. Prince Charles finally married Camila Parker-Bowles, who had been identified by Diana as his long-term mistress. As they settled into a life together of public engagements and tours, the British public came around to their union. By the end of the first decade of the new century, the palace and the government were working on a state visit which would inaugurate a new chapter of relations between Britain and Ireland, which had been troubled for generations. This personal diplomacy was conducted with memorable style in the Queen's visit to the Republic of Ireland in 2011. It was the first by a reigning British monarch and it stood out for cementing a rapprochement between Dublin and London that would have been inconceivable during the tensions and conflicts of the preceding century. "These events have touched us all, many of us personally and are a painful legacy. We can never forget those who died or have been injured and their families. To all those who have suffered as a consequence of our troubled past, I extend my sincere thoughts and deep sympathy". This was one of the Queen's most closely watched speeches. She began it in Irish Gaelic, winning over the audience with charm, but her clearly genuine expression of regret for the past left the deepest impression. She knew of the difficulties first hand; Her uncle Lord Mountbatten had been murdered by the provisional IRA in 1979. Now though, she was looking ahead. The extent of the change was confirmed when she later met privately with Martin McGuiness, then the Northern Ireland Deputy First Minister, who fought with the IRA. It was an astonishing evolution, but it also said something about her own role. It is an example of what can be done symbolically, her capacity to choose the right moment when history can move on, by means of a symbolic gesture. She knew these changes were necessary and willingly supported these efforts of the government in bringing about peace to Northern Ireland.

There was inevitably another dimension to that Dublin visit; a day was devoted to her love of horses, breeding and racing.

It was to be a global sporting event a year later that brought out an aspect of the Queen's character seldom seen. Like her father and grandfather, she opened the Olympic Games when they came back to London in 2012, but she did so in a way that was unthinkable. During the Opening Ceremony of the games, the Queen herself appeared in a cameo alongside Daniel Craig as James Bond. During the skit, the James Bond escorts the Queen from Buckingham Palace to the Olympics in a helicopter. An actor playing the Queen was then shown jumping out of the aircraft fit with a Union Jack parachute. This was change at a monumental level with the Queen agreeing to be played for the audience. It was however a super success marking the Queen's sixty years on the throne. They confirmed the atmosphere established at the golden jubilee ten years earlier, more relaxed and less remote and stiff. The sons of Prince Charles and Diana too brought a different tone to the monarchy; Prince William married his longstanding girlfriend Kate Middleton in 2011 and the Queen's first great-grandson, Prince George, was born in 2013.

Prince Harry wed the divorced American actress Meghan Markle in 2018. Her welcome into the royal family, notably by the Queen herself, contrasted remarkably with the way the proposed marriage of the divorced Wallace Simpson to Edward VIII had been seen in establishment circles eighty years before.

Another television performance the previous year had also prompted a decisive intervention from the Queen. Prince Andrew spoke on BBC Newsnight about his relationship with the convicted sex offender Jeffrey Epstein, who later took his own life in an American prison. These included allegations of sex with a teenage girl. To many people, the lack of empathy the Duke of York showed to Epstein's victims was shocking. The Queen had reportedly been in favour of the interview, but as criticism of her second son intensified, she, with the Prince of Wales, forced a rethink. Three days after that broadcast and with his mother's explicit agreement, Prince Andrew announced he would no longer perform royal duties. Sensing deep public anger The Queen changed tact and ensured Prince Andrew was out, and there was little to conceal his deep humiliation. Later, the Duke had to reach a substantial out of court settlement with a sex accuser, although he denied her claims. Along with Prince Harry's exile, the episode seemed an extension of the fictional royal melodrama being portrayed in the long-running series, the Crown, first seen on Netflix in 2016, a sumptuously portrayed story that began with the Queen's marriage in 1947. The exceptionally popular series follows the Queen's life through to modern times. Public interest in the queen and the royal family grew as a result of the widespread popularity. "There's no doubt that The Crown has changed our perceptions of the monarchy," says historian and royal expert Robert Lacey, who is a historical consultant on The Crown. "It's made it into a sort of entertainment, which it wasn't before, but I think it's also allowed people to appreciate both the challenges and the benefits of being in the Royal Family." Lacey argues that one of the show's key aspects is the way in which it allows us to reconsider both our past and how we feel about the nation. "The monarchy is a tremendously important part of British identity for good and ill and I think The Crown makes people think about that," he says. "The strength of the Queen is that the constitutional monarchy is ultimately supposed to stand for the power of the people in that even the grandest of prime ministers must answer to the people. The Queen's great skill is to embody that well and The Crown in turn conveys that challenge really skilfully." The Crown's greatest appeal is the way in which humanises the Royals, often in the most surprising of ways. While Buckingham Palace retains a discreet distance from The Crown, never allowing us to know what members of the Royal Family might think of the show (or even if they watch it), it also understands that its existence helps burnish the royal image.

THE FUNERAL OF THE QUEEN

Whilst the Queen's life embraced change in many ways her funeral was held following generations of traditions. It was in keeping with her wishes to follow in the foot step of her father and grandparents.

The funeral ceremony was held in Westminster Abbey on September 19, 2022 marking the first time that a monarch's funeral service had been held at the Abbey since George II in 1760. More than a million people travelled to London to line the streets and witness an old and established ceremony, an unprecedented event almost none of them had seen before in their lifetimes. The day was declared a holiday in the UK and in several Commonwealth countries. Some four billion people watched worldwide, probably the largest television audience in history. The day comprised three separate services in 12 hours, starting in Westminster Hall and ending with a private burial in St George's Chapel, Windsor. The service in Westminster was conducted by the Dean of Westminster and the sermon and the commendation were given by the Archbishop of Canterbury. During the service, the Prime Minister and the Secretary General of the Commonwealth read lessons. The Archbishop of York, the Cardinal Archbishop of Westminster, the Moderator of the General Assembly of the Church of Scotland and the Free Churches Moderator said prayers. To mark the end of the Service, the last post sounded, followed by two minute's silence observed in the abbey, and throughout the United Kingdom. The national anthem drew the service to a close. At the end of the Service, Her Majesty's coffin was borne to Wellington Arch, via The Mall on the State Gun Carriage. The King and Members of the Royal Family again followed The Queen's Coffin in Procession. Following the procession to Wellington Arch, during which Big Ben tolled, the queen's casket was borne by hearse to her final resting place in the Royal Vault in St. George's Chapel at Windsor Castle for the Committal Service. Her son King Charles III said the death of his beloved mother was a "moment of great sadness" for him and his family and that her loss would be "deeply felt" around the world. He said: "We mourn profoundly the passing of a cherished sovereign and a much-loved mother. "I know her loss will be deeply felt throughout the country, the realms and the Commonwealth, and by countless people around the world." A Private Burial took place in The King George VI Memorial Chapel later that evening, conducted by the Dean of Windsor. The Queen was buried together with The Duke of Edinburgh, at The King George VI Memorial Chapel.

The state funeral for the Queen was not only an opportunity for the nation to join together to pay its last respects to a much-loved and admired monarch. It was also a significant diplomatic occasion, hailed as the "biggest diplomatic occasion in a century". King Charles played host at Buckingham Palace on the eve of the Queen's funeral to presidents, prime ministers, royals and ambassadors from almost every country with which Britain has diplomatic relations — on a night that most heads of government expected to be spending at the UN general assembly in New York. More than 500 dignitaries received handwritten invitations for themselves and their spouses for the evening reception. The reception was called a "mini-United Nations", in some respects overshadowing the official gathering at the UN general assembly in New York later in the week, to which some leaders cut short their visits to attend the funeral. The event was tightly policed by the Foreign Office's intricate seating plan. The funeral itself was perhaps the largest gathering of world leaders in the UK since the funeral of George VI. The last such gathering globally was Nelson Mandela's funeral in Johannesburg in December 2013. Foreign Office officials handwrote around 1000 invitations to the funeral.

That so many world leaders travelled to Britain for the funeral is in large part a tribute to the Queen herself. Among them, Joe Biden became the first serving American president to attend a British state funeral, is in large part a tribute to the late Queen Elizabeth herself. Emmanuel Macron, the French president, put it best in his elegant tribute, when he said that "to you, she was your Queen; to us, she was The Queen". Throughout her 70 years on the throne, Elizabeth was a figure of global fascination and admiration, as much a symbol of dignity, continuity and devotion to duty for the world as she was in Britain. The cast of world leaders present in London was also testimony to the continued strength of Britain's place in the world. It is a form of soft power that has endured despite the loss of empire during the late Queen's reign, and it is reflected in the decision of so many of those former imperial territories to retain links with Britain via the Commonwealth after independence. It is also a soft power that Britain has kept despite the challenges and changes of recent years that have been beset by political volatility and strained relations with allies. King Charles III demonstrated in his first days on the throne that he understands the important role that the crown can play, both as a source of soft power and in projecting it. In his packed schedule of domestic appearances since his accession, the King found time to speak to many world leaders. It helps that the King already knows many world leaders as a result of his own years of service to the country and the causes close to his heart. His commitment to the Commonwealth, an important forum for engagement among its 56 members, is clear.

On the day of the funeral, 2,000 mourners began filing into Westminster Abbey two hours before the service began; amongst them royalty, presidents, prime ministers, diplomats, dignitaries, representatives of the realms and the Commonwealth, holders of the Victoria Cross and the George Cross, members of the government and parliament and devolved parliaments and assemblies, representatives of the emergency services, the civil service, the professions, the Christian churches and other faiths (Jewish, Muslim, Buddhist, Hindu, Sikh). President Biden came by armoured Cadillac, "the Beast"; most of the other world leaders arrived by coach, bussed in from a temporary car park for limos at the Royal Hospital Chelsea. Here was Emmanuel Macron, president of France, Olena Zelenska, the wife of the Ukrainian president, the royal families of Monaco, Denmark, Norway, Sweden and the Netherlands, along with King Philippe and Queen Mathilde of Belgium. King Felipe and Queen Letizia of Spain attended — as did former king Juan Carlos I, who abdicated in disgrace in 2014 and now lives in exile in the United Arab Emirates. Emperor Naruhito and Empress Masako of Japan also attended, as did the king of Jordan, Abdullah II. On top of the current prime minister, every living former British prime minister, including Boris Johnson, Theresa May, David Cameron, Tony Blair, Gordon Brown and John Major. Other high-profile politicians included the Labour leader Sir Keir Starmer, the Liberal Democrat leader Sir Ed Davey; Scotland's first minister Nicola Sturgeon; the first minister of Wales, Mark Drakeford; and Michelle O'Neill, vice-president of Sinn Fein and first minister-designate of Northern Ireland was in attendance. Commonwealth realms, including Canada and Australia, who retain the British monarchy as head of state, enjoyed the greatest representation at the funeral with ten delegates each.

CONCLUSION

Continuity had always been important to the Queen; after her coronation, she looked back to the vows she had made publicly in

1947. Those words expressed what she saw as a sacred inheritance. "When I was 21, I pledged my life to the service of our people, and I asked for God's help to make good that vow. I do not regret or retract one word of that vow". The key to her reign was that she was and saw herself as a servant; her faith was utterly central; a huge sense of duty.

The Queen epitomised change which happened sometimes at glacial pace and sometimes at breath taking speed. The Queen inherited the throne at a time when it had been strengthened by victory in war and when it was accorded automatic respect, even some veneration. But the following seventy years would not allow the old ways to persist; she adapted sometimes willingly, sometimes under pressure, with the resolve that became her trademark. It is that stoicism, the pursuit of a resolute course, that history will celebrate in her reign. It was remarkably long and sometimes troubled, but always devoted, and most of all, always true to who she was. It is therefore fascinating to study her as a subject of change both slow and fast.

SOURCES:

https://www.bbc.co.uk/sounds/brand/p09l47b7
https://www.bbc.co.uk/sounds/play/p0cz8jg5
https://www.royal.uk/early-life-and-education
https://www.royal.uk/the-queens-life-and-reign
https://www.bbc.co.uk/sounds/play/p0cz8k0q
https://www.bbc.com/culture/article/20191117-how-the-crown-has-changed-the-worlds-view-of-the-royals
https://www.bbc.co.uk/sounds/play/p0cz8b7f

THE WORLD IN OCTOBER 2022

Introduction

October 2022 was a month during which Russia's invasion of Ukraine entered its seventh month. There was an explosion on the Russian-built bridge across the Kerch Strait to Crimea, which Russia called an act of "terrorism" and blamed on Ukraine. Putin annexed four regions of Ukraine bordering Russia, as Ukrainian forces continued counteroffensives in other occupied areas of Ukraine. Russia also suspended its involvement in the UN-backed deal to export grain through the Black Sea. Brazil held presidential elections, in a tight race between two polarising candidates. In Asia, South Korea entered a period of national mourning after a stampede in its capital left over 150 mostly young people dead. China held its Communist Party Conference, paving the way for President Xi Jinping to enter his third consecutive presidential term. In North Africa, both Egypt and Tunisia reached deals with the IMF for multibillion dollar loans to help their flailing economies. Protests continued in Iran over the death of 22-year-old Mahsa Amini, who died in police custody. Iraq broke its year-long political deadlock, electing as new president. In the UK, Liz Truss resigned as prime minister after a calamitous 44-day term. Rishi Sunak

RUSSIA AND UKRAINE

An explosion on Russia's bridge spanning the Kerch Strait to **Crimea** resulted in the death of at least three people and caused severe damage to its structure, dealing a major blow to Putin's during his invasion of Ukraine, which has entered its seventh month. The explosion was triggered by a truck on the bridge's roadside, causing seven fuel tanks on the adjacent railway bridge to ignite. In response, Putin issued orders to heighten security measures at the bridge and conduct an investigation. The incident led to massive clouds of smoke and a raging blaze, resulting in the collapse of two road spans and scorching of a section of the railway. The 12-mile bridge was constructed when Russia annexed Crimea from Ukraine in 2014 and was completed in 2018. It stands as an impressive engineering feat and had come to symbolize Russian prestige. The bridge plays a crucial role in shipping, connecting export ports on the Azov Sea to the Black Sea, and serves as a significant conduit for supplying Russia's war effort in south-eastern Ukraine. In recent times, Russian troops have experienced substantial retreats from territories that Putin claimed as Russian after annexing four Ukrainian regions, adding to Russia's humiliation. Putin accused Ukraine of orchestrating a "terrorist attack" on the bridge, asserting that there was "no doubt" about Ukraine's involvement in the explosion. However, Ukraine has not taken responsibility for the attack, although some officials posted derogatory comments about Russia on social media, and the Ukrainian post office issued a commemorative stamp.

In response to the escalating situation in **Ukraine**, Vladimir Putin declared martial law in four occupied regions and granted sweeping powers to security forces. The measures include broad travel restrictions, vehicle checks, and "economic mobilization" in large parts of western and southern Russia. Putin also authorized Russia's governors to ensure public order, supply the armed forces, and protect critical infrastructure in eight regions bordering Ukraine, including the Crimean Peninsula. These actions were taken as a response to Kyiv's continued successes in counteroffensives in occupied regions, including the advance on the southern city of Kherson, and growing tensions over Russia's faltering invasion.

In another significant development, Ukrainian troops successfully liberated the key eastern city of **Lyman**, marking yet another military defeat for Russia. Russia's Ministry of Defense acknowledged its troops' retreat after Putin's earlier claim that the city in the Donetsk region would forever belong to Russia. In a ceremony held at the Kremlin, Putin announced the annexation of the province along with Luhansk, Kherson, and Zaporizhzhia. However, Ukrainian forces managed to encircle the city entirely, trapping thousands of Russian soldiers inside.

Russia's suspension of its participation in the UN-backed deal with Kyiv further escalated tensions and threatened to worsen the **global food crisis**. Russia linked its decision to an attack on ships in Sevastopol, Crimea, attributing it to the Ukrainian armed forces. The attack allegedly involved Ukrainian drones being shot down by air defences, while autonomous explosive boats caused damage to navy vessels and energy facilities. Putin expressed dissatisfaction with the deal, claiming that it was not adequately benefiting the "poorest countries." The UN data revealed that rich countries received the majority of the shipment volumes, led by Spain, with middle-income countries like Turkey and China accounting for about a quarter. Lower and lower-middle income countries, including Egypt and Ethiopia, received just over a fifth. The UN clarified that the agreement was intended to make grain purchases more accessible for poorer countries and to lower market prices affected by Russia's invasion of Ukraine. However, Ukraine disputed Russia's pretext for pulling out of the deal.

Putin announced an end to Russia's mobilization drive to bolster its forces in Ukraine but defended the draft army from criticism. According to Russia's president, around 220,000 men had been drafted into the army since he called up reserves and moved to annex four occupied regions in south-eastern Ukraine. He believed this effort was sufficient to strengthen the forces on the battlefield. Despite Putin's threats of using nuclear weapons to defend the regions now considered part of Russia, Kyiv's forces continued to advance, with the draft proving deeply unpopular in Russia. More men fled to Kazakhstan in the first two weeks following Putin's decree than joined the army. However, despite these challenges, Kyiv's forces made significant progress since the ceremony held in the Kremlin and the rally on Red Square to celebrate the annexation.

THE AMERICAS

Brazilians headed to the polls to choose between two politicians with markedly different visions for Latin America's most populous nation. The run-off vote between the current right-wing populist president, Jair Bolsonaro, and the leftist former leader, Luiz Inácio Lula da Silva, is expected to be a close result after a protracted and acrimonious campaign. This election holds significant importance as it will shape the political trajectory of the country. Bolsonaro, an ex-army captain, is seen by his supporters as a champion of freedom and defender of traditional values, protecting the nation of 215 million people from what they view as godless socialism. On the other hand, Lula, who served two terms as president between 2003 and 2010, has formed a broad coalition that includes centrist politicians, arguing that Bolsonaro poses a threat to democracy.

In **Venezuela**, opposition parties are considering a plan to dissolve their "interim government" and abandon Juan Guaidó's claim as the country's legitimate leader, recognizing that the US-sponsored attempt to overthrow President Nicolás Maduro has failed after nearly four years. The end of Guaidó's "interim government" would mark the conclusion of an unusual diplomatic experiment, wherein a coalition of more than 50 mainly Western nations established formal relations with a shadow opposition administration to push for regime change in Caracas, following allegations of election rigging by Maduro in 2018. Additionally, this move could lead to the US easing oil sanctions on the Maduro government, providing an alternative supply source for Western nations boycotting Russian crude due to its war in Ukraine.

The congressional committee investigating the **US** Capitol attack from last year has voted unanimously to issue a subpoena to former president Donald Trump, holding him responsible for the violence that occurred that day. This marks the seventh instance in history that Congress has issued a subpoena to a sitting or former president and sets the stage for a potentially high-stakes legal battle. Some of Trump's closest aides have already refused to comply with subpoenas to testify before the committee, leading to their prosecution. Steve Bannon, for example, is facing sentencing for contempt of Congress later this month. Trump might choose to attend a hearing but refuse to answer questions, following the lead of some of his supporters. Speculation suggests that Trump could launch a legal challenge that might prolong the congressional investigation until after the midterm elections in November. During a recent televised hearing on the January 6, 2021, Capitol attack, the committee presented fresh evidence that Trump believed he had lost the election but continued with efforts to overturn the results.

ASIA

South Korea's President Yoon Suk Yeol has declared a national mourning period following a tragic incident in a popular Seoul nightlife district, where at least 151 people lost their lives, and many others were injured in a crush. Around 100,000 individuals had gathered to celebrate Halloween in Itaewon, an area known for its concentration of bars and restaurants in narrow streets and alleyways. A surge in the crowd within a tight passageway left numerous people unconscious, prompting emergency workers and passers-by to rush to perform CPR amid distressing scenes. The cause of the initial surge remains unknown.

Amid heightened tensions on the Korean peninsula due to recent **North Korean** missile launches, South Korea initiated a series of military exercises. These annual drills aim to simulate various threats from North Korea, including the use of nuclear weapons, and involve troops from the South Korean armed forces as well as some US soldiers. In response, Pyongyang conducted artillery drills near the inter-Korean border and flew military jets south of a reconnaissance boundary set by the South Korean armed forces. This came after North Korea launched long-range cruise missiles, with state media reporting that leader Kim Jong Un wanted to test the "rapid reaction ability of our nuclear combat force." North Korea blamed the escalation on joint military exercises between the US and South Korea in recent months, a stance supported by allies Russia and China. The UN Security Council failed to condemn North Korea's firing of an intermediate-range ballistic missile over Japan, as Russia and China accused the US of disregarding North Korean security concerns.

In **Pakistan**, the election commission has barred Imran Khan from holding office, alleging that he incorrectly declared his assets, leading to a contentious case that may heighten political tensions in the country. Khan's party, Pakistan Tehreek-e-Insaf, confirmed the election commission's ruling and stated their intent to challenge the decision in Islamabad's high court. The case revolves around accusations that Khan violated the law by selling gifts he received while serving as prime minister. Khan denies any wrongdoing, and some legal experts question whether the case will withstand a challenge. This decision sets the stage for a tense stand-off between Khan and Prime Minister Shehbaz Sharif, with PTI leaders calling on their supporters to protest nationwide. Sharif assumed office in April after Khan lost a no-confidence vote in parliament, but Khan's popularity has surged as he alleges a foreign-backed conspiracy to remove him. Many analysts believe Khan is the most popular candidate for the upcoming elections, scheduled to be held by late next year.

President Xi Jinping urged the 97 million members of the **Chinese** Communist Party to brace themselves for a critical time in the country's history as he inaugurated a congress that will further solidify his position as the most powerful ruler since Mao Zedong. Xi highlighted the party's glorious mission, which includes goals such as waging an all-out people's war against the Covid-19 pandemic and achieving the unification of China and Taiwan. The week-long congress will conclude with the formation of a new leadership line-up and Xi's reappointment to a third term as party leader and head of the Chinese military, despite controversial policies that have slowed down China's economic growth and strained its relationship with the US and its allies. The party congress will also usher in a new 200-member central committee, a politburo comprising the top

25 party officials, and a seven-seat Politburo Standing Committee, led by Xi.

Shanghai is implementing stricter Covid-19 restrictions in response to an increase in cases, sparking concerns about potential disruptions in China's financial center just a few months after emerging from a prolonged lockdown. Various districts have confirmed the closure of entertainment venues, including bars and cinemas, as authorities work to contain the latest outbreak while keeping case numbers relatively low. Close contacts of positive cases are being sent to quarantine hotels and centers, and their residential buildings are temporarily locked down, demonstrating the city's determination to stamp out any virus outbreaks. This situation reflects a broader state of agitation across the country ahead of the opening of the quinquennial event, which has led to the adoption of stricter measures, especially in Beijing.

Sri Lanka is now importing significant quantities of oil from Russia, signalling a notable shift in supplies as cash-strapped nations take advantage of price discounts resulting from Western sanctions on Moscow. Due to a financial crisis, Sri Lanka has been heavily reliant on Russian crude since May, with more than half of its oil sourced from Russia for the first time since at least 2013. This move reflects a trend where financially stressed countries are seeking to reduce import costs in response to rising inflation and the strength of the US dollar. Following Russia's invasion of Ukraine, the G7 nations pledged to phase out or ban imports of Russian oil. However, countries like India, China, Pakistan, Bangladesh, Cuba, and Sri Lanka have continued to buy Russian oil despite the geopolitical situation.

Myanmar's deposed former leader, Aung San Suu Kyi, and Nobel Peace Prize winner, has been sentenced to an additional three years in prison for corruption by a court in the military-run country. This sentence extends her total prison term to 26 years, adding to a series of punishments handed down to the 77-year-old, a prominent figure opposing decades of military rule. Suu Kyi was accused of receiving $500,000 in bribes from a local tycoon, but she denied the charge, and her lawyers claim that the allegations against her are politically motivated. Currently held in solitary confinement at a prison in Naypyidaw, the capital, Suu Kyi continues to face legal challenges after being removed from power in a military coup in 2021.

A deadly incident occurred during an **Indonesian** league soccer match, resulting in at least 131 fatalities and marking one of the world's deadliest stadium disasters. The tragedy unfolded when clashes erupted between supporters of Arema FC and rival Persebaya Surabaya, two major soccer teams in Indonesia, following a match in the city of Malang, East Java. The losing team's supporters invaded the pitch, prompting the police to use tear gas, leading to a stampede and suffocation cases. Tragically, two police officers were also killed during the chaotic event.

Thailand is in mourning following a gun and knife attack at a nursery, leaving children dead and triggering calls for stricter gun control and a crackdown on illicit drugs. The assailant opened fire and stabbed sleeping children at a preschool in Uthai Sawan, resulting in 37 fatalities. After the attack, the perpetrator shot a bystander and returned home, where he killed his wife, child, and himself. The country's monarch, King Maha Vajiralongkorn, and Queen Suthida expressed condolences to the victims and their families, meeting them personally. The tragic incident has sparked public gatherings, demanding justice and action against such heinous acts. The attacker, Panya Khamrab, a 34-year-old former police lieutenant colonel who was previously dismissed from the force for drug possession, has raised concerns about the need for more stringent measures to prevent such violent acts in the future.

AFRICA

The IMF and **Egypt** have reached a $3 billion loan deal after Cairo fulfilled a key bailout condition by floating its currency. The decision caused the Egyptian pound to slide as the central bank abandoned its policy of using reserves to support the currency, aiming to reduce import costs and maintain social stability in a country where 60% of the population faces economic vulnerability. The loan agreement comes after months of talks with the IMF, prompted by soaring commodity prices and a foreign currency crisis exacerbated by Russia's invasion of Ukraine, leading to significant outflows of foreign debt investors. This marks Egypt's fourth loan agreement with the IMF since 2016, with the economy witnessing growth despite the pandemic, largely driven by state and military investments in infrastructure projects while private sector investment and manufactured exports continue to lag.

Tunisia has reached a preliminary agreement with the IMF on a $1.9 billion loan to address food and fuel shortages in the North African economy. The deal is expected to unlock loans from other donors, pending assurances of Tunisia's commitment to reforms. This marks the third agreement between Tunisia and the IMF since 2013, and the country is urged to implement previously agreed reforms, including subsidy reductions, state-owned enterprise privatization, and civil service wage cuts. The reform program includes increasing targeted cash transfers to the poor and expanding the social safety net to help vulnerable families affected by price increases. Tunisia is also committing to reforming state-owned companies to improve the economic situation.

Nigeria is facing severe flooding, affecting 33 of its 36 states and the capital Abuja, resulting in over 600 deaths and 1.3 million people displaced from their homes. The government attributes the situation to an unusually heavy rainy season exacerbated by climate change and excess water release from a dam. The floods have submerged over 108,000 hectares of farmland, destroyed critical infrastructure, and caused partial or complete destruction of over 200,000 homes. The affected areas include rice-producing states, raising concerns about food shortages as annual food inflation reaches 23%. The situation has led to a tragic incident where a boat carrying people fleeing rising water levels capsized, causing fatalities.

Sam Matekane, one of **Lesotho's** wealthiest individuals, is set to become the country's prime minister as his newly established party, the Revolution for Prosperity, secured 56 seats out of 120 in the elections. Despite falling just short of a parliamentary majority, Matekane's party is in a strong position to form a government. He aims to prevent Lesotho, an enclave surrounded by South African territory, from becoming a "failed state" and vows to step back from his business interests if he becomes prime minister to avoid conflicts of interest.

Burkina Faso's army captain Ibrahim Traore has been officially designated as the country's transitional President after staging the second coup of the year to seize power. Officials are working on plans to restore the country to constitutional rule in the face of a violent insurgency linked to Al Qaeda and Islamic State groups. Burkina Faso has been grappling with political instability and violence, leading to thousands of casualties and massive displacement. Traore commits to a democratic transition timeline to restore constitutional order by July 2024, as agreed with his predecessor and the Economic Community of West African States (ECOWAS).

THE MIDDLE EAST

Israel and **Lebanon** have reached an agreement on their maritime border, ending a long-standing dispute after months of US-brokered talks. The deal allows both countries to develop gas fields in the eastern Mediterranean, easing tensions that have arisen in recent months. Negotiations restarted this year after London-listed Greek oil and gas explorer Energean arrived at the Karish gas field in the Mediterranean, prompting conflicting claims from Israel and Lebanon. The lack of bilateral ties between the two countries means the deal will be conducted through separate agreements between each country and the US.

Thousands of protesters in **Iran** marked 40 days since Mahsa Amini's death in police custody, resulting in clashes with Iranian riot police across the country. The largest demonstrations were in Amini's hometown of Saqqez, with the internet shut down in response. Protests have erupted across Iran following Amini's death, with demands for social change and opposition to the regime. Iran's government has been facing challenges in ending the wave of anti-regime protests, sparked by Amini's arrest and death in the hands of the morality police.

Saudi Arabia's sovereign wealth fund is set to invest $24 billion in six Arab countries to strengthen its soft power and economic presence in the region amid an oil boom. The fund will establish companies in Iraq, Jordan, Bahrain, Oman, and Sudan, seeking investments in various sectors. The wealthier Gulf states, including Saudi Arabia, UAE, and Qatar, have been aiding their allies with loans and central bank deposits to support their economies amid deepening economic and social pressures.

Western team captains at the World Cup in Qatar plan to wear rainbow-themed armbands in support of the "One Love" anti-discrimination message, promoting diversity and inclusion. FIFA has not clarified whether this action would result in punishment, as it strictly prohibits political action on the pitch. The gesture has drawn both support and criticism, with some dismissing it as a mere token gesture in a country where homosexuality remains illegal.

Iraq's political deadlock has been broken with the election of Abdul Latif Rashid as the new president. Rashid, a veteran Kurdish politician, defeated incumbent president Barham Salih, paving the way for a government formation within the constitutionally mandated 30-day period. The political feud between Shia cleric Moqtada al-Sadr and his Iran-backed rivals had caused a year-long crisis in Iraq, resulting in street protests and instability.

Syrian soldiers suffered a deadly attack when an explosive device detonated on a military bus in Damascus countryside. The attack caused numerous casualties and is one of the deadliest against government forces in recent years. Syria has been grappling with a long-running civil war, and while government forces have regained control of much of the territory, attacks and violence continue to persist in regime-held areas.

OPEC+ has announced plans to slash oil supply, with **Saudi Arabia** clarifying that the decision was unanimous and not influenced by its stance on Russia's invasion of Ukraine. This decision came amid backlash from the US, and the Saudi government suggested that the Biden administration had asked for a delay in cutting oil production to avoid impacting crude prices before the midterm elections.

Turkey's official inflation rate reached a 24-year high, rising to 83.45% in September due to President Erdogan's unorthodox economic policies. Despite established economic consensus, Erdogan has pushed for interest rate cuts to boost growth ahead of critical elections. This has led to a heavy pressure on the Turkish currency and rampant inflation, raising concerns about the country's economic stability.

EUROPE

Rishi Sunak, the former Chancellor, has become **Britain's** youngest and first non-white Prime Minister in modern times, promising to tackle the profound economic challenges facing the country. Chancellor Jeremy Hunt is encouraging Sunak to proceed with a new debt-cutting plan. Sunak was elected Tory leader after Boris Johnson and Penny Mordaunt dropped out of the contest. Liz Truss, who had a 44-day tenure as Prime Minister, resigned. The combination of Sunak and Hunt, both seen as fiscal conservatives, is hoped to reassure markets and lower borrowing costs, benefiting mortgage rates.

French President Emmanuel Macron's statement that France would not respond with nuclear weapons if Russia used its atomic arsenal against Ukraine or the region caused criticism within the NATO alliance. This broke from the standard policy of "strategic ambiguity" followed by nuclear-armed countries. Macron cited the "fundamental interests of the nation" and France's nuclear doctrine. Such explicit declarations are rare to avoid giving adversaries a playbook for possible attacks. France is a critical part of NATO's deterrence against Russia, and Macron's words were discussed at a meeting of NATO defense ministers in Brussels.

Austria's President, Alexander Van der Bellen, secured a second six-year term in office after winning a majority of votes in the election, avoiding a runoff. The former leader of the Greens projected calm during national crises, earning broad popularity. The far-right Freedom Party (FPO) was the only party to present a candidate against Van der Bellen, who received backing from other parties' leaders. The President's role is largely ceremonial but involves overseeing periods of transition and turbulence.

The **German** government has hinted at permitting personal possession of up to 30g of cannabis, with the measure yet to be approved by parliament and the European Commission. Health Minister Karl Lauterbach presented the initiative, aiming to make it law by 2024. The plan would also allow adults to grow three cannabis plants at home. Lauterbach argues that decriminalization would protect young people's health, as the current cannabis ban has not been effective in curbing usage or adult drug addiction. The government is also considering limiting the maximum potency of cannabis products available to individuals under 21.

SOURCES:

https://www.ft.com/content/d3db052a-2471-4c45-849d-21c58e58ffd9

https://www.ft.com/content/8cdb1346-0950-41aa-b3e2-fbc28542f506

https://www.infoplease.com/current-events/2022/october-world-news

https://www.ft.com/content/3e700f18-81bc-4336-b944-ba7c1146c6e5

https://www.bbc.co.uk/news/world-asia-63344059

https://www.ft.com/content/134adedd-844c-425d-b706-1248b5be5080

https://www.theguardian.com/world/2022/oct/29/dozens-of-people-crushed-by-large-crowd-at-halloween-festivities-in-south-korea

https://www.ft.com/content/95ee40c1-110c-4b25-bf00-8518a6d9d650

https://www.ft.com/content/2f6f2e4f-8a2e-4b7d-9203-3debbec52e54

https://www.ft.com/content/e4b5827e-26da-49eb-aa04-4a4198631f48

https://www.ft.com/content/dbb7db99-d78f-4dde-8e49-4d0e6732e484

https://www.theguardian.com/world/live/2022/oct/23/chinas-president-xi-jinping-expected-to-secure-historic-third-term-in-power

https://www.ft.com/content/b8f0c047-fff3-4860-b8d7-ccd7dcba8da8

https://www.ft.com/content/59e4ff01-f8eb-4ba1-95e9-bcaa76bcbb10

https://www.reuters.com/world/africa/gunfire-heard-burkina-faso-capital-day-after-coup-reuters-reporter-2022-10-01/

https://www.ft.com/content/5b5360b4-e34e-4c1d-9886-82e653fb2111

https://www.ft.com/content/049654de-708d-4582-9305-96a10e5627f5

https://www.ft.com/content/4806dbc6-d920-4dc3-9895-8974b2521875

https://www.aljazeera.com/news/2022/10/11/israel-lebanon-agree-on-draft-deal-on-maritime-borders

https://www.ft.com/content/dc619255-609f-4859-90b0-2a2a84157d2a

https://www.ft.com/content/fefe4857-10b8-497b-9904-da86daf5c7bb

https://www.ft.com/content/d6e1f062-309f-4649-b557-ab6cf2edc499

https://www.aljazeera.com/news/2022/10/13/iraqi-parliament-elects-new-president-abdul-latif-rashid

https://www.reuters.com/world/middle-east/several-soldiers-dead-wounded-explosion-targeting-military-bus-syria-state-media-2022-10-13/

https://www.ft.com/content/48d61b60-6fc0-4ea2-8cc9-79ee580f7044

https://www.ft.com/content/5eaea58f-d04f-40d6-aae5-f0b39ab324c0

https://www.aljazeera.com/news/2022/10/24/rishi-sunak-becomes-uks-new-prime-minister

https://www.ft.com/content/f08c920d-84db-4c91-89f7-e23a1329edef

https://www.infoplease.com/current-events/2022/october-world-news

THE WORLD IN NOVEMBER 2022

Introduction

November 2022 was a month during which the world continued to grapple with the consequences of Russia's invasion of Ukraine. As the war entered its ninth month, Russia ended its draft of citizens to fight in the country's war in Ukraine. As the Ukrainian counter-offensive continued, Russian forces retreated from the city of Kherson in southern Ukraine, a major setback for Russia which captured the strategic city early in the war. A missile that landed in Poland killing two people caused tension between NATO members over its source. The blast had threatened to escalate the Ukraine war into a conflict between Russia and Nato, causing moments of panic at the G20 summit in Bali. In Europe, Turkey continued to block Sweden's bid to join NATO and Germany signed a long-term gas supply deal with Qatar, the first long-term agreement for LNG supplies to an EU country since Russia's invasion of Ukraine. Tensions continued between the European Commission and Hungary over transparency in the country's finances. In the Middle East, the FIFA World Cup began in Qatar, becoming the first Arab nation to host the tournament. Benjamin Netanyahu won a decisive majority in the Israeli parliamentary election after 18 months away from power and protests continued on the streets of Iran. In Pakistan, ousted leader Imran Khan began a week-long march through the province of Punjab. Malaysia elected a new Prime Minister after a chaotic election and President Tokayev consolidated his grip on power after elections in Kazakhstan. US President Biden announced plans to run for a second term as president, as former president Donald Trump launched his third presidential campaign. In Africa, the Ethiopian government and the regional forces of Tigray agreed a peace deal after two years of civil war. At the UN COP27 climate summit in Egypt G20 nations pledged to strive to limit global warming to 1.5C.

WAR IN UKRAINE

Russia has declared the completion of its "partial mobilization," which involved mobilizing hundreds of thousands of citizens to join the war on Ukraine, thereby ending a controversial draft that sparked protests. The Ministry of Defense in Russia confirmed the suspension of all partial mobilization activities, including summons deliveries and conscription for military service. Going forward, the country will only accept volunteers and contractors. The mobilization was announced by Russia's President, Vladimir Putin, in late September, following a significant setback on the battlefields in Ukraine. Officials confirmed that the draft's target of recruiting 300,000 personnel had been met. However, the chaotic execution of the draft led to hundreds of thousands of people fleeing Russia.

In a significant shift, President Putin publicly called for the evacuation of civilians from the Russian-occupied city of **Kherson**, recognizing Ukraine's advancements in recapturing the city. This marks the first acknowledgment of such an evacuation by President Putin. Ukraine has launched a fierce counter-offensive to regain Kherson, the only regional capital that Russia has captured during its nine-month invasion. The counter-offensive has faced challenges due to renewed efforts to target Ukraine's energy infrastructure, particularly as winter approaches. Ukrainian President Volodymyr Zelenskyy accused Putin of engaging in "energy terror," resulting in widespread power outages affecting 4.5 million people across the country. These outages were caused by massive Russian missile barrages and drone attacks on Ukrainian power facilities, plunging much of Kyiv and other parts of the country into darkness. Kyiv's mayor, Vitali Klitschko, reported that 450,000 residents of the capital were without power. Russia has acknowledged that its armed forces targeted critical infrastructure as part of an attempt to "neutralize military infrastructure facilities." In response to the situation, the Pentagon announced a $400 million military aid package for Ukraine, which includes the delivery of Hawk air defense systems and tactical Phoenix Ghost drones, as well as the refurbishment of advanced tanks from the Czech Republic.

A dispute arose between Ukraine and its Western allies regarding the origin of a missile that exploded in **Poland**. Nato, Warsaw, and the US suggested that Kyiv's air defense forces likely fired the weapon during a Russian attack. However, Ukraine's President Volodymyr Zelenskyy disagreed, asserting with certainty that the missile that landed in the village of Przewodów near the Ukrainian border, resulting in two fatalities, was not Ukrainian. Nato Secretary-General Jens Stoltenberg stated there was no indication that the missile attack was a deliberate act by Moscow. He emphasized that the western military alliance had no evidence of Russia preparing offensive military actions against Nato.

In response to the incident, **Ukraine** called for increased Western air defenses after a Soviet-era missile seemingly misfired, leading to casualties in Poland and raising the potential for a confrontation between Nato and Russia. The Ukrainian Deputy Defense Minister highlighted the need for more sophisticated weaponry to protect Kyiv from the daily bombardment of Russian cruise missiles and kamikaze drones.

President Zelenskyy expressed his country's readiness to apologize if the missile turned out to be Ukrainian. However, he added that Ukraine's military General Valerii Zaluzhny assured him it was not their missile or strike. Military experts analyzed debris from the incident site in Poland, indicating that a Soviet-era 5V55K missile, used with the S-300 system dating back to 1978, may have veered off course, leading to the explosion in Przewodów. Nato held the Kremlin responsible for the explosion in Poland, raising concerns that the incident could escalate the Ukraine war into a conflict between Russia and Nato. The situation even caused moments of panic during the G20 summit in Bali.

EUROPE

Turkish President Erdogan asserted that **Sweden** must take additional actions to convince him to withdraw opposition to its bid to join the Nato alliance. These actions include deporting asylum seekers wanted by his government for terror-related offenses. In May, Sweden and Finland, after ending their longstanding military non-alignment, applied for Nato membership. However, Turkey, with Nato's second-largest army, has refused to endorse their joint bid. Turkey accuses Sweden of harboring individuals with alleged links to Kurdish militants and a religious network connected to a failed military coup in 2016. Erdogan appreciated Sweden's recent decision to lift an arms embargo on Turkey, imposed in 2019 after Turkey's Syria invasion targeting Kurdish militants. Nevertheless, he expects Sweden to fulfill the commitments agreed upon in a memorandum signed with Finland and Turkey by the end of November.

Qatar and **Germany** have entered into a significant long-term supply agreement for liquefied natural gas (LNG). This represents a significant step for Germany as it aims to reduce its reliance on Russian gas. The deal entails the annual supply of 2 million tonnes of LNG to Germany for at least 15 years, with deliveries scheduled to commence in 2026. Notably, these are the first long-term LNG supply agreements with an EU country since Russia's invasion of Ukraine in February. European countries have been cautious about such deals as they seek alternatives to Russian pipeline gas in their transition away from fossil fuels.

Hungary faces potential delays in receiving EU payments amounting to up to €13.3bn, following accusations from Brussels that the country has not fulfilled its commitments to combat corruption. The European Commission recommends freezing €7.5bn in cohesion payments after finding Budapest's delivery of 17 pledged reforms to the rule of law unsatisfactory. Despite endorsing

Hungary's €5.8bn Covid-19 recovery plan, the commission insists on no disbursements until the promised reforms are implemented. This stance deals a blow to Prime Minister Viktor Orban, who is eager to access EU funding as Hungary's currency, the forint, faces challenges amid a budget deficit exceeding 6% of gross domestic product this year. Hungary has had longstanding disagreements with the EU over concerns about its rule of law record, with critics, including a majority in the European parliament, expressing worries about the fair and transparent distribution of EU taxpayer money.

MIDDLE EAST AND NORTH AFRICA

The 2022 FIFA World Cup tournament began in **Qatar**, the first Arab country to host the tournament. There have been various tensions in the lead up to Qatar's hosting of the tournament, mainly centring over Qatar's treatment of its migrant labour force and decision to ban the sale of beer in stadiums.

Benjamin Netanyahu and his allies secured a decisive majority in **Israel's** parliamentary election, setting the stage for his return to power as the leader of one of the most right-wing governments in the nation's history. According to the final tally released by the election committee, a bloc comprising Netanyahu's Likud party, the extreme-right Religious Zionism, and two ultraorthodox parties, Shas and United Torah Judaism, would hold 64 seats in the 120-seat Knesset. Meanwhile, the Yesh Atid party, led by outgoing Prime Minister Yair Lapid, obtained 51 seats, and the non-aligned Hadash-Ta'al alliance secured five seats.

In **Iran**, people filled the streets of various towns and cities across the country to mourn those who lost their lives during significant rounds of protests against the Islamic republic. Ceremonies were held to mark the 40th day since the deaths of some young protesters, a traditional Shia Muslim period of mourning. Demonstrations took place in Karaj, Qazvin, Arak, Amol, and Fuladshahr, with protesters chanting anti-regime slogans and engaging in clashes with riot police. The protests, triggered by the death of 22-year-old Kurdish woman Mahsa Amini in police custody, have grown in size and scope, with many young Iranians demanding a secular, modern government to replace the country's Islamic theocracy. According to Amnesty International, more than 200 protesters, including 30 children, have been killed in what they call a "lethal crackdown." The demonstrations have spread to other cities such as Rasht, Tabriz, Mashhad, Kermanshah, and various neighbourhoods in Tehran.

In response to a rebuke from the UN's watchdog over alleged undeclared nuclear sites, **Iran** has announced an expansion of its nuclear enrichment program, including enriching uranium to 60% purity at the underground Fordow facility, just below weapons-grade levels. The International Atomic Energy Agency's board had passed a resolution calling on Iran to cooperate regarding traces of uranium found at undisclosed sites in the country. Despite facing international criticism for the crackdown on protesters within the country and alleged missile and drone sales to Russia for attacks on Ukrainian cities, Iran has consistently maintained that its nuclear program is for peaceful purposes. However, experts view uranium enrichment to 60% as a significant step towards reaching weapons-grade levels of 90%.

A new resolution criticizing **Iran** for inadequate cooperation with the International Atomic Energy Agency's investigation has been adopted by the agency's board of governors, with Iran objecting to it. The resolution, introduced by the United States, France, Germany, and the United Kingdom, urges Iran to cooperate fully with the IAEA's investigation into traces of uranium found at undisclosed sites. The West and the IAEA have repeatedly called on Iran to provide comprehensive explanations for the traces of man-made nuclear particles discovered at various Iranian sites in 2018, and to fully restore agency monitoring capabilities. This is the second such resolution against Iran, with China and Russia being the only countries to object to it. Tensions increased after the US withdrew from the 2015 nuclear deal, known as the Joint Comprehensive Plan of Action (JCPOA), imposing severe sanctions on Iran. Talks to restore the deal have stalled in recent months.

Turkey has attributed a bombing in central Istanbul that resulted in six deaths and numerous injuries to Kurdish militants, and has pledged retaliation. Turkey accused the US of supporting Kurdish rebels in Syria, likening the US to a "murderer" due to this alleged support. The Istanbul police department detained 46 people in connection with the attack on İstiklal Avenue. The primary suspect, identified as a Syrian national, left an explosive device containing TNT near a bench on the pedestrian street. She claimed to be a "special intelligence officer" for the armed Kurdistan Workers party (PKK) and its Syrian affiliate, stating that she entered Turkey illegally from the north-west Syrian province of Afrin.

ASIA

Convoys of motorcycles and vans adorned in red, green, and white colours travelled along **Pakistan's** historic Grand Trunk Road, led by ousted Prime Minister Imran Khan. Khan has initiated a week-long march through Punjab, the country's largest province, heading to Islamabad, with the aim of rallying enough support to topple rival Shehbaz Sharif's government and push for early elections. This "long march" represents Khan's determined efforts for a political comeback. Despite facing challenges, such as being barred from holding office over mishandling gift allegations and facing proceedings for accepting foreign funds, Khan's populist messaging has resonated with the public amidst economic difficulties and inflation. He also encountered dropped terrorism charges, a stand-off with the military, and is navigating a turbulent political landscape.

In **Malaysia**, Anwar Ibrahim has been sworn in as the country's Prime Minister after the king intervened to resolve post-election chaos, bringing significant political change to the nation. Anwar, a former protégé of former Prime Minister Mahathir Mohamad, faced two decades in opposition and controversies that led to imprisonment on sodomy charges and political disqualification. Following a general election with a hung parliament, Anwar's appointment follows five days of uncertainty and signifies the culmination of political divisions and economic challenges due to the pandemic.

Kazakhstan's President Tokayev secured a landslide re-election victory, further solidifying his control over the central Asian country. The elections, held under tight media controls criticized by human rights groups, saw Tokayev garnering more than 81% of the preliminary vote. With limited access to major media, the president's competitors earned single-digit percentages in the polls. The elections witnessed a significant turnout of nearly 70%, while some opposition activists who held protests were detained.

North Korea fired at least 17 missiles into the sea, with one landing less than 60 km off South Korea's coast, leading to tensions in the region. It was the first time a ballistic missile had reached near South Korea's waters since the peninsula's division. South Korea issued an air raid warning and responded by launching missiles. This escalation marks the most missiles North Korea has fired in a single day, and the situation remains tense with South Korea's military actively responding.

THE AMERICAS

Joe Biden expressed his desire to run for a second term in the White House and will make a final decision early next year, following a stronger than expected performance by Democrats in the midterm elections. Although Democrats avoided sweeping defeats in Congress, they still face the risk of losing control of both chambers to Republicans, as Americans did not grant a strong political mandate to either party. Biden and his party found some comfort in the election outcome, as they were predicted to suffer heavy losses. However, the results dealt a blow to Donald Trump's presidential ambitions, as victories by Republican candidates he endorsed were not enough to fuel his potential run for the White House in 2024. Ron DeSantis, the Florida governor, emerged as the clear winner for the Republican presidential nomination, considered a likely challenger to Trump. Biden, who turns 80 this month and has faced low approval ratings, has been questioned about his willingness to seek a second term, with exit polls showing that more than two-thirds of Americans do not want him to run again.

The **Colombian** government and the leftist guerrilla group, the National Liberation Army (ELN), will initiate peace talks to put an end to the over half-century-long war that has caused numerous casualties. This fulfils a campaign promise from Colombia's first leftist president, Gustavo Petro, a former guerrilla fighter with the now-defunct M-19 rebels, who seeks "total peace" with various armed groups in the conflict-torn Andean nation. The first round of talks is set to take place in Caracas, Venezuela, following a diplomatic improvement between the two neighboring countries. Petro visited Venezuelan President Nicolás Maduro this month, breaking from the policy of his predecessor, Iván Duque, who recognized the US-backed opposition leader Juan Guaidó as Venezuela's legitimate leader. Cuba and Norway, both experienced in mediating negotiations between the Colombian government and rebel groups, will join Venezuela as guarantors of the peace process. The location of talks is expected to rotate between the three countries, although Cuba and Norway have not confirmed this. Previous talks between the government and ELN were broken off by Duque after the rebels carried out a car bomb attack that killed 22 police cadets in 2019, as they refused to halt attacks against the state.

The **Venezuelan** government and the country's opposition will recommence talks in Mexico, raising the possibility of easing US oil sanctions in exchange for progress towards free and fair elections. Amid a severe economic collapse and allegations of human rights abuses, President Nicolás Maduro has managed to withstand Washington's sanctions and a diplomatic boycott, thanks to support from Russia, Cuba, China, Turkey, and Iran. Norway, acting as a mediator, announced the resumption of talks, which also involve a $3 billion fund from various frozen Venezuelan accounts to be managed by the United Nations for healthcare, infrastructure, and education needs. Previous talks that started in September 2021 were disrupted when the Maduro government walked out following the extradition of key ally Alex Saab to the US on money-laundering charges.

The Cuban leader met with President Putin in Moscow to reaffirm mutual support, evoking memories of the Cold War era. **Cuba**, among the few countries not condemning Russia's invasion of Ukraine at the UN, has complicated its recent efforts to thaw relations with the US. Cuba's increasing dependence on Russian oil, due in part to Venezuela's production slump, has led to multiple oil shipments from Russia to the island. Moscow has extended repayment terms for a $2.3 billion loan to Cuba. Currently facing its deepest economic crisis since the early 1990s, Cuba experienced food shortages and mass migration during its "special period" after the dissolution of the Soviet Union, its main trading partner and benefactor.

Donald Trump launched his third campaign for the US presidency, aiming to "save our country" and build the "greatest economy ever." The former president, despite two impeachments and disappointing Republican results in the midterm elections, made the announcement at his Mar-a-Lago residence in Florida. Trump, 76, avoided his usual complaints about the 2020 election being fraudulent and reviewed his accomplishments while accusing President Biden of failures. He also proposed eye-catching ideas for a second term, including the death penalty for drug dealers, planting the American flag on Mars, and advocating for term limits for members of Congress.

After losing the bitterly fought election to Luiz Inacio Lula da Silva, **Brazil's** President Bolsonaro broke his two-day silence, refusing to concede but stating he would abide by the constitution. Following the election, roadblocks organized by his supporters paralyzed the nation, with lorry drivers blocking roads and affecting food supplies. Bolsonaro had made unfounded claims of possible electoral fraud before the election, and while Lula secured 50.9% of the vote to Bolsonaro's 49.1%, it marked the narrowest victory since Brazil's military rule ended in 1985. Environmentalists welcomed Lula's victory, as they were concerned about rising levels of Amazon deforestation during Bolsonaro's tenure. Lula is expected to attend the Cop27 climate conference in Egypt.

AFRICA

The US and EU have expressed approval for the "permanent cessation of hostilities" between the **Ethiopian** government and the regional forces of Tigray, ending a two-year civil war that caused significant loss of life and pushed millions of civilians to the brink of famine. The agreement came after eight days of peace talks between Ethiopian Prime Minister Abiy Ahmed's government and the Tigray People's Liberation Front. The EU's foreign policy chief called for a swift implementation of the African Union-brokered agreement, focusing on restoring humanitarian access and basic services in Tigray, which has been under blockade since the conflict began in November 2020. This breakthrough is crucial for Ethiopia, as the war posed a threat to the country's unity and economic stability.

Ghana's currency has faced a substantial devaluation against the dollar this year, inflation reached a 21-year high at 40%, and debt servicing is projected to consume 47% of revenue in 2022. Despite its previous economic success, with an average GDP growth rate of 6% annually between 2000 and 2019, Ghana's economy is expected to grow by only 3.5% this year due to the impacts of the Covid-19 pandemic and the repercussions of Russia's invasion of Ukraine. The country has sought an IMF loan of up to $3 billion to mitigate the economic challenges exacerbated by rising food and energy prices globally, driven by the Ukrainian conflict and the US Federal Reserve's tightening monetary policy. The significant depreciation of the cedi against the dollar, over 50% in 2022, has further intensified the import-heavy economy's struggles.

The UK is withdrawing its entire military force from **Mali**, including about 250 troops stationed since 2020 as part of an anti-jihadist UN peacekeeping mission. The decision follows France's announcement of ending its nine-year operation in the region due to increasing hostility from Islamic militants. The UK and France's withdrawal has raised concerns about the growing threat from al-Qaeda and Islamic State in the region. Mali's relationship with France has been strained since a military coup brought the army to power in 2020. In response, Mali's military leaders have turned to the Wagner Group, a Russian mercenary group with close ties to the Kremlin, to stabilize the country. However, this involvement has been marred by allegations of atrocities, including accusations of Russian fighters participating in a massacre that killed at least 13 civilians.

CLIMATE CHANGE

At the UN COP27 climate summit in **Egypt**, negotiators welcomed the G20's commitment to strive for limiting global warming to 1.5C. The G20, which includes major emitters like the US, China, Saudi Arabia, the UK, and Germany, recognized that the impacts of climate change would be significantly reduced with a temperature increase of 1.5C compared to the less ambitious goal of 2C set in the Paris agreement. Including a reference to the 1.5C target in the final COP27 agreement has become a contentious issue, with some unidentified countries opposing its inclusion. Scientists have warned that even fractions of a degree in warming can lead to more frequent and intense extreme weather events. The world has already warmed by at least 1.1C compared to pre-industrial levels. According to top climate researchers, if rapid emissions cuts are made, warming could exceed 1.5C by 2060, but taking all recommended actions could potentially lead to cooling to 1.4C by 2100.

SOURCES:

https://www.infoplease.com/current-events/2022/november-us-news

https://www.ft.com/content/0e6d0d72-2e6f-40be-b27b-2fed1f753870

https://www.ft.com/content/d417ea8f-62ee-4bb8-966b-a85a98fc6b3a

https://www.ft.com/content/d417ea8f-62ee-4bb8-966b-a85a98fc6b3a

https://www.thetimes.co.uk/article/ukraine-pleads-for-western-air-defences-after-poland-missile-strike-2q9js6ghs

https://www.ft.com/content/e54ae496-9438-4bd5-8501-4d194eba3b26

https://www.ft.com/content/43f60031-c0cf-41f7-8a93-cf931006507a

https://www.ft.com/content/5ece6ecc-5973-40ac-9ba2-4193f042dacd

https://www.aljazeera.com/news/2022/11/3/netanyahu-and-far-right-declared-winners-in-israeli-elections

https://www.ft.com/content/d0f6df50-c52e-4e72-847e-3514b230728f

https://www.ft.com/content/d0f6df50-c52e-4e72-847e-3514b230728f

https://www.thetimes.co.uk/article/tokayev-tightens-grip-in-kazakhstan-after-winning-uncontested-election-83x8rtlxs

https://www.ft.com/content/36a5d96e-4c66-4dea-8aef-2ddd3f198a77

https://www.aljazeera.com/news/2022/10/25/pakistans-former-pm-imran-khan-announces-march-on-capital

https://www.ft.com/content/cd060035-5003-44d8-9b5c-33370f69f7f4

https://www.ft.com/content/f79918bb-93b7-4fcc-8250-91d0d2012583

https://www.ft.com/content/f12163f2-705e-4ef5-bf09-34da40be8cc0

https://www.thetimes.co.uk/article/cuba-stands-with-moscow-against-shared-enemy-as-president-meets-vladimir-putin-k8tm3x5s0#%3A~%3Atext%3DThe%20communist%20island%20nation%20of%2Cthaw%20relations%20with%20the%20US

https://www.thetimes.co.uk/article/cuba-stands-with-moscow-against-shared-enemy-as-president-meets-vladimir-putin-k8tm3x5s0 *https://www.thetimes.co.uk/article/britain-to-withdraw-troops-from-mali-bqj3jd98w#%3A~%3Atext%3DThe%20British%20army%20has%20stationed%2Cincreasing%20hostility%20from%20Islamic%20militants*

https://www.thetimes.co.uk/article/britain-to-withdraw-troops-from-mali-bqj3jd98w

https://www.ft.com/content/63865d24-c788-424a-a21f-76cd0ba6069a

https://www.ft.com/content/88f606c3-03af-4de3-a91d-67af6ebf7f47

https://www.thetimes.co.uk/article/lorry-protests-bring-brazil-to-a-halt-after-bolsonaro-election-defeat-996cs9mp6

https://www.thetimes.co.uk/article/donald-trump-annonucement-president-2024-run-statement-jr09xf6wc

https://www.ft.com/content/f1feb965-dfad-4bcc-9fc4-0d0aa85a47dd

https://www.ft.com/content/f1feb965-dfad-4bcc-9fc4-0d0aa85a47dd

THE WORLD IN DECEMBER 2022

Introduction

December 2022 was a month during which the world continued to grapple with the consequences of Russia's invasion of Ukraine, as the war entered its tenth month. President Zelenskyy of Ukraine arrived in the US to plead for more aid from congress. Western diplomats talked of plans for a settlement with Russia, as a break in fighting led to fears of a renewed assault by Russia early next year. In Europe, tensions flared between Serbia and Kosovo stemming from a dispute over the issuing of car licence plates. Scandal rocked the EU Commission, as Belgian police raided a European parliamentary office in a widening corruption investigation involving Qatar and Morocco. Croatia's membership of the border-free Schengen bloc was approved. The World Cup continued in Qatar, with Morocco making history to become the first African team to reach the semi-final of a World Cup. Argentina were crowned champions after an exciting final against France, their third World Cup win. Chinese President Xi Jinping visited Saudi capital Riyadh for three days, pledging to boost oil and gas trade between the two countries. Hong Kong dropped the last of its strict covid-19 restrictions. In South America, Peru's president Pedro

Castillo was ousted after trying to shut down congress before a vote on his impeachment. Argentina's ex-President Cristina Fernandez de Kirchner was convicted of corruption. The UN COP15 biodiversity summit reached an agreement to protect almost a third of the planet's lands and oceans by 2030.

WAR IN UKRAINE

Vladimir Putin has acknowledged the "extremely complicated" situation in **Ukraine**, hinting at the possibility of a prolonged war as Russia's invasion approaches the 10-month mark. The Russian president admitted facing difficulties in the four regions of Ukraine that are partly occupied by Russian forces. In September, Putin annexed these regions in an effort to consolidate Russian gains and deter Western support for Kyiv. However, Ukraine's counter-offensive, backed by advanced Western weaponry, has resulted in the recapture of territories claimed by Russia, including the regional capital, Kherson.

NATO chief Jens Stoltenberg stated that the conditions for a peaceful resolution to the war in Ukraine are currently absent. He urged Western alliance members to continue supplying weapons to Kyiv throughout the winter, as Russia is reportedly preparing for a spring offensive. US President Joe Biden expressed his willingness to engage in discussions with Putin to end the conflict. German Chancellor Olaf Scholz also appealed to Putin for a diplomatic solution that involves the withdrawal of Russian troops. While talk of a potential settlement with Russia has raised concerns among Kyiv and its more hawkish Eastern European allies, Western defense and intelligence officials privately believe that neither side seems inclined to initiate peace negotiations at the moment. They note that Ukraine's recent success in reclaiming previously occupied territory indicates momentum in Kyiv's favor. Stoltenberg cautioned that Moscow may be seeking a temporary cessation of hostilities to regroup for a renewed assault early next year.

Russia has indicated openness to peace talks but asserts that they will be complicated due to the West's refusal to recognize the new territories seized from Ukraine. The possibility of a meeting between the US and Russian presidents has been mentioned, but the Kremlin is firm in its stance that it will not withdraw from Ukraine at the West's demand.

Kharkiv, Ukraine's second city, experienced a prolonged power outage as Russian forces targeted energy stations across the country, firing 76 missiles and conducting drone attacks. As many as nine power facilities were struck, causing "colossal" damage, according to the city's mayor. By the evening, approximately 55% of residents had electricity restored.

Ukraine's President, Volodymyr Zelensky, arrived in the United States for his first foreign visit since the invasion began. During his visit, he addressed the US Congress, emphasizing that aid to Ukraine is not charity but an investment in democracy. Zelensky sought further support from the United States for Ukraine's war efforts. In response, the US Secretary of State, Antony Blinken, announced an additional $1.85 billion in military aid to Ukraine, which includes the provision of a Patriot air defense system to counter Russian missile threats. The United States has already sent about $50 billion in assistance to Ukraine since the invasion started. However, there have been concerns expressed by Republicans about the cost of such support, especially considering that they will take control of the House of Representatives soon.

In response to the G7's attempts to cap gains from Russia's oil revenues, **Russia** retaliated by signing a decree that prohibits sales under contracts complying with the $60 price ceiling imposed by Western allies of Ukraine. This move allows Russia to continue selling crude to countries like India and China. The price cap aims to undermine funding for Russia's invasion of Ukraine by targeting the oil and gas revenues that constitute a significant portion of Russia's budget. So far, the cap has not affected actual oil prices, as Russia's main crude blend, Urals, continues to sell below $60 a barrel. Russia has disregarded the G7's actions, focusing instead on maintaining its oil shipments through a "shadow fleet" of vessels to avoid the impact of targeted sanctions on oil insurance.

EUROPE

Kosovo has taken the step of closing its main border crossing with Serbia as tensions between the two nations escalate. Serbia has put its military forces at the border with Kosovo on high alert, and Belgrade has issued threats to intervene to protect ethnic Serbs if peacekeepers fail to defuse the situation. The conflict stems from a dispute over car license plates issued by Pristina. The Serbian president accused Kosovo of preparing to attack ethnic Serbs in the north of the country and vowed to protect Serbia's people. Protests by ethnic Serbs against Pristina's authority have been ongoing for weeks, including walkouts in government offices and the installation of roadblocks. The international community's control over the situation appears to be weakening.

In a racially motivated attack, a gunman killed three people near a Kurdish cultural center in central **Paris**. The assailant, a 69-year-old man with a history of violent attacks, was arrested at the scene. The motive behind the attack was not immediately clear, but the interior minister alleged that it was racially motivated. The gunman was not associated with any organized far-right movement.

The **UK** government's plan to remove asylum seekers to Rwanda has been deemed lawful by the High Court. The policy, announced in April 2022 and endorsed by Prime Minister Rishi Sunak, means that people who arrived "illegally" in the UK since January 2022 could be eligible for removal to Rwanda, where their asylum claims would be assessed. The decision has been met with criticism from many MPs and rights groups, and the groups behind the lawsuit are considering an appeal against the ruling.

Four people lost their lives in an attempt to cross the Channel in an inflatable boat off the Kent coast, reminiscent of a tragedy that occurred a year earlier, claiming 27 lives. The home secretary, Suella Braverman, confirmed the deaths and mentioned an ongoing multi-agency rescue operation. The incident occurred just after **UK** prime minister Rishi Sunak unveiled a new strategy to address the backlog in the asylum system and curb the record numbers of small boat crossings. Despite government efforts to deter such journeys, more than 40,000 crossings have occurred this year, the highest number since records began in 2018.

Slovakia's minority government faced a parliamentary vote of no confidence, potentially leading to a snap election amid increasing inflation and economic slowdown. The vote followed internal conflicts among ruling politicians, leading the SaS party to withdraw support from prime minister Eduard Heger's government. The no-confidence motion was approved by 78 out of 150 Slovak legislators. Whether Heger can continue as a caretaker prime minister now depends on the President, who may appoint another leader, likely facing difficulties in garnering enough parliamentary support to avoid an early election.

In a corruption investigation involving World Cup host Qatar, **Belgian** police raided a European parliamentary office, while top politicians pledged to combat corruption. The Belgian federal prosecutor conducted searches and seized about €1 million in cash from 20 premises, including homes and offices. Four individuals, including a member of the European Parliament, have been charged with various crimes related to the investigation. In response to the scandal, the European Commission president called for the establishment of a body to uphold integrity and ethics rules across all EU institutions. Leading ministers from EU member states demanded a thorough investigation into the alleged payments, raising concerns about the credibility of the EU.

European interior ministers have approved **Croatia's** accession to the Schengen zone, enabling the removal of border checks at the frontiers of the country, known for being a popular tourist destination. However, bids from Balkan neighbours Romania and Bulgaria were rejected. Austria expressed concerns about Romania, while the Netherlands blocked Bulgaria's entry, deferring their approval until the following year, citing worries about migration and corruption. Despite the lack of consensus, both Bucharest and Sofia remain committed to joining the free travel zone in the future. Countries seeking Schengen membership must demonstrate reliable border checks and a functioning criminal justice system. Austria called for Schengen rule reforms to better manage undocumented migration. Croatian trade associations welcomed the decision, anticipating a boost in tourism and retail consumption, especially after the country adopts the common European currency on January 1.

In a move that deepens the divide between **Hungary's** Prime Minister Viktor Orban and Brussels, Hungary has blocked an €18 billion package of EU financial support for Ukraine. The decision adds financial pressure on the war-torn country, as it requires significant external funding to maintain public services. In response, Brussels has put on hold a decision regarding Hungary's access to €5.8 billion worth of Covid-19 recovery funds, citing concerns over corruption in the country. The conflict reflects the rift between Orban and his EU partners concerning support for Ukraine. Additionally, Orban is using his veto power to block the EU's attempt to introduce a minimum corporate tax in the union, which necessitates the unanimous approval of member states. Some EU capitals suspect that Hungary is using its veto as a means to pressure allies into endorsing its €5.8 billion share of the EU's Covid-19 recovery fund.

MIDDLE EAST AND NORTH AFRICA

Morocco made history by becoming the first African team to reach the World Cup semi-finals after securing a 1-0 victory over Portugal, continuing their impressive performance in Qatar. Youssef En-Nesyri scored the match's only goal just before halftime, while Morocco maintained another clean sheet. Manager Walid Regragui expressed pride in the team's growing support, not just from Moroccans but also from Africans and Arabs. For Portugal, the defeat marked the likely end of Cristiano Ronaldo's World Cup journey, as he was unable to break through Morocco's defense. The Atlas lions celebrated their now-trademark victory in style, launching Regragui into the air. The two teams previously faced off at the 2018 World Cup, with Cristiano Ronaldo scoring the sole goal of that match.

Benjamin Netanyahu was sworn in as **Israel's** prime minister, completing a remarkable comeback for the veteran leader, who will now head the most right-wing administration in the country's history. His coalition government, consisting of Jewish ultranationalist and religious parties, has ambitious plans to overhaul the country's judicial system, accelerate settlement construction in the occupied

West Bank, and emphasize Jewish identity in public life. These plans have drawn significant criticism from various sectors of Israeli society, including the defense establishment, business community, education system, LGBT+ rights groups, and legal officials. Netanyahu's return for a sixth term as prime minister extends his more than decade-long dominance in Israeli politics, following 18 months in opposition. The recent general election provided a clear majority for his coalition, which includes the right-wing Likud party, the Religious Zionism alliance, and two ultra-Orthodox factions.

Iran's foreign minister engaged in talks with his Saudi counterpart at a regional conference, indicating Tehran's efforts to ease tensions with its arch-rival amid ongoing protests in the Islamic republic. Hossein Amirabdollahian held "friendly talks" with Prince Faisal bin Farhan at the gathering in Jordan, believed to be the first meeting between Iranian and Saudi foreign ministers since 2017. The extent of the meeting was not fully disclosed. The conference, attended by officials from various regional countries and French President Emmanuel Macron, aimed to address regional matters. Tensions between Iran and Saudi Arabia have escalated recently, with Iran accusing Saudi Arabia and other foreign powers of fueling the protests in the country. Western officials also suspected that Iran was planning an imminent attack against Saudi Arabia.

A senior **Qatari** diplomat has expressed concerns about the EU's handling of a corruption scandal that has impacted the European Parliament, warning that it could have negative implications for security cooperation and discussions on global energy security between the bloc and Qatar. However, Qatar clarified that it was not considering cutting LNG supplies to Europe or using gas exports for political purposes. The scandal revolves around allegations of attempted bribery by Qatar and Morocco to influence EU legislators. Four individuals have been charged with corruption, money laundering, and involvement in a criminal group, with police seizing almost €1.5 million in cash from the homes of a current and a former MEP in Brussels. The Qatari government denies any involvement and criticizes the EU's decision to suspend legislative work related to Qatar but not Morocco, believing it has been unfairly targeted. Qatar, the world's largest exporter of LNG, emphasizes that it has never used its pivotal role in gas markets for diplomatic gains.

Tunisians have witnessed a record-low turnout in the first parliamentary election held since President Kais Saied's power grab in July 2021. Only 8.8 percent of registered voters cast their ballots, the lowest turnout since the country's uprising against the rule of Zein al-Abidine Ben Ali in 2011. Most candidates ran as independents, and many political parties boycotted the poll. The low voter participation occurred amid an economic crisis characterized by soaring food prices and delays in securing an IMF loan agreement. After suspending parliament in July 2021, President Saied ruled by decree and restructured the political system, granting the president significant powers. A new constitution shaped by Saied was adopted in July this year through a referendum with a 30 percent turnout, reducing the authority of parliament and enhancing the president's control over the government and judiciary. Tunisia was once viewed as the region's only successful democratic transition, but Saied's actions have caused divisions among the population and impacted the country's political landscape.

During a summit with Chinese President Xi Jinping, **Arab states** pledged closer ties with China, with Saudi Arabia stating it would balance its relationships between Beijing and its traditional partner, the US. Xi emphasized China's intention to strengthen cooperation with the region and enhance oil and gas trade during his three-day visit to Riyadh. The summit came after strained ties between the US and Saudi Arabia, particularly due to the Saudi-led OPEC+ oil production cuts earlier in the year. President Joe Biden's previous visit to the kingdom aimed to assure that the US would not leave a void in the region, potentially filled by China, Iran, and Russia. Both China and Saudi Arabia hailed the recent meetings as a new chapter in their relationship. Beijing has become the kingdom's largest trading partner, while Riyadh serves as China's primary oil supplier. The two sides signed a comprehensive strategic agreement and more than two dozen deals during the summit, covering areas like construction and a broadband contract with Huawei.

ASIA

Hong Kong has eased most of its remaining Covid-19 restrictions and eliminated compulsory testing for arrivals as the city aims to revive its pandemic-hit economy and align with Beijing's approach of moving away from zero-Covid. Chief Executive John Lee announced that travelers will no longer need to undergo PCR testing upon arrival and will only require evidence of a negative rapid antigen test. Additionally, the ban on gatherings of more than 12 people will be lifted, although the outdoor mask mandate will remain in place. Hong Kong had previously implemented some of the strictest measures globally to control the virus, including lengthy mandatory quarantines and policies that separated Covid-positive children from their parents, which raised concerns among residents and businesses.

Imran Khan, the former Prime Minister of **Pakistan**, has pledged to dissolve two of the country's four provincial legislatures, a move likely to intensify political tensions as the nation faces a worsening balance of payments crisis. Khan's party, Pakistan Tehreek-e-Insaf (PTI), plans to dissolve assemblies in Punjab and Khyber Pakhtunkhwa provinces, where it holds government control. These regions account for around 70 percent of Pakistan's population, and Khan believes that PTI can strengthen its hold on power through new elections. While Prime Minister Shehbaz Sharif is scheduled to face voters in a national election in October 2023, Khan has been advocating for an early poll. If the legislatures are dissolved, new elections will need to be held within 90 days. Khan's popularity has surged despite his previous ousting from power, amid economic challenges, natural disasters, and IMF bailout efforts.

Indonesia's parliament has approved a new criminal code that outlaws extramarital sex and imposes restrictions on political freedoms. The new laws, set to take effect in three years, will penalize sex outside marriage with up to a year of imprisonment. The changes reflect a rise in religious conservatism in the Muslim-majority country. Critics view these laws as detrimental to human rights and potentially harmful to tourism and investment. Protests against the legislation occurred in Jakarta, and legal challenges against the laws are expected. The new regulations apply to both locals and foreigners in Indonesia, including popular tourist destinations like Bali. The laws not only ban sex between unmarried couples but also criminalize living together without marriage and adultery.

In the Gulf of **Thailand**, a Royal Thai Navy warship, HTMS Sukhothai, capsized and sank during a storm, leaving 33 out of 106 sailors missing. Three sailors were rescued in critical condition as search operations are underway to locate the missing crew members. The ship's electrical system failed due to seawater entering the exhaust pipe when strong winds caused the ship to tilt. Consequently, the crew could no longer maneuver or pump out the seawater entering the hull. The Sukhothai, a 960-ton corvette commissioned into the Thai navy in 1987, was built in the United States.

THE AMERICAS

Argentina has been crowned World Cup champions after defeating holders France in a penalty shootout, in what is being hailed as the most memorable final in recent history hosted by Qatar. This victory marks Argentina's third World Cup win and serves as a fitting finale for captain Lionel Messi. The match concluded with a 2-2 draw after 90 minutes and a thrilling 3-3 tie after extra time, with Messi scoring twice for Argentina and Kylian Mbappé of France netting a hat-trick. Argentina emerged victorious in the penalty shootout with a score of 4-2. Following the triumph, thousands of ecstatic fans flooded the streets of Buenos Aires adorned in sky-blue and white to celebrate their team's first World Cup victory since 1986.

Peru's president, Pedro Castillo, faced removal by lawmakers after attempting to dissolve congress before an impeachment vote, intensifying a longstanding political crisis. Dina Boluarte, the vice-president, was subsequently sworn in as Peru's first female president. Castillo was taken into custody and accused of "rebellion" following his attempt to dissolve congress, and lawmakers overwhelmingly voted to remove him from office. The president of Peru's constitutional court referred to Castillo's actions as a "coup" during a live broadcast. The armed forces and police distanced themselves from Castillo, stating that the dissolution of congress could only occur after two votes of no-confidence in one government, and any other action would violate the constitution.

The president of the **Dominican Republic** has urged the international community to intervene in Haiti urgently to address the escalating gang violence, rather than making mere promises to aid the distressed Caribbean nation. In October, Haiti's interim prime minister called for an international military force to curb the terrorizing activities of armed gangs and prevent a major humanitarian crisis. The US attempted to secure agreement on a multinational force, but regional allies showed resistance, concerned about supporting Haiti's unelected interim government, which assumed power after President Jovenel Moïse's assassination in July of the previous year. Regional allies seek a broader political consensus within Haiti before committing to intervention. However, the Dominican Republic's President, Abinader, argues that the situation demands immediate action. The Dominican Republic's thriving economy has attracted a large number of Haitian migrants in recent years, leading to increased border crossings, and the government has responded by deporting record numbers of Haitians.

The **US** House of Representatives has approved legislation safeguarding the rights of same-sex and interracial couples to marry, and the bill is now headed to President Joe Biden's desk for his signature. The House, currently under Democratic control but soon to be controlled by Republicans, voted 258-169 to advance the Respect for Marriage Act. A significant number of House Republicans, 39 in total, joined Democrats in supporting the bill, while most House Republicans voted against it. This move follows the Senate's approval of the bill last month. Democratic lawmakers led the effort for this legislation after the US Supreme Court's decision to overturn Roe vs. Wade, which led to concerns that other landmark rulings, such as Obergefell vs. Hodges, recognizing same-sex marriage, and Loving vs. Virginia, rejecting state laws banning interracial marriages, could be revisited by the court.

Cristina Fernández de Kirchner, **Argentina's** vice-president and a prominent figure in Latin America's political left, has been found guilty of corruption in a divisive case that has stirred public opinion, with her supporters vowing to protest and paralyze the country. A three-judge panel in Buenos Aires delivered the guilty verdict, and prosecutors sentenced Fernández de Kirchner to six years in prison and a lifetime ban from holding public office on fraud charges. She was among many accused of leading a criminal scheme that allegedly diverted approximately $1 billion in government funds through public works contracts during her presidency from 2007 to 2015. As vice-president and head of the Senate, the 69-year-old politician enjoys legal protections and is unlikely to face immediate imprisonment. According to Argentine law, she retains her right to serve and run for public office until all avenues of appeal have been exhausted. However, the federal court's ruling will have significant repercussions in Argentina's tense political landscape as the left-wing government prepares to face a challenge from the conservative opposition in next year's presidential elections. An anticipated appeals process could extend over several years as the case proceeds through higher courts.

AFRICA

Ghana has reached a $3 billion loan agreement with the IMF, moving the heavily indebted nation in West Africa closer to a deal with creditors aimed at stabilizing its economy and finances after a year of turbulence. The three-year funding loan is a staff level agreement between the IMF and Ghanaian authorities.

South Africa's ruling African National Congress (ANC) has thrown its support behind President Cyril Ramaphosa amidst a damning report accusing him of abuse of power. As Ramaphosa asked the country's highest court to dismiss the report, the ANC's backing secured his position as president. The report had raised pressure on him to resign over allegations of law-breaking related to a theft at his private game reserve. In his court filing, Ramaphosa requested the constitutional court to dismiss the report and also sought an order declaring any further parliamentary actions on the report as "unlawful and invalid." The ANC announced that its MPs would vote against an impeachment investigation in parliament, reinforcing Ramaphosa's position as the party's head. Ramaphosa is widely expected to be re-elected as ANC leader in the upcoming leadership elections, which come five years after he won a power struggle against Jacob Zuma and began efforts to tackle corruption following a major post-apartheid scandal. The panel's findings, however, have shaken his grip on power, suggesting serious misconduct regarding a cash theft incident in 2020 at his Phala Phala farm.

In the **Chadian** desert, the bodies of 27 migrants, believed to have died of thirst, have been discovered. According to the International Organization for Migration (IOM), these migrants reportedly left Moussoro, a central town in Chad, 17 months ago on a pick-up truck. The truck is believed to have become lost in the deep desert, broke down due to mechanical issues, and the migrants subsequently died of thirst. Among the deceased, four were children. The IOM has documented deaths and disappearances of over 5,600 people transiting through the Sahara since 2014, with 148 deaths recorded in 2022 alone. In Chad, 110 migrant deaths have been reported since 2014, but due to many deaths going unrecorded, the actual death toll is suspected to be much higher.

CLIMATE CHANGE

The **UN COP15** biodiversity summit has achieved a consensus to protect nearly one-third of the world's lands and oceans by 2030, despite the longstanding divide between wealthy and developing nations in UN climate and nature negotiations. The framework, which was approved by nearly 200 countries, aims to safeguard at least 30 percent of the planet's land, inland waters, coastal areas, and oceans by the set deadline. Currently, only 17 percent of land and 10 percent of marine areas are under protection. Unlike the legally binding Paris Agreement, this pact does not carry the force of law. The summit was presided over by China's environment minister and COP15 president, and co-hosted by Canada after it was moved to Montreal due to Covid-19-related delays of two years. However, during the final UN session to adopt the agreement, some African nations expressed their dissatisfaction with the process, feeling that it was pushed through without proper debate. The Democratic

Republic of Congo voiced its unhappiness, although it did not formally object. The push for adoption without further comments led Cameroon to accuse a "force of hand," and Uganda described the procedure as a "fraud" and "coup d'état." Nevertheless, COP15 legal advisers asserted that the process followed the established rules.

SOURCES:

https://www.theguardian.com/world/2022/dec/27/russia-bans-oil-exports-to-countries-that-imposed-price-cap

https://www.bbc.co.uk/news/world-europe-63997749

https://www.infoplease.com/current-events/2022/december-world-news

https://www.ft.com/content/a3a35c7e-258e-455a-9197-09360b6e129d

https://www.ft.com/content/b7815d37-97e4-4658-bed4-402b4811f012

https://www.ft.com/content/b7815d37-97e4-4658-bed4-402b4811f012

https://www.ft.com/content/4f5c4eb2-a8d3-46b6-8fdc-8a363ab52b87

https://www.politico.eu/article/european-parliament-under-attack-roberta-metsola-police-launch-fresh-raids-qatar-corruption-scandal-eva-kaili-socialist-democrats-ursula-von-der-leyen-visentini-giorgi-panzeri-margaritis-schinas/

https://www.ft.com/content/9b3912d2-9f5e-48c2-bddc-51aafd92205d

https://www.ft.com/content/83630128-0ebc-4703-accd-64d3ff87e170

https://www.ft.com/content/97cdc53d-02ee-4c56-91b5-717309173793

https://www.ft.com/content/4124c6ca-b8ee-4cd4-8f0b-11f49b5d685c

https://www.ft.com/content/0adb2fb9-9f9f-4a56-b0f0-3fce08456cd3

https://www.politico.eu/article/croatia-join-schengen-area-eu-visa-free-travel-zone-2023/

https://www.ft.com/content/5ac5e2ec-c4b9-404c-b8e5-8b72f96c4568

https://edition.cnn.com/2022/12/29/middleeast/israel-benjamin-netanyahu-swearing-in-intl/index.html

https://www.ft.com/content/beff5178-f8c7-4172-b121-f4d6356f7d16

https://www.ft.com/content/28fa5d28-228e-4ef9-9d50-d5771c794e8a

https://www.ft.com/content/28fa5d28-228e-4ef9-9d50-d5771c794e8a

https://www.ft.com/content/992f98d3-f6da-4d8b-817a-6ad3438fbe6a

https://www.ft.com/content/ed8734cd-1866-4b28-82c8-367ad6a85b21

https://www.ft.com/content/a489fdc2-7b2e-4842-9b91-f822ed6b60be

https://www.ft.com/content/274aaa6b-073b-4e35-9983-64ce16e185aa

https://www.bbc.co.uk/news/world-asia-63869078

https://www.ft.com/content/b25bc6e3-d977-46ab-a0e2-de4fe93a0cc3

https://www.ft.com/content/ae1f6141-fd8c-4b5f-9c48-8d6979a6418d

https://www.reuters.com/world/africa/bodies-27-migrants-found-chadian-desert-2022-12-13/

https://www.ft.com/content/9bb13b79-c2d8-41e7-965f-467729109558

THE PALESTINIAN-ISRAELI CONFLICT IN GAZA

I was about to submit this book for publication when I had to pause again to include a fast-moving story happening in Gaza in the Middle East. As I have explained, history is littered with incidents which burn slowly for months and years but turn into quick-paced and catastrophic events in a short period of time. The situation in Gaza is an excellent example of this and over the course of this chapter, I will discuss how such events have changed history forever.

OCTOBER 2023

On October 7th 2023, Hamas, based in Gaza, fired hundreds of rockets into Israel and in a breath-taking and audacious move entered Israel and massacred more than 1,000 Jewish residents near the border.

Never in the long history of this conflict has there been such a successful attempt by Hamas to inflict a devastating blow to the state of Israel.

The entire world was taken by surprise and Hamas' attack inflicted pain and anguish brought humiliation to the Israeli army and its intelligence service, Mossad.

On 8th October, the day following Hamas' attack, Israel declared war and warned Hamas it would "teach them a lesson" as never before and began to amass troops on the border with Gaza, in preparation for a ground offensive. The world watched with horror over the next few weeks to witness the revenge pounding of Gaza by the Israeli Airforce which went into overdrive flattening buildings with its overwhelming air power.

Israel also announced a "complete siege" of Gaza, cutting off supplies of food, water, fuel and other essential items.

As of 19th October 2023, according to Israeli officials, 1,400 Israelis had been killed, 4629 injured and 203 were being held hostage in Gaza.

On the same day, the Palestinian Ministry of Health stated that 3,785 Palestinians had been killed in Israeli airstrikes with 12,500 injured.

Gaza is one of the most populated places on Earth with over 2 million Palestinians packed into a small area of land measuring only 25 miles long and 6 miles wide.

It has the Mediterranean Sea on one side blockaded by the Israeli army and the land of Israel on the other, protected by a steep wall and electrified fences. It is therefore trapped on all sides and has heavily restricted access to both Israel and Egypt.

At the time of writing, Israel has given the residents of Northern Gaza several warnings to move south of Gaza City. This is effectively displacing over one million residents and causing a humanitarian crisis of mammoth proportions. The Secretary General of the United Nations along with numerous world leaders has asked Israel to respect the conventions of war and not kill or injure innocent noncombatant civilians. It has also asked Israel not to inflict collective punishment on over 2 million Palestinians with many women and children at risk of starvation and death.

There is a perception amongst many people in the West that Muslims are responsible for a lot of terrorist activities. It is therefore important to consider some of the terrorist activities committed on innocent ordinary people.

One of the most famous events in the last 50 years is the 1972 Summer Munich Olympic attacks by the Palestinians when 11 Israeli athletes were attacked in their dormitory: two were killed and nine were taken hostage. After a botched plan, all of them were killed.

More recently, there were the 9/11 attacks by Osama bin Laden and Al Qaeda on 11th September 2001. Four aircrafts were hijacked. Two planes were flown into New York's World Trade Center twin towers, destroying them completely. One plane was flown into the Pentagon in Washington and the fourth and final plane was brought down in a field by the passengers. More than 3,000 people were killed and this iconic event was a turning point for American policy. The invasion of Afghanistan and the American military involvement was a major reason for subsequent events in the Middle East and ironically the growth of terrorism.

In November 2008, the world witnessed the attacks by Lashkar-e-Taiba on the Taj Mahal Hotel and other locations in Mumbai and murdered and injured hundreds in cold blood.

In June 2014, hundreds of ISIS members took control of the city of Mosul, the second largest city in Iraq and murdered over

500 people. In addition, there were numerous attacks in India by terrorists connected to Pakistan targeting Hindus in Kashmir.

However, it is also pertinent to point out the King David Hotel in Israel when members of the Zionist terror group Irgun detonated a bomb in 1946 in the basement of the hotel which was serving as the base for the British.

It is difficult to predict the future, but it looks extremely grave and dangerous.

However, it is important to place it in context by looking back on how this conflict began and examining the roots of the issues we perceive today.

PALESTINE BEFORE 1948

Jerusalem is one of the oldest places on Earth and the religious seat of three ancient Abrahamic religions – Judaism, Islam and Christianity. The Islamic Temple mount sits on top of the Jewish Temple. Jews and Muslims worship at the same structure separated only by a wall metres away. Close by, Christians worship the crucifixion of Christ in this Holyland. Jews considered this their homeland from 1,000 BC before the advent of the Arabs and Christianity. The Jews were driven away by the Romans and settled in various parts of Europe. Thereafter, only a small number of Jews lived in Palestine and the adjoining areas, with more Arab Muslims living in the region.

During World War I, British forces took control of large areas of Palestine and at an Allied Peace Conference in April 1920, it was formally given the administration of the land. The majority of inhabitants at that time were Arabs. There was a Jewish presence alongside other ethnic groups. This was problematic as the role of Britain in the region was to establish "a national home" for the Jewish people. This aim was enshrined in the Balfour Declaration of 1917, a pledge made by the British foreign secretary and supported by the League of Nations (a predecessor of the United Nations) five years later. However, Palestinian Arabs had lived in this area for hundreds of years, with only a small number of Jews. The "Jewish National Home" policy caused the Arabs much anger and resentment as this was their ancestral home and they therefore opposed the move. This became the start of numerous struggles and wars between the two sides over the last century.

Between the 1920s and 1940s, the Jewish population of Palestine significantly increased with many escaping persecution in Europe, especially the Nazi Holocaust in World War II. Jews and Arabs attacked each other and there was rebellion against British rule. Britain supported in many ways, the arrival of Jews in this disputed land.

In 1947, there was a vote at the United Nations (UN) which came out in favour of Palestine being divided into separate Jewish and Arab states. Under this proposal, Jerusalem would become an international city. That plan was accepted by Jewish leaders but rejected by the Arab side and never implemented. The Arabs could not accept the proposed partition because they felt it was their land which was being given to the Jews. In other words, the indigenous Arab people were being asked to give away their ancestral land to the Jews who had just arrived.

1948

In May 1948, unable to solve the problem, Britain withdrew in a hurry, not properly handing over the keys to two warring factions. This followed a similar pattern to what Mountbatten did in India by hastily withdrawing from a land they had occupied for over two hundred years.

Wealthy immigrant Jews from Europe were arriving in shiploads. They had the tacit support of Britain where they had connections with the British establishment. Moreover, Britain and America were siding with the Jews who they felt were more European and there was a sense of racism in not trusting the indigenous Arab population. The Jews therefore had the resources to quickly spread themselves and occupy more and more of the Arab land.

On May 14, 1948, Jewish leader Ben-Gurion announced the creation of a Jewish State, and it was immediately recognised by US President Harry Truman. These events caused a war. Two days after Ben-Gurion's declaration, Jordan, Syria, Egypt and Iraq invaded Israel. However, Israel won the war and 700,000 Palestinians fled from their homes in what they still refer to as Al Nakba, or "the Catastrophe".

In 1949, the war ended in a ceasefire, leaving Israel controlling most of the territory.

Jordan controlled the land now referred to as the West Bank, and Egypt was responsible for Gaza. West Jerusalem was occupied by Israel and Jordan occupied the East. No peace agreement was ever signed between the various countries, and this led to numerous conflicts over more than 70 years.

The heart of the current situation is the plight of these displaced Palestinian refugees whose numbers have now soared to over five million. They claim the right to return to their land which Israel currently occupies. The millions now living in the Gaza Strip and the West Bank are highly regulated by the Israeli defence force leading to much frustration and anger.

1967: THE SIX-DAY WAR

The Six-Day War (also known as the Third Arab-Israeli War) took place between 5th and 10th June 1967. It was precipitated by Egypt's closure of the Straits of Tiran to Israeli shipping in May and the mobilisation of Egyptian forces as well as the ongoing Palestinian refugee issue.

On 5th June 1967, Israel launched pre-emptive airstrikes against Egyptian airfields, destroying nearly all its aerial capabilities. At the same time, the Israeli army invaded the Sinai Peninsula and Gaza Strip. Jordan joined the war by launching specific attacks rather than an all-out war on Israel while Syria shelled some Israeli forces.

By 10th June, Israel had taken control of the whole of the Sinai Peninsula, having agreed to a ceasefire with Egypt and Jordan two days earlier and Syria on 9th June. The ceasefire was signed on 11th June. The Six-Day War resulted in 20,000 Arab fatalities and less than 1,000 Israeli fatalities.

At the end of the conflict, Israel had captured the Golan Heights from Syria, the West Bank including East Jerusalem from Jordan and the Sinai Peninsula and Gaza Strip from Egypt. This had long-term consequences: between 280,000 and 325,000 Palestinians and 100,000 Syrians left their homes or were expelled from the West Bank and the Golan Heights.

Since then, the situation has become more complicated because the right-wing Israeli Likud government has been building settlements in the West Bank. Much of this land on the Jordan River is fertile, causing more resentment among the Palestinians.

THE CLINTON OSLO PEACE ACCORD

This accord was hailed as a breakthrough with high expectations of an improved relationship between the two. However, when both sides read the fine print, disagreements began to emerge with the assassination of Yitzhak Rabin the Israeli PM in November 1995. Hard-liners felt that he had sold out to the Arabs.

The Arabs were unhappy that the West Bank was divided into three areas:

Area A would be under Palestinian control under a new governing body which was established by Oslo.

Area B will be joint control between the Palestinian and Israeli governments.

Area C which was the largest, occupying over 60% of the West Bank and covering some of the most fertile pieces of land.

The problem was that the Palestinians who wished to move from one area to the other needed the approval of the hated IDF (Israeli Defence Force). Further, the commercial part of the agreement gave Israelis access to the Palestinian market but not vice versa. Israel also had control of tax collection and imposed their currency on this area. All these gave legitimacy to Hamas and other militant groups to become the voice of the Palestinians who were frustrated people.

Over the years, an increasing number of settlers have occupied the West Bank, with estimates of over 700,000 Jews now living there. The United Nations Security Council has stated that these settlements are illegal under international law. Needless to say, Israel rejects this position.

There are several difficult issues which include:

- What should happen to Palestinian refugees?

- Whether Jewish settlements in the occupied West Bank should stay or be removed.

- Whether the two sides should share Jerusalem.

- And perhaps most tricky of all, whether a Palestinian state should be created alongside Israel.

2000–05: SECOND INTIFADA

The Second Intifada was precipitated by the failure of the 2000 Camp David Summit to create a lasting peace plan which was acceptable to both sides and the visit by Israeli opposition leader Ariel Sharon to the Al-Aqsa compound in Jerusalem, a holy site for the Palestinians. The Palestinian uprising began in September 2000. As prime minister, after February 2001, Sharon refused to negotiate with the Palestinians.

The Second Intifada lasted for five years and there were more than 4,300 deaths. The Israeli army took on a more central role after a suicide attack on a hotel in Netanya on 27th March 2002, which killed 30 Jewish Israelis. Operation Defensive Shield was instigated with the aim of Israel retaking the West Bank and areas within Gaza. A year later Israel placed a "separation barrier" on the West Bank: much of this barrier was placed on land officially belonging to the Palestinians and it did significantly reduce the number of attacks by Palestinians on Israel.

In January 2003, Ariel Sharon's Likud Party won the Israeli national elections, in part as a reaction to the security situation in the country. This led to a temporary ceasefire between Israel and the Palestinians and in May of that year, the Aquba Summit. This was significant because Sharon endorsed the Roadmap for Peace, a plan proposed by the US, EU, and Russia, which enabled dialogue with Mahmoud Abbas, whom Yasser Arafat had installed as Palestinian prime minister in March. The terms of the Roadmap for Peace meant the creation of a Palestinian State at some unspecified future date. A further development was the establishment of the Quartet of the Middle East, an intermediary body formed of representatives of the US, UN, EU and Russia.

There were issues in the Palestinian leadership including conflicts between Mahmoud Abbas and Yasser Arafat. These led to accusations from both Israel and the US that Arafat was undermining Abbas. Arafat retained control of the Palestinian security services, making it impossible for Abbas to uphold parts of his commitments to the Roadmap for Peace in cracking down on militancy on the Palestinian side. Abbas resigned as Palestinian prime minister in October 2003.

By the end of 2003, Ariel Sharon was taking Israel in a new political direction – the unilateral withdrawal from the Gaza Strip. Israel would still control both the coast and airspace. The withdrawal plans gained approval from both the left wing in Israel and the Palestinians and were opposed by elements within Sharon's own Likud Party. In response, in January 2005 Sharon established a National Unity Government, composed of representatives of Likud, Labor and Meimad and Degel HaTorah. As part of his disengagement plans, in August 2005, Sharon expelled 9,480 Jewish settlers from 21 settlements in Gaza and four settlements in the

West Bank – a controversial move in Israel. The withdrawal of Israel from the Gaza Strip led to shelling and mortar attacks on Israeli communities near the border.

2005 TO 2019

Events took a dramatic turn in 2006 when Hamas crossed into Israel from Gaza and attacked Israeli Defense Force (IDF) soldiers, killing two and kidnapping a third. This act, in conjunction with rocket attacks from Gaza into Southern Israel, led to conflict between Israel and Hamas in the Gaza Strip.

The following year, Hamas took control of Gaza after battles against the rival Palestinian group, Fatah. This effectively divided the two Palestinian areas: Hamas controlled the Gaza Strip and Fatah governed the West Bank. Mahmoud Abbas was now president and critics argued that his governing coalition based in the West Bank excluded Hamas, which had been victorious in the Palestinian Authority elections in 2006.

Israel and Hamas agreed to a six-month ceasefire in the summer of 2008. However, this was fragile at best and was not extended when it expired in December of that year. Hamas accused Israel of still blockading the Gaza Strip and Israel blamed Hamas for continuing to attack Israeli cities with rockets.

After the ceasefire ended, Israel bombarded the Gaza Strip attacking Hamas bases, police buildings and civilian infrastructure including mosques, hospitals and schools. The Israelis alleged that Hamas was using these buildings to store weapons. On the other side of the conflict, Hamas stepped up its rocket attacks on Israel. At the beginning of January 2009, Israel launched a ground invasion of Gaza which resulted in the deaths of around 1,400 Palestinians. Israel stated that most of the Palestinians killed were Hamas fighters, However, the Palestinian Centre for Human Rights contended that almost 1,000 of the casualties were civilians.

From the time that US president Barack Obama took office in 2009, his administration tried to persuade Israel to re-engage with the peace process and stop building settlements on the West Bank. Obama even went as far as to state that "The United States does not accept the legitimacy of continued Israeli settlements" and "This construction violates previous agreements and undermines efforts to achieve peace. It is time for these settlements to stop" when addressing Muslim nations. This may have precipitated a more conciliatory response from Israeli president Benjamin Netanyahu who endorsed a "Demilitarized Palestinian State" for the first time – as long as Jerusalem remained the capital of Israel. This was rejected by Hamas and other Palestinian leaders. However, it did lead to a pause in settlement building on the West Bank for ten months from November 2009 and direct negotiations between Israel and the Palestinian Authority overseen by the US the following year.

September 2011, saw the Palestinians attempt to get official international recognition for the State of Palestine with East Jerusalem as its capital city. This included submitting a United Nations (UN) resolution. In November of the following year, Palestine gained non-member observer status on the UN Security Council. It also acquired admission as a UN non-member state after the draft resolution was passed by 138 votes to 9 with 41 countries abstaining. However, although recognised, the Palestinian State is still only theoretical and symbolic as Israel has stated that a functioning, practical Palestine cannot come into being until peace is achieved between the two sides.

In October 2011, Israelis and Palestinians agreed to a prisoner exchange. One Israeli soldier, Gilad Shalit who had been kidnapped in 2006, was exchanged for 1,027 Palestinian prisoners. This remains the largest prisoner exchange to date and a Hamas leader stated at the time that the released Hamas prisoners had been responsible for killing more than 500 Israelis.

Military engagement between the two sides continued. In November 2012, Israel launched Operation Pillar of Defense in Gaza, targeting militants to stop the rocket attacks. The Israeli Defense Force stated that it attacked 1,500 military sites but the Palestinians countered that civilian targets were deliberately hit. Palestinian militants fired 1,456 rockets into Israel, 875 of which fell in open areas of the country. During the conflict, 167 Palestinians were killed, and more than 200 Israelis were injured.

The 2014 Gaza War was triggered by the murder of three Israeli teenagers by Palestinian militants among other issues. This led to the arrest of 350 Palestinians including Hamas fighters. Hamas stepped up its rocket attacks and a seven-week conflict ensued including a full-scale Israeli ground invasion of Gaza. Seventy Israelis and more than 2,000 Palestinians were killed. The UN has estimated that more than 1,400 of those were civilians.

2020s

May 2021 saw yet another conflict between the two sides which lasted 11 days, killed 250 Palestinians and displaced a further 72,000. Part of the reason for the violence was the entry into the Al-Aqsa Mosque compound by Israeli forces. The fighting may have reduced the possibility of renewed Israeli-Palestinian negotiations.

Eighteen months later, in November 2022, a new coalition government headed by Benjamin Netanyahu, gave power to far-right politicians. This inevitably led to an increase in violent conflict, not helped by events such as the Israeli incursion into the Jenin refugee camp in the West Bank in July 2023, which was the largest military offensive in the area in 20 years. This military action was undertaken to target militants sheltering in the camp. Twelve Palestinians were killed, 9 were injured and up to 500 left their homes, voluntarily or otherwise.

This chapter ends where it began: with recent events. On 7th October 2023, Hamas launched its surprise large-scale offensive, launching thousands of rockets and kidnapping and murdering Israeli civilians and soldiers. Israel has retaliated and at the time of writing on 28th October, exactly 3 weeks after Hamas' attack, Israel has begun an expanded ground operation in Gaza and the Palestinian Health Authority in Gaza has announced that more than 7,700 Palestinians have been killed since Israel's retaliation to Hamas' incursion began.

WHY ARE ISRAEL AND GAZA AT WAR NOW?

Gaza is controlled by Hamas. Hamas has been designated as a terrorist organisation by the UK, US and other countries because it is an Islamist militant group committed to the destruction of Israel. It gained power in Gaza in 2006 by winning an election, seizing control of Gaza from its Fatah rivals the following year.

For the last 16 years, Gaza militants have been involved in several conflicts with Israel which has instigated a partial blockade of the strip to isolate Hamas and attempt to stop rocket attacks on Israeli cities. The Palestinians insist Israel's restrictions and air strikes on Gaza amount to collective punishment.

Between the years 2008 – 2023, around 308 Israelis were killed in the occupied Palestinian territories. In comparison over 6400 Palestinians were killed.

2023 has been the single most deadly year for Palestinians in the occupied West Bank and East Jerusalem, who are also affected by restrictions and military actions being carried out in response to deadly attacks on Israelis. The numbers affected by the current conflict are huge compared to the deaths over many years and hence this conflict is one of the most serious in the long history of the Palestinian-Israeli conflict.

- Many western countries have condemned the Hamas attacks on Israel.

- The US has given Israel more than $260bn in aid, and a pledge for more equipment and ammunition. The US also announced that it was sending an aircraft carrier, plus other ships and jets to the eastern Mediterranean.

- Russia and China will not condemn Hamas, apparently maintaining contact with both Palestinians and Israelis.

- Russian President Vladimir Putin has attributed the lack of peace in the Middle East to US policies.

- Iran is a major supporter of Hamas, and the Lebanese Islamic Hezbollah movement.

- Iran's role in the recent attacks is being questioned after reports that it gave permission for them days earlier.

In discussing the subject of change this is a fascinating and horrific subject. The situation in Gaza and for its residents is dire with hundreds of thousands on the brink of starvation. Gazza and its neighbouring Palestinian areas were an idyllic land of sheep grazing farmers filled with beauty. It produced bountiful fruits and vegetables but this land has changed so fast into a land of bloodshed. Millions of Palestinians are today displaced without a roof amongst their head. The Israeli Defence force continues its daily bombardment with tens of thousands of innocent women and children being killed or mortally wounded. It is a very sad conflict with no winners in sight and one can only hope that the two-state solution that is practical is accepted by all sides as a way to live in peace in the region.

ENDNOTES

1   Israel formally declares war against Hamas as more than 1,000 killed on both sides –
    The Washington Post
    Israel-Hamas war updates: Death toll rises as Israeli jets pound Gaza. – Al Jazeera
    'Complete siege' of Gaza: satellite map of worst affected areas – The Guardian
2   Hostilities in the Gaza Strip and Israel | Flash Update #13 - United Nations Office for
    the Co-ordination of Humanitarian Affairs (OCHA)
3   Israel Gaza war: History of the conflict explained – BBC News
4   Jewish state - Wikipedia
    David Ben-Gurion - Wikipedia
    Why Nakba is the Palestinians' most sombre day, in 100 and 300 words - BBC News
5   Six-Day War Middle East [1967] – Encyclopaedia Britannica
    The 1967 Six-Day War – Wilson Center
    Six-Day War- Wikipedia
6   Israel Gaza war: History of the conflict explained – BBC News
7   Second Intifada – Wikipedia
    The second intifada - Encyclopaedia Britannica
8   Roadmap for Peace in the Middle East: Israeli/Palestinian Reciprocal Action, Quartet
    Support – US Department of State
    Road map for peace – Wikipedia
9   Ridiculed and betrayed: why Abbas blames Arafat – The Guardian
    Mahmoud Abbas - Wikipedia
10 Israeli disengagement from Gaza – Wikipedia
    Israel's disengagement from Gaza 2005 – Encyclopaedia Britannica
11 Fatah–Hamas conflict – Wikipedia
    Hamas-Fatah Conflict (2006 -) University of Edinburgh
12 Israel Agrees to Truce with Hamas on Gaza – New York Times
    Hamas ends Israel truce early – The Guardian
    2008 Israel–Hamas ceasefire - Wikipedia
13 Remembering Israel's 2008 War on Gaza – Middle East Monitor
    Gaza War 2008-2009 - Wikipedia
14 A New Beginning (speech) – Wikipedia
    Transcript: Obama Seeks 'New Beginning' In Cairo – NPR
    2010–2011 Israeli–Palestinian peace talks - Wikipedia
15 History of the Question of Palestine – United Nations
    Palestine 194 - Wikipedia
16 Gilad Shalit deal: West Bank prepares to welcome Palestinians home – Christian
    Science Monitor
    Israel and Hamas Are Both Winners and Losers in Shalit Swap Deal – Haaretz
    Gilad Shalit prisoner exchange - Wikipedia
17 Operation Pillar of Defense (Gaza) - November 2012 – Anti-Defamation League
18 2014 Gaza conflict – United Nations (UNWRA)
    2014 Gaza War – Wikipedia
19 2021 Israel–Palestine crisis – Wikipedia
    Life Under Occupation: The Misery at the Heart of the Conflict – New York Times
    UN: There is no 'safe place' in Gaza, 72,000 people displaced – The Jerusalem Post
20 July 2023 Jenin incursion – Wikipedia
    Israel attacks Jenin in biggest West Bank incursion in 20 years – The Guardian
21 Live updates | Palestinian officials say death toll rises from expanded Israel military
    operation – The Associated Press

REFERENCES

Israel formally declares war against Hamas as more than 1,000 killed on both sides -The Washington Post - *https://www.washingtonpost.com/world/2023/10/08/israel-hamas-war-gaza/*

Israel-Hamas war updates: Death toll rises as Israeli jets pound Gaza – Al Jazeera - *https://www.aljazeera.com/news/liveblog/2023/10/8/israel-palestine-escalation-live-israeli-forces-bombard-gaza*

'Complete siege' of Gaza: satellite map of worst affected areas – The Guardian - *https://www.theguardian.com/world/2023/oct/20/complete-siege-of-gaza-satellite-map-of-worst-affected-areas*

Hostilities in the Gaza Strip and Israel | Flash Update #13 – United Nations Office for the Co-ordination of Humanitarian Affairs (OCHA) - *https://ochaopt.org/content/hostilities-gaza-strip-and-israel-flash-update-13*

Israel Gaza war: History of the conflict explained – BBC News - *https://www.bbc.co.uk/news/newsbeat-44124396*

Jewish state – Wikipedia - *https://en.wikipedia.org/wiki/Jewish_state*

David Ben-Gurion - Wikipedia - *https://en.wikipedia.org/wiki/David_Ben-Gurion*

Why Nakba is the Palestinians' most sombre day, in 100 and 300 words – BBC News - *https://www.bbc.co.uk/news/world-middle-east-44114385*

Six-Day War Middle East [1967] – Encyclopaedia Britannica - - *https://www.britannica.com/event/Six-Day-War*

The 1967 Six-Day War – Wilson Center - *https://www.wilsoncenter.org/publication/the-1967-six-day-war*

Six-Day War- Wikipedia - *https://en.wikipedia.org/wiki/Six-Day_War#*

Second Intifada – Wikipedia - *https://en.wikipedia.org/wiki/Second_Intifada*

The second intifada - Encyclopaedia Britannica - *https://www.britannica.com/event/second-intifada*

Roadmap for Peace in the Middle East: Israeli/Palestinian Reciprocal Action, Quartet Support – US Department of State - *https://2001-2009.state.gov/r/pa/ei/rls/22520.htm*

Road map for peace – Wikipedia - *https://en.wikipedia.org/wiki/Road_map_for_peace*

Ridiculed and betrayed: why Abbas blames Arafat – The Guardian - *https://www.theguardian.com/world/2003/sep/08/israel*

Mahmoud Abbas – Wikipedia - *https://en.wikipedia.org/wiki/Mahmoud_Abbas*

Israeli disengagement from Gaza – Wikipedia - *https://en.wikipedia.org/wiki/Israeli_disengagement_from_Gaza*

Israel's disengagement from Gaza 2005 – Encyclopaedia Britannica - *https://www.britannica.com/event/Israels-disengagement-from-Gaza*

Fatah–Hamas conflict - Wikipedia - *https://en.wikipedia.org/wiki/Fatah%E2%80%93Hamas_conflict*

Hamas-Fatah Conflict (2006 -) – Peace Agreements Database, University of Edinburgh – *https://www.peaceagreements.org/view/conflict/5/Hamas-Fatah+Conflict+%282006+-+%29*

Israel Agrees to Truce with Hamas on Gaza – New York Times - *https://www.nytimes.com/2008/06/18/world/middleeast/18mideast.html*

Hamas ends Israel truce early – The Guardian - *https://www.theguardian.com/world/2008/dec/18/hamas-israel-truce-end*

2008 Israel–Hamas ceasefire – Wikipedia - *https://en.wikipedia.org/wiki/2008_Israel%E2%80%93Hamas_ceasefire*

Remembering Israel's 2008 War on Gaza – Middle East Monitor - *https://www.middleeastmonitor.com/20181227-remembering-israels-2008-war-on-gaza/*

Gaza War 2008-2009 – Wikipedia - *https://en.wikipedia.org/wiki/Gaza_War_(2008%E2%80%932009)*

A New Beginning (speech) – Wikipedia - *https://en.wikipedia.org/wiki/A_New_Beginning_(speech)*

Transcript: Obama Seeks 'New Beginning' In Cairo – NPR - *https://www.npr.org/2009/06/04/104923292/transcript-obama-seeks-new-beginning-in-cairo*

2010–2011 Israeli–Palestinian peace talks – Wikipedia - *https://en.wikipedia.org/wiki/2010%E2%80%932011_Israeli%E2%80%93Palestinian_peace_talks*

History of the Question of Palestine – United Nations - *https://www.un.org/unispal/history/*

Palestine 194 – Wikipedia - *https://en.wikipedia.org/wiki/Palestine_194*

Gilad Shalit deal: West Bank prepares to welcome Palestinians home – Christian Science Monitor - *https://www.csmonitor.com/World/Middle-East/2011/1017/Gilad-Shalit-deal-West-Bank-prepares-to-welcome-Palestinians-home*

Israel and Hamas Are Both Winners and Losers in Shalit Swap Deal – Haaretz - *https://www.baaretz. com/2011-10-12/ty-article/israel-and-hamas-are-both-winners-and-losers-in-shalit-swap-deal/0000017f-e0d2-d568-ad7f-f3fb43900000*

Gilad Shalit prisoner exchange – Wikipedia - *https://en.wikipedia.org/wiki/Gilad_Shalit_prisoner_exchange*

Operation Pillar of Defense (Gaza) - November 2012 – Anti-Defamation League - *https://www.adl.org/ resources/backgrounder/operation-pillar-defense-gaza-november-2012*

2014 Gaza conflict – United Nations (UNWRA) - *https://www.unrwa.org/2014-gaza-conflict*

2014 Gaza War – Wikipedia - *https://en.wikipedia.org/wiki/2014_Gaza_War*

2021 Israel–Palestine crisis – Wikipedia - *https://en.wikipedia.org/wiki/2021_Israel%E2%80%93Palestine_ crisis*

Life Under Occupation: The Misery at the Heart of the Conflict – New York Times - *https://www.nytimes. com/2021/05/22/world/middleeast/israel-gaza-conflict.html*

UN: There is no 'safe place' in Gaza, 72,000 people displaced – The Jerusalem Post - *https://www.jpost.com/ middle-east/un-there-is-no-safe-place-in-gaza-72000-people-displaced-668489*

July 2023 Jenin incursion – Wikipedia - *https://en.wikipedia.org/wiki/July_2023_Jenin_incursion*

Israel attacks Jenin in biggest West Bank incursion in 20 years – The Guardian - *https://www.theguardian. com/world/2023/jul/03/palestinians-killed-israeli-strike-west-bank-jenin*

Live updates | Palestinian officials say death toll rises from expanded Israel military operation – The Associated Press - *https://apnews.com/article/israel-hamas-war-live-updates-10-28-2023-3348f0544aa6d66b28 0c8cab1637a3db*

COVID 19 PANDEMIC 2020

The pandemic brought immense changes on a scale not seen before and therefore an interesting chapter for this book.

I restricted my research only to understand the various changes witnessed as a result of this unexpected event as the pandemic itself is a very large subject which has been covered by various writers.

Human beings have evolved to the top of all species on earth. We are hugely talented with immense creative skills. We have evolved over centuries by creatively finding solutions to various problems encountered over generations.

The pandemic was no different and although it was deeply disturbing, depressing and challenging mankind found various solutions and that is what I will discuss in the coming pages.

1. CHANGES TO MEDICAL RESEARCH

Covid 19 helped researchers use mRNA technology using platform-based research into finding a vaccine at spectacular speed. The world's scientific community for the first time worked in close cooperation in a race against time to safely bring a vaccine to market. This would have taken many years in the normal course of a vaccine's development, but the pandemic forced our scientists to bring about change at a spectacular level to save mankind from the dreaded Covid 19 epidemic Although there were very significant deaths and illnesses changes to medical research brought spectacular success in preventing millions of people from succumbing to the illness by rushing through vaccines.

WHAT IS mRNA?

MRNA is genetic material, similar to DNA, so its "code" is expressed with letters.

mRNA—or messenger RNA—is a molecule that contains the instructions or recipe that directs the cells to make a protein using its natural machinery. That is why it is called a messenger as it sends a message to the cells with instructions on how to make proteins.

mRNA travels smoothly within a protective bubble called a Lipid Nanoparticle. Once inside, our cells read the mRNA as a set of instructions and then building proteins that match up with parts of the pathogen called antigens. The immune system sees these foreign antigens as invaders—dispatching defenders called antibodies and T-cells—and training the immune system for potential future attacks. So, when the real virus comes along, the body might recognize it—it sounds an alarm to help defend against infection and illness.

The Potential of mRNA to Deliver New Vaccines and treatments. The scientific community was not new to mRNA technology but the pandemic changed all that. For decades, scientists have studied mRNA, looking for ways to unlock its potential to prevent and treat disease. While the mechanism of action for mRNA technology is relatively simple—once inside cells, it instructs them to build proteins—researchers have had to work for years to develop technologies to allow mRNA to work in the real world. mRNA has proved to be a great platform for vaccine development (and potentially therapeutics), so that our own cells can do the hard work of producing proteins, resulting in an immune response which helps protect us against diseases.

The approval of the first mRNA-based COVID-19 vaccines was a scientific turning point, establishing mRNA as a versatile, flexible technology. The focus and drive companies like Pfizer gave to developing our COVID-19 vaccine in partnership with BioNTech gave us a wealth of scientific knowledge in just one year.

Pfizer's next wave of mRNA scientific innovation is expanding in the infectious disease arena with vaccine development programs in flu (influenza) and shingles, as well as exploring respiratory combination vaccines.

Pfizer is also exploring the versatility of this technology in areas of rare genetic diseases. Pharma companies like Pfizer will stay close to other opportunities where the scientific rationale for using mRNA is strongest and their disease and biology area expertise is deepest and where the potential impact on patients could be greatest.

The pandemic accelerated our capabilities, collaboration and partnership in key areas of mRNA strategy. A variety of licensing and research collaborations have been initiated to further the development of mRNA-based vaccines and treatment options such as :

- An ongoing collaboration with BioNTech to advance candidates including COVID-19 and shingles. Pfizer and BioNTech also have a collaboration on flu that was initiated in 2018.

- A Development and Option agreement with Acuitas Therapeutics, which will provide an option to license Acuitas' lipid nanoparticle delivery system for up to 10 targets for vaccine or therapeutic development.

- An exclusive research collaboration with Beam Therapeutics, which is focused on *in vivo* -based editing programs for a range of rare genetic diseases of the liver, muscle and central nervous system.

- A strategic research collaboration and license with Telesis BIO to access and further develop Telesis Bio's enzymatic DNA synthesis technology for potential application by Pfizer for its mRNA-based vaccines and other biopharma products.

https://www.pfizer.com/science/innovation/mrna-technology

https://www.mayoclinic.org/diseases-conditions/coronavirus/in-depth/different-types-of-covid-19-vaccines/art-20506465

https://www.nature.com/articles/d42473-022-00159-1

2. CHANGES TO THE WAY WE SUCCEEDED IN REDUCING THE TIME NEEDED TO BRING OUT A VACCINE WITHOUT COMPROMISING SAFETY ISSUES.

Driven by a global urgency and underpinned by decades of work on vaccine research developers found a way to chop not just days or months, but years off the timeline There was no compromise on the science or on safety tests, but rather the wait time baked into the development process — waiting for results and waiting for regulatory approvals

For instance, it took just under 16 weeks to recruit and enrol more than 43,000 volunteers for the final phases of testing Pfizer's vaccine. When volunteer recruitment began for clinical trials of the rabies mRNA vaccine in 2013, it took 813 days to get 101 participants enrolled. Based on this comparison, that's roughly 730 days — nearly two years — saved in recruiting alone.

The Pfizer Phase II/III coronavirus trial, in contrast, got initial efficacy results for the first of its two doses in just 105 days, when it hit a nearly 2.4 percent infection rate in the placebo group. That's 424 days faster than an HPV trial. The urgency to find a cure faced by most of the world's governments meant the race to find a cure was immense .

Typically, it takes the FDA (USA) 10 months to review a new drug. However, with the COVID-19 death toll rising, the FDA rushed all coronavirus vaccines to the front of the review lines. The Pfizer vaccine got reviewed and authorized for emergency use only 21 days after submission and the Moderna vaccine in just 19 days. Compared with a more typical 10-month wait time, that's about another 283 days saved.

In total, that's 1,437 days, or 3.9 years, cut off the normal timeline for a new vaccine. And that doesn't include other time savings, such as putting the ethics reviews at the front of the line. Add that saved time to the 11 months it actually took to get the first COVID-19 vaccines and it would add up to nearly five years — remarkably close to the six years needed to test and approve patisiran. https://www.sciencenews.org/article/covid-coronavirus-vaccine-development-speed

Other pharma manufacturers like Moderna's mRNA Covid vaccine development moved quickly. What Moderna did over many of those years was develop mRNA on a bioplatform, which allows for speedier vaccine development. Bioplatforms are systems that can be easily scaled and tailored for many different diseases. Traditionally, developing any vaccine has been a bespoke effort.

"The benefits of a bioplatform is the ability to quickly redeploy the platform once established and refined — in the case of Moderna's mRNA platform, to create and test new vaccines based on new viral sequences," says Moderna co-founder Noubar Afeyan. All of this makes mRNA vaccines virtually programable.

"The only difference between" mRNA vaccines is "the order of the letter; the zeroes and ones of life. The manufacturing process is the same, the equipment is the same, with the same operators. It's the same thing. And so this is why we could go so fast." Moderna

CEO Stephane Bancel https://www.cnbc.com/2021/07/03/how-moderna-made-its-mrna-covid-vaccine-so-quickly-noubar-afeyan.html

COVAX was a historic multilateral effort co-led by Gavi, the Vaccine Alliance, the Coalition for Epidemic Preparedness Innovations (CEPI), the World Health Organization (WHO) and UNICEF from 2020 through 2023. During the COVID-19 pandemic, COVAX aimed to accelerate the development and manufacture of COVID-19 vaccines and to guarantee fair and equitable access for every country in the world. COVAX came to a close on 31 December 2023.

By the end of 2022, COVID-19 vaccines delivered by the global vaccine access initiative, COVAX, helped to avert 2.7 million deaths across 92 lower-income countries, according a new report based on modelling by researchers from Imperial College London.

COVAX's biggest success was in low-income countries, where its vaccines were responsible for three-quarters of all deaths averted, with 73% of COVID deaths averted in Africa from COVAX vaccines.

Between January 2021 and December 2022, COVAX delivered 1.9 billion vaccine doses to countries supported by the Advance Market Commitment (AMC), a financing mechanism where doses were largely funded by donor governments to countries that could not afford them. By the end of 2022, over half the populations in AMC countries had received their full primary vaccines.

Since 2020, vaccine development has been expedited via unprecedented collaboration in the multinational pharmaceutical industry and between governments. According to the Coalition for Epidemic Preparedness Innovations (CEPI), the geographic distribution of COVID19 vaccine development puts North American entities having about 40% of the activity compared to 30% in Asia and Australia, 26% in Europe, and a few projects in South America and Africa. https://en.wikipedia.org/wiki/History_of_COVID-19_vaccine_development

CHANGES IN THE WAY THE WORLD HEALTH ORGANISATION (WHO) PLAYED.

The World Health Organization (WHO) has played a vital role in acting as a hub to centralize and share information on data and research results. WHO has prescribed guidelines for national governments to test and trace COVID-19 cases and launched innovative initiatives to accelerate the development of therapies and vaccines through international collaboration. Notably, the Solidarity trial collects data from multiple hospitals in over 90 countries that enrol their patients through the WHO website, following simplified procedures to enable even overloaded hospitals to participate. The website then randomly assigns patients to a trial drug among the four currently being tested (including hydroxychloroquine and remdesivir, which had already been undergoing tests for use in treating Ebola and SARS), allowing reliable comparisons of large-scale samples by an independent scientific board. According to WHO, the trial can reduce the time necessary to design and conduct clinical trials by 80%.

Complementing WHO, an array of specialized global research partnerships are also playing an important role in coordinating global efforts. These include:

- The Coalition for Epidemic Preparedness Innovations (CEPI), an international alliance to finance and coordinate the development of vaccines for emerging infectious diseases, cofounded by the Bill & Melinda Gates Foundation, the Wellcome Trust, and a consortium of nations.

- The Global Research Collaboration for Infectious Disease Preparedness (GloPID-R), a network of research funding organizations from various countries to facilitate research on infectious diseases with pandemic potential.

- The International Severe Acute Respiratory and Emerging Infection Consortium (ISARIC), a global federation of clinical research networks to provide a coordinated research response to outbreak-prone infectious diseases.

- The Innovative Medicines Initiative (IMI), a public-private partnership between the European Commission and the European Federation of Pharmaceutical Industries and Associations, to speed up the development of urgent medical treatments.

- The Global Alliance for Vaccines and Immunization (GAVI), a public-private partnership involving various multilateral organizations, philanthropies, pharmaceutical firms, and national governments, focusing on creating equal access to vaccines for children in developing countries.

3. CHANGES TO FUNDING RESEARCH

Observers say the renewed promise of vaccines, and of mRNA technology — which delivers instructions to cells to produce proteins — has revived an industry that had lost some of its lustre as other approaches were adopted to treat many infectious diseases. Although [mRNA vaccines] have always shown promise, the infrastructure and experience for large scale manufacturing was lacking. The pandemic has seen governments invest and also share risk in the development of vaccines, which was key in speeding up the process."

After the pandemic began in early 2020, the US made historic financial investments in completing clinical trials and provided advance purchase guarantees for hundreds of millions of doses of vaccines even before their safety and efficacy were fully demonstrated. The US government invested at least **$31.9bn** to develop, produce, and purchase mRNA covid-19 vaccines, including sizeable investments in the three decades before the pandemic in 2022. These public investments translated into millions of lives saved and were crucial in developing the mRNA vaccine technology that also has the potential to tackle future pandemics and to treat diseases beyond covid-19. To maximize overall health impact, policy makers should ensure equitable global access to publicly funded health technologies.

In addition to decades of government funding for research prior to the pandemic, the US taxpayers added significantly more support during the pandemic to further accelerate vaccine development and capacity. Operation Warp Speed (OWS) invested billions of dollars in conducting rigorous clinical trials and in manufacturing with the participation of Moderna, AstraZeneca/Oxford, Johnson and Johnson, and Sanofi/GSK. In total, over $18 billion dollars of US public funds have been invested in 6 vaccine candidates. https://www.ncbi.nlm.nih.gov/pmc/articles/PMC8426978/

UK Research and Innovation (UKRI) is a non-departmental public body sponsored by the Department for Science, Innovation and Technology (DSIT). When the pandemic arrived in 2020, UKRI reacted with unparalleled scale and speed to ensure all investments were ready and able to respond to the challenge, and that they were plugged into the UK's wider vaccine, life sciences and pharmaceutical ecosystems. An additional £131 million investment was announced by UKRI in May 2020, bringing its total investment in its Vaccine Manufacturing Innovation Centre (VMIC) to £196 million (the VMIC had been established in 2018 with an investment of £66 million).

At least 97% of the funding for the development of the Oxford/AstraZeneca Covid-19 vaccine has been identified as coming from taxpayers or charitable trusts. Using two different methods of inquiry, researchers were able to identify the source of hundreds of millions of pounds of research grants from the year 2000 onwards for published work on what would eventually become the novel technology that underpins the jab, as well as funding for the final product.

The overwhelming majority of the money, especially in the early stages of the research, came from UK government departments, British and American scientific institutes, the European Commission and charities including the Wellcome Trust.

Less than 2% of the identified funding came from private industry, the researchers said. https://www.theguardian.com/science/2021/apr/15/oxfordastrazeneca-covid-vaccine-research-was-97-publicly-funded

BILL & MELINDA GATES FOUNDATION

(JANUARY 2022)

This charity allocated **US$770** million in new funding to support the growing public health emergency.

US$264 million was made available to fund the development and production of new diagnostics, treatments, and vaccines for COVID-19, including:

US$20 million was made available to advance additional candidate vaccines, through the Coalition for Epidemic Preparedness Innovations (CEPI) US$50 million to the COVID-19 Therapeutics Accelerator, to evaluate existing drugs that could be repurposed to treat COVID-19 and to scale up new treatments for use in low- and middle-income countries

US$309 million to ensure equitable, timely, and large-scale delivery of COVID-19 diagnostics, treatments, and vaccines, including:

US$200 million was given to Gavi, the Vaccine Alliance, to support COVID-19 vaccine purchasing through Gavi's COVID-19 Vaccine Advance Market Commitment (COVAX AMC) as well as delivery of those vaccines to 92 lower-income countries https://www.gatesfoundation.org/ideas/articles/covid19-contributions

4. CHANGES TO ENTREPRENEURIAL APPROACH

Many important changes took place to rapidly respond to science-based entrepreneurial businesses.

DnaNudge, the world's first lab-in-a-cartridge consumer nutrition business, rapidly responded by re-coding its diagnostic chip for COVID-19 RNA. Its founder, Chris Toumazou, Imperial College's Regius Professor of Engineering, redeployed the company's entire team to create an in-field test that provides results in around an hour, rather than having to send samples to a central lab and wait hours or days. This life-saving technology has already been through the first round of successful trials on COVID-19 patients in London and is being validated on a much larger group. Its original design as a consumer technology makes it easy to use, offering a quick solution for testing healthcare staff every day as they come to work. It also holds potential to provide confidence in bringing employees back to work as lockdown ends.

The agility of such science-based entrepreneurial companies to leverage their networks and repurpose their expertise and equipment shows how ingenuity and resources can be combined to help create a safer and more certain future. These examples hold lessons for larger organizations that need to increase their capacity to adapt, improving their flexibility, resiliency and responsiveness.

https://www.weforum.org/agenda/2020/04/how-an-entrepreneurial-approach-can-help-end-the-covid-19-crisis/

5. CHANGES TO THE WAY WE WORK

The Covid-19 outbreak led to a rapid shift to working from home in many occupations. The change may have a negative impact on productivity, but this ignores workers' perceptions and effects on their wellbeing.

Covid-19 changed how many people work. During the pandemic, there was a rapid move towards working from home (WFH) in many occupations. This is very likely to be a permanent shift in how work is organised in at least some advanced economies.

But this development has raised questions about the effects on workers' productivity. A review of recent evidence indicates that policymakers should be sceptical of general claims being made about the impact of home working on productivity, either negatively or positively.

Some quantitative studies indicate that the pandemic has had a negative effect on labour productivity. But at the same time, more qualitative studies provide important insights that are relevant to public and private decision-makers.

Indeed, productivity is a complex variable to determine, and different studies have applied varying approaches to capture the impact of Covid-19 on labour productivity. Recent studies have used three main approaches, which appear to give different results. These are based on: accounting data; systems for monitoring the activities and hours worked by employees; and self-assessment by workers.

While the first two approaches show a mainly negative relationship between working from home and labour productivity, the self-assessment approach reports mixed results.

Specifically, although some research seems to imply that a return to the workplace is necessary to recover economic performance, the preferences and perceptions of employees seem to suggest that working from home at least some of the time ('hybrid working') may become a permanent option.

https://www.economicsobservatory.com/the-shift-to-working-from-home-how-has-it-affected-productivity

It is becoming clearer that remote work does not necessarily harm productivity. Robust research suggests a fully remote workforce may be about 10 per cent less productive than a fully in-person one, though losses can be offset by big savings on office space and hiring staff globally for lower local wages. But hybrid working seems to have a zero or slightly positive impact on performance.

There is the big surprise about the type of countries where working from home is taking off. Researchers, such as Stanford University economist Nicholas Bloom, expected to see a rich-poor pattern like that in individual countries, where homeworking levels are highest among high earners and fall as income declines. But for countries, the data suggests language, not income, makes a bigger difference. Research that Bloom and others just published shows levels are distinctly above average in English-speaking countries: the US,

UK, Canada, Australia and New Zealand. In all five nations, work from home levels were higher than in other rich, but non-English-speaking countries such as Japan, France and Italy. "This is striking and not what we predicted," Bloom told me last week. So what explains the difference? "We honestly don't know." There are several theories. Roomier US homes might make it easier to work remotely than squishy flats in northern Europe and Asia. Asian countries that conquered Covid faster had shorter lockdowns and thus less time to experiment with homeworking.

US FOCUS

There are companies and employees that love the new WFH economy, while others are having a hard time making it work. The general consensus is that it works in the right situations. Consider that WFH is not new. Even before the pandemic, there were over 5 million U.S. employees working from home at least half the time. According to Kate Lister, president of Global Workplace Analytics, 56% of the U.S. workforce have jobs that are at least partially compatible with remote work. Furthermore, she predicts that 25-30% of the workforce will be working from home multiple days. People can be very productive when working from home, sometimes even more so. Both companies and employees save money. Lister's research estimates that a typical employer can save about $11,000 per year for every person who works remotely half of the time. The employees save on gas, clothes, cleaning and more.

https://www.forbes.com/sites/shephyken/2021/02/28/the-impact-of-the-virtual-work-from-home-workforce/

UK FOCUS

Analysis from ONS in January 2022, on how home working has affected people's spending, found almost half of homeworkers in the UK (46%) reported spending less as a result of working from home. However, likely in response to rising energy prices, the majority of homeworkers reported an increase in their spending on utility bills (86%). Nevertheless, half said they spent less on fuel and parking for commuting (50%), and two-fifths said their spending on commuting on public transport had reduced (40%). It has been raised that while some costs may be offset by reduced commuting costs, the longer term considerations of the financial impacts of being at home on a full-time basis may include increased heating and lighting.

Having a designated space to work at home with minimal distractions was also related to employees' adjustment and their improved work-life balance. This is related to the fact that the blurring of work and personal boundaries can make it harder for some employees to 'switch off' and stop thinking about work related issues when not working.

https://www.gov.scot/publications/working-home-during-covid-19-pandemic-benefits-challenges-considerations-future-ways-working/pages/3/

6   CHANGES AND IMPACT ON OFFICE SPACE

About half of large multinationals are planning to cut office space in the next three years as they adapt to the rise of homeworking since the coronavirus pandemic. A Knight Frank survey of executives in charge of real estate at 350 companies round the world that together employ 10mn people found that, among major groups cutting their footprint, the largest number was aiming to reduce space by 10 to 20 per cent.

A Savills study predicted that US cities like San Francisco and Washington DC will have the most surplus office space in the next decade, while the Asian market will be tighter and Europe will "sit in the middle of the pack". "This isn't about offices just becoming empty due to some cities seeing lower return to work levels post-pandemic. It's about how long-term economic, demographic and development trends interact with working patterns," said Savills research associate Kelcie Sellers. In London, companies agreed a record number of office moves last year but took less space than the pre-Covid average, according to data from Cushman & Wakefield.

https://www.ft.com/content/276c26f2-889c-4e08-8f33-ce170890765b

Demand for office space has slumped further, with vacancies reaching at least 20-year highs in the US and London, as people continue to work from home despite companies' attempts to get staff back in the office after the height of the Covid-19 pandemic. Vacancy rates have risen to fresh highs and investment in offices fell sharply in the third quarter this year compared with the same period in 2022 in London, New York and San Francisco, according to preliminary data from CoStar, a research company focused on commercial real estate. The sustained slowdown in the office market comes as higher borrowing costs and low occupancy are compressing building valuations while companies including Amazon, BlackRock, Lloyds Banking Group and JPMorgan have in recent months introduced staff attendance mandates on given days.

Jonathan Gardiner, head of real estate agent Savills's central London office agency, said large companies were holding off pulling the trigger on real estate deals because they were "still trying to understand their spatial needs" as working patterns shift from Covid-induced work from home to hybrid working and an increase in mandated office attendance. Vacancies in San Francisco offices hit a two-decade high and reached a 20 per cent rate in the third quarter — up from 6.3 per cent at the onset of the pandemic. The Californian tech hub only generated £454mn worth of investment in office space in the period, less than a third of its pre-pandemic average. "Places like San Francisco have been hit particularly hard given the level of hybrid working and levels of tech occupation over there," said Stansfield. Tech workers have embraced remote working more than other office workers, according to analysts. Investment in London rebounded slightly to £2bn in the third quarter thanks to a flurry of deals in the City fuelled by appetite for green, modern and newly refurbished offices in central London which are in short supply. However, it remains far below its pre-pandemic levels and more than a fifth lower year on year.

The tech and media sectors historically boosted London's office take up, but companies in those industries are shedding space as they experience slower growth, said Gardiner. London's vacancy rate hit 9 per cent in the third quarter, the highest since CoStar started recording the data in 2003. The picture in New York was similarly grim in the third quarter, according to CoStar data. Investment in the city's offices fell by 60 per cent on the previous quarter while its vacancy rate remained at 13.4 per cent, hovering near a two-decade high. In a positive sign for the commercial real estate sector, leasing showed signs of renewed activity in the third quarter. Large deals in London's City and West End drove a 19 per cent quarterly jump in leasing activity in the UK. In the US, leasing activity rose by 13 per cent overall despite falling in San Francisco. Copyright The Financial Times Limited 2024

https://www.ft.com/content/698f41af-0d88-424b-80b0-241be01dac35

7. CHANGES TO THE IMPACT OF THE REDUCTION TO OFFICE SPACE

The economic dislocation goes much further with the reduced need for office space. There is a whole industry of office cleaning, maintenance, repair and decoration. It is huge and covers everything from replenishing the loo paper, to watering the pot plants and emptying the bins, almost every single day of the year. Fewer offices with fewer people mean less work.

Offices across the country are also surrounded by cafes, coffee shops, sandwich bars, pubs, bars and restaurants, not to mention dry-cleaning outlets, newsagents, shoe repair bars and card shops. All of these outlets are dependent on thousands of people working right next door to where they are sited, or huge numbers of people passing them on the way from the tube or railway station. But if office use is down by 20%, their takings will fall accordingly.

In the centre of large cities like Birmingham, Manchester, Edinburgh, and London it is far worse. All those department stores, clothes and shoe shops, jewellers and perfume retailers are there for a reason; millions of people visit the centre of those cities to work. If they can fit in some retail therapy during their lunch hour, or on the way home, they do just that. Now those shopping centres have to work even harder to attract weekend shoppers – this means out-competing the retail parks, which are often easier to get to, where the parking is better, and everything is conveniently located in one place.

Then there is the loss of revenue to almost every provider of transport in the country. If millions of people are working from home there are fewer passengers every day on commuter trains, trams, buses and tube lines. The transport companies relied heavily on commuters buying their season tickets. Now, not only are many people not travelling regularly, but they are also avoiding the office on Mondays and Fridays – and when they do pop into work, they are often arriving later and leaving earlier in order to avoid peak time fares. As a result, while nationally rail passenger numbers are back to pre-Covid days, revenue is still 10% lower.

https://www.theneweuropean.co.uk/the-death-of-the-office/

8. CHANGES TO THE WAY WE COMMUNICATED.

Although some of us used the internet to have video conferencing Covid accelerated the use of video conferencing. The Zoom App brought video conferencing even to grannies by introducing very easy to use technologies. Earlier video conferencing was the privy of large companies with dedicated staff and office space to assist in having meetings over the internet. Zoom, Teams and other internet-based protocols ushered in the mass use of video conferencing to having meetings. This was the result of necessity because people were unable to travel. Necessity became the mother of invention with the vast number of Apps aimed at conducting meetings over the net. 'Microsoft Teams' further revolutionized this by offering features to share slides and information making meetings more efficient, fast and effective. One more advantage of having video conferencing was most participants arrived on time and meetings became less of idle chat and more of getting to the details of the meeting. Companies and individuals also saved substantial amounts on travel and time.

Video conferencing improved communications, helps build relationship as one could conduct more meetings in a day. it saved money on both travel and time costs. Sharing of slides and other information helped collaboration, improved efficiency and productivity.

ACKNOWLEDGEMENTS

I have many to profusely thank in my journey thus far in the world of publishing.

My loving family have supported me all my life. My wife Rajni has been my rock for over four decades, guiding me in her gentle way.

My daughter and mother have been pillars on whom I can always lean on.

My eminent friend Prof Lord Parekh has guided me in this new journey. A hugely respected academic he has helped me in my new enterprise and encouraged me all the way.

My background as an entrepreneur taught me different skills which has been most useful. However the whole process of creating a subject and executing a book has taught me different skills.

In this journey the eminent Professor has been most helpful.

Lastly I thank my research assistants Maria and Heidi and my publishers for all their support in bringing this book.

Milton Keynes UK
Ingram Content Group UK Ltd.
UKHW020254020824
446458UK00002B/33

9 788119 263837